Pat Booth, formerly a top model, is now a well-known fashion photographer as well as an established writer. She has had three previous novels published, THE LADY AND THE CHAMP, RAGS TO RICHES and SPARKLERS.

She lives in London and Palm Beach with her psychiatrist husband and young son.

D0130157

Also by Pat Booth in Futura:

SPARKLERS

PAT BOOTH

Big Apple

Futura

A Futura Book

First published in Great Britain in 1984
by Futura Publications, a Division of
Macdonald & Co (Publishers) Ltd
London & Sydney
Reprinted 1986, 1990 (twice), 1991

ISBN 0 7088 2578 8

Printed and bound in Great Britain by
BPCC Hazell Books
Aylesbury, Bucks, England
Member of BPCC Ltd.

Futura Publications
A Division of
Macdonald & Co (Publishers) Ltd
165 Great Dover Street
London SE1 4YA

A member of Maxwell Macmillan Publishing Corporation

To Michael Fragnito

Chapter One

It seemed like some exotic conjuring trick as the long sculpted legs cascaded endlessly from the back of the sleek, black Cadillac limousine. Every day for the past few months the cynical street vendor working the rich 51st and Fifth Avenue location had watched this scene unfold, and he ran a leathery tongue over dry lips in anticipation of what he knew was coming. The vicious New York winter was already over, its brutal cold replaced by the crisp, early morning air of the City's spring. That had advantages in terms of the visuals. Less clothes. No longer were the exquisite limbs protected by tight-fitting boots, the tantalizing upper reaches swathed in fur, hidden from the prying eyes of street trash. 'For what we are about to receive . . .'

The legs' owner got out of the limo as if she was clambering from a pick-up truck in a turnip field, the despair of a charm school proprietor and feast for the voyeur. The tight-fitting, immaculately cut blue serge suit, slit generously to mid-calf, rucked up on the leather seat of the car and for a second black stocking tops were exposed showing a flash of white suspenders against milky skin. Not for the first time the lowly citizen of the Big Apple wished that his mind was a camera.

Anne Carrington stood on the sidewalk running both hands over her small, tight bottom as she smoothed the errant skirt into place. She looked up at the vastness of St Patrick's Cathedral. In Europe it would have been a colossus. Here, despite its 300-foot spires, it looked like a rabbit hutch, dwarfed by the enormity of the surrounding buildings. She strode briskly up the steps towards the church, the clinging skirt straining against her muscular buttocks.

On the corner, her secret admirer, unknown and unseen, sighed in admiration as he watched. Clearly there had been cheating in the lottery of life. This girl had too much. Tall and athletic, her long, dark shoulder-length hair was cut in a style which emphasized finely chiselled features which were saved from cold classicism by twinkling brown eyes and a voluptuous mouth. Generous breasts made their presence known despite the severe cut and thick material of a navy-blue coat, which tapered down from broad shoulders to a deliciously thin waist. It required no Sherlock Holmes to deduce that she was rich, no Emily Post to declare that she had class. Wrestling with the heavy brass door, Anne Carrington stepped into the quietness of the cathedral.

It was 7.30 in the morning and already in the side altars hundreds of candles burned their testimony to the faithful. Anne made her way to her regular pew, wondering what made her choose again and again this particular position in the vast cathedral. She knelt to pray and at once felt the familiar feeling of peacefulness pass through her If only it could always be like this: her restless mind stilled, the churning thoughts slowed, protected, insulated from the problems and difficulties of the outside world. Yet even as she wished it, Anne knew it could never be. Moments like this made the struggle possible. They couldn't replace it. For her, church provided a temporary refuge from the demanding realities of the outside world.

The disembodied voice, strangely soothing, drifted into her consciousness. Its source, a tiny white speck at the end of the long nave, was chanting the time-honoured phrases.

'He has confused the proud in their inmost thoughts,' the priest intoned.

Was that her problem? thought Anne. Was intellectual pride her chief sin? If so, she should confess, but how?

What words should she use? 'Father, I have committed the sin of pride.' It sounded insufferably pretentious, an example of pride itself to have such a problem. Anyway, Anne wasn't at all sure that pride *was* the source of her difficulties. It was, above all, *doubt* that bothered her. That was it – intellectual doubt was the core of her dilemma.

Such philosophical speculations were no new thing for Anne and she had all but given up hoping for an intellectual explanation of her emotions, or an emotional one for her intellect. So now, as she leaned back against the polished pew, she pushed the gearstick of her mind into neutral. Anne longed for satisfaction of an entirely different sort, and as she thought of it the muscles of her pelvis tensed against the hard wood and her long legs squeezed together beneath her clinging skirt.

Back on the streets of the raw city, Anne walked fast, breathing in deeply at the intersections. Was this the heart of New York City? she wondered as she passed the glittering Fifth Avenue shops – Cartier, Tiffany's, Van Cleef & Arpel's. Here in New York City luxury and squalor stood side by side, an often uneasy but seemingly inevitable relationship. What was unique wasn't so much the buildings and their high-priced goods, but the people of the city who were rushing to inhabit them. It was hard to believe that the sidewalk crowds came from the same species as the congregation in the church. On this street in particular, despite the quality of the clothes, there was no mistaking the racing of the rats as the Big Apple's abrasive inhabitants struggled to get to work, to make their dreams come true. Eyes fixed on some point in the middle distance, they looked through each other as they hustled to meet deadlines, to placate bosses, to bully inferiors. More than anywhere else, it was in the cold eyes of these determined faces that the pulsing heart of the city could best be seen.

Anne looked at her watch. Eight a.m. Passing the swish Pierre Hotel she watched porters loading Louis Vuitton luggage into the trunk of a Kennedy-bound limo. Across the street a black man fought to stay asleep on a park bench, knees drawn up to his chin in a forlorn attempt to preserve body warmth. The surly shop and office workers of midtown had now been replaced by a different class of city-dweller. This was the land of the early-morning jogger, a weird cross-section of humanity ranging from super-fit narcissists heavily into body worship, to half-dead, crinkly wrinklies – old men whose faces shouted their determination to bolt the door of the stable long after the horse had gone

Intermingling with the joggers were the walkers out with their dogs. Dogs: in China a meal; in England and America an obsession. It was a funny world.

At the Knickerbocker Club Anne turned right on to Madison. Caffeine withdrawal, the occupational hazard of all New Yorkers, was now a threat. However, Anne was a highly organized person and all needs were catered for in her early-morning timetable.

Under the friendly, benevolent gaze of the craggy-faced Irishman behind the counter, she strode into the coffee shop.

'Top of the mornin' to you, Annie me love,' he said, beaming his welcome. 'And I'll suppose you've been bending the ear of poor St Patrick again at some unearthly hour of the morning?' The steaming coffee arrived at the same time as the cheerful greeting.

'Listen, Tom, one of us has got to keep the hot-line open. Liver transplants are a risky procedure, you know.'

Tom affected a mournful air. ' 'Tis a terrible thing to be sure that a man's little weakness can have such a terrible consequence.'

'At this rate I'll be gone from starvation before the cirrhosis gets you.'

Two eggs, sunny-side up, rye toast and a glass of orange juice restored Anne's blood-sugar level, and at exactly 8.25 a.m. she was back at the junction of Fifth Avenue and 62nd Street, standing in front of the big metal door. A discrete and highly polished brass plate announced in small black capitals, CARRINGTON-ISAACS MEDICAL ASSOCIATES. She stepped inside. Her working day had begun.

White Carrara marble, a carefully lit Henry Moore sculpture and a handsome Matisse line drawing gave an understated opulence to the medical offices. A white uniformed receptionist stood up from the corner desk as Anne walked into the lobby.

'Good morning, Dr Carrington.'

'Morning, Paula.'

'Your first patient telephoned to say she'd be fifteen minutes late – something about oversleeping. That's Miss Weissman.' Paula's attitude was brisk, matter of fact. Her jealousy of the beautiful doctor was not a million miles from the surface.

Anne switched on her professional mind and was at once the psychiatrist. Classically, this was considered an attention-seeking mechanism, to announce lateness in advance doubly so.

Anne suppressed a frisson of irritability that her day had started in disorderly fashion. 'Let me know when she arrives. Is Peter in yet?'

The receptionist nodded and Anne walked down the beige carpeted corridor. Knocking briefly, she entered the door marked DR PETER ISAACS, M.D.

'Don't tell me your 8.30 patient cancelled,' Peter Isaacs laughed his welcome. Small, Jewish, with friendly horn-rimmed glasses, he actually looked like a psychiatrist. The herringbone jacket, quiet tie and sensible brogues were standard New York Psychoanalytic Institute issue, yet, despite appearances, Peter Isaacs was far from being a psychodynamist.

'God knows what's going on,' replied Anne. 'She telephoned to say she'd be fifteen minutes late – typical obsessional. When the doorbell rings it will be 8.45 precisely.' Anne mimicked the talking clock.

Peter's face said that he would've settled for a lot longer than that. Anne's presence in the room seemed to turn him on like an electric light. Nothing new there – she'd had the same effect on him since the moment of their first meeting as medical students at Johns Hopkins. She hadn't changed much since those days – still bright, sparky, enthusiastic, still incredibly beautiful with the same almost magical ability to make his juices flow.

'Well, I just love that patient of yours. I get fifteen minutes of you all to myself. Marry me.'

Anne laughed. She was used to this. But behind the laughing exterior the alarm-bells sounded. The comedy had a way of wearing thin.

'Come on,' said Anne, 'it's your mind I'm after – not your body or your alimony payments.'

Peter winced. Couldn't she see he was a man as well as a mind? But he knew that the flash of internal anger changed nothing and pretended to enjoy the joke.

'You'd sure be disappointed if you had my mind. The only thing in here is an X-rated vision of you.'

It wasn't far from the truth. There she sat – damn her – perched on the corner of his desk, long legs dangling voluptuously with all the decorum of a hard-hat construction worker. Great areas of immaculate thigh taunted him, their owner seemingly oblivious to the havoc they were wreaking with his hormonal balance.

'Tell you what – when I fall out of love with my work I'll fall in love with you. How's that?'

Peter smile ruefully. That was probably true, and there was some small satisfaction in it. At least there was nobody else. No man had ever been able to compete with Anne's love of her profession. She was obsessed by psychiatry, fascinated by the problems of her patients. Sex in comparison offered little.

Peter held up his hand in mock resignation. 'I know, I

know, don't tell me. Sex is a boring little procreative process full of sound and fury, signifying nothing.' Anne often said that at this point in the banter.

Anne smiled. 'You know, I think you revel in this role of spurned lover, Peter.' Her tone was teasing. 'It must let you off a lot of hooks, and you know how lazy you are. Think of all the money you save on wining and dining. It's the oldest lie in the world that two can live as cheaply as one.'

It was Peter's turn to laugh. Of course she was right. After all these years there had to be some action in it for him. Perhaps it simplified life, excused him from the hard work involved in getting relationships together, the even harder work in keeping them together. He let the laugh die, replacing it with what he hoped was a mildly pained expression.

Anne saw the 'little-boy-hurt' look and immediately began to lose patience. There was nobody on earth of whom she was more fond than Peter, but if he was in love with her and his love was unreciprocated, it was scarcely her fault. He was a big boy now.

Anne's face said it was time to change the topic of conversation. Peter had seen that look before; it wasn't one to ignore. At moments like this he would go for Anne's weak spot and talk about her work. It was the one sure way to provoke a reaction, and any emotion was better than none. Sometimes this took the form of a subtle wind-up, couched in strictly scientific terms so that it was seldom evident to Anne that anything other than a discussion between professional colleagues was taking place.

'How are you getting on with that obsessional? What was it she felt compelled to do – give head to the adolescents in her class?'

Anne suppressed a momentary flicker of irritation. Had Peter got it wrong on purpose? It was unlike him to use language inaccurately.

'No, no. She has a recurrent and resisted obsessional

impulse to shout 'I want to suck cock' when she's teaching class. She has no impulse to *act*, other than to scream out that particular sentence. The thought of fellatio fills her with disgust. She's petrified that she'll succumb to the impulse. God, it's a funny illness. Her whole life is turned upside down and yet we know that the least likely thing in the world is that she'll actually go ahead and tell the boys she wants to give them a blow. It's like all those puerperal women who have the thought that they might kill their babies. The true obsessional never gets round to doing it.'

' "What, never? Well, hardly ever".' Peter sang the snippet from 'HMS Pinafore'. 'Do you remember when we saw that show in Baltimore?' The subtle wind-up had gone on long enough. The appeal to shared memories marked its end.

Anne remembered and for a second silence descended. Visions of student days, of the *alma mater* flooded back. Mostly, it was the Baltimore winter that had the power to evoke the most poignant memories – the feverish dash across the mugger-infested streets of the black ghetto from the hospital to the warmth of the dormitory. Then there were the long talks over beer and pepperoni pizza late into the night, as blueprints for a brave new psychiatric world were refined and polished.

'Sure,' said Anne at last, her smile nostalgic. 'Boy, were we the brave young Turks in those days. Heresy was the name of the game.'

The sound of the doorbell cut into their reverie. They both laughed. It was 8.45 a.m.

'Well, you haven't shifted all her obsessional symptoms.'

Anne looked back over her shoulder on her way to the door. 'Listen, you're a bit thin. You'd better come and have some dinner with me tomorrow night at Washington Square. Can't have one half of the partnership starring in the journals as the only male menopausal example of anorexia nervosa in the history of the disease.'

Eyes twinkling, she was gone.

Freda Weissman sat perched on the very edge of the chair in a position of supreme discomfort, back ramrod straight, hands clasped tightly in the lap of her neat tweed skirt. She was twenty-three going on forty-five, an impression heightened by the severity of her hairstyle and the weight of her shoes. She was blushing to the very roots of her being.

'Frankly, it's so *disgusting*, Dr Carrington. It's the last thing I'd actually want to *do*. I can't think of anything more revolting than putting one of those . . . things inside my mouth. I can't think where the awful idea comes from. It's quite mad. Maybe I am mad. I must be, mustn't I?'

'Of course you're not mad. No way. This is an isolated difficulty. We're getting on top of it already. It's not even that unusual. Also, Freda, you must realize that nobody is suggesting for one minute that you want to do these things. I don't think that, and you mustn't feel guilty. Try to think of it like the 'flu, as a temporary illness which we can cure. There's no blame attached to having it any more than there is to having the measles.'

'But I'm so afraid I might actually say those words. It would be the end of everything if I did. I'd just die. It's all I can do to resist it. I just stand there biting my lip, unable to speak or do anything, and I just feel faint with worry as if I'm going to collapse, fall over or something. It's just so *ghastly*.'

Anne liked to use a two-pronged attack when dealing with obsessional illness. Firstly, you had to get the brain biochemistry right and treat the symptoms of anxiety and depression. The next thing was to deal with the obsessional thoughts themselves, and that meant behaviour therapy.

'Right, Freda. Now I'm going to use a behavioural technique during this session. The theory is that anything that has been learned can be unlearned with practice. We're going to start with something called "desensitization". Firstly, we have to get you to experience the awful impulse to shout out the obscenity – and then, while you are actually experiencing it, we practise new emotional and physical reactions to the unwanted thoughts.'

Freda Weissman caught on right away. Her voice sounded a little panicky. 'What – you mean you're going to go right into the class with me? I . . . don't think that's really possible. I mean, nobody knows I'm being treated . . .' Her voice trailed off. Teachers who were known to be psychiatric patients had a habit of becoming ex-teachers.

Anne laughed. 'No, no. I'm sorry. I haven't explained properly. In this technique we can get good results by using imagination. You have to imagine you're in class, right here in my office. Then as the anxiety levels begin to rise I'm going to get you to relax. By constant repetition we're going to get you to associate the impulse with relaxation rather than terror. That way we can break the vicious circle.'

Freda looked relieved. 'OK,' she said.

The first step was to get Freda stretched out on the couch.

'Now, you must relax completely. Start at the tips of your toes and work upwards, letting the muscles go, one by one. That's it. Take deep breaths. Very slowly.'

Gradually, Freda began to respond to the soothing monotone, and Anne watched her tense body begin to unwind.

'OK. Now you're in the classroom, standing up in front of all those young boys. Tell me their names.' Hesitantly, Freda began a rough-and-ready roll call.

'You feel calm, peaceful. Concentrate on letting everything go loose. You're feeling sleepy. Imagine lying in the sun after a delicious lunch. What does Dobson look like?'

'He's sort of tall, and dark. Rather thin. Brown eyes, I guess.'

'What are you teaching?'

'Oh, I'm telling them about Hemingway's novels.' Freda had begun to blush. She shifted uncomfortably on the couch. Her hands opened and closed.

'You're so warm, deliciously warm, the sun beating down. Your whole body is totally relaxed. Let the tension ooze out of your muscles. Isn't there something you feel you have to tell the class. What do you want to suck? Say it very quietly, very gently.'

At first it was barely audible, a conspiratorial whisper. 'I want to suck cock.' Then Miss Weissman said it again, a little louder this time.

'Say it again. Tell the class what you want to do. Tell them so they'll remember it.'

Freda Weissman's face was now twisted in hatred as she spat out the words with, pure, naked aggression in her voice. 'I want to suck cock,' she screamed at the top of her voice. Immediately she was weeping. 'But I don't. I don't. Oh God, it's so filthy. It makes me sick to think of it. Those poor young boys. What am I going to do?' She had an overwhelming desire to get up and run to the bathroom, to wash herself, to clean off the dirt that was all over her hands and face.

'Sit still.' Anne barked the command.

And then, quite suddenly, Anne had a conceptual hit, a blinding flash of neat, undiluted intuition. Before her eyes a window of opportunity had opened up. In a second it would be closed. There was no time to weigh the pros and cons.

'Freda, I think you really do want to have a boy in your mouth. You want to feel it, to taste it.'

For a long moment of unbearable doubt, Anne waited. If Miss Weissman rejected this interpretation then Anne would reap the whirlwind. The therapeutic alliance would be in ruins. At a stroke Anne would be transformed from friend into enemy.

Freda Weissman sat bolt upright on the couch. Slowly she turned to face Anne, a puzzled, quizzical expression on her face. 'You know, I think there's a part of me that does,' she said simply.

At a stroke the obsessional impulse had been transformed into another much less sinister and more easily managed animal – it had become a statement of desire. If Freda could admit to herself that the impulse was not mad, to be resisted with every fibre of her being, but was instead the manifestation of a real sexual longing, however perverted and inappropriate, then much, though not all, of the associated anxiety would fade.

Anne breathed a great sigh of relief. This was the sort of thing that made it all worthwhile.

Chapter Two

'I went to this restaurant called Gnolo's.
It's a sheeeeety place, it's a fucking disgrace'

The small, effervescent man belted out the words of the song to the tune of the Eagle's 'Hotel California', bouncing up and down as he wrapped his tongue indulgently around the syllables. Despite the fact that he was clearly very drunk, he sang extraordinarily well. The fruity baritone with its exuberant Mexican accentuation made Speedy Gonzales sound like a gringo, but the singer was pure prep, from his short, tousled sandy hair to his highly polished, tasseled Weejuns. The song's contents were so far from being complimentary that they constituted the purest and most unadulterated slander, as the singer traced the rise of the legendary restauranteur Nick from his lowly position as one of Elaine's waiters to the proprietorship of first Nicola's and now the new and trendy Gnolo's. Sexual favours of a somewhat debasing kind to the mighty Elaine had, according to the song, smoothed the path to fame. Crude gestures simulating masturbation and oral sex accompanied the appropriate lines of the song, and beads of sweat stood out on the singer's glistening brow as he bent and twisted his stocky frame in the frantic and explicit pantomime.

To the uninitiated it may have seemed strange that this performance, not obviously flattering in content, should be permitted amongst the tables of Gnolo's. That was to miss the whole point of the 'in' joke. As the audience roared its appreciation, none was more enthusiastic than the large, round, swarthy man whose ingratiating sexploits formed the subject matter of the ditty. As the saga of Nick's dubious journey to power and influence n the kingdom of New York's night crashed to a close amid thunderous applause from the cognoscenti and bewildered and perplexed smiles from the outsiders, he embraced the singer in an appreciative bear-hug.

'Petey, you win the $1.98,' he roared.

Peter Danforth staggered towards an empty seat at the large centre table and allowed his head to loll forwards on to the white tablecloth. A muffled cry came from the back of his throat.

'Champagne, champagne.'

Without hesitating the girl next to him grabbed at the neck of the Dom Perignon and in a single sweeping movement extracted it from the silver bucket and upturned it over Peter Danforth's head and shoulders. For a second or two he didn't move except to turn his head from side to side under the golden cascade amid gales of laughter from the rest of the party. Finally, the bottle empty, he surfaced, shaking his head like a wet dog and covering everyone with about $100 worth of champagne. Far from being upset, he seemed to be enjoying the joke enormously.

'Next time you give me a golden shower, I insist on the real thing, Mariel,' he shouted.

Mariel O'Sullivan allowed her eyebrows to rise in a mock quizzical expression as a knowing smile played round the corners of her mouth. She drawled her reply.

'Fer shuuuurrre. I didn't know that was your bag, Petey.' Despite the jokey atmosphere, the flame of sexuality flickered briefly, then disappeared.

Mariel O'Sullivan looked good, even looked as if she could do you good, but in fact she wasn't really good at all. This took a bit of finding out, and many didn't bother to dig that deep, being quite content to sample the inviting exterior. After all, who cared that beauty was only skin deep? For that matter, so was ugliness. Whatever, beauty was a commodity which Mariel possessed in almost obscene abundance. The green eyes sparkled dangerously above the high cheekbones, which in turn fell away sharply to

20

the corners of a long, inviting but rather cruel mouth. Her blonde hair, a whiter shade of gold, looked as if it had been moulded by a chisel, chopped and layered by a consummate artist long on self-confidence and with an unerring eye for shape. Though she was sitting at the table, it was obvious that she was tall. There was little mystery, too, about the quality and cut of her breasts. From time to time, when she shifted position, one or the other of them was clearly visible to the most shortsighted of observers. Such myopia as was present at the large table at Gnolo's was exclusively due to alcohol. But although everyone was flying high for the moment, nobody was blind drunk. Mariel's semiconscious peep show was far from unnoticed. Now, as she leaned back and let a rough laugh explode from the back of her throat, her deep-blue satin jacket bent away from her naked chest revealing a perfectly formed breast.

Peter Danforth ogled it shamelessly. The pale pink nipple was a triangle of temptation as it rubbed gently against the heavy, sapphire-coloured material. The confident muscles of extreme youth projected the pointed breast outwards and upwards – arrogant, daring, calling stridently for the touch of hands, of lips. Or so it seemed to Peter Danforth's fevered brain as he revelled in the spectacle. Milk-white and peach-pink. Peaches-and-cream. The words went round and round in his mind.

Mariel held the position a little longer, far from unaware of its effect, and then abruptly withdrew the tantalizing visual. Shifting in her seat she pushed back her chair and unwound long, smooth legs as her pencil skirt slithered upwards towards her thin waist. Now there was a new focus of attention, a mystery of infinitely greater fascination than where the rainbow ended. Where and how did Mariel's legs end? Through the champagne mist in his mind, Peter sought the bionic vision, fought to experience visually the thrusting boyish buttocks, to imagine the contents of the white cotton panties, if indeed such things existed.

The mocking voice cut into his lascivious thoughts. 'For Christ's sake, Petey, stop mind-fucking Mariel and get us some more shampoo.'

The languid drawl conjured up thoughts of a bygone age as spirits of aristocracy were summoned from some vasty deep. To describe the accent as Boston Brahmin was to do it little justice. It was far too original for that. Unmistakably American, there was a solid percentage of English, too, and it was this which gave it a unique distinction. No one could *learn* to speak in this way. It was passed on in the genes, taken in by osmosis from nursery walls, filtered into the vocal chords from the damp mists of the river Thames. The speaker had to be an Old Etonian American.

Adam Phipps was twenty-three and looked like an angel. Dorian Gray would have slunk away at the suggestion of a beauty contest. His fair hair was slicked back from a high forehead in a rakish style, shining and glowing beneath the restaurant lights. Deep Cambridge-blue eyes flanked an immaculately structured nose. Even, snow-white teeth flashed between delicate, full lips set in a firm, square jaw. What soft skin was visible from the deep V of the open blue cotton Turnbull and Asser shirt to the hair line had been sun-basted to a delicious light honey-brown.

Adam stared across the table at Mariel. His good-natured rebuke to Petey had been a statement of claim.

Mariel smiled back at him, continuing an ancient and ritualized charade. Knowingly, but apparently unwittingly, she'd excited Adam's friend. As intended, a spark of jealousy had flashed. Adam had made a public statement of seigneurial rights. Objective achieved.

Such behaviour was second nature to Mariel. Sometimes it seemed to her that she'd been born with this ability to manipulate men – and women, too. That was often a more valuable skill. Right now she was playing for very big stakes indeed, and she didn't intend to lose. Adam Phipps was her target, her ambition, her goal. Mrs Adam Phipps. There were riches beyond the dreams of avarice for the girl who hooked the Phipps fortune – and he even looked good! But she wasn't home yet. Rich aristocrats, even those with dead parents, had a way of sliding out of the ultimate commitment to street-sharp girls with no background like Mariel. Just when you thought you had them by the balls, that they were addicted to what you could provide, they upped and married distant relations with faces like buns and names like Muffy and Bitsy.

Mariel had been caught like that before. She'd ignored the challenge, underestimated the opposition when Mary Stevenson had muscled in on Harry Brewster III. Mariel had decided quite rightly that Mary couldn't fuck her way out of a paper bag. In view of the fact that it took Mariel herself about an hour to make the impotent lush come, she'd dismissed the plain-jane preppy out of hand. She'd ignored the pedigree stretching back to the Mayflower, the mighty trust fund, the acres in Virginia and the New York brownstone – but Harry had not. In a tearful farewell he'd had the gall to offer to set Mariel up in a Madison Avenue duplex if she'd continue as his mistress after the wedding. It had not been an auspicious occasion.

So Mariel had been bitten, and now, with Adam in her sights, she'd profit from her experience. She'd answered Brewster's offer with a knee in the groin, which, she later heard, had not contributed greatly to the enjoyment of his honeymoon. When she'd left his apartment it was with nothing but the addresses and telephone numbers of four or five of his richest friends. Adam had been at the top of the list and she hadn't had to try any of the others. Now, as she gazed warmly across the table at $100,000,000, she said a silent prayer of thanks to Mary Stevenson and the third Harry Brewster. Her son, a Phipps, would be able to buy the whole stinking lot of them.

She'd read Adam like a book, discovering his weaknesses and insecurities as if hunting for the most precious of gems. Through his faults she could control him, through

23

his desires and needs dominate him, through his inadequacies and his ambitions manipulate him.

Mariel might have been surprised to learn how well Adam knew her thinking. She'd have been surprised, too, at the conclusions he drew. She'd been on the scene for a couple of years now, and at the Racquet Club she had something of a reputation as a golddigger. It was far from the only reputation she had. All who had been afforded the privileges of her bedroom, and occasionally of more unlikely venues, testified to the mindbending uniqueness of the experience. The bottom line was that in bed Mariel was extraordinarily good, a virtuoso performer. For that alone he was happy to overlook the fact that in other respects she was a very bad girl indeed. Adam knew exactly where she was coming from and where she intended to go. He knew, too, that ultimately their plans didn't coincide. For the moment, however, she suited him just fine.

For the moment. For the moment. That was the problem. Nowadays he lived only for the present, scarcely daring to look at the future, which day by day looked increasingly unpromising. It hadn't always been like this. Once there had been plans, dreams – hope. Adam stared morosely into the bubbles of his champagne, their cheerful irreverence in direct contrast to his suddenly gloomy thoughts. And then he was going back, the restaurant and its raucous inhabitants receding, drifting away, their senseless shouting stilled as he escaped into the land of memories.

The adrenalin pumped and the feeling of unreality was intense. Was it really he – Adam – standing above the sea of expectant faces? Was that his voice – so cool, so commanding – saying all those brilliantly clever things? He felt completely depersonalized, his thoughts divided into watcher and watched. The amazing thing was that the thought processes which produced the words seemed to be

24

on automatic pilot, and it didn't seem to matter a bit if the proud, smiling face of Professor Hicks was anything to go by.

'And so I must make the prediction that in one or two short years we will see nothing less than a computer revolution in this country. Personal computers will sit in every living room and the whole family – even the children – perhaps especially the children – will know how to use them.'

That speech had represented the ultimate accolade. To graduate *summa cum laude* in computer sciences from Harvard had been done before. To be asked to address the faculty because of the excellence and originality of the research work he'd done as an undergraduate was unheard of. That the department would offer him a job was baked in the cake. A glittering future in the groves of academe was all but assured.

He was getting to the end of the address now. Old Hicks was in ecstasy. Adam had been his protégé and he hadn't been let down. When he'd suggested that Adam talk to the department, feathers had been ruffled and more than one of his colleagues had been predicting and hoping for disaster. They'd been totally confounded by Adam's triumph, and now Hicks was basking in the reflected glory. Almost before Adam had stopped talking he'd been on his feet to lead the applause.

It was only when he'd sat down that Adam had remembered his parents. How strange it was that the two people he cared about more than the world itself had been absent from his mind at the moment of his greatest achievement. He'd done it for them as much as for himself, and now at last his eyes scanned the hall to find them, to share with them his happiness, to experience theirs. They had flown in from New York to be with him, a tight schedule meaning they had missed the faculty lunch that had preceded Adam's address.

What was that flurry at the back of the lecture hall, the

cluster of academics, the nervous glances directed backwards towards the rostrum? Yes, those furtive, huddled whisperings had been the first harbingers of the disaster. Then there had been the purposeful, heavy steps of the Dean walking towards him, and Adam had felt the sick dread well up within him as he'd contemplated the face of tragedy's messenger. An airplane crash . . . great sadness . . . no survivors . . . pray for strength . . . if there was anything he could do . . . The Dean's words sounded the death-knell of Adam's world. His mother and father dead. A fatherless, motherless child. Alone. The audience gone, the light gone out, the actor mouthing meaningless words. It had been the end of happiness for him, the beginning of hopelessness. Before that awful moment there had been nothing in his life that had gone wrong; afterwards it seemed nothing had gone right.

Awesome riches, before never even considered, enlarged rather than filled the void created by the loss of his parents. Gripped by a deep depression, he'd let all the good things go – his work, his ambition for excellence, his kindliness, his love of life. And, slowly but surely, he'd found seductive surrogates to replace them. Mariel had come into his life like a white tornado. At first she'd shown him how to laugh again, how to enjoy himself in a way that required no self-discipline, no effort, no energy. There had been the drink, and then, in increasing quantities, the drugs. Finally, and most importantly, she'd begun to turn him on, to wind him up sexually as she led him on a journey of sensation and discovery. Gradually the pain of his grief had lessened. But at a terrible price – his self-respect.

So here he sat, a fugitive from excellence, in Gnolo's restaurant, with his bitter memories of the days when it had all been possible.

Hell. Dammit. He was back. But in the here and now there was champagne. Lots of it. And other substances, too.

'I think I could cope with a little divine dandruff, Mariel

– and young Petey looks to be in need. I think the sight of your tits has unnerved him.'

The small, exquisite, George II snuff box hit the table dead-centre. Mariel had undoubtedly been its origin, but the exact location of its former hiding place – a pocket? Some more secret place? – remained a mystery. Adam leaned forwards slowly and grasped it between long, delicate fingers.

'You're a star, luv,' he said paternally.

He stood up and, casting disdainful looks about him at the other diners, picked his way delicately towards the lavatory. Petey, like a faithful dog responding to his master's voice, stumbled unsteadily in his wake.

Mariel poured herself a glass of champagne. In a place like Gnolo's, you did your own pouring.

Danforth's date, the pretty daughter of an English MP, who had made the fashionable transition into the New York modelling scene, shifted seats to sit next to Mariel. Open admiration shone from her eyes.

'Oh, Mariel, you're really *wild*.'

Mariel acknowledged the compliment by flicking a drop or two of Dom Perignon in the general direction of the girl. She was used to being held in awe by men, women and children. It was nothing new, and it was deserved as well. After all, she'd scored the coke. It was she who had to make the trip downtown, to mix with the scum, pretend she was their friend and take the risks that acquaintance with pushers always entailed. OK, so Adam peeled off the scoots. But when you had megabucks, that was no big deal. She usually made a turn on the deal, too – in effect ripped him off a bit. So what? Adam's weird value system would've approved of that. It was fine for Mariel to put her hand in his pocket – but gross for a Vanderbilt to do the same. One law for the 'quality' another for the . . . ? Mariel wondered what the right word was. Rubbish? Outlaws? Space cadets?

Anger flashed briefly across the firmament of her mind.

27

There was more. She had to carry the drugs and if there was a bust she'd take the rap, get touched up in the cells and fingered by the cops until ten o'clock the next morning when the Phipps family lawyer would finally make it to the precinct, nose in the air and asshole puckered in distaste. She'd be sprung all right, and later at Lutèce they'd all giggle and congratulate themselves on how clever they'd been as they sucked back their gin and tonics and quarrelled about the choice of the claret. Fuck-rats. She'd sit there playing it for all it was worth, letting them in on the low-down from the other side of the tracks, when all the while the stench of the drunkards' vomit would be in her nostrils, the urine stink of the night holding-cage, the grubby fingers picking at her body, the supercilious shit from the cops, the unspoken scorn of the Phipps legal eagle.

Mariel forced herself to stop the silent scream of protest. She unwound tight white fingers from the arms of her chair, invisible beneath the tablecloth. She mustn't blow it. Stay light. Stay fun. After she'd made it – and only then – there would be time for revenge. Boy, would there be blood on the walls.

So little Sarah from Wiltshire thought she was wild, did she? And awesome? And *terrific*? Well, that was fine. In a way she was right, but she hadn't seen anything yet. In the meantime, all adulation was gratefully received. It could be used – perhaps sooner than anyone imagined.

Mariel slipped into acting gear. Head cocked to one side, expression questioning and lips slightly parted, she looked straight into Sarah Gurney's eyes, taking in the wide-open pupils, the misty haze of intoxication and the respect that flowed out from them.

'Well, I think you're pretty cute yourself, Sarah.'

Her voice was deliberately husky, with the faintest hint of a catch – as if it hadn't been entirely easy to make this little statement. Mariel's tongue darted out to wet an implied dry lip as she sized up the girl. She probably wouldn't have made it on to Wilhemina's list without daddy's connections, but it would've been a close run thing. She had most of the English qualities, some of their disadvantages. The face was definitely aristocratic, the features undoubtedly fine. Skin superb, tits big – if just a little floppy. Marginally on the short side, perhaps a hint of broadness in the beam. Swimming suits? Forget it. Ball gowns? Perfection.

For a split second Sarah looked perturbed. That had sounded just a little too sincere for comfort, and people like Sarah reacted to sincerity in the same way they did to social clumsiness. They ignored it. She gave a short, whinnying laugh. A bit like a frightened horse, thought Mariel.

'I wonder where the boys have got to?' she said by way of changing the subject.

Forget 'the boys'. This one doesn't get off the hook. No way, thought Mariel. 'What you need is a popper,' she said.

Suddenly there was power in her voice. If Sarah wanted to remain a 'regular guy', she wouldn't turn down a noseful of amylnitrite. They both knew what Sarah 'wanted'. Both knew that Mariel could and would queer her pitch with Danforth, with the whole group, if the idea appealed to her. But there was something else. Mariel radiated a strange strength, frightening and yet oddly alluring, her siren voice making the rocks sound like exciting places indeed. If taking drugs made you more like Mariel, then they couldn't be all bad. A more perceptive observer than nineteen-year-old Sarah Gurney might have noticed that, despite all appearances to the contrary, Mariel herself was a pretty abstemious person. She always seemed to be drinking and yet was never drunk, and the drugs always ended up inside somebody else's nose. While other minds bent, her psyche remained frighteningly straight; while other consciousnesses expanded, hers remained within strictly patrolled boundaries. All the while she remained conductress of the orchestra, mistress of ceremonies, life and soul of the endless party.

'What, here, at the table?' Sarah sounded and looked uncertain but didn't want it to show.

'Fer sure.' Once again the drawled reply, reassuring, threatening – the carrot and the stick.

'OK, great.' Generations of Gurneys turned in their graves at their kinswoman's lack of backbone.

'Come here.'

There were lots of different ways of saying that. Mariel gave the two words an undeniably sexual connotation. The words were like a caress, and as Sarah leaned across towards the disturbing beauty she felt tingling electrical sensations shoot up and down her long, thin neck.

Obediently, she lowered her face into the crisp cotton napkin, heard the brisk snap as the ampoule exploded between Mariel's fingers, breathed in the disgusting fumes which always reminded her of the smell of her brother's socks in the gunroom after a wet day's shooting. Then the feeling took her – freedom, liberation, desire, a lightness in the brain, a pounding of the heart. The room spun round as she leaned back laughing against her chair, her legs splaying open lasciviously, Mariel's face, so beautiful, inches from her own. She could feel the other girl's breath upon her, was mesmerized by the delicious looking tongue as she began to reach forward, wanting only to taste it with her own. But as she moved towards her objective, oblivious to the other inhabitants of the crowded restaurant, Mariel put out a restraining and at once caressing hand, its finger on Sarah's searching lips.

'Later, honey. Not now, later,' she said, eyes twinkling with mischief at the effect she had conjured up out of thin air. Little Sarah Gurney would be a pushover. No sweat. No sweat at all.

Sarah, coming down from her brief but far from uneventful high, was already trying to cope with the ramifications of her feelings, with the meaning of Mariel's

30

words, with the presence of Mariel's fingertip on her dry lips.

Peter Danforth's jaunty comment didn't help at all.

'Hey, Mariel, what's all this? You going for a little tongue sushi with my girl? Boy, it's really sin-city round here.'

Adam joined in the fun. 'You leave them for a second or two and they're all over each other like a hot rash – swapping spit – you name it.'

The deep red glow started on Sarah's neck and, as the audience watched, crept up to suffuse chin, cheeks and forehead. Mariel remained cucumber-cool, totally in control.

'Listen, assholes, girls need a bit of affection when the only cock that's about is hanging on a couple of wacked-out dope-fiends.'

The comment drew noisy enthusiasm from the two men. Wow, could Mariel ladle it out!

And so it went on. Jocular rudeness. Raucous shouting. In jokes. The occasional thing thrown. One party of out-of-towners, unlucky enough to have been seated at a nearby table, attempted to complain to Nick when a fine spray of champagne suffused them.

'Oh, that's Mr Phipps,' had come the jaunty reply. 'Mr Phipps is *allowed* to throw champagne.'

Adam, Peter, Mariel and Sarah formed the nucleus of the party, but were by no means its only members. Screams of welcome would erupt as new friends stopped for a bit on their way towards the innards of the restaurant or had one for the road on the way out. Others, less favoured, were ignored completely and told to 'walk on' if they didn't get the hint. Trips to the bathroom became more regular as nasal membranes withstood a sustained assault. Food came and went, largely untouched, in a token gesture to the fact that they were all supposedly 'having dinner'. This didn't prevent a stream of abuse about its quality, all steadfastly ignored by a Nick long impervious to such careless insults.

31

'That chicken really *sucked*, Nick.'

'Those ribs have given me the runs already, and I didn't even *try* them yet.'

'Listen, Petey, when you hit the bathroom it's not to ride the porcelain Honda.'

No prizes for the wit of the repartee here. Still, the wine check was pushing a $1,000. No business like good business.

Nick was quite happy to put up with most of the bad behaviour, and when it went totally over the top he'd throw them all out, deaf to their threats of revenge and retribution. In a day or two they'd be back, the row forgotten. For when the chips were down they respected a firm hand, a man who had the courage to stand up to them, to spit in the face of their money and class. Raffish, rich, carefree, rude and young, they were also creatures of habit. At Gnolo's they knew what to expect and that was always a bull point.

It wouldn't be long now before the jeunesse d'ore passed on in their movable feast. A row started with people at the next table, Petey felt sick, a waiter was slow in replenishing the drink, an ice bucket made it to the floor.

'We're out of here,' said Adam.

'We're history,' agreed Peter.

'Want to swing by Area on the way back?' asked Adam.

'No. Let's go straight home. I've got girls waiting.' Mariel looked at her watch as she said this. It was going to be a long night.

The sleek black limo was waiting for them outside the restaurant. Bob, the black driver, immaculate in grey uniform and peaked cap, was already opening the doors as the noisy group erupted on to the sidewalk. In the front passenger seat sat another black man, his role not immediately clear but hinted at by his monumental size. He wore jeans, a white sweat shirt, a black leather jacket and an expression of transcendental nastiness. This was Andy, the muscle. Adam and his friends felt it was chic to travel around with their own bodyguard, and on one or two occasions the affectation had more than paid off. This evening Andy would almost certainly be superfluous.

In Tribeca or Soho, and points further downtown, he was as essential a piece of kit as the car itself. In such places there were more than enough 'good citizens' who'd consider it the high-point of their evening to splatter the likes of Adam and Petey all over the sidewalk before walking off with their women.

They drank brandy from Waterford cut-glass goblets as they drove the few blocks to Adam's duplex at the corner of Fifth Avenue and 72nd Street. That put Petey through the ceiling. Muttering 'Boy, I think I'm going to woof,' he passed out.

The liveried doorman hurried out to meet them. 'Good evening, Mr Phipps. There's two ladies waiting for you in the lobby. Wouldn't give their names but they said they was expected. I hope I done right letting them wait.'

The doorman's voice was riddled with uncertainty. Mr Phipps' Christmas bonus was so substantial that it actually figured in his mortgage calculations. The two women sitting in the sumptuous foyer of the apartment block hardly qualified for the title 'ladies' in his book, although both were undeniably good looking, but he felt it was wise to describe them as such. There might easily be problems about his letting them in, especially as Miss O'Sullivan was in Mr Phipps' party. Mariel dispelled all doubts.

'Oh, it's all right Frank. They're friends of mine. We were expecting them.'

'What are we going to do about Petey? He's really *zoned*, you know.' Sarah had taken to using such expressions, her Oxford accent giving them a faintly surreal quality. Somehow, it was to Mariel that the question was addressed.

'Oh, we can send him home in the limo. You'll put him to bed won't you, Andy?'

The sullen Andy grunted his acquiescence. It wasn't the first time he'd performed this function, and it wouldn't be the last. It was the sort of thing he was paid to do. He had a healthy respect for Mariel. She was his sort of people – tough and ballsy, knowing where she was going and yet not for one minute forgetting where she'd come from. She might not have a nickel to her name today, but he had the hunch she was going to take these rich mothers for a whole bundle of cash. If there had been a taker he'd have had had money riding on it.

Sarah protested mildly, 'I think really I ought to see him home,' she said without conviction.

'Nonsense,' said Adam. 'If he's going to puke it's certainly not going to be all over my Shirvans. Give him a call in the morning. If he makes it through the night, that is.' He laughed cheerfully.

Mariel took Sarah's hand, leading her towards the marbelled hallway as the limo slid away from the kerb. She gave it an encouraging squeeze. 'Hey, this is really great. We've got you all to ourselves.'

She ushered Sarah ahead through the swing doors. It was shaping up well. Things were falling neatly into place. Petey had taken himself out of the game and now young Sarah was all alone. Mariel eyed her professionally, model appraising model. The full, ripe bottom moved nicely. There was a sort of seductive innocence to the walk – grouse moor-hiking and high fashion making uneasy but interesting bedfellows. A thrill of anticipation coursed through her. The same stone would be hitting two birds this evening – or should she say three? The truth was that Mariel really liked to make it with girls, and Adam liked to watch her do it. In pleasing herself she tightened her hold on him. It all made sense.

The two girls sitting in the giant foyer beneath the vast crystal chandelier got up uncertainly as the little group walked in. The taller one went over to Mariel. She seemed very nervous.

'Miss O'Sullivan, I'm sorry we were a little early. I hope you didn't mind us waiting here.'

It seemed a polite if rather unnecessary apology. Her tone was thoroughly subservient, almost ingratiating. Neither Adam nor Mariel said anything. Instead they stood back as if surveying a mildly interesting piece of sculpture at the Met. Sarah, knowing that manners maketh man, prepared some innocuous phrase to put these two rather overawed friends of Mariel's at their ease.

'Oh, not at all. We . . .'

Mariel's voice, hard as nails, cut her off in mid-sentence. 'Have you got all the gear?' she asked rudely.

The girls pointed towards a large suitcase.

'OK Let's get this show on the road. Follow me.'

Nobody made any attempt to help with the suitcase, which appeared to be quite heavy. There were no introductions.

In the elevator the tension rose as they sped upwards in total silence.

Sarah opened her mouth to murmur some inanity, then thought better of it.

Mariel continued to look the two girls up and down, a producer casting for a Broadway show. Not bad, not bad at all. The tall girl was good-looking rather than pretty. Raven black hair cut short in a boyish bob, dark-brown eyes, olive skin, very delicate hands and what looked like great tits beneath the cheap 'fur' coat. She wore shiny black boots of imitation leather whose tops were invisible under the fake chinchilla. She stood straight, avoiding the walls of the elevator and the eyes around her, hands clasped in front of her. If it hadn't been for the clothes she could have passed for a schoolteacher, the sort that the history master was in love with and over whom the adolescents in the senior class had wet-dreams. Even more remarkable, that was exactly what Rachel was.

The other girl was more obviously pretty, with a pert all-American face and a hint of freckles clustering around an upturned nose. Her hair was also short, but this time a rather obvious bleached-out blonde. Her best feature was a remarkably generous mouth, through the parted lips of which white tombstone-like teeth were visible. Jenny looked as fresh and innocent as an eighteenth-century milkmaid but she, too, kept her head down, away from the curious eyes which bored into her. She wore a tweed hacking jacket tapering at the waist over a white cotton shirt open to a cleavage of medium-sized, pointed breasts. Tight Levis accentuated a small, well-rounded ass. Clean, seemingly brand-new Nike running shoes finished off the somewhat unlikely ensemble. What, Mariel wondered, did this one do in her spare time, or rather her real time? She knew the other chick was some sort of freaked-out teacher. She speculated briefly. The coat said 'suburbs' or 'country', the shoes quite definitely 'city'. The rest was neutral. Whatever, she looked terrific and had 'amateur' written all over her. No way had she seen 25 yet. She was a real scoop.

With a sudden movement Mariel reached forwards and put two fingers beneath the blonde's jaw, lifting up her face towards hers.

'And what do you do, honey, when you're not being a wicked little girl, like tonight?'

'I'm a nurse at Bellevue.' The girl's face was a delicate rose pink by the time she had finished the sentence. She began to breathe faster, breasts rising and falling beneath the cotton shirt. 'I'm married to an architect,' she added. A bead of sweat appeared on her upper lip.

'Don't tell me,' said Mariel. 'He likes you to come on jaunts like this, and you have to give him all the juicy details. Right?' She took her hand away as the other girl nodded shamefacedly. Christ, thought Mariel, she's ripe. The elevator stopped on the 17th floor.

In a city where space wasn't given away, the area in which the party now found themselves seemed a colossal extravagance. The floor was of Italian marble and the giant anteroom was totally empty except for two ornate Louis

36

XVI chairs standing guard on either side of the eighteenth-century carved oak door that led to Adam's apartment. A cut-glass Georgian chandelier of incredible delicacy provided light for the windowless anteroom. High in the corner of the ceiling, wide-angle, closed-circuit TV cameras scanned the room. From both inside the duplex and from the doorman's room on the ground floor visitors were carefully monitored. If street people were going to make it into the Phipps place, it would be strictly by invitation.

As if by some unheard command the massive door opened as the group approached, revealing a small, parchment-coloured Oriental dressed in white coat, pinstriped trousers and highly polished black walking shoes. He conducted himself as if it was two o'clock in the afternoon rather than two in the morning. Nor did Adam see fit to apologize for keeping the Chinese servant up.

'No need to stay up, Wan-Tu. We'll fix our own drinks. Goodnight.' That meant, on no account come anywhere near the drawing room, study, bedrooms, theatre or sauna and jacuzzi area on pain of instant dismissal. Wan-Tu, whose application for US citizenship was already lodged in the bowels of the bureaucracy, would do as he was told. Even the most exotic of noises wouldn't draw him from bed.

Sarah Gurney collapsed in mock exhaustion on the slubbed silk sofa and looked around appreciatively. This was English country house-style decoration, and she felt instantly at home. No queer designer, no afficionado of the avant garde had been in on the organization of this apartment. For Adam, despite his tender years, was a traditionalist in such matters. In vain would one look for mirrored walls, perspex, brass, leather and strip-lighting. No cheap tricks, apart from its occupants, marred the eighteenth-century gentility of the duplex.

Before setting off for the excitement of the New World, Sarah Gurney, like so many of her contemporaries, had done a stint as a trainee at Christies, that famed emporium where gentlemen maintained their upper-class pretensions while behaving like used-car salesmen. She took in a quartet of Venetian oils. Canaletto or Guardi? She'd only lasted at the London auctioneers six months. Couldn't be sure. The silk Persian carpets were extraordinarily fine. A Tabriz, a Kirman, three or four Shirvans – the ones Adam had not wanted ruined by poor Petey's puke. The furniture was predominantly Sheraton – a superb colour, condition immaculate. Carpets, walls, table lamps – all faultless.

'What a beautiful apartment, Adam. Did you fix it up yourself?'

'Nope. Sister Parish.'

That figured. The septuagenarian doyenne of American decorators worked only for the richest and grandest families in the land. She'd made an exception to that rule in agreeing to do the Kennedy White House.

Mariel, however, was not about to lose the evening's momentum in a precious discussion about design. Gesturing to a door she issued an imperious command.

'OK you two. Shift ass. Get your act together in one of the bedrooms and wait till I call you.'

Dutifully, Rachel and Jenny moved off, totally obedient, every movement proclaiming their subservience. Sarah Gurney could contain her curiosity no longer.

'Who *are* those girls?' she asked seconds after the door had closed behind them. 'What on earth are they going to *do*?'

Mariel laughed, delighted by Sarah's confusion. 'They're submissives,' she said shortly, knowing that the word would mean nothing at all to the English girl.

'Oh,' said Sarah, unwilling to expose her lack of sophistication.

Adam came to her aid. 'What Mariel means is that these two charming ladies of the night get their rocks off by being dominated, humiliated and made to 'do things'. Like they actually enjoy being degraded – sort of like they dance to the masochism tango.'

38

'Oh!' Sarah repeated the exclamation, not at all sure what to make of this information. Was it good news or had she just heard a discouraging word? Clearly the two girls were going to mount some sort of an exhibition. That would be interesting – quite exciting, actually. And yet she had a strange feeling that somehow a little more than merely playing the role of enthusiastic spectator might be required of her. It made her feel uneasy, nervous. But at the same time the mild anxiety was far from being unpleasant, in fact possessed distinct elements of that delicious fear felt at the heart-stopping moment before the Big Dipper plunged into its hair-raising descent. The champagne had loosened her up but she needed some more to keep up flying speed.

Mariel was ahead of her. 'Have you got any of that Pol Roger rosé on ice, Adam?'

'Should be some. I'll go see.'

The two girls were alone. Time to move things along a bit. Mariel slumped on to the sofa beside Sarah. The movement was deliberately out of control, with the end result that she ended up closer to the English girl than would have been acceptable otherwise. This way it looked like the proximity was accidental. Their knees were touching. Would Sarah move her leg away? She didn't. OK. Mariel's mind was in overdrive. She really liked this – the chase, hunter and hunted. One false move and it could be blown. Get it right and this pretty aristocrat could be blown in the most delightful way. She felt the juices begin to move within her, the familiar squirting of adrenalin into her system. She had some time. Adam knew the score – the champagne wouldn't be 'found'. His re-entry to the room would be discreet, possibly secret. Sarah had had just about the right amount to drink, but something else would be needed to soften her up. A toot of coke? Another popper?

Sarah Gurney was in an agony of indecision, emotions pulling her in all different directions at once. She'd been with girls before. At school, crushes had been far from uncommon. On at least two occasions she'd kissed another girl, but it had never gone further than unprofessional fumblings, guiltily indulged in and later ignored by both participants. Since then she'd considered herself to be heartily heterosexual. Until Mariel. Until the moment in the restaurant. Until now. It was the weirdest feeling. Mariel was the strongest, most powerful personality she'd ever met. It seemed pointless, ridiculous to resist her in anything. Moreover, resisting Mariel was oddly undesirable – the idea of pleasing her positively pleasurable. But what did Mariel want and why? That she was a lesbian was a ridiculously facile explanation. It went deeper than that. Then there was the awful possibility that Sarah had simply misread the signals – that Mariel's behaviour was just an extrovert's display of innocent affection. If so, the desire welling up inside her was her own production entirely. Since arriving in New York City, Sarah Gurney had some experience of living life to the full. She had to clear up the mystery of Mariel's intentions, of her own needs. She would hang in there and see what developed.

The manifestation of this decision was that Sarah's leg stayed exactly where it was. The ball was back in Mariel's court. Conspiratorially, she leaned towards Sarah, encouraged by the twin patches of flushed skin that had suddenly appeared high up on the alabaster-white cheekbones.

From the corner of her eye the English girl saw the sapphire coat balloon out, revealing a perfectly symmetrical breast, its pink nipple unashamedly erect, pointed, conical, extraordinarily alluring. In a flash of frightening intuition Sarah realized that there was nothing in the world that she wanted to do more than to have it in her mouth, to taste it, to love it, to suck it. She swallowed nervously, her mouth as dry as the desert sands. She didn't know what to do, how to behave.

Mariel's scent was in her nostrils, her warm, sweet breath on her cheek. One hand sneaked behind Sarah's

40

neck, the fingers resting lightly on the cool skin, sending little explosions of pleasure into her brain. Mariel's lips brushed against the lobe of the other girl's ear and she breathed the words into Sarah's consciousness.

'I'm going to give you another popper, honey. Remember? Like in the restaurant.'

In her mind Sarah had already surrendered but the doomed protests went on. What about Adam? What about her reputation? Would Mariel tell anyone? How would Mariel react towards her in future? God! She was *wet*, really *wet*, and her tits were standing out like beacons. Her whole body was burning up. She fought back a desire to reach out and touch the tantalizing breast, alternately visible and invisible beneath the half-open coat.

A voice that might or might not have been hers said, 'I'd like that.'

The sound of breaking glass accompanied her words and dutifully she bent her head to sniff in the pungent fumes. In a second all of her doubts dissolved, all objections were instantly abandoned. She felt herself open out to embrace the ultimate experience which was about to engulf her. Her heart banged against her chest as the arteries dilated, the blood pressure dropped and the fountain of her desire began to play between her legs, drenching the cotton panties, threatening to burst through the thin silk dress and stain the delicate fabric of the sofa. She fell back, a low moan bubbling from the depths of her throat.

'Oh, Mariel. I want to be fucked.'

Mariel's face relaxed in a look of pure unadulterated triumph. Sarah had fallen. From now on Mariel had her. The pleasure trip on which she was about to embark would hook her more surely than the finest heroin. She'd become one of Mariel's creatures to dispose of as she wished, a valuable ally in her journey towards the Phipps fortune.

'Don't worry, baby. Don't worry about a thing.'

She had about a minute before the effect of the amylnitrite wore off. By that time Sarah would've reached the point of no return. With a quick movement Mariel spread the English girls legs wide apart, the short silk skirt racing up to expose the long white limbs and tiny panties. Later there would be time, all the time in the world to explore the delights of Sarah's body. For now it was important to concentrate on the very centre of her universe, to build her fast to a peak of desire from which the only possible retreat would be a massive, shuddering orgasm.

Mariel allowed her eyes to feast on the delicious vision before her. Sarah was wide open to her, pelvis pushed out in anticipation, almost in supplication, as if willing Mariel's fingers to touch her, to give her the gift of awesome pleasure. She was dripping with excitement, her panties glistening with moisture.

'Sarah Gurney, you are *really* hot.'

And then Mariel put her out of her agony. The fingers of her left hand slid beneath the elastic of the panties into the jungle wetness of Sarah's vagina. Unerringly they found the epicentre, parting the full lips, tenderly caressing the tiny, erect pleasure-source. Sarah thrust herself out at the sublime fingers, alternately crushing Mariel's hand between her thighs and splaying them wide to enable Mariel to reach deep within her. Mariel felt the heat of the English girl's passion radiating out from between her legs and breathed in deeply to savour the heavy scent of her desire. Mariel wanted it all – to taste it, to have it – but not yet, not yet. For now she wanted to concentrate on the breaking down of barriers, the destruction of any lingering inhibitions. Talking was one way of achieving that.

'Do you like it, Sarah? How does it feel? Tell me how good it is.'

'Don't stop, Mariel. For God's sake. Oh, I'm coming. I'm going to come. Ohhhhhhhh!'

Sarah's head thrashed from side to side, lips bared in an expression of blissful anguish, sweat standing out in little beads on her tall, snow-white forehead. Both hands beneath her generous buttocks, she pushed herself desperately against Mariel's probing fingers as she reached towards orgasm. Mariel, ice calm in the heaving storm of sexual ecstasy, watched for the tell-tale signs – the faraway look in the eyes, the beginnings of the muscular spasms, the intensification of the liquid deluge. Sensing them she formed her hand into a fist and plunged it with all her strength into the ever-widening opening. A strange whinnying shout of pure joy burst from the English girl's throat as she dived gratefully into the orgasm. Mariel felt the vaginal musculature clamp down hard on her fist, imprisoning the pleasure-giving invader. Then it relaxed before tightening once again, milking the knowing fingers of every last ounce of satisfaction.

'It looks as if everyone could do with a little Pol Roger,' said Adam with earth-shattering nonchalance. Nothing like a little lesbian fist-fucking for working up a healthy thirst, was the inescapable inference.

Clockwork, thought Mariel. This evening her timing was right on target. Adam had secretly watched her seduction, as she'd hoped he would. That really turned him on.

Sarah lay back exhausted, buffeted by the jingle-jangle aftermath of the orgasm. At the sound of Adam's voice she groaned gently, covering her face with her hands, legs still wide open, Mariel's hand buried deep within her. Shame and guilt rushed into the vacuum left by the evaporation of sexual passion.

Mariel was no help, no help at all. Slowly, she extracted her dripping hand and ran her fingers in a gentle caress across Sarah's parched lips, moistening them with the juices of her own orgasm.

'Hey, baby, do you like to *come*.'

As Sarah felt the flickerings of rekindled desire at this crude talk and the feathery touch of Mariel's fingers, she knew at once that it was far from over, that guilt and embarrassment would have to be shelved for the time being. In Churchill's words, it was only the end of the beginning. Gratefully, she took the delicate champagne glass and downed its contents like a hard-hat taking out a Budweiser at a ballgame.

'More,' she said, holding out the empty glass. She had decided to go for it – all the way.

Time for stage two, thought Mariel. The Limey girl was game for anything now. She'd better be!

She opened the door leading off to the long corridor. 'Hey, you two – get your asses in here in a hurry.'

Sarah's eyes widened perceptibly as the two girls entered the room. To say there had been a transformation was an understatement. Both were dressed in heavy bondage gear – black leather bikini bottoms, skimpy and revealing large areas of buttock, black boots to mid-thigh and black leather bras with round holes cut out to reveal protruding, erect nipples. Wound tightly around their torsoes were brown thongs, restricting and cutting into straining breasts. Both girls wore leather collars and matching wristcuffs studded with smooth silver buttons to which long leads were attached. Somehow they managed to look desperately ashamed and highly excited all at the same time.

'OK, you tacky little girls – get down on your knees and crawl over here.'

The schoolteacher and the nurse from Bellevue did exactly as Mariel said, quivering in anticipation of the humiliations they knew they would now be forced to undergo. Mariel leaned down and picked up the leads to the collars of both girls, yanking them sharply as she did so. Rachel and Jenny's heads darted upwards like two dogs learning how to do it the Woodhouse way.

'You call me mistress, right?' Both girls nodded, minds racing. What would it be? Would it be painful? Would the man take part?

'You!' Mariel kicked out sharply at Jenny's pert ass, catching her a glancing blow. 'Beg for permission to take off my pants.'

Jenny turned her innocent face upwards. 'Please, mistress, may I take down your pants?'

Mariel stood astride her, legs apart like some Amazon warrior, proud and commanding. The leather leash was wound tightly round her hand and Jenny's face was held immobile at the level of her crotch, inches from the blue skirt. Slowly and with infinite reverence, as if unveiling the statue of some respected statesman, Jenny lifted the material upwards. Mariel's thighs fulfilled the promise of her lower legs, perfectly complementing the well-turned ankles, the rounded but not muscular calves. Jenny shivered her excitement as the soft, white skin came into view above the dark Christian Dior silk stockings. She pushed the skirt higher revealing the red frilled suspender belt, and the bikini-style panties clinging tightly to the contours of the firm, upturned bottom. Jenny fumbled with trembling fingers at the elastic waist of the panties, and as she did so Mariel shortened the leash further so that Jenny's mouth and nose brushed against the soft silk, feeling the warmth of the forbidden territory beneath.

'Slowly,' said Mariel sharply.

Jenny could smell the musky, delicious scent. All she wanted to do was to give pleasure, to be used, treated merely as a mechanical source of sexual ecstasy. As commanded, she inched the pants down with deliberate slowness, feeling the pubic hair against her face as it sprung from the tight briefs. With her right hand she reached behind Mariel and freed the round, hard bottom. A few more inches and her objective would be exposed. Jenny knew exactly what she'd be forced to do. There it was – the flash of pink nestling in the damp hair, the glistening lips of Mariel's vagina.

Imperceptibly, Mariel shortened the leash still further. 'Kiss it,' she commanded. 'Gently, very gently.'

Jenny pressed her lips forwards, running them lightly over the soft, shiny skin. She inched out her tongue and licked tenderly, tasting the salty warmth, the indefinable flavour of feminine sexuality Mariel arched her back and, throwing back her head, closed her eyes to concentrate on the delicious sensations. But she was still in control – the dominant and cruel mistress for whom these two sluts existed only to please. With her left hand she grabbed hold of Jenny's hair and crushed the nurse's face deep between her legs so that her mouth, nose and tongue were crammed against Mariel's vagina. With her right hand she wound the long leather leash tightly round her own waist, back round Jenny's neck and once again round the back of her own thighs, before tying it roughly to the studded leather collar. In this way Jenny's head was fixed in position, stuck irretrievably between Mariel's legs, her face buried in the wetness, hardly able to breathe.

Both hands free again, Mariel grasped Rachel's collar, pulling her roughly behind her back. The schoolteacher could see at once what was coming. She'd been singled out for especially humiliating treatment. Mariel's pert bottom thrust out towards her face.

'Put your tongue in it,' she said shortly.

Rachel swallowed nervously, heart racing, adrenalin flowing. This girl was really something. Vicious and beautiful all at the same time. Dutifully, she leaned her head in towards the commanded destination, pushing aside the smooth buttocks with her cheeks, searching with her lips for the secret orifice. In the fetid darkness she found the illicit place and, as ordered, reached out with her tongue to touch and taste it.

'I said "inside",' shouted Mariel. With a sudden movement she pulled with both hands on the other girl's hair, at the same time bearing down hard on her face, forcing Rachel's tongue deep into her bottom. Quickly, she found the long lead to Rachel's collar and wound it tightly round her hips before fastening it to Jenny's collar on the other side of her body. Although still standing, the two girls kneeling beneath her provided a sort of a seat for Mariel with their heads. Strapped to her by the tight leather, they were forced to support her weight with their faces, tongues and lips imprisoned against her two most potent pleasure-zones.

Mariel braced her legs, pulling the captive tongues upwards. Then she bore downwards with her pelvis, testing the tightness of the thongs. Satisfied, she made a writhing, squirming movement, checking the delightful sensation of the tongues in her vagina and bottom.

'OK, you turds,' she panted, 'now make me come.'

A body surfer riding the crest of her own personal pleasure-wave, buoyed up on a sea of tongues, Mariel hovered, suspended in space and time. She was dimly aware of delicious noises as beneath her the two girls struggled to give her what she wanted as they fought for breath in the damp world of her private places – sucking, licking, working her towards orgasm, desperate to please. Mariel sensed the time-bomb ticking within her and felt its fuse shorten as she headed towards the explosion. The leather thongs cut into her body as the bobbing heads danced to the tune of her desire. Any moment now the mighty wave would begin to break, the surf explode in a bubbling cauldron of passion.

And then, quite suddenly, Adam was beside her. With a shock of horror Mariel saw the gleaming kitchen knife in his hands. For a split second pure panic fought with sexual ecstasy for control of her mind. What on earth was he going to *do*?

With two deft sweeps of the blade Adam cut through the leather thongs which pinioned the two 'submissives' to Mariel. The unexpected release of their bonds threw both girls off balance and they fell away from Mariel, leaving her crouching, teetering on the precipice of orgasm. Suddenly she knew what was happening and her heart leaped at her triumph. Adam couldn't bear to be a spectator for a second longer. He wanted her – and was about to have her.

Quickly he moved behind her and his strong arms

snaked round her waist, gripping her tightly in a bear-hug. At almost the same moment she felt him drive into her as simultaneously she was swept up into the air. Mariel, a second before infinitely powerful, was reduced at a stroke to a marionette dancing on a string, a plate circulating precariously on a juggler's stick. Not for one instant did she allow her change of role from dominator to dominated interfere with her objective. Drawing her legs up to her chest, Adam's hands clasped together behind her knees, she concentrated all her attention on the pleasure-giving invader. It seemed as if her orgasm was an almost tangible thing, existing a fraction beyond the furthest reaches of Adam's thrusting penis. Both were united in their desire for the twain to meet. As Adam pushed into her he forced her down hard on him, his knees buckling with the effort of suspending Mariel's entire weight. At the same time, Mariel squeezed her legs tightly together, wriggling from side to side to increase her pressure on Adam. Slowly Adam took one step forwards, his muscles straining with the exertion, his pelvis jerking forwards strongly, his penis punishing Mariel's tightly clamped vagina. The extra effort created the fusion that both so desperately sought, and the match and gunpowder met as their mutual orgasm began.

When Adam walked, or rather staggered, through the vast arched entrance to 370 Park Avenue, it was with the quiet desperation of the parched traveller arriving at a desert oasis. Although the opening through which he passed was large, there were many New Yorkers to whom it appeared smaller than the biblical eye of the needle. Adam was a fully paid member of the upper-class élite, but non-gentiles, non-gentlemen and the nouveau riche found the stringent entry precautions of the Racquet Club an insurmountable obstacle.

Adam didn't have much of a plan for his morning. In fact his mind was on automatic pilot, his legs carrying him towards the cure for the ills which afflicted him, unbidden and undirected. He'd woken early to the familiar scream of steam engines in the very depths of his brain. His mouth had felt as if it had been liberally coated with Araldite, which toothpaste had been only partially successful in shifting. His Brooks Brothers pyjamas had been soaked in sweat and the icy fingers of nausea had plucked and picked at his stomach and throat. Wan-Tu, well used to such awakenings, had done his best and the breakfast tray had looked like a hypochondriac's heaven: heavy-duty Tylenol for the headache, vitamin C and fructose to aid liver metabolism, kaolin and morphine mixture for nausea, iced tea for dehydration, Librium for psychological angst, dry toast for an empty stomach. That little lot had been mere first aid, only scratching the surface of the problem. Its main use had been to make possible the second stage of operations for which the Racquet Club was the location.

Wearily, Adam pressed the elevator button for the second floor. Like a blind man in familiar surroundings, he made a left turn and headed right at the end of the corridor. This was it. Nirvana. The womb-like world of the Turkish bath and plunge pool. Here he'd lay his hangover to rest.

He threw off his clothes, leaving them in a crumpled heap on the cubicle bench. Screw the creases, what he needed to straighten out was his *mind*. He grabbed grumpily at a couple of rough, white towels from the generous pile at the entrance to the hot rooms before stepping across the threshold into another world. As the warm, humid air enveloped him he felt immediate comfort. Here was a quiet sanctuary of white marbled peace, far from the reality of the raw, angry city with its fiendish and dangerous pleasures. Here all problems were reduced to those of temperature. Was one too hot or too cold?

To the left was the steam room. Powerful stuff, but the only way to go. Adam stepped into the misty gloom, peering through the dense moisture to see if he'd be alone.

Great – empty. He stretched himself out luxuriously on a hot marble slab, wincing while his body acclimatized to the temperature. He checked mentally on the proximity of the green hose pipe. There were few more delicious sensations in the world than to stand naked amid the intense steam-heat and play the icy water over his body.

For the moment the physical problems were being dealt with. The mental ones weren't so easily treated. With a little sigh of resignation he allowed his tortured brain to dwell on the events of the previous evening. Then the world had indeed seemed a wonderful place, full of laughter and gaiety, good friends and good times. Now, in the dim twilight of the steam room, there was a different perspective. The coke and booze had conjured up the illusion of contentedness and then, capriciously and cruelly, had destroyed it, leaving the wicked pain of withdrawal symptoms as a punishing legacy. Last night Adam's spirits had soared, his self-confidence had been unassailable as he'd forced the pernicious substances into his body with reckless abandon. Today it was time for the doubts and fears, the dreadful insecurities, as the coke paranoia plagued his senses and guilt ravaged his besieged psyche.

He hadn't been brought up to behave like this and considered it in no way admirable, but somehow it seemed impossible to get off the speeding merry-go-round, to shift position into one of life's slower lanes. Always siren voices, Mariel's predominantly, lured him towards the easy pleasures and with every fall from grace the rocks crept closer. In terms of life's lottery, anyone but he would consider him a big winner. He had looks, money, class and brains – but Adam knew they meant nothing. When the chips were down the truth was that he was throwing it all away, blowing it, one of life's most durable clichés – the poor-little-rich-boy for whom money hadn't bought happiness.

He was beginning to sweat now, the drops of perspiration unable to escape into the already saturated atmosphere. He brushed the accumulated wetness from his flat, hard stomach, flicked the beads of sweat from his eyes. Letting his legs swing off the marble slab, he reached for the hose, turned on the tap and let the cold jet play on the top of his head in a vain attempt to wash away the cobwebs in his mind.

Two short years and so much had changed. In those now far-off halcyon days his parents had been alive and life had been very different. Tears filled Adam's eyes and he blinked them away. His parents. Oh God. Thinking about them always tore him apart. How he'd loved them. How proud they'd been of their brilliant son – the man whom the professor of computer sciences at Harvard had once described as the brightest student he'd ever had the good fortune to teach. Old Fred Phipps, who had never done a stroke of work in his life nor done or said a mean thing, had always marvelled at the quirk of genetic fate that had enabled him to father Adam.

'My son's apparently a bloody genius,' he'd been fond of saying, 'and that's odd enough in the Phipps family. But what's really rum is that he's one hell of a guy at the same time.' What would he have found to say about Adam today? It was not a happy speculation. Could he know what Adam had become? Was there a way the dead could learn these things? Adam's insides tightened and then churned at the ghastly thought. He had revelled in his father's pride and worshipped the gentle, unassuming man whose whole life had been living proof that to be grand and rich was no obstacle to being good. His father had always encouraged him, always supported him and had imbued him with the value system that he'd now chosen so completely to discard.

And then Adam thought of his mother. Not a day passed when he didn't experience the dreadful void created by her loss. Calm, intensely practical, endlessly reassuring, kind but stern, she was the rock on which Adam had constructed his life. When she died his foundation stone had been rent asunder and, at a stroke cruelly exposed to the rough weather of life, he had been found wanting.

Moodily Adam withdrew from the steam room. He flopped down in the comfortable chaise-longue covered with a crisp, warm white sheet and stared out through the thick glass picture-window at the inviting 35-foot plunge pool. Later, when it seemed as if his body was about to catch fire, he would hit the pool and swim as though his life depended on it, swim his black mood away. By that time, perhaps his hangover would be severely dented and the future would look brighter.

While enduring a tough twenty-minute deep Swedish massage he would plan his lunch. Spicy Bull-shots or Bloodies in the club bar to soften up the psyche for the next round. Then lunch in the dining room or at Le Relais, instant friends available at both to stop one thinking about the past.

Damn! He'd almost forgotten. He'd promised to have lunch with his uncle at the Union Club at 69th and Park. Christ, how depressing! The Union Club and Uncle Charles were an unattractive combination at the best of times, and these were far from the best of times. At the appalling thought Adam felt his hangover making a comeback. Charles Phipps, cold, hard, supercilious and patronizing, his tone contemptuous, would really put him through the hoop. Usually Charles was no match for Adam's superior intelligence and quickness of mind, but feeling like this he would be cannon-fodder. There was only one possible course of action. He'd cancel. No question.

But even as he decided to walk away from the lunch he knew that it was another step down the slippery slope to disaster. Charles Phipps ran Adam's $100-million investment portfolio on a discretionary basis. Since his parents' death, Adam had taken only a minimal interest in the way in which his assets performed under his uncle's supervision. That had been partly due to laziness and partly to Adam's distaste for things financial. However, each month they'd meet to discuss investment policy.

The lunches were always dull, occasionally intolerable,

but to Adam they represented the taking on of at least some form of responsibility. He was now the sole legatee of the Phipps fortune, that mighty body of money which had survived from the late eighteenth century when his English ancestor had founded the banking business of Phipps and Co. Generations of Phippses had managed to hang on to the bulk of the fortune through such disasters as the Civil War and the Depression. So durable had it been that latter-day Phippses tended to view the family fortune rather in the way that English aristocrats saw their relationship to their ancestral homes – that of curator, of temporary custodian, rather than of outright ownership. They believed it to be their role to hand it on, enlarged if possible, to the son and heir, the baton of gold passed on interminably to the next Phipps runner in the relay-race of life. Because of this attitude the Phipps family tended to adopt the European tradition in which the money went in its entirety to the first son and to nobody else. So his uncle Charles, being the younger son, had been cut off totally from the bottomless Phipps cookie jar, receiving not one red cent.

For Adam to disassociate himself from the management of the family assets would be to fly in the face of tradition, to insult indirectly the memory of his beloved parents, who had paid him the considerable compliment of leaving him the money outright rather than tied up in some trust fund. He just couldn't let his parents down again. No, however ghastly it might be he'd have to keep the luncheon appointment with his hated and despised uncle. The line must be drawn somewhere. This was as good a place as any.

Resignedly he checked his watch. Eleven-fifteen. There would be time for the swim but none for the massage if he was to make it to the Union Club bar in time for a couple of straighteners before his uncle arrived.

Adam traipsed unhappily into the gloomy marbled halls

of the Union Club with all the enthusiasm of a convicted murderer preparing himself for a lethal injection. This was his least favourite lunchtime venue – a place where rich businessmen told cruel racist jokes in nasal accents they imagined to be anglicized. He felt The Union Club was about as grand as Ole Opry. Typically, his uncle would eat nowhere else.

He turned a sharp right past the depressed-looking porter and descended the steps to the basement bar in the East Room. The windowless cellar, all polished wood and dim, religious light, was not his idea of a proper bar at all. Past experience had shown the barman to be unreliable with any concoction more ambitious than a gin and tonic.

He took the first drink fast, savouring the delicious bubbles at the back of his throat, the warm glow as the hard liquor hit his empty stomach. Dehydration was still a problem, exacerbated by the earlier steam-heat. He ordered a second. At least they were strong, he thought, as the welcome alcohol began to unwind his tightly coiled psyche.

A small, high-pitched whining voice filtered over his left shoulder, as welcoming as a fruity fart in a crowded elevator.

'My word, Adam, getting stuck into the booze already, are we? I'm sure I know of no young man who drinks as much as you.' The tone was bantering, in a traditional 'what's-happened-to-the-youth-of-today' style.

Adam turned slowly, his pale blue eyes staring malevolently at his uncle. Charles Phipps, short, corpulent, aggressive and smelling strongly of Eau Sauvage, gazed balefully back. His small size, generous paunch and dainty, effeminate hands gave him a Pickwickian appearance, but with no trace of jollity. An uneven, rather beaky nose separated the two tiny eyes, twin piss-holes in the snow, from which throbbing pulses of pure evil beamed into the room like radio waves from Hades. The dark, immaculately fitting suit didn't disguise the slack, flabby bottom or the dough-like muscles, while the rather daring shirt, the stripes a little too wide, failed to achieve an intended moderately rakish look. The overall impression, thought Adam, was one of unwholesome femininity, sort of 'haute business camp', into which a generous slug of nastiness had been injected, neat.

Adam lounged back against the polished wood bar, and took a long, deliberate pull at his drink. Let the battle commence.

'Really? You surprise me, Uncle Charles. I would've sworn that among the very *large* number of personable young men of your acquaintance there was at least one less abstemious than myself.'

Fifteen-all. Adam saw the arrow strike home. Twin specks of heightened colour appeared on Charles Phipps' otherwise, sallow, parchment-coloured cheeks.

It was an open secret in the Phipps family that Charles was possessed by the brown habit. At family gatherings there had been a time when the teenage contingent, long on daring if short on wit, would yell the traditional 'Backs to the wall, boys' on his approach. However, like many of the closet-queen fraternity, Charles Phipps remained convinced that his 'little weakness' was completely unknown to anyone else. Indeed, inside the solemn bastions of the Union Club, where, at least in theory, sodomy was held to be a capital offence, Charles' preference for his own sex was unsuspected. No way could he have remained a member, let alone chairman of the all important Candidates' Committee, if he ever decided to 'come out'.

In fact, open declaration of his homosexuality was the very last thing on Charles' mind. He liked to keep his life in three very different and totally watertight compartments. By day he was Charles Phipps, social gadfly, respected investment banker and pillar of the Establishment, a man of impeccable character, if of dubious personality. Sometimes this persona would extend into the evenings, when he filled to perfection the role of 'walker' to ballsy hostesses who wanted to be escorted rather than fucked, and who couldn't persuade their husbands to play the part of lapdog at which Charles was something of a virtuoso performer.

On other evenings Charles indulged his secret passions. These, completely separate from his Washington and New York social life, underwent a further subdivision. In a loft in Greenwich Village he kept his homosexual 'mistress', a classically good-looking but highly neurotic twenty-four year old called Skip. Charles and Skip were technically 'lovers' and the relationship was perfectly straightforward. Charles gave Skip money and 'presents', and in return Skip satisfied Charles' sexual desires, or at least most of them.

Charles, however, had other, more exotic, longings. From time to time he would feel dark urges coursing through him and would give in to the black, forbidden lust. At such times he would empty his pockets of all identification and travel incognito to the Lower East Side, to the wild and woolly sexual demi-monde of the S & M district leather-bars. There he'd enter into strange and dangerous financial transactions with hairy truck drivers, meaty construction workers and violent iron-pumping blacks – and deeds without names would be performed. In such situations of the most extreme degradation and humiliation would Charles Phipps experience the ultimate pleasures, scaling the peaks of his weird sexual desires.

The White House Chief of Protocol and the Chairman of the Union Club didn't know about Skip. Skip, in turn, wasn't supposed to know about the rough creatures of the night who satisfied Charles' basest needs. Last, and far from least, the sadistic male prostitutes had no inkling of Charles' exalted status in the corridors of power. Charles intended to ensure that their blissful ignorance wasn't replaced by the folly of wisdom.

Now he chose to ignore his nephew's innuendo.

'I do think you could have bothered to get your suit

pressed, Adam. It's not as if you can't afford the laundry bills. In this club we do try to keep up appearances, you know.'

Adam peered round the room allowing his eyes to flicker disdainfully over the members gathered in the small bar. The unmistakable inference contained in his look of withering scorn was that appearances were just about all that this motley crew were capable of keeping up. On the other hand, he was prepared to concede that a couple of hours of lying in a heap on the floor in the humid air of The Racquet Club's hotroom had not improved the shape of his suit.

'So, Uncle Charles, what news from the Rialto?' he said at last, watching the quotation from 'The Merchant of Venice' go right over the top of his uncle's head. He wondered if he could get away with ordering another gin and tonic and tried to catch the barman's eye. Charles Phipps saw the gesture

'No time for any more, Adam. Some of us have to work, you know. Earn money rather than just spend it.'

Bastard, thought Adam. That one was right on target.

Charles scented blood. As they walked towards the elevator he pressed home his advantage.

'I often think of how disappointed your father would've been that all those academic triumphs of yours came to nothing in the end,' he said maliciously. 'Your mother, too. Always had the highest hopes for you with all that computer nonsense.' He twisted the knife in the wound.

Adam stood his ground, reeling with the psychological blows. The parent bit really got to him. He affected a devil-may-care attitude, which he in no way felt.

'Well, you know how it is, Uncle Charles. When you're as rich as I am it rather takes away the incentive to race along with the rats. Quite different for you, as the poor relation, as it were.'

Charles Phipps clenched the sensitive fingers of his lily-white hand. He began to throb with anger, the venom rising within him as he sought an appropriate response to Adam's direct hit. The dreaded words kept resounding in his brain: 'Poor relation . . . poor relation . . .' It was exactly what he was and had always been, the poor, fucking relation. God, how he hated them all, the whole self-satisfied crew, his supercilious brother Fred, his stuck up Limey sister-in-law, his own senile father, who had cut Charles out of the will on grounds no better than that he was the second son. Most of all he hated this little prick of a nephew who owned what was rightfully his, who had the gall to insult him in his own club. If only some divine thunderbolt would descend from on high and spread him all over the sidewalk, or possibly some inspired mugger would take him out with a Saturday night special. Was twenty-three too young to die of drink? With a sinking feeling in the pit of his stomach, Charles faced the fact that he was clutching at straws. The bottom line was that Adam would see him boxed, would drink champagne at his funeral and would dance on his grave. It was a sickening thought.

As if reading his mind, and still hurting inside from the reference to his parents, Adam piled on the pressure. Speaking as if to himself, he said, 'Come to think of it, I suppose I really ought to think about getting married one of these days. Secure the inheritance, you know.'

He followed his apoplectic uncle out of the lift and together they headed towards the vast dining room.

Charles Phipps forced himself to cool down. Adam had a far quicker mind than he could ever hope to have, but he possessed some powerful ammunition.

Through clenched teeth he managed to ask Adam what he wanted to eat. Adam didn't really want to eat anything – wasn't very sure he would be capable of keeping food down. What he needed was a drink. However, he was at a disadvantage. He was a guest at his uncle's club. He would be kept short of drink, no doubt about it.

'Red or white wine?' said Charles wickedly.

Adam peered into his uncle's face trying to read his mind. If Charles wanted red he'd take the white. That way at least he wouldn't be forced to share. Charles had already expressed an intention to eat a steak.

'I'll have some white,' said Adam cunningly.

'I think I'll join you. Never hold with this business of choosing the wine to go with the main course.' Charles allowed himself a beatific smile.

'We'll have a *small* carafe of the club white wine,' said Charles Phipps to the waiter, his spirits rising once more at this little success. He knew how small the club carafes were. Adam would be lucky if he got a decent glass. That would make him nervous.

Talk turned to business. Charles Phipps was a partner in an old, patrician firm of Wall Street investment bankers. In the early part of the twentieth century it had been part of the Phipps financial empire until a canny ancestor had sold off ninety per cent shortly before the Crash. The bank had weathered the storm and now, under the name of Seabury Phipps, was one of the most respected and stable banks in New York.

It had become the tradition that the bulk of the Phipps money should reside at this bank, and through a mixture of Machiavellian scheming, plain stubbornness and Adam's lack of interest, Charles had managed to gain complete control of the Phipps account. Within Seabury-Phipps he and he alone decided on the disposition of the $100 million portfolio. Adam of course had the ultimate right to override him, and at least in theory was free to remove the entire account from the bank any time he liked. However, Adam, despite his erratic behaviour, remained a traditionalist and Phipps blood ran in his veins. Phipps money had always been kept at Seabury-Phipps and was largely controlled by whoever had been nominated the Phipps partner. Like the laws of the Medes and Persians, *that* would remain unchanged despite Adam's personal feelings for his uncle. Charles was counting on it.

Still, it would be wise not to push the little creep too far. To get it wrong would be a tragedy of horrendous proportions. No more lunches in the oak-panelled partners' dining room, goodbye expense account, farewell $150,000 a year. It would be the coup de grâce to his glittering social career, death to the little cottage in Newport from which he pursued the nation's blue-bloods during the summer months and most emphatically the end of his relationship with the money-loving Skip. He would have to slink away from the world he had created, tail between his legs. Cold fingers danced along his spine and sepulchral organ music sounded in his ears at the awful prospect.

'I think perhaps we ought to get you a little more wine, Adam,' he said quickly, noting the hunted look that had crept into his nephew's face at the sight of the empty carafe.

Adam nodded in relief. He felt terrible, all strung out, the hangover re-establishing itself in full force after the brief lull. What he needed was one of Petey's dry martinis, for which the vermouth was dispensed from an eye-dropper. Christ, a little toot would help as well – that wonderful life-giving feeling as the line went right up the nose and into the depths of the brain. Hey, this was dreadful, really awful. This was addiction. Usually he never got to feel this bad. Mariel was always there, doling out the goodies, high priestess of the coke bag, divine dispenser of substances – uppers, downers, quieteners, sideways-pills. Now, in the uncompromising respectability of the Union Club dining room, a little sour, thin white wine on the way, Adam was confronted with the fact of his dependency. He leaned forwards on the table, both hands on his clammy forehead, wondering if he was going to make it through the lunch. He was all fucked up. Totally screwed, and it didn't feel good. Even his dreaded uncle was taking pity on him. Where the *hell* had Mariel got to? Why on earth had she chosen today to do one of her moonlight flits? Just like her: predictable in her unpredictability. Always unavailable when most needed. With effort Adam forced himself to concentrate on what his uncle was saying.

'Do you have any time these days for your computers? They seem to be all the rage.'

Charles Phipps' face softened. He was trying to be nice. That in itself was one of the nastiest sights a man could experience. Great waves of hypocrisy slurped across the table, sending little ripples of nausea through Adam's already uncertain stomach. Still, if Charles had decided to suspend hostilities momentarily, he should accept the olive branch. The terms of truce were agreed.

'Funnily enough, I do. I've just installed an Apple Five, the one they call "Linda". Buckets of random access memory, all the peripherals. It's really neat.' Was that a trace of enthusiasm in his voice?

'Do you write programs in BASIC?' Charles was rather proud of this. He knew the question was phrased right but he wasn't entirely sure what it meant. He was just showing that his was a head not exclusively in the sand.

Adam resisted the temptation to expose his uncle's lack of knowledge.

'I usually write in PASCAL for run-of-the-mill stuff. Lately I've been playing around with COBOL.'

Charles peered at him suspiciously. Was his nephew putting him on? Not impossible. He decided he wasn't.

Not for the first time Charles thought how good looking his nephew was. Infuriating, maddening, but really very attractive indeed. He felt the familiar stirrings.

'You know, we really ought to see more of each other, Adam. After all I'm your nearest family now – we ought to stay close.' He made little waving movements with his tiny hands as he said this, his voice oily and ingratiating. Not for the first time Adam caught the intimation of suppressed desire. God, how gross he was. What was it Mariel called him – a zod, a nerd? Whatever they meant, he was both.

Charles was warming to his theme. Close relations with

his nephew. The hard, young body hanging out at the Newport house. Not an unattractive thought. Make friends rather than keep fighting this endless battle. Tie up the vital Phipps account once and for all. Once again he allowed himself to dwell on the disastrous effect on his finances if the money was withdrawn from the bank. Quite apart from the danger to his job, there was another angle. Unable to get his hands on the capital itself, there were a couple of ways that Charles could and did use the account to feather his own nest. He sipped contemplatively at the vinegary wine and allowed himself to make a very serious mistake indeed.

'Yes, Adam, in the summer you must come up to Newport. The pool is very private, very charming – we never bother with clothes, you know.' He leaned across the table and patted Adam's hand.

Adam withdrew it as if he'd been electrocuted. Christ, this revolting poof was as good as propositioning him, the filthy faggot. This was the last straw. He sat up straight. That was enough. Fuck Phipps tradition, he was going to pull the account. Blow his fairy uncle clean out of the window. He didn't need this crap.

'Uncle Charles, you're kind, but you know I don't think I would be strong enough to deal with the sight of you in the nude,' he said simply.

Charles Phipps opened and then closed a fish-like mouth. His eyes widened and then narrowed. The red glow of anger rushed upwards, diffusing his podgy neck and colouring his unhealthy complexion. With a superhuman effort he held on to his tongue.

They munched the rest of their way through the meal in total silence.

The check signed, Charles Phipps rose slowly to his feet, puffing himself up like a frog as he prepared to deliver his Parthian shot.

'I can't say I have enjoyed our lunch, Adam. Certainly we haven't had a chance, due to your, ahhhhh, obvious indisposition, to discuss the business which was its original purpose. However, I do feel that, as your uncle, and in the absence of your dear parents, it's my duty to give you some advice. It would appear that you've got yourself into a mess. It seems to me that you need help – professional help. Now it so happens that a friend of mine has been visiting a psychiatrist, who has given him excellent advice. The doctor's name is Carrington, the office just a few blocks from here on Fifth Avenue. You'd do well to listen to what I have to say.'

Charles beamed his satisfaction. How ashamed his brother Fred would be if he knew that his son needed a shrink. And that snob of an English wife of his would turn in her grave. Purposefully, he had failed to mention that Dr Carrington was a woman. Somehow that made it even more pleasurable. He'd also concealed the fact that the person who had recommended Anne Carrington was none other than Skip, his Greenwich Village 'mistress'. What was indubitably true was that Anne Carrington had managed to calm Skip down, no mean achievement, and for that alone her bills were worth paying.

Adam remained sitting exactly where he was. Looking straight into his uncle's eyes he said, 'Fuck off, Uncle Charles.' He reached out and caught a passing waiter by the sleeve. 'Will you bring me a large glass of Hine as quickly as you can – and put it on Mr Phipps' account.'

With grim satisfaction Adam watched his uncle waddle petulantly from the dining room, the ugly duckling, the runt of the Phipps litter. Good riddance, he thought. But the name Carrington kept going round and round in his mind. Maybe he should give this doctor a call.

Chapter Three

Anne Carrington was not looking forward to the session. Occasionally psychiatrists really disliked one of their patients, despite the popular professional wisdom that held that if you took the trouble to get to know someone, then everyone was potentially lovable. Skip Demery, Anne had long since decided, was just plain nasty.

It was Anne's custom to see all new patients at least twice before agreeing to take them on full-time. It allowed her time to separate the ill from the merely bored and fed-up because, unlike many psychiatrists practising in the immediate vicinity, Anne believed in saving her time for those who really needed it. No way was she going to be a paid friend, fitted in between the hairdresser and lunch at Le Cirque, pandering to the narcissism and loneliness of the stinking rich.

During his two initial interviews, Skip had given voice to some rather remarkable fantasies involving his homosexual lover, a closet queen and society figure by the name of Charles Phipps. These had involved castration with cheese wire and the subsequent feeding of the detached genitalia to the pigeons in Central Park. Anne, fascinated by the colourful imagery of this bizarre desire and the total lack of self-consciousness with which it was offered, had immediately concluded that Skip was teetering on the brink of serious illness, and had agreed to monitor him on a twice-weekly basis for an initial period of six months. Now she bitterly regretted her decision.

She'd revised her initial diagnosis in light of later sessions. In her book Skip was undoubtedly suffering from a severe hysterical personality disorder, far from unusual in homosexuals of his ilk. When thwarted or in any way criticized, he would become very angry, often viciously rude.

For this reason, and because he appeared to have the morals of an alley-cat, Anne had come to dislike him intensely. As far as personality went, Skip had made his own bed and now had to lie in it. Actually, his parents, farmers in the midwest, sounded extraordinarily decent, as did Skip's many brothers and sisters, most of whom were still at home working the land. But that sort of decent life hadn't been good enough for Skip. He'd headed for the bright lights of the Big Apple, fame and fortune in his sights. When he'd failed to hack it, like so many country boys before him, he'd fallen back on his natural assets, on his blue eyes and heavily muscled body. In the meat market lottery he'd drawn Charles Phipps, and was now feverishly trying to hang on to him.

'You see, doc, Charles is really very *important* to me. Actually quite *vital*. Of course we have the most *terrible* rows – the worst in *history*, but afterwards we make the most *wonderful* love. You know I'd just *die* without him.'

Anne stared at him in astonishment. Skip would cheerfully cut this Phipps guy's throat for a few thousand bucks, might easily get around to it, and yet for some reason today he was playing the role of romantic lover. She noted the hysterical exaggeration. Typical.

'You mean that without him you'd have no existence, that by leaving he'd be murdering you.' Anne had no faith in the interpretation, but she felt she'd better keep the ball rolling. The brutal truth was that she was stuck with Skip until the six-month period was up. It was a matter of professional pride that she never went back on her commitment to a patient.

'Oh, come on, doc, I don't mean *literally* die. It's just a way of saying something. Sometimes it seems you don't really *concentrate* on what I say And it costs so much *money*.'

Anne winced with displeasure. God how she hated the 'doc' bit. Of course he was right. He wasn't really getting value for his boyfriend's money, but how typical of him to point it out. Briefly she debated whether or not to defend the insight she'd just offered. 'Very often in apparently casual speech we use phrases or words which are indicative of hidden unconscious fears or desires . . .' She decided against. No point dancing to the patient's tune. That was a beginner's mistake.

'What makes you think Charles is going to leave you?' she asked instead.

Skip became conspiratorial. Not a pretty sight.

'I've made it my business to know a thing or two about Charles' life. Sort of keeping tabs on him. Not his high society life, but . . . the darker side.' He paused for effect. 'The darker side' had been delivered in a stage whisper, the purpose being to conjure up dank Transylvanian forests, witches, cauldrons – and worse.

Anne gazed back at him evenly. No applauds from the audience. Skip was unfazed by her lack of visible interest.

'Charles is into heavy leather, and he doesn't know I know.' He sat back in the chair proudly, the man who'd revealed the ultimate secret.

At first Anne thought that Charles Phipps liked to dress up in leather gear, perhaps encouraged Skip to do the same. Then suddenly she understood. How naive could she be! He meant S & M, the violent underworld of the gay scene, the downtown bars of homosexual hustlers, cheap tricks and one-night, perhaps even ten-minute, stands. Suddenly she was interested. She knew precious little about this scene and in her professional capacity, at least, she should know more.

'Tell me more,' she said, her voice heavy with boredom. Skip was enough of a contrarian to clam up tighter than a virgin's ass at any intimation of interest.

'It would appear that my faithless love takes himself off to charming little places like The Anvil and The Snake-Pit, where he pays a whole lot of weirdos to do unpleasant things to him. I wonder if he discusses his predilections with Jackie when he takes her to the theatre.' Sarcasm dripped from Skip's every syllable.

Anne remained silent, the old psychiatrist interviewer trick. Nobody could stand silence. Always had to destroy it by babbling the first thing that came into their minds.

'Luckily I have an acquaintance who hangs out in those sorts of places from time to time. Of course it's not my bag. I just happen to know this fella from places in the Village. Anyway, he says Charles is often around, cruising for a bruising, flashing handkerchiefs – the whole bit. Really it's so incredibly *degrading*.' Tears welled up in Skip's sky-blue eyes and he shrugged his shoulders helplessly.

'What do you mean, "handkerchiefs",' said Anne sharply.

The misty film left Skip's eyes like morning fog vanishing in the sun. Dispensing information was always fun. The jealous lover routine would keep on the back burner.

'Oh, but, doc, you lead such a sheltered life. I thought you shrinks knew about things like that.'

Anne let it go. She tapped a pencil impatiently on her desk, saying nothing.

'Well, you put a coloured handkerchief in your back trouser pocket so that everybody gets to know what you fancy. It's a kind of code.' He looked at Anne slyly. 'Blue handkerchief, back left pocket means you like to give blow jobs; right pocket, you want to be given head. Green, back left, you're a hustler and charge for it; back right, you're a punter, a buyer. Yellow, back left, you give golden showers; back right, you like the fellas to piss all over you.' He peered at Anne intently. Had he succeeded in shocking her? She was very pretty if you were into chicks. Sex had to mean something to her.

Anne was giving nothing away, her face as inscrutable as Wan-Tu's. She stored the information away in her memory bank. So Skip felt Charles might abandon him for one of the heavy-leather brigade, for several of them, perhaps.

67

And that would mean goodbye Greenwich Village apartment and, possibly, hello Minnesota. A fate far worse than death to the citified Skip, whose Gucci loafers alone had left no change from 120 bucks. She looked him up and down. He was right to worry. An off-duty truck driver might well be preferable to this insipid specimen of humanity.

'Has he got into anybody special in that world?' she asked, assessing the immediacy of the threat.

'Word is there's a couple of freaks who work him over quite regularly. I'm keeping tabs on it. If he gets too heavily into it, those fucking pigeons are going to have one hell of a high-protein lunch. You'd better believe it.'

'Looks like time's up,' said Anne with scarcely disguised relief.

Adam's mind was alive again, vibrating with enthusiasm. He sat in front of the Apple Five computer monitor peering at the numbers flickering on the screen, fingers occasionally punching a staccato rhythm on the electronic keyboard. This was his area of expertise. All around him, in apparently careless confusion but actually arranged with total precision, were the tools of his trade. It was the room of an academic – papers, journals, books and piles of computer print-outs were scattered everywhere. Wires trailed across the room from the central processing unit to the expanded memory banks, to the floppy-disc system, tne printer and microprocessor, the tentacles of an octopus carrying electronic charges backwards and forwards to the minuscule chips of silicon with their vast accumulations of information.

Nobody was allowed into this room except Adam and what he liked to call his Big Apple. It was his inner sanctum, his retreat from the world where he could recharge his batteries, escape from his hard-living hedonism into a world of ROMS and RAMS, and purge his excesses in the rigorous intellectual disciplines of computer programming. To the uninitiated the exotic equipment looked unbelievably complex, but to Adam these electronic pathways were well-trodden, familiar ground. He gazed intently at the high-resolution colour video monitor, watching the green hieroglyphics dance before his eyes.

This was really very interesting. All morning Adam had been feeding the details of stock-exchange transactions on his Seabury-Phipps account into the machine's memory. He'd been at it since dawn, as there seemed to have been a phenomenal number of trades over the two-year period since he'd inherited the assets from his father. He wasn't absolutely sure that this was unusual, but strongly suspected that it was. At mid-morning he had telephoned an old friend, who worked at the downtown office of Merrill, Lynch, and asked for some information. A lot could be achieved on the old boy network. After lunch he'd telephoned back with the data Adam needed. Now he was committing to the machine's memory storage the details of the frequency and volume of private client's account transactions at Merrill, with the intention of getting the Big Apple to compare them with his own. The program for this had taken him only a couple of hours the previous evening.

This was it. He sat back, punching the PRINT button as he did so. It was all there, displayed graphically and in colour, as he'd arranged. A four-year-old couldn't have failed to get the message. His account had been three times as active as those of the biggest Wall Street firm. That might be forgiven if performance had been significantly superior. No problem to discover the answer to that. Adam's long fingers raced over the keyboard. PRINT. The graph was summoned up on the monitor as if by magic.

Both the Dow-Jones Industrial Average and the New York Stock-Exchange All-Share Index were plotted against time over the two-year period. A quick glance told Adam that his own portfolio had underperformed by 30 per cent.

In short, his uncle's performance as an investment advisor had been worse than disastrous. Any cretin with a pin could have done better. In the light of this sort of result, the unusually high turnover was definitely sinister. At best Charles was incompetent, at worst a crook.

As he had sat sipping his cognac after his uncle's departure from the Union Club dining room, Adam had made a few decisions. His initial impulse had been to pull the account and place it elsewhere, but gradually a more enticing proposition had occurred to him. The first thing to do would be to discover just how good or bad Charles Phipps' management record had actually been. If, as Adam suspected, he'd hardly covered himself in glory, then Adam would take over the running of the account himself.

Now, thanks to the Big Apple, it was crystal-clear that not only had the account been grossly mismanaged, but it was almost certain that Charles had been ripping him off in the biggest possible way. Obviously Charles had an arrangement that he personally would receive a commission on all stock-exchange transactions placed through the bank for the Phipps account. By churning the investments constantly, buying and selling with careless abandon, Charles had clearly made a packet in commissions. Sometimes the stocks had apparently been bought and then re-sold in the space of a few days. Because the buying and selling of investments was itself a costly business, this had put the skids under the account's performance.

Bastard, thought Adam. What's more – foolish, untalented, bastard. If Charles had had the remotest ability some of the trades he'd made should've shown a profit, but time and time again he seemed to have bought high only to sell low.

And then the thought hit him. What was it he'd read about the other day? Something about that English merchant-banker who'd been a distant cousin of his mother's – the guy who'd topped himself after being caught with his hand in the till. It had been known as 'the suspense account

70

scam'. That was it. When you bought a stock you booked the deal to a discretionary account – in this case an account through which Adam's and Charles' own personal transactions were passed. The name of the buyer wouldn't be booked until a week or two later. If during this period the price of the stock had risen, then Charles would book it to his own account and take the profit. If the price of the stock fell, then it would be booked to Adam's account and he'd be stuck with the loss. It was a foolproof way of ensuring that Adam got stuck with the rotten apples while Charles made off with the goodies. No wonder performance had been so dismal. The Big Apple had told him everything. Well, revenge was a dish best served cold.

Of course, to manage the account himself he'd have to learn all about investment, but that shouldn't be a problem. After all, it was a fact that his IQ was in the genius range, whereas most of the stockbrokers he knew were not conspicuously endowed with grey matter. Excitement coursed through him as he contemplated the challenge. He'd need a tutor, somebody whom he could trust to put him on the right track and show him the snakes and ladders of the investment game. There was an obvious candidate. John Dukes. Adam and he had worked together at Harvard. Now he was with First Boston and word was that his track-record was good, very good. Adam picked up the telephone and in a minute or two was talking to his old friend.

The two Harvard graduates sat opposite each other in deep, dark-brown leather chairs on either side of the fireplace in the library of Adam's huge duplex. Two antique reading lamps illuminated the faces of the two men as they talked earnestly in low Boston Brahmin. They used a minimum of gesture, a maximum of clan shorthand. In their right hands, like some obscure emblem of rank, were identical Irish Waterford cut-glass tumblers. Adam had acquired the English perversion regarding Scotch whisky. He drank Bell's, half-and-half with room-temperature Malvern water. John Dukes played it straight. He drank Dewars, on the rocks, with a splash of soda.

John Dukes had been very pleased to hear from his old Harvard friend. Adam's wealth was legendary. Phippses, Vanderbilts, Whitneys, Du Ponts and Rockefellers were in the very forefront of American plutocracy, and ambitious investment bankers like Dukes stuck as close to the megabucks as was conceivably possible.

'So, if I can summarize what you're saying, John, broadly speaking you can divide nearly all investment advisors into two categories, both of which tend to look down their noses at the other.'

'Yes, that's about it. The fundamentalists and the technicians. And they're usually ridiculing each other.'

'Now, am I right in thinking that the fundamentalists adopt what one might call the common sense approach?'

'In a nutshell, yes. The fundamentalists say that in the end it all depends on how much money the company makes. If earnings go up, then eventually the share price will go up, and vice versa. So the name of their game is to predict changes in the sort of things like interest rates, which must ultimately have an effect on profits.'

'What about these other yo-yos – the technicians?' Adam was enjoying himself. It was great to be spending some time understanding all this with someone of John's intellectual calibre. He had a first-class mind and Adam was beginning to realize how starved he'd been lately of intellectual stimulus.

'The technicians claim that the fundamentalists are labouring under a misconception. The harder they work – ferreting out information, gazing into their crystal balls, peering into the future – the easier they make the technician's job. These people say that every bit of information of possible relevance to a company is already contained in its current share price, which, in the last analysis, represents the sum total of all investors' knowledge and hopes for the shares up to the present time. These people believe that the market has a language, a psychology, all its own, and that by studying the charts of past market behaviour one can predict future price movements.'

Adam's mind was way ahead. He liked this technician thing. If one could predict future market performance from mathematical analysis of past information, then his beloved computer could be brought into the equation. He could turn Big Apple loose on the market and forget all the other factors which the fundamentalists held to be so important. It was a very attractive prospect. Adam raised his glass and drank deeply. He hadn't felt this good in years. John Dukes continued, seeing he had a totally attentive audience.

'Of course, in the end the market makes fools of everyone, although it doesn't stop hundreds of thousands of people from making a good living out of pretending to understand it.'

'I guess if there was a way to know for certain what was about to happen it would be the end of everything. Nobody would bet against the guy who had the answer. When he wanted to buy something nobody would sell it to him and vice versa. The market would break down completely – come to a full stop. Of course he'd make a killing until his success gave him away,' said Adam reflectively.

'Right on. That's if someone didn't kill him for his secret. To have the market Midas touch would be pretty damned dangerous, as he'd be creaming billions off the other poor punters.'

Adam sat back staring into space, the germ of an idea hatching in the incubator of his fertile mind. Could the stock-market be made to yield up its hidden secrets? If the market did indeed signal its future, then it would, at least in theory, be possible to crack it. It would be a question of constructing a computer program in which appropriate variables were each given the correct weighting.

73

It had to be the longest shot in the world, but it would be a fascinating intellectual puzzle of the very best sort. He took a long pull at the lukewarm Scotch and watched the reflection of the reading lamp bounce off the South Carolina pine panelling. And then, quite suddenly, he felt the confidence surge within him. He could do it. He would take the world by the balls and shake it. He would expose the market's secret. Nothing less. While the whisky warmed his stomach, the sudden knowledge warmed the cockles of his heart.

Charles Phipps had felt the excitement rising within him all day. He hadn't been able to concentrate on the views of the well-respected economist who'd been the guest of honour at the Seabury-Phipps partners' lunch. All the inside talk, the dropped names, the intimations of Presidential confidences – usually food and drink to him, the very stuff of life – had passed him by. At five o'clock he had hurried home. There he'd bathed carefully, washing every inch of his flaccid, corpulent little body as his skin tingled in anticipation of the delicious horrors which lay in store for him. Carefully, he'd shampooed his thinning hair, and now, rubbing himself reverently with the thick, rough towel, he felt like a virgin ready for sacrifice. Sacrifice, that was it. He'd be an instrument of pleasure, giving his body as a precious gift for others to use and abuse. He emptied generous amounts of Eau Sauvage cologne over his unhealthy flesh, smoothed down his sparse, brittle hair and surveyed himself in the long bathroom mirror. Not too bad. Distinguished, anyway.

What should he wear? Charles was certainly not a jeans man, and yet a suit would be way over the top. The Spouting Rock Beach Association blazer was hardly appropriate for the type of venue he'd be frequenting tonight. He settled for a nondescript black sailing anorak and some dark-grey Brooks Brothers trousers. Keep a low profile.

He checked through his pockets carefully. Mustn't have any ID. He should be totally untraceable – the two worlds must never meet. All he needed was cash – lots of it. His transport to delight.

Outside he hailed a Yellow Cab and whispered the address furtively to the driver, who eyed him knowingly as he did so. And then Charles Phipps settled back on the uncomfortable torn seat to savour the surging mixture of fear and desire that coursed through him. What would it be? How would it happen? Would he be hurt? Would there be marks? He shuddered with the thrill of these speculations. He'd be helpless, at the mercy of others, totally controlled, an animal. Charles Phipps, social lion, grovelling on the floor among the sweat and the sawdust, the lowliest pawn on the chessboard of the night.

The taxi pulled up at last outside the red neon sign. Heavy-metal rock blared out across the sidewalk calling stridently to those bent on illicit pleasure. Charles paid off the driver and flashed guilty eyes up and down the street. Quickly, like some frightened cockroach, he darted across the sidewalk and disappeared down the stairs into the bowels of the club.

At once the smell hit him, the powerful stink of degradation, acting as a potent aphrodisiac to his already souped-up psyche. Charles sidled down the stairs, squeezing apologetically past muscle-building faggots, necking queens and the hungry eyes of butch hustlers. Purposefully, he avoided the questioning glances, the looks containing unspoken invitations or, delectably threatening, the unuttered commands. His whole demeanour spoke his purpose, while his unwholesome physique declared that he had money to spend.

A frisson of excitement sparked round the crowded bar at the arrival of such an obvious customer. The bees prepared to gather about the honey pot. But Charles was looking out for someone special. He peered round the smoky basement for the familiar face. The restless eyes stared back at him, flashing their diverse messages. Charles felt his adrenalin flow. It was a dangerous place for a man like him. He was powerless to protect himself, a pushover for any kid who'd taken too much bad stuff and decided on a whim to go 'all the way' with the pompous little fag from uptown. If he played it wrong he could wind up very dead, or in the city hospital with a lot of explaining to do. For this reason he liked to deal with the same person each time, or with people introduced to him by his contact. That way risks were minimized, although by no means abolished.

A huge man detached himself from the group at the bar and walked over towards Charles. In desperation Charles twisted his head away to avoid eye-contact, but the stranger kept coming. Christ! This was trouble. The unknown man was unknowable because he wore a black leather mask covering his whole head like the visor on a suit of medieval armour. A zip ran up the side of his fearsome piece of headgear and there was another corresponding to the position of his mouth. Through leather slits dark eyes moved ominously. He was naked to the waist and thick, matted black hair, glistening with sweat, covered his torso, extended over his shoulders and down the tops of his arms. A brief leather jock-strap scarcely contained what was obviously a vast penis. The hair continued down his powerful legs, which ended in short, black leather ankle boots. Charles couldn't remember when he'd seen muscles to compare with this. The man obviously pumped more iron than Saudi Arabia did oil. The voice came out like sandpaper being drawn across rough wood.

'Seems to me, scum bag, you ought to come into the back room and smoke my pork. I'll let you give me $50 for the privilege.'

Charles gulped. His eyes flicked nervously over the man-mountain that loomed over him. There was no way he could refuse. It had been that sort of offer. Dubiously he eyed the jock-strap and its awe-inspiring contents while an orchestra of desire began tuning up deep within his body.

In the humiliation stakes you couldn't do a lot better than be used by a thing like this. Fear and foreboding fought with passion for possession of his emotions as, like a pet Pekinese, he followed the mighty stranger across the dance floor to the Snake-Pit's infamous back room. Red Sea-like, the gyrating dancers parted to allow the unlikely duo to pass. A hand goosed Charles' slack ass, another tweaked his ear, an unknown voice called out, 'Go for it, fag-bag.'

Like a sinner entering the gates of purgatory, Charles followed his leader down the two or three steps into the dank cellar, his eyes straining to adjust to the dim, flickering light. The interior decor of this place was never going to make it to the pages of *Architectural Digest*, its inhabitants would never be asked to grace the pages of *People* magazine. The place smelled like a public lavatory from which the attendant had long been absent. All around unspeakable scenes of debauchery were being enacted as the miserable prisoners of perverted desire struggled to turn their sordid fantasies into reality. Animal groans, short screams of pain interspersed with the vilest of curses and crude abuse provided the harrowing soundtrack. As always in such situations, Charles allowed himself to speculate what his upper-class friends would think if they could see him now – the judges, the partners in the bank, the society hostesses, the Senators' wives, the regular guys at the Union Club with their jokes about fags and degenerates.

'What's the difference between kinkiness and decadence?'

'Kinkiness is with a feather. Decadence is with the *whole* chicken.'

That was the sort of joke he laughed at in the Union Club bar, WASP holy-of-holies. Well, the joke had got it wrong. Decadence was the back room at the Snake-Pit. No contest. Forget chickens.

Would this fearful figure want more than head? Was Charles in for a dreaded fist fucking? His heart almost stopped at the thought. The pain would be excruciating, unbearable, he'd pass out. And yet as the cold, clammy hand of naked terror touched his heart, he knew that there was a part of him that cried out for the awful pain and humiliation of that ultimate degradation. Whatever happened, he was deliciously out of control, no longer in charge of his own destiny. In this room his life, his fate, was ruled by others – men for whom morals were a word without meaning, truth and trust symbols of some alien language bearing no relationship to their warped world. Danger darted and lurked in the fetid corners, evil dripped from the walls, the stench of original sin pervaded the humid air. Aubusson carpets and tinkling teacups, sawdust and cries of delighted anguish represented the distant polarities of Charles Phipps' universe.

The masked muscle-man turned to face him and held out a spade-like hand. 'Come with the bucks,' said the unpleasant, gravelly voice.

With fumbling fingers Charles found a fifty. He'd paid his entry fee to the game.

With a slow, deliberate movement the man reached into his jock, revealing the monstrous semi-erect phallus, the foreskin half retracted, its pink head glistening in the gloom of the cellar.

Charles Phipps stared at it transfixed, hypnotized by the cobra-like penis. Fascinated, he watched it jerk upwards as the blood rushed into the distending veins under the mysterious command of the stranger's sexual urge. His mouth, the intended receptacle of this mighty weapon, was dry, parched – his tongue desiccated like some crystallized fruit.

'On your knees, you disgusting piece of blubber. Make it smooth, and good.' In slavish obedience Charles did as he was told and leaned forward to receive the offering.

The new voice cut into his consciousness like a horsewhip biting into flesh. 'Find someone else to eat you,' it said, 'this one belongs to me.'

Charles looked up. He knew this voice. It was Mickey, the guy he'd been looking for earlier, the one with whom over the weeks he'd come to an unspoken understanding. Now it looked as if Mickey was protecting his patch against a potential poacher. A thrill rushed through him at the ridiculous, obscene implications of the scenario. He'd become a commodity, a possession to be haggled over by the lowest of the low. Like some damsel in distress he awaited the outcome of the confrontation, helpless and demure, prepared to offer himself up willingly to the victor of the battle.

'Who says so?' The erection was beginning to wilt.

'I say so, motherfucker.'

Charles throbbed with anticipation. They were going to fight over him. No way out. Mickey would be murdered, broken to pieces by this muscle-bound hulk. Dr Death couldn't have taken him. He looked up at his would-be protector. Mickey's lean, tight body was coiled like a spring, the wiry tendons and ligaments standing out, anchoring the sleek, hard muscle to angular bone. His skin glistened in the twilight, giving off the shiny patina characteristic of a man at the very peak of physical condition. There wasn't an inch of spare tissue on the flat, rippling stomach, while the sculpted quadriceps bulged through the clinging leather trousers. But it was in Mickey's eyes that the discerning observer would have seen the factor that evened up the contest. Cold anger shone from them like a laser beam, the terrible wrath of the frustrated psychopath, of a man with the lowest possible flash-point. Mickey had the emotional age of a child of five. Imprisoned within a body that qualified as a dangerous weapon, the combination spelled trouble of the most violent kind. Somebody was trying to muscle in on Mickey's territory, to take away his candy-bar, his woolly toy. Mickey didn't like that – didn't like it at all. He'd asked nicely, and then not so nicely. He wouldn't ask again.

The big man peered through the leather slits at his adversary. In the semi-darkness he failed to take in the glinting eyes, the steel-like muscles, seeing only the smaller stature, the discrepancy in weight. In his fist was Charles' fifty-dollar bill – it was worth a fight for that alone. The man who liked to hide behind black leather visors during his nocturnal meanderings tonight failed in two other respects: he failed to notice the five dull-bronze spikes that poked like periscopes from between the fingers of Mickey's clenched right hand, and he failed to sense the presence of the other man, who stood stock-still directly behind his left shoulder. During the many long and painful weeks he would spend in hospital he was to regret those two significant failures.

'Go eat shit,' he said.

But it was he who was to do the eating. Nor was excrement to be his meal. At the precise moment that his biceps and triceps received the mental command to move in the direction of the smaller man's throat, their capacity for motion was inexplicably withdrawn. Two rope-like arms encircled him from behind, holding him immobile. In dreamy slow motion he watched the fist arcing up towards his face, a passive spectator speculating on its exact destination. He knew there would be pain, but that it would come later, much later. He even found time to wonder, before the explosive impact, what he'd look like in the years to come. Different, he concluded. He heard his teeth splinter, tasted the salty rush of blood, felt suddenly very light and very tired, as if he wanted to go to sleep. Kiss mommy goodnight. Good night, darling. The lead pipe took him behind the ear, fracturing the bone and rupturing the eardrum before continuing upwards, peeling back the scalp to the pearly white skull beneath. And then he was a skydiver, stretched out in space, making a jump from the World Trade Center. What a pity that the parachute had failed to open. Such a nuisance. And the sidewalk was rushing up towards him so very fast.

Mickey leaned over the prostrate hulk. Roughly he prised open the still-clenched fist and extracted the fifty-dollar bill. He wiped a bloody hand across the sawdust floor.

'You get twenty-five, Fritz. You took him out good.' The wielder of the lead pipe grinned his agreement.

'Like, the harder they fall,' was all he said.

Both men turned their attention towards Charles, the bone of contention, the victor's spoils.

'The way I see it, it's a hundred for knocking over the gorilla, another for what you're going to get now.' Charles nodded his acquiescence, weak with excitement. Mickey unzipped his fly, oblivious to the bleeding, unconscious man at his feet.

'Lips or hips, you little bastard,' was all he said.

Chapter Four

Anne Carrington's house on the North side of Washington Square was listed as an historic landmark by the New York Community Trust. Built in 1830 in the so-called Greek Revival style, or in what the English preferred to call Late Georgian, it stood on five floors, the top and bottom of which were rented out to faculty members of New York University, at which Anne held an honorary teaching post.

Anne lived on the middle three floors in a warm, intimate triplex. From the tall windows she could look out over the trees of the Square she loved and drink in the atmosphere of student life. Here she could imagine the ghosts of Henry James, Walt Whitman and Mark Twain stalking among the trees, seeking inspiration for their work, and could see the latter-day students loitering, dallying, speculating and endlessly socializing in the traditional style of this universal species.

Anne needed this contrast. Here people were interested in the arts, in letters, in discovery and creation. On the Upper East Side where she worked there were different priorities. There the god was Mammon. She herself wasn't immune to an interest in money and the things it could buy, but she liked to think she hadn't sold out, as so many of her colleagues had. For her clinics at Bellevue there was no charge, while part of her teaching salary from the University was donated to charity.

It was 7 o'clock. As Anne stared out across the Square she heard the doorbell chime. She pictured Peter Isaacs, scrupulously punctual as usual, standing in front of the black double doors beneath the stone portico with its Ionic columns. She buzzed down on the entry phone.

'Come on up, Peter.'

He greeted her warmly. 'Really, Anne, you must be more careful. I could have been a rapist, or worse. You should ask who's there before opening the door.'

Anne punched playfully at his arm. 'Peter, how many times have I explained to you that there is *nothing* worse than a rapist.'

He laughed. 'I've never been able to believe in a fate worse than death.'

'That's because, unless you make it to Sing-Sing, you're statistically unlikely to be raped. Most red-blooded males, however, would be only too happy to rape me. It's only the law that prevents them. They do it with their eyes all the time!'

She liked to wind Peter up a bit, pretending he had chauvinistic tendencies, whereas in fact he made Marx look like a John Bircher on most political issues. Funny how he always got the conversation turned round to sex.

Peter looked around him. He loved Anne's home, but then he loved the colour of her car, had adopted her brand of toothpaste and was enough of a realist to admit that his objectivism was questionable. The tall room had the immaculate proportions of the house's exterior and Anne had had enough respect for the Neoclassical architecture not to swamp it in designer rubbish. The drawing room was sparsely furnished, but the furniture was all period, and the right period. It was comfortable, too, intimate but stylish – there was no easy way to analyse how this happy combination had been achieved. The painting over the Adams fireplace was of an eighteenth-century hunting scene – appropriate in view of the fact that the marshy area on which the house was built had once been used for the flighting of duck.

Peter sat down in a deep arm chair. He loved these evenings. Just the two of them. No boring strangers 'fascinated' at meeting a psychiatrist, who spent the whole evening poaching a free consultation before telling you that they didn't really believe in 'shrinks' anyway, always thought that they were madder than their patients. It was always their 'friend' who had the 'interesting' problem. 'You know, this friend of mine has this really *weird* desire to dress up in women's clothes, and do you know, he's a *dentist*.' 'May I ask your profession, sir?' Peter would reply. 'Well . . . actually, I'm a dentist, too. I'm not quite sure why you ask.'

Tonight, as always, they'd have a candle-lit dinner, good, simple food, a superb claret, and afterwards they would set the world to rights over a decanter of vintage port, for which the highly polished mahogany table would always be ceremoniously cleared. Both Anne and Peter loved the anachronistic ritual, the clockwise circulation of the flat-bottomed ship's decanter, the rich, ruby-red liquid with its intimations of distant sun-baked Portuguese fields. Before dinner they'd drink a dry sherry, a manzanilla or a fino, chilled and delicious in thin, tulip-shaped glasses.

He gazed fondly at her now as she poured the amber liquid. Christ, she was amazing. Despite the formality of the surroundings, off duty she wore tight blue-jeans and a cotton shirt. Peter could hardly remember seeing her in anything else. It was OK by him, always had been. The imagination was not overworked by Anne's attire. The fit, lithe body was scarcely concealed as the thin, faded material moulded into the skin of her thighs, calves, of her extraordinary upturned bottom. How did she find the time to do the work necessary to get her body into this sort of shape? Did she work out all night instead of sleeping? Was it kind to her patients to present them with a figure like this? How on earth could they think about their problems sitting across the desk from this one. And what about those tits in the gymnasium. Did people applaud?

He accepted the drink with a nod of thanks, catching her fresh, just-washed scent. Thank God he'd got used to all this, had learned to deal with the hopelessness of his love. Later, over the port he'd probably come out with the same tired old speech and Anne would laughingly defuse it, redirect his attention to something else.

'Did you see the accountant's report that came in this morning? Seems Carrington-Isaacs is a pretty successful corporation. I hope our commercial success is reflected in the quality of the claret,' he said by way of changing the subject of his disturbing thoughts.

'You're the business man, I'm the connoisseur,' she joked back at him. 'We've got a Pétrus '61.'

'How's the fall-out going from the *Journal* article?' Peter asked. Anne wouldn't want to stay away from shop talk for long.

'You wouldn't believe it. Boy, it seems I really stirred up a hornet's nest there, and quite unintentionally. I reckon that about three-quarters of those who've responded haven't read the original article.'

Anne had recently written an article in the prestigious *New England Journal of Medicine* and it had caused quite a stir. In it she'd argued passionately for the abandonment of narrow, stereotyped positions and blinkered vision in psychiatry. The article had been especially critical of the more rigid of the psychodynamists, and especially of the classical Freudians. *The Daily News*, ever ready to jump on any bandwagon that enabled them to sell more papers, had put the cat among the pigeons by publicizing the article in sensational terms under the banner headline 'Doc argues for shocks, pills: Scorns talk.'

'I guess some of those boys at the American Psychoanalytic Association could do with a little more analysis,' said Peter supportively.

Peter knew Anne had taken a lot of flak over the article. At the same time he couldn't suppress a slight feeling of satisfaction that a little pressure was heading Anne's way. Since medical school at Hopkins there had been an element of competition between them in professional matters and Peter was the first to admit to himself that Anne had usually come out ahead. Her reputation within the profes sion was that of a brilliant innovator, an original mind, whereas he was known chiefly for his painstaking analysis of problems.

'The Mitcham case seems to sum up the whole ridiculous situation.'

'Yes, I've been meaning to ask you about that. What's the latest?'

Anne thought for a moment and Peter watched her expression cloud over.

John Mitcham was an out-of-work stockbroker in his late fifties and Anne was treating him for depressive illness. Recently she'd noticed the tell-tale worsening of symptoms. This meant an increased danger of suicide and Anne was monitoring Mitcham closely, while treating him with standard antidepressant medication. At the moment she didn't think his condition serious enough for him to be hospitalized, especially in view of the fact that he had serious financial problems, no medical insurance and was too proud to consider a public hospital.

The fly in the ointment was that until very recently Mitcham had been in prolonged psychoanalysis with Dr Aaron Ishmael, an eminent, vocal, and messianic member of the American Psychoanalytic Association. In Anne's view the exorbitant cost of four years of therapy had been a major precipitating cause of Mitcham's depression. It had led to difficulties with mortgage payments which in turn had caused marital problems with a pushy, ambitious wife. A friend of Mitcham's had recommended that he see Anne for a second opinion, as his mood seemed to be getting progressively worse under Ishmael's regime. Anne had immediately diagnosed a reactive depression in response to financial and marital problems. She recommended that he discontinue analysis at least for the time being and had written immediately to the psychoanalyst to tell him of her diagnosis and advice. She'd ended by mentioning that, in view of the patient's straitened financial circumstances and the relevance of these to his illness, she would be charging no fee.

Anne's action had infuriated Ishmael. A shiver ran down her spine when she thought of the conversation she had had with the irate doctor and his furious words echoed in her ears. At first she'd been unable to get a word in edgeways as Ishmael's words had tumbled out in a torrent of rage.

'How dare you call my professional opinion into question! Are you trying to tell me, young lady, that I don't know my job? Are you daring to suggest that psychoanalysis is rubbish? . . . you're young and inexperienced . . . of course I charge him a fee . . . Freud charged fees . . . it's part of the therapy . . .'

For a full minute Anne had listened to the diatribe and then had started to lose her temper. Her voice ice-cold, she had cut into the stream of invective.

'Your trouble, Dr Ishmael, is that you look at life through the distorting spectacles of Freudian theory. Haven't you heard of antidepressants? Let me tell you *my* professional opinion. I think your psychoanalysis has brought Mitcham to the very edge of psychological ruin. I think it's been life-threatening.'

Ishmael had fought for words. 'I promise you, Dr Carrington, you will have every cause to regret what you have just said.'

Anne had put the phone down on the threat. Screw him, she'd thought, and dismissed the matter from her mind.

So what was the latest on the Mitcham case? Peter's question needed answering.

'I'm afraid the latest isn't too hot on the Ishmael front. He followed up that telephone call with an extremely rude letter. He accused me of poaching his patients and finished by saying that the pills wouldn't work and that I'd put the patient at risk. I'd accused *him* of that.'

'Was that wise?' Peter smiled.

'Probably not. I guess I went a bit over the top, but he

sure asked for it. Anyway, as far as Mitcham's concerned I know I'm doing the right thing. The depression's going biological. Used to have difficulty getting off to sleep, now it's early morning waking. Mood's worse in the mornings whereas before, if anything, it was marginally worse at night. He's right off his food and beginning to lose weight.'

'Looks as if you caught him with the antidepressants in the nick of time. No way are dream interpretation and free-association going to shift symptoms like that. A guy like Ishmael shouldn't miss a depressive illness of that severity.'

Peter drained his glass, well aware that Anne needed a little reassurance. To be locked in combat with a man like Ishmael was no easy thing. And if anything went wrong with Mitcham's treatment there would be a *lot* of explaining to do.

'Why not stick him in hospital? Why take the risk?'

'No Blue Cross. No cash. Wife wants to keep up 'standards'. Besides, I don't think he's that bad yet. I'd like to give the medication a chance. Don't think I haven't thought about it. But I'd be treating my own anxiety rather than doing what's best for the patient in the circumstances. I couldn't do that.'

No, thought Peter, she couldn't do that. Never had. That was one of the things he envied about her. It made her a tricky partner at times but she'd always been the same – the body of a goddess, mind as sharp as a Gillette blade. But where were the emotions, the passion? Where did Anne's sexuality lie? That they existed was beyond doubt. He could sense them, smell them, almost feel them. But they remained intangible, hidden. He'd never discovered the key to the door that contained them despite years of searching. One day a sublimely lucky voyager would stumble across the means of unlocking that door, and enter the promised land. The idea didn't make Peter happy.

'Frankly, Anne, I think you're a saint. Most people would have given Mitcham the brush-off rather than get into a tangle with a guy like Ishmael, especially for no fee. As it is, you've gone out to bat for him in a situation that's no-win to you.'

'I guess winning would be curing his depression and preventing that head-in-the-sand Freudian from murdering him. Anyway, let's go eat. I'm starving. It's roast lamb and apple pie.'

As they walked towards the candle-lit dining room, Peter put his arms round her shoulders. It was coming earlier than usual tonight.

'Marry me,' he said.

Anne laughed gently. 'Come on, Peter, not before the port.'

Peter smiled wryly. 'Boy, when you go you're really going to go. Couldn't it be me? Think how safe you'd be with a psychiatrist.' He was only half serious, but he was a very good psychiatrist, indeed.

'Damn!'

Anne slammed down the telephone. Paula, her secretary, had called in sick. Bad prawn – that universal euphemism for a late night or hangover.

Anne sighed resignedly. She liked the patient interviews to start and end crisply, in her office. Saying hello and goodbye to patients at the front door, and the small talk that the journey necessitated, made it more difficult to get down to the nitty-gritty of the doctor/patient dialogue: 'Good morning, Mr Jones. Did you manage to miss the rain?' 'Tell me, Mr Jones, how often do you masturbate?' 'Goodbye, Mr Jones. Hope little Johnny gets over his homesickness at summer camp.' The change of gear often grated.

She walked downstairs and opened the big red leather appointment book. The first patient appeared to be a new one. Good. Anne liked the challenge of diagnosis. She found the referral letter in the file, grudgingly admitting that Paula, despite her 'bad prawn', was not inefficient. The letter was brief. She noted the doctor's name – Evans, a good man. Fashionable, but competent. Hadn't it been Evans who'd come up with Skip Demery?

'Adam Phipps. Twenty-three. Drink problem.' Bells started to ring in Anne's head. Was this boy any relation to the Charles Phipps who was screwing Skip Demery? The same family doctor argued that there might easily be a connection. Christ, if this Adam was Charles Phipps' son, no wonder he had a drink problem. He would've had to have been a psychological superman not to have strung himself up years before. The insistent ringing of the doorbell cut into her thoughts.

Adam tended to lean on doorbells, his natural arrogance leading him to assume that doors would always be opened by lesser mortals. He was expecting a white-coated nurse, semi-pretty, rather stern, businesslike, mildly superior. He was scarcely prepared for the vision that confronted him. Boy, old Carrington sure had an eye for a pretty receptionist. Anyone who could hire a chick like this couldn't be all bad. He let his eyes do the walking. They said it all as they roamed up and down Anne Carrington's voluptuous body, stripping off her clothes piece by piece, flinging them into an untidy heap on the sidewalk. If this one played her cards right she just might get a luncheon invitation – or better. Things were looking up. Clearly nurses' uniforms were out these days.

Anne had been feeling rather stern, businesslike and mildly superior. But she was now thoroughly taken aback. Nobody had prepared her for this blond Adonis who posed nonchalantly on her doorstep, undressing her with his eyes. With a little rush of alarm she realized that she'd never seen such a good-looking man. Somewhere in the depths of her she felt a strange biochemical shift, sensed her control of the situation drift gently away.

Adam, well used to making a good impression on women wasn't at all surprised by her apparent discomposure.

'Is this where Dr Carrington hangs out?' he said, the faintest curl of condescension dancing round the corners of his lips.

'It is indeed,' Anne replied with all the coldness she could muster. Immediately she saw what had happened. Not unnaturally he'd mistaken her for Paula. Could it be that he didn't know that Dr Carrington was female? If so, she could take this pretty, cocky boy down a few pegs and reassert herself. With mounting alarm Anne sensed the inappropriateness of her reaction. Christ, this was a *patient* and she was already into the business of scoring points. That was ridiculous.

'Actually, I'm Dr Carrington. You must be Mr Phipps.'

It was Adam's turn to blush. He was totally thrown.

'I'm terribly sorry. I had no idea . . . no idea . . . that . . .'

'I was female,' Anne finished the sentence for him, touched by Adam's sudden change in tone from supercilious man-about-town to charmingly apologetic. 'Don't worry, it happens all the time,' she added by way of absolution, noticing a weird tingling sensation somewhere on the inside of her thighs as she did so.

'You'd better come in. The receptionist is sick today and I'm jack-of-all-trades in consequence.'

That was better. Control definitely reasserted. The cool, calm, confident doctor once more. There was a sense of relief. But why? Where had been the threat? Would there have been a problem if Adam had been fifty and with seborrhoeic dermatitis? That was a question which didn't require an answer.

'Follow me. My office is upstairs. I'll lead the way.'

Adam hadn't got over his confusion, but he was beginning to recover. His eyes, like rabbits' in the glare of oncoming headlights, stared fixedly at the tight swaying bottom as he followed her upstairs and along the corridor. She was disturbingly beautiful, and that was both exciting and threatening all at once. Soon, within minutes perhaps, she would be in possession of all his innermost secrets, would know him inside-out and backwards, better, maybe, than he did himself. He would be totally vulnerable, wide open, at her mercy. What would that be like? At the mercy of a woman who looked like this. He hadn't taken in her breasts.

Anne half turned as she spoke. 'I hope you've set aside an hour or two. The first session is always the longest.'

Adam took them in. Full, pointed, in perfect proportion with the rest of her body.

'All my time is your time, Doctor,' he managed. It came out distinctly flirtatious.

Anne didn't reply. The tingling sensation on her inside thighs had now crawled all over her buttocks. It wasn't at all unpleasant. Quite the opposite.

Somehow it was a relief to both of them to reach the office, where familiar props reasserted hierarchic relationships. The big oak desk looked like a barrier that only the foolhardy or desperate would attempt to cross. The soft leather, tall-backed chair, which would be Adam's had 'patient's chair' written all over it. Would Anne wear hornrimmed spectacles? Would she smoke a pipe? Anne collapsed into her chair with the decorum of a brick-layer hitting a bar stool. She straightened the papers on her desk and made a little speech. She'd done this one before.

'What I like to do is to have a general conversation for about half an hour while we discuss the reasons why you're here. Then for about half an hour I take what we call a formalized history, asking a whole lot of questions which might seem to you irrelevant but which are a great help to me in providing background, excluding things, and so on. After that I do a physical examination and take some blood for testing. Does that sound OK to you?'

Physical examination, Christ. Wasn't she supposed to be a psychiatrist? Was this woman going to *examine* him?

'After all that I'll have a good idea of what the problems are and together we can discuss the best way of dealing with them. This first session is always a bit of a marathon, but when we see each other again it'll be for shorter periods.'

Anne leaned back in her chair and placed the tips of her fingers together. She looked straight at Adam. 'So, Mr Phipps, perhaps you'd start by telling me in your own words why it is you've come along to see me.'

Where to start. With his parents' death? With the morning when he'd finally decided to call Dr Evans? What to mention first – the cocaine, the drink, the sex, the globalized angst, the self-disgust, the waste or the lack of direction? Were these the problems, or symptoms of the problems? That's what he supposed he was there to discover.

Adam splayed his hands open, signifying the difficulty of encapsulating his problem in a few well-chosen words.

Anne helped out. 'Dr Evans mentioned a drink problem. Let's start there. How much would you say you drank during a normal day?'

Ah, that was relatively easy. Adam started off. 'Well, let's see. I make it a rule not to start much before twelve, unless I'm in the country. I suppose two or three Bloody Mary's before lunch, that sort of thing. Then I guess most of a bottle of wine with lunch, perhaps a kummel or cognac afterwards. In the evening it's usually martinis before eating, a couple or more. Wine with dinner, of course. If it's champagne I usually stick to that until bedtime.' He reckoned that was about it.

Anne made some notes.

'How long have you been drinking as much as this?'

'Oh, about two years, I'd say.'

'What happened two years ago?'

'My parents were killed in a plane crash.'

It seemed to be straightforward. This boy was still mourning his dead parents. Phipps. Plane crash. Of course. This had to be the heir to the Phipps fortune. The tragic accident had been big news at the time. Anne stared at him hard. No doubt about it.

A watery film covered Adam's eyes. While he'd been relating the details of his drinking day he'd almost regained his doorstep self-confidence. Now, suddenly, there was no sign of it at all. She felt a wave of sympathy grow within her, noticed with growing alarm that there were feelings of tenderness, too. She was beginning to get the picture. The young man-about-town with the hard, tough exterior was all broken up inside, longing for the love and affection which had been so cruelly and so abruptly withdrawn – searching for its replacement but looking in all the wrong places. He'd move in fast circles, be surrounded by n'er-do-wells, be taken for rides by golddiggers and fleeced by unscrupulous wheeler-dealers. And all around him like moths would be the pushers of substances who promised temporary oblivion from the pain of his heartbreak; a one-way ticket to instant happiness at the price of his self-respect.

Anne was pretty sure there was nothing fundamentally wrong with Adam. It wasn't a psychological illness. He was just deeply unhappy, and had good reason to be. Normally, Anne wouldn't have taken on a patient like this. What he needed was help and advice from a wise and concerned friend, even the family doctor. Evans could be relied upon to be suitably supportive, to arrange counselling of some sort to get over the alcohol problem. If she took on every patient with problems like Adam's there would be no space at all for the John Mitchams or her obsessional schoolteacher – those with genuine psychiatric conditions. And yet Anne knew with certainty that she would decide to take Adam on. There was no question about it. The interesting question was why.

Anne avoided the issue by busying herself with the familiar routine history-taking and the mental-state examination. As she did so, Adam's personality began to come alive as the events that had shaped it were uncovered one by one. An only child, apple of his phenomenally rich parents' eyes; the sheltered, pampered childhood, the brilliantly successful academic career, the tragedy that had destroyed his world. Anne felt herself liking the boy more and more as she began to realize his remarkable achievement in rising above his privileged background to his remarkable success in computer sciences at Harvard. She was charmed by his open laugh and his revelation of the $100-million worth of assets in response to her routine question about 'means of support'. And all the time she was disconcerted by the deep blue eyes, the lustrous blond hair, the Dorian Gray beauty which had defied the self-inflicted wounds of his hedonistic life-style. Boyish charm allied with a brittle vulnerability spoke directly to Anne's latent maternal instincts, and with mounting alarm she realized that other instincts were being aroused as well.

As the minutes ticked away the physical examination began to acquire connotations it hadn't held previously, and Anne found herself putting off the moment of approaching this usually unthreatening hurdle. Adam, too, sensed its approach and felt intuitively that for some reason it was being delayed, a metaphysical time-bomb ticking invisibly in the corner of the room. He found Dr Carrington wonderful in every way – sensitive, funny, incredibly bright – and, above all, fantastically exciting. Women like her didn't exist in Adam's world, and he reacted to her as if she was some exotic, alien species, some creature of superior aesthetic construction who had fallen to earth from outer space.

Anne steeled herself. Usually at this stage she'd call Paula, a trained nurse, to 'chaperone' the physical examination of both male and female patients. It was standard procedure for all wise doctors, especially for psychiatrists. But Paula wasn't there, damn it! Or did she really mean 'damn it'? She could ask Peter to stand in, but he was with a patient and anyway, wouldn't that be a bit over the top? No, she would go through with it by herself.

'I'd just like to have a quick look at you.' That was what she always said, but it didn't sound quite right this time. 'You can leave your underpants on.' God, what if he didn't wear any? Anne gestured casually towards a couch, the end of which protruded from behind a Chinese lacquered screen in the corner of the room. She waited for a minute or two while Adam undressed.

He lay there in his white cotton boxer shorts like a patient in pre-op waiting for surgery, heart beating a little faster, thoughts coming a little more quickly than usual. He smiled nervously as Anne approached, extending a stiff arm for her to take his pulse.

'Relax,' she said, both to herself and Adam.

Anne followed her usual routine. Radial pulse. BP. Check the neck veins. Feel for the heart's apex beat. Listen with the stethoscope. In a young, fit man of Adam's age it was routine, but Anne had learned to take nothing for granted in medicine. He looked in good nick. Not anaemic, no tell-tale yellowing of the eye whites indicating jaundice from liver damage. Next, the central nervous system – always important for patients with a drinking history. Pupils equal, reacting to both light and accommodation. Anne noted that she breathed in as she bent over to peer into Adam's eyes with the ophthalmoscope, taking the masculine scent of him down deep into her lungs, her jutting breasts brushing the honey-coloured skin of his chest. Careful, doctor, chimed the alarm-bells in her psyche. Patients could sense this kind of thing.

Adam was too preoccupied with his own feelings to be much aware of Anne's. He was finding her ostensibly disinterested professional touch extraordinarily erotic – the cool, business-like hands probing, prodding. As she looked into his eyes she was almost lying on top of him, and he could feel the warmth of her breath on his cheek, her subtle fragrance insinuating itself into his consciousness. Beneath the boxer shorts he felt the first impossible stirrings and with mounting horror fought desperately to suppress them. To get an erection now would be a disaster, a humiliating tragedy. Surely she had nearly finished. Adam tried to make his mind go blank, counting numbers in his head, trying to visualize them as he did so.

Oblivious to his seething thoughts, Anne continued the examination. Reflexes, muscle-power, bulk, sensation, coordination – all within normal limits. Time to have a look at the abdomen. No masses. No tenderness. No rigidity. Check the liver for enlargement.

'Breathe in deeply.'

Adam did as he was told and Anne's fingers pushed in under his right rib cage. Panic. He'd lost the battle. His penis was on the move. Adam sensed rather than saw it rear up beneath the loose shorts. God. The ultimate embarrassment.

Suddenly Anne, too, was aware of it. For a split second she stared in fascination, not at all sure how she would react. With amusement? A little. Pleasure? More than was appropriate, if indeed any was appropriate. Desire? That thought was too hot to handle. She dismissed it at once. The boy had a hard-on. So what? She was hardly Dracula's sister. It was no big deal. Normally she'd feel the inguinal lymph nodes, have a quick look at the genitalia. Of course it was out of the question, although a part of her wanted to do just that.

'Sorry,' mumbled Adam.

'No problem,' said Anne.

But she knew as she said it that there *was* a problem. A very big problem indeed. And it didn't get any smaller when she felt herself decide that this young man would need a long course of supportive psychotherapy. At least two sessions a week.

Anne wrapped up the session quickly, and neither referred again to Adam's little lapse of self-control. But the fact that it wasn't discussed didn't cover up the truth: that Adam had expressed his physical desire for Anne in the most fundamental of ways – and that Anne had not minded one tiny bit. What was it that Peter Isaacs had said the night before?

At the front door she tried to be as business-like as possible.

'Well, I'll see you in a few days time. Perhaps you could call tomorrow and make an appointment. My receptionist will be back by then.' She smiled briskly as she shook his hand.

But Adam held it just a fraction of a second longer than was strictly necessary, and his deep blue eyes beamed into her own. 'I look forward to it very much.'

As she closed the door behind him, Anne sensed that drastic changes were in store for her. For better or for worse, she didn't know.

Three o'clock in the morning and while one Big Apple slept, another worked on tirelessly. Adam poured over the display console and watched intently. Something very interesting was happening. Ever since his meeting with Dukes, Adam had been reading everything he could get his hands on about stock-exchange technical analysis.

Now, to his astonishment, a significant pattern seemed to be emerging. It appeared that he'd constructed a computer program that was able to predict within two or three points the daily fluctuations in the Dow-Jones Industrial Average. Time and again, as he fed in the twenty pieces of daily information from the pile of old *Wall Street Journals* which littered the floor of his computer room, the Big Apple came up with a figure that corresponded closely to the following day's stock-market movements, as measured by the Dow. He could hardly believe his eyes but the predictions were consistently and uncannily accurate.

The excitement began to mount within him as he continued the tests. Had he by chance stumbled on the latter-day equivalent of the philosopher's stone, the ability to squeeze undreamed of amounts of money from the

98

circuitry of a computer? Certainly his system seemed to work for the past. Would it do the same for the future?

There was only one way to find out. Adam punched in the relative information from the day's trading gleaned from the Dow-Jones Information Service, to which he was now directly linked by telex. Day's volume: 63,000,000. Ratio of New Highs to New Lows: 27 to 368. Winners/Losers ratio: 1/3·65 etc. etc. The flashing screen digested the figures in seconds and there, on the display, was Adam's prediction for the direction of the following day's trading on the New York Stock Exchange: Dow-Jones Industrials. Up 11·65.

If that came true a lot of people would be surprised. On the inside back page of the *Journal* the pundits were looking for continued market weakness. 'Expect further falls, possibly substantial ones', had been the message from the investment strategist at Goldman, Sachs.

How would the market behave? Was he now, at a stroke, better informed than any investment advisor anywhere in the world? Or just a fool who had put too much belief in computers? A mischievous idea suddenly occurred to him. After all, he was a Phipps and Phippses took chances, didn't play safe. Despite the fact that it was the middle of the night, he dialled his uncle's number. The answering service came on the line.

'I have an important message for my uncle, Charles Phipps. It's imperative he get it before nine o'clock tomorrow morning – so call him with it before then.'

'State your message,' said the sleepy, irritable voice.

'Adam predicts the Dow will close 11·65 higher on today's trading.'

Charles could make of that what he wished. He would have the information before the opening bell on Wall Street.

The electric toothbrush sailed through the air, cord and

battery-pack attached, like some fiendish missile designed to garrotte its objective. Charles Phipps ducked in the nick of time, watching it float past his startled eyes before being brought to a precipitous stop by the screen of the TV set. His mind never far from things financial, he was already computing the damage. The toothbrush – a few dollars only, no sweat. The TV, its screen misty at the point of impact, was another matter altogether.

Skip Demery followed up the toothbrush with a large jar of B-complex vitamin tablets and a high-pitched scream of pure, distilled anger and irritation. The bottle caught Charles a glancing blow on the shoulder, painful but not unendurable, before crashing to the floor where it splintered, distributing hundreds of little parcels of potential goodness all over the neat apartment.

'You filthy, fucking . . . faggot,' yelled Skip, oblivious to either the alliteration or to the fact that this was clearly a case of the pot calling the kettle black. 'If you want pain, I'll give it to you,' he added as he launched himself bodily from the bathroom and fell upon the cowering Charles.

This wasn't really Charles' scene at all. He liked pain and humiliation in monitored doses, dished out by people whose emotions were carefully under control. Disinterest was what he looked for in his tormentors. Also, the degradation was inseparable from the wonderful anticipation of it. This sudden assault had come out of the blue, without warning and, to say the very least, was heavily laden with emotional overtones. Hedgehog-like he rolled himself into a small round ball to withstand the pummelling attack. Charles felt the fists crash into his back, his buttocks, the tops of his legs. Hopefully, face and hands would be spared for his luncheon appointment at Le Cirque. A few superficial bruises on the body were par for the course.

Skip managed to keep up the stream of invective while working out on his punch-bag routine.

'If I hear you've peddled your stinking ass around those

shitty, fucking clubs again, I'll chop your filthy little prick off with a meat cleaver and make you *eat* it. Do you hear, shit-bag?'

Charles heard all right. So, he imagined, did most of Greenwich Village. Would someone call the cops? Probably not. Lovers' tiffs of this sort created about as much interest in the local precinct as small earthquakes in Chile. Not much longer now, thought Charles, noticing that the punches were beginning to lose some of their strength as the insults got louder and more colourful.

'One more time, you little piece of frigging dirt, and I'm going to stuff your fat little behind with a ·45 Magnum, and blow your rotten bowels to kingdom-come.'

Then quite suddenly, the infuriated, demented lover, bent on terrible revenge, became at once the saddened, wronged, mistreated partner. The pummelling stopped and Skip began to weep.

'Charles, how could you *do* this to me, when I love you so much. After all we've been *through* together. I never dreamed you could be so unfeeling, so unfaithful, and with all those *terrible* people. Promise me . . . promise me you'll never do it again. Swear. Tell me you won't leave me.' Sincerity dripped from his lips. He'd got one hell of a lot to lose if some wild leather-boy got his fangs into Charles Phipps.

Charles recognized the lull after the storm. There was a traditional way to handle this situation, usually rather pleasant. The old familiar feeling rushed through him.

'Skip, Skip,' said the nasal accent in what passed for soothing tones. 'Don't even talk about it. Nothing could come between us. I wouldn't let it. You're safe with me.' 'I'll never leave you,' he added. I'll keep him on for another six months and then axe him, said the corresponding subterranean thought. Time for the coup de grâce, the remark that would bury the hatchet, clear the way for the next, more enjoyable, phase.

'Listen, Skip. You go out this afternoon and get yourself

a few things. Run along to Ralph Lauren, fix yourself up with some new clothes. Put it on that Express Card I gave you.'

Homicidal lover, wronged 'mistress', fawning concubine – Skip's repertoire was endless. He positively simpered with delight, his tears drying like slugs under a blowtorch. A conciliatory hand snaked out and began to massage the back of Charles' short, squat neck.

'What say we make up?' The remark was a loaded one.

'That would be nice,' said Charles, feeling his penis begin to throb with anticipatory desire.

'Here, on the floor.' Cocquettish, flirtatious, daring – this was Skip the versatile lover, the man who knew a thing or two when it came to pleasing men. Charles was not going to make difficulties over the geography.

Skip was already ramrod stiff. Being promised the run of an Express Card at the Ralph Lauren boutique had that sort of an effect on him.

Charles rolled over on the floor and arching his back, offered up his pink rump as if it was the dish of honour at a cannibal's banquet.

Skip needed no invitation to the feast, didn't stand on ceremony. His mission was simple – to see Charles Phipps well and truly fucked.

Like a Bengal lancer taking out a mountain tribesman Skip Demery went for it, savouring the little squeak of pleasurable pain that Charles emitted at the rough invasion of his nether regions. The warm tightness gripped his tense weapon and he thrust forwards with his hips, pinning the little round figure to the floor, skewered, transfixed, stuck like the pig he was. Rhythmically he began to grind away, working for maximum friction to cause the greatest possible amount of pain, tearing at the tight circle of muscle, his penis an avenging dagger, a sword of retribution. Faster and faster, deeper and deeper he plumbed the depths, his engorged phallus sunk to the hilt in Charles' patrician ass.

Charles liked to be taken like this. Skip could really sock

it to him after a row. No K Y jelly, nothing. Just the alien presence on the rampage within him, a bull in the china shop of his bowels. Not long now and the delicious pump would begin to squirt within him.

The insistent warbling of the telephone wafted over the copulating couple. For a few short seconds Skip ignored it as he calculated how far he was from orgasm. Too far. He'd answer it. Letting it ring was something he found extraordinarily difficult. He stopped his violent motion and, pushing up on his muscular arms, pulled his still erect penis out of Charles Phipps' bottom like a wine waiter pulling the cork from a bottle of burgundy.

'Telephone,' he said unnecessarily.

Charles, his rectum suddenly empty howled in irritation. 'Christ, Skip, you didn't have to answer it.'

Charles was right – it was nothing more exciting than the Phipps answering service. Petulantly he held the receiver out towards the half-undressed Charles. 'It's for you. Your answering service, I think.'

Charles took the telephone. 'Yes?' he barked into the mouthpiece, infuriated at the interruption of his fuck. This had better be important. The answering service had been given this number with the strict instruction that only urgent messages should be passed on.

'What?' he shouted in disbelief and frustration. 'Adam Phipps says the Dow is going up 11 points today? That's the message? Listen, who decided to bother me with this piece of garbage?'

Charles listened irritably as the operator explained that Adam had said the message was urgent and that he should have it before nine o'clock without fail. He slammed the phone down, knowing his bad mood would last all day. His fucking nephew had unlimited power to drive him mad. What the hell did he mean? He knew nothing about the Dow, about anything remotely important like that. Adam had clearly been overdoing the drink again, and on some ridiculous whim had decided to irritate his uncle.

Well he'd succeeded. Coitus interruptus. Blast his eyes. Quite apart from that, any fool knew that the market decline was gathering momentum. The Dow had as much chance of gaining 11 points as Adam had of getting through the day without a drink.

'I'd better be getting off to the bank,' said Charles sullenly, his roving eye taking in the semi-wrecked apartment, the sulky Skip, flaccid penis dangling between his legs, the mounds of vitamin pills like miniscule marbles cluttering the floor. This was suddenly a bad scene. Time to split. Morosely he buttoned his trousers as little messages of frustration from his tingling anus trickled through to his consciousness.

The taxi ride to Wall Street was not a long one, an advantage of the Village love nest. Gloomily, Charles ran over his day. Lunch at Le Cirque with a well-connected fag-hag, whose vicious tongue was neatly offset by the splendid hospitality available at her Southampton home. That would be tiring but useful. Otherwise nothing until the charity gala at Sotheby Parke-Bernet that evening. How to pass the morning? Adam's message kept running through his mind. Dow up! Balls. Crap. The market was going down like an old poof on a fourteen-year-old chorister. Nothing more certain. That's what he'd do: sell some stock for his own account, take out a few short positions in the volatile brokerage houses, maybe accumulate a few 'put' options in the faltering airlines. It would be money for old rope. And he'd let that little prick of a nephew of his stay fully invested, let the famous Phipps portfolio take it on the nose.

As soon as he was at his desk Charles started to deal, betting against Adam's prediction, counting on a falling market. 'These are personal deals,' he had emphasized to the head dealer, 'book 'em to me.'

All morning Charles watched the tapes. Everything was

going according to plan. The market was very weak – down more than 12 points by mid-morning, off 19 by twelve o'clock – and on decent volume, too. It looked like a bloodbath. The Phipps fingers punched the details of his sell orders on to the Hewlett-Packard calculator. He was showing nearly $25,000 profit. Not bad for a morning's work. He chuckled to himself. Up 11 points. Rubbish!

At lunch Charles was expansive, ordering a particularly fine Aloxe Corton burgundy from Le Cirque's comprehensive wine list. He'd made a packet during the morning's trading and it looked as if he'd be making more just sitting there chomping away cheerfully on his steak Mouton Cadet. At times like this it was good to be alive. Here he was, enjoying 'most favoured customer' status in one of the world's, or at least New York's, best restaurants, entertaining a social lioness who could break people's careers with her tongue. Charles Phipps: master of the markets, confidante of the rich and well-born, the man with the golden touch.

'You know, it's really about time we got you married, Charles – though God knows what we'd all do if you were withdrawn from circulation.'

Charles preened. If only this bag of leathery bones knew the truth. Stupid fucking cow. She should've seen him this morning on Skip's Mexican rug, taking a length. That would've given her something to talk about. Still, it was great to be thought of as an eligible bachelor, very much the image he cultivated. No way was some superannuated old geriatric going to withdraw him from circulation like a dirty, crinkled bank note. Unless, of course, there were megabucks around.

'My dear Nan,' he said unctuously, reaching out to touch the hoary, weather-beaten old hand, 'how could I think of marriage when you still have a husband?' Was the decrepit, drunken sot still alive, or had she moved him on like she had all the others? Charles would rather have slept with a boxful of black widow spiders than with Nan

Danvers. What he didn't know was that she suspected just that.

Nan Danvers' laugh was like tearing tin-foil. She'd reached the stage where all compliments were gratefully received, whatever their source. Charles added his high-pitched nasal whine to the general mirth. He would have a cognac. Why not? Yes, a large brandy, and then back to the office just before the closing bell to calculate his winnings.

Charles and Nan continued their analysis of the shifting fortunes and status of the various players in the New York social game in the limo after lunch. After dropping her off at Cartier he headed downtown towards Wall Street. In the corridor on the way to his office he passed one of the partners.

'Boy, what a day,' said the younger man. 'Roller-coaster time.'

Charles felt the first awful moment of doubt. He quickened his step, feeling the uncertainty begin to gnaw at his insides. Off 19 points before lunch. Had the market turned? Would the loss be a mere few points after all? He switched on the television.

'So it was a see-saw day on Wall Street as the bulls and the bears slugged it out. Down nearly 20 points at lunchtime, the market turned right around to end showing an impressive gain of 11 points.'

Hell and damnation. Charles' small, tight fist exploded against the leather-topped desk. He'd fucking blown it – and Adam, by some ridiculous fluke, had got the market right. Fuming his indignation, he dialled Adam's number. The laid-back voice answered.

'Adam, what the hell is this ridiculous stock-market business? You ring me up, irritating my answering service in the middle of the night, wasting my time. Really, haven't you got *anything* better to do? Some of us have to earn a living, you know.'

For a moment there was silence at the other end of the

line. It was followed by a loud gargling noise and what sounded like a burp.

'Sorry, Uncle Charles. I'm just starting a cold and a guy I met at the Racquette Club said the thing to do was to gargle with Jack Daniels. Works every time apparently. Funny thing is it has to be Jack Daniels. No other bourbon will do. Oh, by the way, the market'll be up 18·75 tomorrow, Charles. Better get a hold of some stock.' He rang off.

Charles stood stock-still, his mind seething with pure and refined hatred, his body vibrating gently with the pulsations of his terrible rage. Somehow, some way, he'd get even.

Anne Carrington had the happy knack of being able to switch off at the end of her working day. Eight hours of gruelling patient interviews left her physically and emotionally drained, and over the years she'd acquired the vital ability to wipe clean the cluttered blackboard of her mind. That way she slept soundly and was ready, early next day, for the next round. Last night it hadn't been like that at all. The problem on her mind was both simple and complex at the same time: Adam Phipps. Last night she'd failed to resolve it, and resolution appeared as far away as ever as she sat behind her desk waiting for her first patient.

The straightforward part was that she knew for certain exactly what she should do. She should tell Adam that she'd decided he didn't need therapy – especially from her. It was so obvious it didn't even require a second thought. But the brutal truth was that she wanted to take Adam on for reasons that were scarcely honourable – because of his deep blue eyes, because of his honey-brown skin, because of those strange little physical sensations he'd conjured up in her, because of the extraordinarily obvious desire she had created in him. OK, so it was well known in psychiatric circles that patients had a better chance of being taken on if they were young, attractive, verbal, intelligent and successful, but Anne tried to rise above such things. Tried and invariably succeeded. Now she felt she was on the verge of conspicuous failure.

Her first two patients had required and received total concentration, and so when Adam's turn came Anne still had not decided how she would behave. As the door opened and Paula ushered him into her office, she felt powerless to control her behaviour; an interested spectator, waiting to see what she would do.

'Good morning, Dr Carrington.' Adam's smile was wide, open, enthusiastic and warm. It said he liked her, had been looking forward to the meeting.

'Good morning, Mr Phipps.' That was a bit formal, thought Anne. Usually by now I'd be on Christian-name terms with a twenty-three year old. I'm trying to keep him at arms length.

Adam slumped down into the big leather chair, arms fully extended by his sides, legs wide apart. It wasn't a patient's position, although he was in the patient's chair. Anne reckoned he'd sit like that in front of the fire in whatever men's club people like him belonged to. He looked in rude health. OK, so he was drinking like a fish, but his body was young and the firm muscles, so well remembered from the physical examination, said he worked out both hard and frequently. Anxiety and depression appeared to be absent.

Ann pursed her lips. Schoolteacher feelings coursed through her. Christ, she was going to give him the bullet. Internally she found herself rehearsing the words. But Adam spoke first.

'Do you mind if I just say what a terrific relief it was talking to you the other day? Somehow it really helped to get things into perspective – and I feel it's made a great difference.'

Adam had been rehearsing this little speech. He couldn't know how important it was to be. He'd said it because it was true. Since the meeting with Anne things had really started moving – and now there was the incredible excitement of the whole computer thing.

Anne had actually got so far as opening her mouth to deliver the equivalent of a 'Dear John' speech. She closed it again.

'Well, I'm glad. We aim to please.' God, she sounded like some cheerleader responding to a compliment from the captain of the football team. This was no good at all. She heard herself trying again.

'Actually, Adam, I was going to start off today by telling you that in my opinion I don't think I have a great deal to offer you – nothing that you couldn't get more easily and more economically elsewhere.' That was *tame*. What about all that 'I *was going* to start off . . .'? And to tell someone who had a hundred million that he ought to be thinking about saving some bucks!

Adam looked startled, disappointed and hurt all at once. It was a winning combination.

'Oh, no. I'm sorry, I think you're wrong. I mean . . . I don't want to tell you your job or anything, but I know it'll be a help. Really.'

The apparent hesitation, implied by the rather halting delivery, was an illusion. Between the words Anne had no difficulty picking up Adam's steely determination. He wasn't used to being given the brush-off and looked as if he wouldn't be prepared to tolerate it.

Inside her head Anne felt she'd both won and lost. Only time would tell if it had been a victory or a defeat. Still a passenger in the cockpit of her own mind she watched herself give it one more try.

'You see, Adam, I'm a trained psychiatrist and I try to deal only with people who suffer from genuine psychiatric illness – depression, schizophrenia – things like that. Obviously you don't fit into any of those categories, so really my training is a bit superfluous in this case. What you need is a good friend to talk to, someone who can give you commonsense advice and some support. Perhaps Dr Evans . . .' Anne's voice trailed off uncertainly.

'I don't have friends like that. I want to talk to you.'

Anne discarded several possible replies. 'OK, you win. Actually, I'd enjoy taking you on. Why not? Let's do it.'

She was far from satisfied with her choice, or with the warm relieved smile that accompanied it.

Adam picked right up on her mood, and staring fixedly into her eyes he echoed her words. 'Right, let's do it, indeed.'

Anne was worried. John Mitcham was pretty depressed. OK, so he'd only been on the antidepressant tablets for a week, which was too early to expect any improvement. But one always hoped for a quicker reaction. She checked his mental state carefully. The early morning waking seemed to be solidifying. Wide awake at 4.30 in the morning and totally unable to get back to sleep again. Lying there, staring at the ceiling, obsessed by morbid thoughts. Appetite hopeless. Weight-loss increasing. It didn't look good.

'Do you feel very guilty, John – almost as if you deserve all these bad feelings?'

There were tears in the stockbroker's honest eyes as he tried to answer the question.

'I do feel I've let everyone down. My wife especially. I must be a pretty pathetic sort of character to crack up like this. Sometimes I wonder if it isn't some sort of punishment for something I've done wrong. I've tried not to be wicked in this life, but I can't help feeling that I'm not a very good person, that I sort of deserve this . . . hell.' He buried his head in his hands and began to sob.

'I know there's nothing much I can say that will help, but I promise you, John, that you're a wonderful person. You've had a terrible time, and you've coped better than many of us would. Try to believe that you feel like this because of the depression, not because of anything you've done, or failed to do. It's like flu, only much, much worse. I promise you we can cure you of this. Just try to have faith.'

He looked up at her through tear-filled eyes. 'I know you're just saying that, Dr Carrington, but thank you. In all the years I was seeing Dr Ishmael I don't think he ever said a kind thing to me.'

Bastard, thought Anne. He wouldn't, would he. As for laying a comforting hand on a patient – well, for a Freudian that was heresy, an unforgivable lapse into the reality of human relationships.

'John, I know we've discussed this before, but I really think you might be better off in hospital where we can look after you. Just for a day or two until the medicine begins to work.'

'No!' It was almost a shout of desperation. 'I couldn't do that to my wife. The neighbours might find out. It would destroy her. I've messed up her life enough without doing that to her. I can't possibly afford a private place, and one of those public ones . . .' His voice tailed off and he began to wring his hands at the awful thought.

'OK, OK, John. I don't want to force you. It just seemed like a good idea to me, but I quite see the difficulties.'

Time to take the bull by the horns. If she was to continue to treat him at home she had to cover the suicide angle.

'Tell me, John, does it ever seem to you that life just isn't worth living any more – that things are that bad?'

'You mean, have I thought of killing myself?' The voice had a break in it.

'Yes,' said Anne simply.

John Mitcham let out a great sigh, his shoulders sagging under the mighty burden of his grief. 'I could never do that,' he said. 'Never. Although I can't see any future for me.'

Just about good enough. Just, thought Anne. 'No

thoughts of suicide,' she wrote in her notes. 'But future looks hopeless.' Then she wrote, 'I can't see any future for me.'

'You're taking the tablets regularly, aren't you?'

Mitcham nodded. Anne believed him.

'OK, John, I'll see you again at the beginning of next week. Don't hesitate to call any time if you feel you can't cope. I mean that. Day or night. My service knows how to get hold of me at all times. Just leave a message and I'll ring right back.'

'Thank you, Dr Carrington. I wish there was some way I could repay you for all of this.'

'Your getting better is all I want from you,' said Anne with a laugh. 'Good-bye, John. Till next week.'

For a few minutes after he'd left, Anne sat lost in thought. In a way she was gambling with a man's life, or rather was allowing *him* to gamble with it. But what else could she do? She'd covered all the angles. She couldn't force him into hospital, couldn't stop him from killing himself if he decided to do it. The doctor could propose and prescribe, but it was always the patient who disposed. Perhaps that was just as well. The God trip had never appealed to Anne. Still, a little moral support was in order. She'd drop in on Peter. Luckily, she was able to catch him in-between patients.

Peter said all the right things, asked all the right questions, backed her to the hilt – but Anne knew that the responsibility for the management of her patient was hers alone. There was no getting away from that, and they both knew it. No point going over the ground ad nauseum.

By way of changing the subject, Peter asked, 'I saw you had a new patient – Phipps. Drink problem. Did you pass him on?'

It was usually partnership policy to give alcoholics a miss, referring them on to Alcoholics Anonymous, whose success rate was far better than that of most psychiatrists.

Anne tried hard not to blush but didn't quite succeed.

'I think I'll give him a few sessions. See how it goes. I think he could use some help.'

Peter looked at her quizzically. He didn't miss a trick. 'My word. Unlike you to spend so much time on a drink problem. I thought you favoured the "pull your finger out" approach.' It was a joke and a probe at the same time.

'Oh, come off it, Peter.' Suddenly Anne was annoyed. Her remark was sharp, full of irritation – and immediately she regretted it. Over-reaction. Plain for all to see, especially Peter Isaacs. No prize for the analysis of motive. Defence. But against what? Guilty feelings, of course. She'd taken Adam on as a patient because she was attracted to him, and Peter was a quarter of the way towards recognizing that. It was time for a tactical retreat.

'Well, I mustn't waste any more of your time, Peter. See you later.'

As the door closed behind her, Peter Isaacs experienced a mild twinge of anxiety, both in his capacity as Anne's partner and, far more significantly, as the man who loved her.

The wall thermometer in Anne Carrington's office registered no increase at all, but in other ways the temperature was rising. Each time Anne looked at Adam she couldn't avoid remembering the disturbing yet beguiling vision of the heaving strength beneath his boxer shorts.

She found him unsettlingly attractive – no point trying to deny that. Damn. It was so incredibly unprofessional and it was totally screwing up the mechanics of the session. Anne was aware that her words sounded strange and stilted as she attempted to understand the basis of his problems. Her voice, too, seemed odd – disembodied, dry, distant, weirdly unreal. All her remarks and observations sounded uncharacteristically formal, patronizing, even prudish. A bit like some tight-assed schoolteacher boring the pants off her long-suffering class. Pants? The session all screwed up?

Christ! Freud would have had a field-day with those associations.

With a mighty effort Anne struggled to regain her objectivity but her emotions were locked in deadly combat with her intellect, and the role of dispassionate observer continued to elude her. Adam wasn't making things any easier. Quite apart from his remarkable good looks he exuded great waves of waif-like vulnerability, interspersed with little splashes of touchingly macho bravado – the little child inside the man shining through like a bright beacon on a dark night. He was charming, funny, obviously incredibly bright, and with the body of an angel and the fortune of an emperor. It was a significant combination and it was playing havoc with Anne Carrington's usually formidable self-control.

So far in the sessions they had covered neutral, unthreatening territory, at least in terms of the overt content of the dialogue. Beneath the surface, however, hidden from view, an emotional volcano bubbled, squirting the occasional spray of passion into the conversation as doctor and patient, man and woman, probed each other's defences.

It was established that Adam snorted a lot of coke, drank too much, mixed with a pretty unsatisfactory crowd, was wasting his life, and had done so since the tragic death of his parents. But Anne had been able to see much further than that, and as he talked about his dead parents, feigning a 'couldn't care less' attitude, her psychiatric training and natural sensitivity allowed her to peer into his very soul, to see the agony and hurt that had accumulated there. As she did so her heart went out to him, and her very essence sought to commune with his. Don't worry. I'll protect you. I'll look after you. Trust me, was her unspoken message.

Despite the undoubted humanity of her emotions, they were feelings of which, as a professional psychiatrist, Anne was far from proud. Sympathy was one thing but why the hell did she feel so damn *tender* towards him? Why did she want to reach out and touch him, to hold him in her arms, to comfort him, to make him feel safe?

Adam picked up on these subterranean vibrations and was intrigued by them. Was this par for the psychiatric course, standard chemistry between doctor and patient? Or had he quite by chance triggered some responsive chord in this stunningly beautiful psychiatrist which had enabled both their feelings to transcend the normal professional relationship – enabling her to react to him as a woman rather than as an untouched and untouchable professional?

Adam remembered the events of their first meeting. Then he'd been totally helpless, unable to dampen the flame of passion which had flowed through him as her cool fingers had roamed over his body. Unintentionally Anne Carrington had summoned desire with the soft touch of her hand and now she must know he found her attractive as surely as if he had a neon sign flashing across his chest. There was a certain satisfaction in that, the ball firmly in her court, as it were. It was her problem and she had to deal with it. She could discourage him, ignore his feelings, or explore them.

With a delicious feeling of anticipation Adam allowed himself to wish for the latter. He permitted his eyes to linger on the full breasts beneath the cream silk shirt, admiring their fine contours, savouring the exquisite mental sensations as the visual data merged into lascivious thoughts.

Anne felt Adam's blue eyes on her, caressing her with the soft paintbrush of vision, and tried to resist the implications of the look and of the thoughts which she knew were accompanying it. With mounting despair she realized that she was flattered by his attraction to her, that she wanted it far more than she wanted his indifference. This was an ambivalence that she must confront, not avoid, if the therapeutic relationship wasn't to dissolve into ruins. So far she'd avoided the issue by concentrating on background, building up a picture of Adam's past life and of the events that had helped to shape it. There had, however, been one glaring omission in her history-taking, and Anne was well aware of it because she had a framework to which she adhered as closely as possible. Somewhere between occupational and medical history she always asked about sex. For some reason she'd avoided this topic with Adam, and Anne was the first to realize that her motives were not entirely worthy. She should rectify the oversight if she wasn't going to let go of the reins altogether. She tried to sound casual.

'Do you have any sexual problems?'

'One thing's for sure, I can't complain about failure of erection.' Adam smiled impishly.

Anne swallowed hard, her mouth suddenly dry. There was no answer to that. 'No, seriously,' she managed at last. It was both a plea and a command.

Sex? Any problems? There were all sorts of ways of answering a question like that. Adam could be flirtatious, honest, evasive, embarrassed or confused. He dipped into the hatful of choices. 'I've been a bit worried about myself recently,' he heard himself say in a halting, serious tone of voice.

Anne leaned forwards. 'Tell me about it.' That was better. Her role as expert was intact.

And then Adam knew exactly what he'd do. She'd asked him about sex. He'd tell her, tell her everything, leaving nothing out. He'd parade the most intimate details in front of her, test her broadmindedness to the limit. A warm glow of excitement coursed through him at the thought of shocking the delectable, rather prim psychiatrist to the very roots of her being. The recent evening with the submissive hookers would be a brilliant place to start.

'Well, you see I have this desire to see women making love – and I suppose that's not particularly normal. Like, for instance, the other night . . .'

Anne could hardly believe her ears. OK, she'd asked for it, but why was he going into such *detail*? It was as if he wanted to involve her in the cobweb of his esoteric sexual predilections as an observer, if not as a participant. She wasn't shocked but she was far from unmoved. She realized that he was trying to wind her up, to unsettle her, possibly trying to turn her on. What was so dreadful was that he was succeeding. As the explicit details poured from him, Anne allowed the truth to break over her. It was almost with relief that she realized that she wanted nothing so much on this earth as to fuck him, to put his rearing prick in her mouth, have him empty himself inside her. There it was. She wanted to taste him, to feel his hardness in her, hear him roar his love as he filled her with his semen, have him push his tongue deep into her, violate her, use her, take her.

Adam's monologue continued and Anne felt herself twist her eyes away from his lest he should see the confusion that had captured her. She should change the subject, break the flow, reach out for some island of neutrality where she could escape the torrent of sexual desire that had engulfed her. But she was powerless to resist. Relentlessly, Adam pursued her, building up the pressure, piling it on as he recounted his sordid exploits, of orgasms, of Mariel's endless inventiveness.

It was a mind-wank, pure and simple, and she was colluding with him in mental masturbation. Any other patient wouldn't have lasted ten seconds on this trip. Adam had been allowed ten minutes. There was nothing therapeutic in it. Nothing at all.

At last he was finished and Anne thought she could see the triumph in his eyes as he contemplated the defeat in hers. She couldn't be certain of that, at any rate she would have to pretend she didn't know what he knew. The vital and immediate problem was to get this session finished, to get him out of her office as fast as possible. She needed to think, to plan her retreat from what was quickly turning into a completely impossible situation. Get rid of him.

Keep him there all afternoon. All evening. All night. What did she really want? She stood up. Her legs felt like jelly.

'Adam, I'm afraid we've overshot a bit. I think we should discuss some of the things you've told me when we meet next time – if that's all right by you.' Get out of here before you make me come, would've been more appropriate, she thought in desperation.

Adam got up quickly, the scent of the fox in his nostrils. The chase had started. There could be no doubt. He was going to make love to Anne. No question. Only the time and the place were uncertain. But there was no hurry, no hurry at all.

As the door closed behind him, Anne sat down hard, burying her face in her hands as she tried to collect her thoughts. What did she feel? What was her predominant emotion? With a blinding flash the unwelcome realization hit her. It was for her a foreign feeling, but with a mounting sense of horror Anne Carrington accepted the fact that she was jealous, jealous of the other women in Adam's life, especially of the girl called Mariel.

Adam was flushed and excited when he hit Fifth Avenue after the session. Anne Carrington. God, she was good looking. Incredible. He couldn't remember when a woman had turned him on like that. He had an appointment to see her in two days' time, and he could hardly wait. He quickened his pace. His life was turning round. Suddenly it was all fun again, as it once had been. The doctor and the computer. Passion and the stock market. What a combination!

He checked the time. Four o'clock. The market had closed. His heart-beat speeded up. It was day two of his market predictions. On day one they'd been extraordinary accurate, but had it all been coincidence? If he was way out today it would begin to look like it. But if he was spot-on a second time then the probability that he'd stumbled on an amazing discovery would be increased dramatically. He hurried into the Knickerbocker Club and waved cheerfully to the hall porter as he made for the Reuter's tape. How did the market close? His heart stood still. He was looking for a rise of 18·75. There it was: DOW JONES INDUSTRIALS. UP 18·42. Christ!

At the Club La Racquette in the basement of the chic Parker Meridien Hotel on West 57th Street, Anne Carrington was working out as if her life depended on it. Trying to lose herself in the music, she pushed her body to the limit, went for the Jane Fonda 'burn' which was supposed to cure all problems. The painful messages from the overworked muscles came screaming into her psyche, crowding out the other thoughts but failing to get rid of them entirely. Maybe she should have tried more traditional remedies. Cold showers, perhaps, or bromide. Aerobics, the panacea of the 1980s. Body fascism. Look good, feel good, be good. Usually it made Anne feel terrific, but today the magic wasn't working.

What should she do about Adam Phipps? Should she discontinue the sessions? No. Whatever the effect on her, there was no mistaking the improvement in Adam's mood and confidence. Anyway, to give up now would be a total admission of failure. Her self-respect would be severely compromised, her faith in herself as a psychiatrist considerably diminished. But she couldn't allow another session like yesterday's, that was for sure.

The class leader's voice cut into her thoughts sharply. 'Go for it. Reach out for it. Feel the pain,' she shouted above the loud rock music, urging the sweating group on to greater suffering as they sought to lose their minds in the physical sensations of exercise, straining to feel rather than to think.

Anne felt wetness explode through her pink leotard as she pushed her superb body into overdrive. Could pain drive out thought? Apparently not. Anne's mental processes were withstanding the physical onslaught, easily defeating the invading army of sensations.

Her feelings for Adam were neurotic. But so what? That realization didn't begin to solve the problem. She was better off with Freud. What had he said about love?

Anne speeded up, forcing herself into double-time as she repeated the words in her mind like some incantation to ward off evil spirits. Love is neurosis. Love is neurosis. Love is neurosis.

Later, as she powered up and down the roof-top swimming pool, she told herself that love didn't enter the equation at all. There was no danger of her falling in love. None. What she needed was some good old-fashioned sex. That would clear the air. But where on earth would she get it? Certainly she knew a lot of men – psychiatrists, hospital administrators, professional acquaintances – but no one who was remotely in a position to service this suddenly awakened desire.

On the massage table after her swim, Anne once again attempted to escape from the disturbing, intrusive thoughts. Usually she could relax completely under the soothing fingers of the muscular masseuse, the tensions of the day vanishing beneath the knowing hands. But now the deeply sensuous experience began to fan already inflamed passions, as if for the first time her whole body had become sensitized to the stimulus of sex. Anne herself was slow to realize what was happening to her and it was almost with surprise that she became aware that her nipples had grown erect, felt the delicious sense of fullness in her breasts and the tingling, titillating sensations of arousal. Slowly other signs and signals of desire, little awakenings deep within her, percolated through to her consciousness.

The probing hands were on her stomach now, smoothing, kneading the flat, hard muscle, sometimes lightly caressing the skin, at others pushing in towards her firm abdominal wall. The delectable stirrings were moving lower, towards the heart of her sexuality, and Anne felt desire begin to flow from deep inside her, sensing the build-up of moisture as her growing passion began to take liquid form.

Her eyes were tightly closed but she couldn't avoid thinking about the girl who, at least indirectly, was the source of these delicious feelings. Short, muscular and rather 'butch', she seemed to remember. Particularly powerful thighs from long hours on the Nautilus body-building machine. An aquiline face, darkish hair. Unre-markable really. But quite attractive. Anne felt a surge of dampness inside her. Hey, wait a minute. What was going on? Women had never been her thing. Why was she feeling like this? Thank God her feelings were carefully concealed. There was no way the masseuse could know of them. It was her little secret.

Or so Anne thought. The masseuse liked women very much, liked the touch of their bodies, the feel of their skin, their feminine smell. And she knew their secret ways. Years of experience had enabled her to play on a woman's body like a fine and delicate instrument, to feel its silent language of contraction and relaxation, smell its musky messages, see its subtle movements. She knew at once that she had flicked some switch, struck some receptive chord in the beautiful doctor whom she had known and secretly admired for so long and she could hardly believe her luck. She would capitalize on the discovery. She piled on the pressure, making the massage more overtly sexual as the tell-tale symptoms of arousal came back to her from the delicious prostrate form.

This was one of the bonuses of the job. From time to time she got to indulge her desire for her own sex. But she had to be careful, couldn't afford to make mistakes. If she read the signals wrong and made an overt and unambiguous advance towards somebody who wasn't ready or prepared to receive it, her job wouldn't last five seconds. With some of her clients there were no problems at all. There were some who expected sex and were prepared to pay for it with a handsome tip. This doctor, though, had 'novice' written all over her. There could be no misunderstandings. It was all deliciously dangerous. The best way.

She reached for more oil. Next the breasts. She swallowed deeply, flames of passion beginning to flicker as her hands roamed over the magnificent conical tits, brushing against the pouting, rock-hard nipples. Her eyes played quickly over Anne's glistening pubic hairs, her nostrils scenting the well-known perfume of feminine need. This girl wanted it all right. But would she be prepared to break through the shackles of convention into the blissful land of feminine lovemaking? That was far from certain, although tantalizingly possible.

To Anne the fever-pitch of excitement to which she was being raised was solely the result of her own mental processes. She didn't know that, inadvertently, she'd given her own game away and was being manipulated as a result. As her body buzzed and vibrated with sexual desire, she remained in blissful ignorance of the masseuse's intentions, was aware only of her own illicit longings for gratification, of her own soaring sexual fantasies. Dancing before her mind's eye were the muscular quadriceps of the anonymous woman whose hands had the freedom of her body. It seemed extraordinary that she'd never noticed them before, taken in the beauty of the sculptured thighs, the product of so much sweat and ecstasy. She'd like to reach out and touch them, feel their hardness, allow her fingers to slip between them, to worship at the altar of feminine lust. Secure in the supposed secrecy of her thoughts, she allowed them to fly free, unfettered and uncontrolled as she vibrated to the masseuse's touch. If only the sublime fingers would reach between her legs, plunge into the depths of her being to scratch the itch that plagued and delighted her. But there wasn't any need to stop at fingers. A tongue was what she needed, even demanded. A woman's tongue to enter her – soft, loving, gentle, insistent, lapping at her, moving her on to the ultimate explosion of pleasure. Yes, that was what she wanted, what she needed to straighten her soaring mind, to bring her back to earth. In the pool she had wondered who would provide her with sexual release. On the massage table she knew the answer. This way was the safest. No commitments. No recriminations. No relationships. No ties. And the beauty of it was that she was alone in her own private world of pleasure. Even the unfortunate girl who was building her towards orgasm was in total ignorance of what was going on. OK, so you could argue that it was depraved to entertain such wild fantasies, to use another human being in this way, but where was the harm? If it allowed Anne to regain her equilibrium, to become the dispassionate psychiatrist once more, to exorcize the demon of sexual desire, then the end would justify the means.

Monitoring all the signals through her sensitive finger-tips, the masseuse began to get the message. The doctor would admit nothing, wouldn't participate in overt love-making, wanted everything to remain ambiguous, uncertain. It was also perfectly obvious that she wanted, intended, to come. Momentary disappointment was replaced by excitement at the contemplation of the game about to be played. To achieve orgasm she'd have to sail close to the wind, skirt the borders of acceptable stimulation, hover on the brink of secret places, not too far, not too close. It would be a delightful service to perform, testing her considerable pleasure-giving skills to the limit. At the same time there would be the dangers, stimulating yet substantial, of over-stepping the mark. She'd have to walk the thin line, subtle yet insistent, daring yet prudent, firm yet gentle. And – as the sexual voyager began to reach towards the destination of orgasm – who knew what inhibitions might be cast aside, what prejudices abandoned in the maelstrom of ecstasy, in the headlong pursuit of the ultimate pleasure?

And so the masseuse leaned low over Anne Carrington's

body as she smoothed her fingers over the alluring breasts and rubbed the thrusting nipples. She sent her fingers up into the warm, wet armpits, covering her hands with Anne's sweat, loving it, luxuriating in it, feeling the sweetness of Anne's breath on her cheek as her breathing quickened with mounting desire. Continually the masseuse fought back the inclination to dip her head down, to take the fascinating nipples between her teeth, to suck at them, to taste the rose-pink tips. Her face inches from the perfect geometry of Anne's chest, she had to summon up all her reserves of self-control. Beneath her hands the masseuse could feel the fluttering heart, the heaving lungs as Anne's whole body reacted to her stimulation. Get the timing right. Not too fast, not too slow. She would take a chance, journey to the edge. With both hands she gently cupped the ripe, eager breasts. Then, with infinite reverence, she moved her hands up towards the tempting, tense nipples. Deftly she took each simultaneously between thumb and forefinger and squeezed firmly but insistently. That was pushing it to the boundaries of conventionality. Only a pretty way-out massage would involve that sort of action – but if both participants ignored it there would be no hard and fast cause for complaint. Instantly relinquishing the throbbing, hot, pointed twin peaks of eroticism, the masseuse's hands journeyed south.

Anne's churning mind received the two messages of sharp but delicious pain with both surprise and gratification. That had never happened to her before but it was nonetheless welcome.

For the first time she allowed herself to consider that this whole thing could be a two-way street. Had she given herself away? Had the masseuse worked out that she was turned on, her mind seething with erotic thoughts, orgasm her ambition? The squeezing of her totally erect nipples said yes, the immediate relinquishing of them, the re-location of the hands, said no, or at least maybe. If yes, then it began to look as if she was on the verge of being made love to by a girl. Dr Anne Carrington, well-known and respected psychiatrist, had by a woman on a massage couch. Her intellect screamed defiance at the thought while her emotions howled for satisfaction. What should she do? As the irresistible force crashed into the immovable object, the two neutralizing each other, she took the line of least resistance. She did nothing. In more than one sense of the word, she was in the hands of another. How would it turn out?

For an almost unbearable moment of suspense the two pleasure-giving hands left her body, leaving Anne longing, aching for their return, dreading the moment when she might be forced to choose between gratification and prudence. And then the hands were back, dripping with warm, sweet-smelling oil, tracing lazy patterns on her beautifully sculptured thighs. The relief at being released from the unbearable state of sexual limbo flowed through her body, increasing her arousal. The hands amplified the change, digging firmly into the muscles of Anne's inner quadriceps. The strong strokes rushed up towards the very edge of her vagina, tempting, threatening, coquettish, before racing away again towards her knees. Endlessly repeated, their piston-like action grew in strength until Anne's whole body rocked rhymically with the force of the movement. On and on in perpetual motion the hands milked at Anne's quivering thighs, and Anne pushed back at them, her desire building at every thrust. As if by accident the masseuse allowed the forward momentum of her hands to overstray the acceptable mark, her fingers pushing into the shining pubic hairs, to the very edge of the glistening pink lips which nestled so invitingly in the abundant wetness.

Anne twisted her head from side to side, running her tongue over her dry lips. She felt the orgasm begin to build. Don't stop. Don't stop. With all her might she concentrated on the screaming centre of her world. If only the strong hands would invade her body, reach inside her, drag the growing orgasm out of her. She fought back the desire to make the first move, to touch herself, or better, to take hold of the other girl's sublime fingers and force them deep into her vagina. With almost superhuman willpower, Anne recoiled from the abyss. Nothing could be admitted. She must take the middle way.

The masseuse sensed Anne's change in sexual gear. Not long now. With both shoulders she leaned in hard, sending her strong arms shooting towards the hot centre of Anne's world. Fingers straight, she engineered the overshoot until, for the briefest of seconds, her fingertips rested on the opening lips of Anne's vagina. As intended, this put Anne right over the top. As the teasing fingers withdrew, the masseuse saw Anne's bottom lift an inch from the surface of the table, took in the whiteness of the clenched knuckles, the half-opened mouth, the darting tongue. At the same time she felt the alternate contraction and relaxation of the muscles beneath her hands, saw the wetness cascade from the secret inner recesses of Anne's body, as the mighty orgasm broke.

Not for one second did the masseuse hesitate. She had earned this and she was safe now, beyond danger. With her right hand she reached up between Anne's heaving, thrashing legs and slipped two strong fingers deep into the moist recess. For a long thirty seconds she held on to the orgasm, riding it, directing it like the conductress of an orchestra.

Anne felt the alien fingers as the orgasm crashed about her, beyond caring, beyond caution, beyond shame. Mercilessly she crushed them between her thighs, squeezed them in the vice of her vaginal masculature, extracting every last drop of pleasure from them. It was too late, far too late, for anything else. She might be a doctor, a psychiatrist, but, for the very first time in her life, she'd been screwed by a woman, and there had been nothing on God's earth that she could have done about it.

Mariel was back. At once she'd noticed the sea-change in Adam. There was a new self-confidence about him and her reception had been distinctly lukewarm. She'd calculated her two-week absence on the European modelling trip with concentration and care. Adam had been taking her for granted. She'd therefore withdrawn facilities. Let him find his own drugs, run his own life for a day or two – he would soon realize how dependent he was on her. And just when he was getting used to it, beginning to find his own feet, she'd reappear and re-enter his atmosphere, reassert control. In this way over a long period she'd break his will until he was prepared to give himself over to her completely, to have and to hold, from this day forth . . . But something had gone horribly wrong. A new and dangerous element had clearly entered the equation. It had to be identified, isolated and neutralized, with all possible speed.

When Wan-Tu had opened the door to her the message had been that Mr Phipps was busy in his computer room and had left strict instructions not to be disturbed. OK, so he hadn't known Mariel was coming back, but the whole idea of Adam working, not wanting to be distracted, had set the alarm bells ringing in Mariel's finely tuned psyche.

Her response to the Oriental's polite message had been typical. 'If you don't get his ass out here in ten seconds, your balls will be chop-suey,' she'd said simply.

Wan-Tu had done as he was instructed. Mariel O'Sullivan didn't conform to the Chinese conventions of what was and was not acceptable feminine behaviour. As far as he was concerned she was a Martian, a creature from outer space, dangerous and unpredictable.

Adam's greeting had been decidedly cool. In the past there had been iced Krug, lines of coke and feverish telephone calls as his life came together again with Mariel's return. Today he managed a wan smile and a half-hearted, 'Hello, Mariel. When did you get back?'

Mariel had been far too cunning to make the mistake of

commenting on his lack of enthusiasm. Her role was to be light, amusing, fun. So she'd pretended not to notice, to be far too interested in her own exciting plans to be aware of Adam's dreary preoccupations. Inside, however, her mind had been seething, hell-bent on gaining information, on discovering the nature of the threat to her great fortune-hunting expedition.

'What's with the computers?' she'd asked.

In the past he would have shrugged her question aside with a languid hand and a drawled 'booooooooring', preferring to concentrate on the serious business of planning creative frivolity, engineering the 'good time'. On this occasion, however, he'd answered her question in some detail.

Mariel didn't know a lot about computers, but she had a working knowledge of the stock-market. In the circles in which she mixed that was vital. A girl like her, who had to make it on her wits, was often in a position to profit from the scraps of information that were frequently dropped from the lips of the megabuck owners with whom she mixed exclusively. Details of mergers and takeovers, insider information of the most choice kind was always available at Manhattan's star-studded social gatherings. Many had been the time when her first call in the morning had been to the small, relatively unknown stockbroker who handled her market transactions, and from whom a large cheque was often forthcoming, payment for her 'horse's mouth' tip-offs.

When Adam had explained the workings of his stock-market computer programme to her she'd at once seen its astounding potential. Suddenly she found herself looking at Adam in a new light and she was a little afraid of what she saw. There seemed to be a new vibrancy in his personality, an urgent excitement in his speech before only she'd been able to evoke. What was the foundation of his new persona? Was the computer 'discovery' the fount of his uncharacteristic self-confidence, of his lack of interest in her return? No. There was something else. Something of far greater significance.

And so Mariel, feeling a little unsure of herself, had wittered on about the scene in Paris, about the models she'd met, about the two loose-limbed beauties she'd persuaded to fly back with her to New York, who were at that very moment tucked up in the big double bed in her tiny apartment. She'd watched Adam closely for signs of awakening interest and had been relieved to see his eyes glimmer at the mention of the two European girls.

'I thought we might all go down to Southampton for the weekend. Catch some wind-surfing. Hit the beach. Do a few jacuzzis. It'd be fun,' she said. It was a promise as much as a prediction.

Adam sat and watched her. She was like a beautiful but infinitely dangerous cheetah, or some other more exotic member of the cat family. Sleek, sharp, deadly, impossible to ignore or discount. Great waves of power and strength shot out from her. Adam had vowed to reduce her influence over him, to diminish the role she played in his life, to cut down on the drugs she procured for him, to avoid the sexual delights she dangled in front of him. But now, confronted with the gorgeous reality of her presence, he felt himself weaken once again as Mariel's spell snaked round him like the seductive scent of jasmine on some magical Arabian night. He'd seen her at work, knew her tricks, watched her as she enslaved and ensnared people, reducing them to putty in her long, delicate fingers. He'd seldom seen her look more beautiful, and as he felt himself succumb once again to her extraordinary sexual charm, he heard himself say, 'Wonderful Mariel. Call your girl-friends. Can't think of anything I'd like more.'

Immediately he began to rationalize his reaction. Southampton *would* be fun. Summer was just starting and the house needed to be opened up. Barbecues, racing Ford Broncos on the beach, communal saunas. He lay back languidly, his long blond hair a burnished gold against the cream silk sofa. Through parted lips he drawled the words that Mariel wanted to hear. 'You're right, Mariel. The beach is exactly what we all need. I've been taking myself far too seriously lately.'

Mariel felt relief course through her. So much for the battle. But the war was far from won.

As Adam lay still, soaking up the mid-morning sun poolside at his Southampton house, his mind, if not his body, was hard at work. Life was on the move again, a careering chariot almost out of control, the reins precariously held between his fingers. He felt the power surge within him like some photosynthesizing plant. It was a good feeling, the very best, better than drugs, than any synthetic high. There had been a time when it had been usual for him to feel like this, and now his spirits lifted him up, making him certain that he'd regain the sense of direction and excitement of days gone by.

On every day of the previous week the Dow-Jones had closed at the level he'd predicted. The odds against that happening by chance were over 100,000 against. Next week would be the biggest test of all. If Adam could correctly call the market's closing levels, then the odds of it being a chance-happening would have risen to a staggering ten billion to one.

It was beginning to look as if his discovery would allow him to corner the market, to extract more money than anyone had ever done before. The way was clear for him to become the richest man in the world, with all the power and influence that position must bring.

It was a mind-blowing thought. Of course it would have to be done carefully. Nobody must know about his secret. If people knew he had cracked the mystery of the market, then they would simply cease to bet against him and the stock-exchange would grind to a close. For every willing seller there had to be a willing buyer – that was what it was all about. If everybody agreed on the direction of prices then share-trading would cease.

The second reason for secrecy was almost as compelling. At a stroke he would become a target, and not just for fan-mail. Anyone who made their living from the market stood to lose – money, prestige, houses, wives. Some people would go to the furthest extremes to protect such things.

It was essential that Adam move with the greatest caution. But he'd already told two people. Charles Phipps had been taken into Adam's confidence at the very beginning. By now, having seen on a daily basis the accuracy of the forecasts, he must suspect that Adam had stumbled on to something big. The feverish messages he'd left with Adam's answering service on Friday afternoon while the market was falling apart were eloquent testimony to that. Then there was Mariel, presently engaged in suggestive horseplay in the pool with the Italian model. He shouldn't have told her. Still, she hadn't appeared particularly interested and probably hadn't understood what he was on about, or hadn't believed him if she had. In future he'd be more careful. Charles would be the problem. How to handle Charles, and how to handle Anne Carrington.

At the very thought of her Adam sensed a subtle chemical shift within him as glands began to secrete mysteriously, and juices gathered. He'd seen her several times now and the disturbing vision of her magnificent body, her finely structured face, her animal attraction was never far from his mind. He supposed that her encouragement and reassurance had helped him to feel better, had been responsible in part for his feeling so good today. But it was more than that. Infinitely more. It was the tension in the air whenever they met, the growing confusion of the usually cool doctor as the sessions had progressed. There was a tantalizing, bizarre quality to the whole business, as if doctor and patient were like sleepwalkers heading irretrievably towards a conclusion which neither had planned and over which both were powerless, even unwilling, to avoid.

When Adam was with her he believed the messages she seemed against her will to be giving him. Now, far from her presence, he could no longer be sure. She had to be in her mid-thirties, he was twenty-three. Could a relationship between two people of such an age difference work? For him the answer was 'yes'. But what about Anne? He smiled inwardly at the absurdity of it all. He'd only just met the woman and he was thinking in terms of a permanent relationship. Adam chuckled out loud at his delicious predicament.

'Petey, for God's sake make yourself useful and make some Bloodies.' Adam didn't open his eyes as he issued the instruction.

Peter Danforth eased himself off the sun-bed, dutifully prepared to earn his keep. Southampton weekends chez Phipps were always fun, sometimes spectacularly so. Mariel's productions, both topless, one already bottomless, seemed creatures of infinite promise. The role of Bloody Mary manufacturer was a small price to pay for the crumbs of feminine beauty, which might later be expected to drop from the master's and his mistress's table.

'Celery salt or horseradish?' he asked. One had to get these things right.

Adam stretched himself like a sleepy cat waking from a fireside slumber. Decisions. Decisions. Stolichnaya, tabasco, Worcestershire sauce, lemon juice, pepper and salt, V8 juice, thank God, were not negotiable.

'I think we'll try a little of each,' he said at last. The wisdom of Solomon, poolside. He could hardly remember when he'd last felt so good.

He cast somnolent eyes out towards the tiny strip of ocean beach which separated the inland water from the sea. Adam loved this place. The Phipps house had been in the family since the 1920s, a huge, rambling mansion whose manicured lawns led down to the water. Since his parents' death Adam had made some changes. The centre of activities was the 60-foot pool and the open-air jacuzzi, laid out in front of the spacious poolhouse with its bar, sauna, showers and relaxation room for when the summer heat became unbearable, a welcome refuge from the rigours of sunbathing.

Anne-Marie, the French girl, had already fled the burning rays and now, her pert and totally naked rump thrusting upwards, she lay in the shade flicking through the pages of French *Vogue* as she waited for something to happen.

Mariel's foraging trip in Europe had been a conspicuous success in terms of female imports. These girls were a class act – no question. They made covers, didn't just crawl in between them, and their high cheekbones, haughty poses and almost fearsome coolness were enough to strike terror into the hearts of all but the most sophisticated.

Luckily, Adam was firmly in the latter category, totally at ease with the sulky indifference, the feigned boredom, the seen-it-all-before effect that the girls cultivated. In the clinches they would scream, moan and swear like anyone else, but next morning at breakfast they'd have forgotten your name, or at least pretended to have forgotten it, would treat you with the warmth of a shop assistant asking you to take your fingers off the merchandise. Were they prostitutes? It was difficult to say, a question of semantics. Today, probably not. No cash would change hands this weekend. Tomorrow – who knew? Would Mariel fix them up in New York with important people from whom they would expect 'presents' – watches from Cartier that could be traded in for money, Concorde tickets for Europe that could be exchanged for a standby seat, rent for an apartment paid on the 'understanding' that the payer would from time to time be 'entertained' there? Mariel probably would. Idly Adam wondered whether in exchange she took a cut. Certainly the cognoscenti at the Racquette Club maintained that Mariel was no stranger to such a world. He supposed that, on the whole, that made her a pimp, 'living off immoral earnings'. Good for her. It was a tough world out there for those who had to earn money.

The high-pitched wine of the blender cut into his thoughts. Petey's only creative act of the day was in progress. A minute or two later the fruits of his endeavour were seeping luxuriantly into Adam's psyche. God, it was a good drink, food, medicine, tranquillizer, consciousness-expander all rolled into one. How would the day unfold? Cracked crab and Pouilly Fumé on the veranda . . . a sleep in the sun after lunch . . . some gentle wind-surfing on the lake around 4.30 – both girls would be sure to want to learn – martinis on the terrace . . . hot baths . . . more martinis . . . a candle-lit dinner . . . a film . . . some Dom Perignon . . . a communal jacuzzi . . . a midnight swim . . . and then, and then . . . unpredictable couplings.

Adam was floating on air, soaring through storm-clouded skies above a dark, threatening sea. He was frightened that he'd fall, crash down into the forbidding waters to be obliterated in the crashing waves. He was a seagull but he had a jet engine instead of wings and he was running out of fuel. How much longer did he have? Could he make the shore? Or was he just seconds from destruction? Charles Phipps was laughing nastily as he sailed along in his Dutch barge. Over and over again he kept chanting, 'You're going down. You're going down.'

Anne Carrington's magic carpet was beneath him now and he was a seagull no more. 'I'm more of a bird than you,' she said and laughed her beautiful laugh, showing perfect white teeth, the lips moist with saliva, the scented breath fanning his face. She reached down and held his penis, her cool fingers stroking its thrusting hardness. At once the sun shone through, the heat fell on Adam's back as she caressed him, as they flew together through the suddenly clear skies.

And then Adam was awake, his whole body tingling at the thought of her, as his mind fought to regain consciousness, to make sense of his physical experiences.

Still inhabiting the limbo between sleep and wakefulness, his clouded mind drifted back over the events of the previous evening which had promised so much but provided so little. There had been no faulting the sexual buffet that Mariel had laid on for him but, untypically, he'd been totally disinclined to indulge in it. There had been no mistaking the reason for his abstinence, and the dream had confirmed it. Anne Carrington. He would see her on Tuesday.

Normally, Charles Phipps would have been slap-bang in the middle of his own personal seventh heaven. Invitations to spend the weekend at Jackie O's Martha's Vineyard hideaway didn't grow on trees. They had to be earned by the sweat of the brow, paid for with a thousand dull evenings, an endless parade of charity galas, committee meetings and intimate dinner parties.

Now, of course, Charles had arrived and was very much a paid-up member of high society, sitting cockily on the top rung of the ladder and peering down with disdain at the climbers below him, preparing to show them his shoe leather, his slack ass. This house party should have been like a heady wine to Charles Phipps – 1961 Chateau Lafite-Rothschild at least – but for all the satisfaction he was getting from the glittering gathering, it might just as well have been Algerian burgundy.

Poor Charles was in a fever-pitch of frustration, his little insides churning like a cement mixer. He couldn't sit still, had lost his appetite, and worse, far worse, had actually lost the thread of conversation at dinner the previous evening when his hostess had been relating a particularly juicy piece of publishing gossip – a morsel he would have normally crawled across five miles of broken glass to receive. A few more lapses like that would result in the door slamming in his face, a humiliating return trip down the ladder to the gleeful crowing of upwardly mobile fellow travellers. That was a thought almost too horrible to contemplate, the ghastly abyss which forever loomed, ready to devour social climbers.

But what could he do? From dawn to dusk, from dusk till dawn the extraordinary events of the previous week rolled round in his mind like marbles. Each morning his answering service had relayed Adam's confident predictions about the outcome of the day's trading on Wall Street. Each day at the closing bell those forecasts had been spot on target. All week Charles had bet heavily against his upstart nephew, and all week he'd been taken to the cleaners. It had cost him a bomb. Adam's cheeky message on Friday morning had been the worst and most expensive of all. Adam's message had said, 'Go short, buy "put" options. The market is going down 26 points.' Wilfully, and feeling that the market would most likely continue its advance, Charles had done exactly the opposite.

Friday, Charles thought, had probably been the very worst day in his life. Not only had he watched the options he'd just sold double and triple during the day as the bottom fell out of the market, but he'd had to put up with the unpalatable truth that Adam had called the market with an accuracy that any market guru would have given his balls for.

But, through the gloom and despondency, as he licked the wounds of his market debacle, a shining vision was beginning to form. Suddenly it began to look as if the impossible dream might have turned into reality, that the age-old secret of the stock-market was a secret no more. What's more, the possible possessor of that magical information appeared to be none other than his own nephew. If cards were played correctly, if humble pie was consumed in large enough quantities, then Charles might yet emerge from the flames. If Adam had indeed cracked the mystery of the market and was prepared to take his uncle into his confidence, into a family partnership even, then his wildest dreams would be fulfilled with a vengeance. Private jumbo jets, a high political office – a governorship, perhaps – the largest private yacht in the world, islands, hospitals and libraries bearing his name, a season ticket to White House dinner parties, the adulation of the glitterati, all would be within the grasp of the man who had mastered the market.

And so on Saturday morning, up at six and unable to sleep, Charles had spent an agonizing three hours before daring to ring the Southampton house. It wouldn't do to irritate Adam. Nine o'clock was pushing it a bit, but he simply couldn't wait any longer. It wasn't until lunchtime that Adam returned his call.

Charles had tried to sound unconcerned and rather amused, by Adam's stroke of 'good luck'. He was the friendly uncle, the regular guy, jokey, witty and generous with his praise. How could he prise the secret out of the little shit?

'Well, Adam. I must hand it to you. In all my years in the market I've never come across a run like that. The good Lord sure showed you a winning streak. I'm not saying that it was mere luck. You clearly have a feel for this game. Natural talent. No question.'

Adam had sounded guarded, polite but distant. At least lines of communication were open. Hostility, if present at all, was mercifully latent.

Charles continued, choosing his words like a prisoner for whom one false move might result in instant execution.

'Adam, it strikes me that we ought to meet, have a little talk. The truth is, I've been feeling a little guilty about my behaviour at lunch the other day. I can't say I behaved very well. After all, we ought to stick together – only real family we've got. What say we crack a bottle of champagne on Monday evening? Let bygones be bygones. Who knows, we might go out for a bite to eat. You could introduce me to one of those gorgeous girls who are always hanging around you.' Charles let out a high-pitched, whinnying laugh which he hoped sounded sufficiently convivial.

On the whole he felt he might have overdone it a bit. Certainly the reference to the girl had gone against the grain. Charles had about as much intention of touching one as he had of picking up a steaming cow-pat. Adam hadn't sounded remotely enthusiastic but he'd agreed to the meet. That was the main thing.

'What price Monday's market, Adam?' He just had to squeeze that one in.

'Straight on down. Off another 16 points on the Dow.'

The adrenalin shot through Charles Phipps as Adam rung off. Monday was going to be a very good day indeed.

Charles Phipps was not the only one looking forward to Monday. For Anne Carrington the weekend hadn't been good. Usually she enjoyed her own company and the quiet peace of the off-duty city. The busy people-packed weekdays were to Anne an overdose of the human race. Now, however, she was worried. The last few days had revealed a side of her personality – a weakness, a vulnerability – which she'd hardly dreamed could have existed. The episode at La Racquette, now shorn of its intense sexual immediacy, horrified and appalled her. Her reaction to the disturbing Adam Phipps was scarcely less frightening.

Several times during the last 48 hours Anne had wondered if she might be ill. Was this the beginning of a psychotic process? Uncharacteristic sexual promiscuity was often a warning sign. Perhaps she should consult Peter. No, that wasn't a good idea. He was her partner and he was in love with her. He couldn't be expected to react favourably to the fact that she'd achieved a racking orgasm while being massaged at her health club – or that she was entertaining sexual fantasies about a 23-year-old patient.

Anne smiled for the first time in days as she imagined Peter's potential reaction to the revelation. She could picture him behind the leather-topped mahogany desk, trying to maintain a detached analytic façade, the wise-old-bird exterior, while inside he'd be anything but cool. God, why couldn't it have been he that her body longed for?

Not for the first time Anne thought about how difficult it was to be a psychiatrist. You were supposed to know all the answers – certainly not expected to crumble at the first experience of passion. She banished the indulgent thought. Come to think of it, it probably wasn't the easiest thing in the world to be a waitress at McDonald's either. Whatever. Here she was, riding the tiger. In the deep end of life at last. God, it was frightening, but it was exhilarating, too.

Chapter Five

To Anne's practised eye John Mitcham's depression appeared to be stabilizing. Although his description of his feelings was as gloomy as ever and he was still riddled with feelings of guilt, he admitted that he was eating and sleeping a bit better. Anne, knowing that the physical symptoms of depression are often the first to respond to antidepressants, was encouraged.

'How are things at home, John?'

'Well, the financial thing is a big mess, of course. I just don't see any way out of that. The bank have been talking about foreclosing again. If I lost the house, I'm sure Mary would leave.'

Anne watched the tears well up in his big blue eyes, heard the catch in his voice.

'Would it be any help if I talked to the bank? Perhaps I could persuade them to tide you over until you've shaken off this illness.'

'You could try, but frankly I don't see a way out of this.' John Mitcham's shoulders sagged under the weight of his problems.

Anne's alarm bells rang at his gloomy response to her offer of help. Her eyes scanned the patient's notes in front of her. She'd asked about suicide last time and received a satisfactory response. She'd have to ask again

'Any thoughts of suicide, John?'

'It would be against my religion,' he said, without a great deal of conviction.

Anne wrote it down. Like Anne, Mitcham was a Catholic. That was a good sign. Catholic suicide rates were significantly lower than those of many other religions.

'And how's Mary reacting?'

This was an important area. So much of Mitcham's sadness and low spirits seemed to revolve around his perceived failure to measure up to his wife's expectations, his inability to satisfy her ambitions. He'd mortgaged himself up to the hilt to buy a house he couldn't really afford, and then had had to fill it with the toys appropriate to the status to which Mary Mitcham aspired. The bills that floated through the front door like confetti had made him ill. Even then Mary had been little help. Determined that her husband should have an exotic and interesting neurosis rather than the infinitely less prestigious diagnosis of 'depressive illness', she'd discovered the flamboyant and fashionable Freudian analyst Aaron Ishmael, leading light of the New York Psychoanalytic Institute. Soon she'd been parading her husband's symptoms and his expensive and trendy doctor with the same zeal with which she displayed the BMW and the video, the dresses from Bill Blass and the bangles from Cartier.

Of course there was another side. There always was. Mitcham had been under no compulsion to marry such a person. She hadn't changed. He had. In the early days he'd gone for her sparkle, her good looks, her enthusiasm for life and the living of it. Naturally lazy, she'd pushed him on, made him stretch himself. The job at the brokerage house had been a good one and he'd been pleased to get it, and had enjoyed the considerable financial rewards it had provided. In those early days they had been very much partners in crime, if to be materially ambitious was a criminal activity.

Then, somewhere along the line, John Mitcham had lost the plot, lost enthusiasm for the relentless struggle and chucked in his cards. When the going got tough, a weak man had got out. Was that his fault? A case could be made that it was. Certainly it was naïve to blame Mary entirely. That would be too obvious. Perhaps the whole notion of blame was irrelevant. Anne was not sure. What was certain was that Mary was the sort of wife who, given the right

141

sort of man, could have turned him into the President of the United States. Poor John Mitcham had just not been made of the right stuff, the tendency to crack under stress perhaps inherited. It was nobody's fault, just an unfortunate fact of life.

Initially Mary had been infuriated by her husband's decision to discontinue therapy. It was a bit like having one's car repossessed by the bank. She had had to do some fast talking at dinner parties to cover things up. However, as the days went by she had begun to notice the marginal improvement in John on the new drug regime and had begun to feel a little guilty about the role she'd played in finding the expensive analyst, in insisting on his continuing the painful analytic process in the absence of any real sign that it was doing any good. From Mitcham's remarks Anne was able to divine this subtle shift in his wife's attitude and was grateful for it. Primarily this was because John would benefit from his wife's better understanding of his miserable predicament. But there was another reason why Anne welcomed some sort of alliance, however tenuous, with Mary. Prominently displayed in her notes on Mitcham was Aaron Ishmael's letter, the angriest and most threatening that Anne had ever received. She already knew its contents by heart, but she'd read it again at the end of the session. For now she was relieved at the appearance of some sort of a break in the formerly strong Aaron Ishmael/Mary Mitcham alliance.

It was time to wrap up. Things were going OK but Mitcham was still deep in the woods.

'I'll write you another prescription for the tablets, John. And I'd like to see you again in three days time.'

On the way to the door she took his hand in hers and gave it a squeeze. 'Hang on in there, John. It's always darkest just before the dawn. We're all rooting for ya, you know.'

As the door closed behind him, Mitcham's legacy of gloom seemed to pervade the room like a fine mist. The empty chair which he'd just vacated seemed to radiate the terrible despair with which it had been in recent contact.

Affected by the atmosphere, she slumped down beside her desk. Was she doing the right thing? She'd better be. Ishmael's letter stared up at her, accusing, unforgiving:

Dear Dr Carrington,

John Mitcham: Age 55

As I have already stated, I find your behaviour in taking on this patient of mine against my advice both unethical and unforgiveable. This matter, as you know, is being taken up at the appropriate level.

My objections to your ethical behaviour, however, are insignificant in comparison with my total opposition to your diagnosis and treatment of his condition which, in my view, represents malpractice.

Before you so irresponsibly persuaded this patient of mine to terminate analysis, against the wishes of both myself and his wife, and indeed against his own interests, treatment was progressing in an extremely satisfactory way. The transference had been well established and the original Oedipal problems were being well channelled and projected on to myself. The failure of the resolution of the transference neurosis upon your untimely intervention can only have disastrous consequences for my patient, consequences for which you must bear full responsibility.

May I add that you have by no means heard the last from me concerning this matter.

Yours sincerely,
Aaron Ishmael, M.D.

Anne sighed deeply as she finished reading. Thank God Mitcham was showing signs of improvement at last. Her position was exposed and dangerous, her head way above the trench. If anything went wrong, Ishmael would waste no time at all in blowing it right off.

'How was your weekend?'

'Great. How was yours?'

Anne smiled. Adam smiled. They both knew that purely professional barriers were breaking down. Neither was sure what was going to happen. Neither was in control.

'Anything you'd like to tell me?' It was safer to change the subject. Or was it?

Adam took a deep breath. This wasn't easy to say.

'I don't know whether or not it's appropriate to mention this – tell me if it isn't – but I had a rather disturbing dream.'

'Dreams are often appropriate to discuss – especially if you feel that they are,' said Anne, wondering with some trepidation what was coming. Were his dreams like hers? Apparently they were.

Adam, wondering from where he'd summoned the courage, told her everything, leaving out nothing. His eyes never left Anne's eyes as he did so.

Anne felt the moisture begin to flow. Below the waist she started to buzz as Adam's erotic fantasies began to cascade from him. Anne felt her nipples thrusting out against the tight bra, accentuating the sense of constriction until it seemed to her that her breasts had grown visibly. She could feel the blood rush to her face, knew that Adam could see the deepening of her colour. She could see his mighty erection beneath the tight blue jeans. Somewhere a strangled voice seemed to be saying:

'It's not unusual for patients to have dream fantasies about their psychiatrists.' It was Anne's voice, or rather a poor imitation of it.

'The problem is,' said Adam simply, 'I get the fantasies when I'm awake too.'

He hadn't let her off the hook. That had raised the ante considerably.

Anne gulped. She could swear that she could see his penis actually throb inside his trousers. She opened her mouth. Nothing came out.

'Do doctors ever feel that way about their patients?' The remark was as innocent as a paedophiliac at a children's party.

This simply couldn't go on. There were ten minutes of the session left, but the only possibility was an immediate retreat.

'If you don't mind, I think we'll end a little early today, and take this up again on Wednesday.' Her mind was all over the place. It had to be obvious to Adam. It was.

Anne sat behind her big desk, safe no more, and tried to get her thoughts straight. He'd been flirting with her. No question. He'd played her like a fish and she'd taken the bait, hook, line and sinker, and then had proceeded to put up no struggle at all. OK, so dreams were fair game in talk sessions, dreams about the doctor less welcome, but acceptable. Inevitable, of course, in a lively transference in classical analysis. But she should have *used* it, not been manipulated by it. Why are you telling me this? What do you think is the significance of this dream? Those were the sort of questions she would have asked normally. And if a patient started to be flippant or suggestive, as Adam had, her usual reaction would have been to cut him off at the knees. She had a neat little speech about the seriousness of sessions, about time-wasting, about threatening with-drawal of facilities if the patient didn't try to pull his weight. After all, there were far too many John Mitchams in this world to mess around with potential attention-seekers and mischief-makers. But what had she done when Adam had stared deep into her eyes and talked about her holding on to his prick? She'd turned a colour that would have made a beetroot look anaemic, then she'd lost her voice, and then she'd looked down, actually *stared*, at the outline of his erect penis. Great. Well played, psychiatrist. A first-year medical student wouldn't have fallen into that trap. Why hadn't she attempted an interpretation? Nothing was ever as it seemed on the surface. She should have gone for the latent content of the dialogue and defused the interchange.

'Listen, Adam. It may well be that you find our relationship rather threatening. The fact that I represent an authority figure, and a female one at that, may be disburbing to you on an unconscious level. It may be that you have to try to trivialize our relationship, turn me into a mere sex object, for instance, in order to neutralize the threat I may represent.'

Yes, that would've done quite well. Or she could have carried the ball further into his court with a few choice Oedipal references. They could always be relied on to take the wind out of a patient's sails.

'It may be there are sexual feelings related to your mother surfacing here, Adam. It's not unusual for male patients to relate to me in that way, to transfer on to me feelings felt in the distant past for other authority figures.'

That, too, would have stopped him in his tracks, wiped the knowing smile off his lips. But Anne had held back, had stuttered and mumbled instead, like some pimply college kid. Why? Because she wanted to make love to him, that was why. Because she wanted to hold him in her arms, to touch his beautiful brown body – not just dream about it. Where did that leave her in terms of the clever insights she was so practised at drawing from others? Why was she having these feelings for this 23-year-old, preppy, blond Adonis? Of what failings in her character and personality were these feelings a symptom?

The awful truth was that Anne had ceased to care. But it was with a sinking feeling that she forced herself to face the truth. These emotions couldn't be dammed up much longer, and when they were unleashed the storm would wreck her world.

Charles Phipps sat eagerly on the edge of the sofa in his cold, characterless apartment. In sharp contrast, Adam lounged easily in an armchair, legs stretched out languidly as he listened to his uncle's sales pitch. Charles was trying hard to be charming, to exude enthusiasm and admiration for Adam's new-found expertise. He wasn't entirely succeeding.

'It seems pretty clear to me, Adam, that you've hit on some sort of a system for predicting the Dow-Jones. God knows how you've done it, but the odds against you getting it right every day last week must be absolutely phenomenal. It couldn't be a coincidence. Well, well, well. Your father always said you were a genius. Now you've proved it.'

Charles was shrewd enough to realize that any reference to Adam's father – as long as it was complimentary – was bound to go down well. He saw Adam's suspicious face ease up a bit. Was this the time for the sting?

'Seems to me,' he continued, 'that we should stick together on this. Keep it in the family. With my expertise and knowledge of the markets, and your system, we could make one of the greatest stock-market coups in history – perhaps the greatest one of all.'

He paused, peering intently at Adam to gauge the effect of his proposition. He was painfully aware that his own contribution to the proposed partnership was hardly an essential one. It was Adam who held the key to the caves of gold.

Adam gazed evenly back, letting his uncle sweat, giving nothing away.

Charles ploughed on. 'Of course you must realize, Adam, that this discovery of yours has potentially explosive implications. It would be essential to keep the whole thing a secret. Just you and me.'

Somehow Charles had made it sound like a furtive activity to be indulged in by consenting males in private.

'With me as a partner, there wouldn't be any problems. Blood thicker than water and all that.' Charles' voice trailed off uncertainly. He could see he was failing to carry his audience with him – was hardly convincing himself. He changed tack completely, his tone now wheedling, ingratiating.

'Come on, Adam, old chap, tell me how it's done.' He spread his podgy hands in a gesture of defeat. He really should've gone the whole hog and bought vintage champagne. Adam wasn't really used to off-the-peg Moët. He was sipping at it as if he felt that this horse ought to be rested.

Adam knew that he held most of the cards, but there was a weakness about his hand, too. Charles knew his secret, or at least knew that he possessed one. If Adam was to cut Charles out completely, then his uncle could exact revenge by blowing the whistle on him and revealing the fact that Adam knew how the Dow was going to perform. OK, so people wouldn't believe him at first, but with the phenomenal stock-market success that the Phipps account was now bound to achieve they'd soon sit up and take notice. So Charles had to be taken along for the ride – at least for part of the way. Adam would be able to keep an eye on him.

Adam briefly outlined the nature of his extraordinary discovery but was careful to tell his uncle only the bare minimum. He trusted Charles Phipps about as much as an alcoholic in a brewery. He had, he said, stumbled by chance on a computer program which appeared to be totally accurate in predicting market movements, adding that the details of the program, although stored on floppy-discs, were useless unless he operated the computer. The

148

vital weightings of the data were, he told Charles, stored in his head.

This was true. From the very beginning Adam had realized that his program had incredible value. Unscrupulous people could be relied on to try and obtain it by fair means or foul. So the vital information was locked away in his memory where no one could get at it. It was as well that Charles Phipps recognized that.

Twin dollar signs clicked into place in Charles Phipps' eyes. Was this the jackpot? Croesus time? Was Adam about to make him rich? Would it be all right, after all?

For one brief moment Adam allowed his uncle's hopes to soar, as he'd soared on Anne's carpet in his weekend dream. It was to be a brief flight. Adam couldn't afford to fall out with his uncle at this stage, but he was determined that this hated and despised adversary shouldn't make one penny out of his discovery. The wounds Charles Phipps had inflicted went deep.

'There's something I've been meaning to talk to you about, Charles. I got a friend of mine to check into the volume of transactions on my account with your bank. It seems that, compared with the action on Merrill customer accounts, turnover on my account is little short of phenomenal. It looks like you've been churning the account to maximize personal commission. That's not a very friendly thing to do.'

Charles watched his luck running out like sand in an hour-glass. His stomach began to rumble ominously, colour flared into his cheeks and he puffed himself up like a fighting cock. As was his habit, he would now explode, unleashing a stream of vicious invective, the words carefully chosen for their cruelty, their aim uncannily accurate. He stopped himself just in time. He mustn't lose the Phipps account. Without it he'd remain on the board of the bank about as long as it took for a traffic light to turn green and the car behind to begin hooting.

He gave an embarrassed, high-pitched laugh – the sort

you give when a country cousin commits a faux pas at your club. Poor Adam, the laugh said, really, you don't understand such things. You might have stumbled on the secret of the market, but the workings of the gentlemanly establishments of Wall Street are clearly still a mystery to you.

'Come, come now, Adam. I think your friend has been misleading you. Certainly the account is managed aggressively. If you don't speculate you don't accumulate. I'm going for performance. The picture is constantly changing, you know. Not at all like the old days when you could buy blue-chips and forget them.

The clichés and mixed metaphors flowed from him as he sought to justify the unjustifiable. On the whole he thought he'd done rather well. He'd especially liked the cunning psychological ploy of heaping the blame for lack of investment sophistication on Adam's 'friend'. He'd like to lunch on that little bastard's balls.

Adam was unmoved by his uncle's attempts at patronization. He'd played his king. The ace was still to come.

'I'm glad you brought up the questions of performance. I was going to raise that matter next. I did some checking there, too. It would appear that over the last year the account has performed thirty per cent less well than the constituents of the Dow-Jones Industrial Average. On that basis the sheep might well wish that the good shepherd would take a long vacation, to put it mildly. It seems to me that the very kindest thing to say is that the choice of investments has been grossly incompetent, and I'm not inclined to take the lenient view. I'm sure that neither of us would want the SEC to look into the booking of transactions on your own personal accounts in comparison with those on mine.'

Christ! The cunning little bastard had rumbled him. The blood vessels in Charles Phipps' face shut down, turning it from red to deathly white. One second on the verge of untold riches, the next teetering on the brink of a prison sentence. Charles Phipps – walker to the cream of high society, successful banker, charity stalwart – sewing mail bags, cataloguing the Sing-Sing library, or whatever one did in prison these days. He fought to stay calm. Deny it, that was always the right thing to do. Desperately he sought for words that would ward off disaster.

'Adam, I must say I am saddened – deeply saddened – by these totally unfounded and unwarranted accusations. I'm surprised and hurt by them. That a nephew of mine should take this completely unfair line is quite remarkable. Frankly, I've worked my guts out on your account. True, it's been an unlucky year – a bad eighteen months actually, but that's the name of the investment game. Next year everything can change. In that eventuality I hope you'll be as generous with your praise as you've been with your accusations and your unacceptable insinuations. I might add that it's lucky for you that ours is a blood relationship. I'm not a litigious man, but remarks such as you've just made must never be repeated in front of a third party, or I would go to the courts without hesitation. After all, unlike you, I have a reputation to protect.' Charles breathed in deeply and thrust out his chest in defiance.

Adam threw back his head and laughed uproariously at his uncle's gall. You had to hand it to Charles – he never gave up.

'Don't worry, Charles, I'm not going to shop you – though we both know you've been milking me. I just point out these things to you so that you can understand what I'm going to do and why. First, the account stays with Seabury-Phipps. It's always been there and I'm not about to change that tradition just because you're a crook. So you get to keep your job. But hear this. I don't propose that in future you'll make one dirty nickel out of any market moves that I make as the result of this computer forecast which I've invented. The second I suspect you are, or attempting to, I withdraw my funds – and you're on the street. I want that crystal clear. Do you understand me?' Adam's voice had acquired a hard, cutting edge.

Charles gulped as he contemplated the sword swinging by a fine thread over his head. He was to be an impotent spectator as Adam cleaned up the market, to be used as a mere instrument, a messenger boy between Adam and the market dealers. Far from climbing on a roller-coaster ride to fabulous riches, he'd be worse off than before. His lucrative commission income would be reduced and the profitable swindle he had used to rob Adam's account would have to be stopped. Every day he'd have to watch Adam growing richer and richer, a gawping bystander, witness to the greatest financial coup in the history of capitalism. For a second he wondered if there might be a way to deal secretly, through Switzerland perhaps, and copy Adam's foolproof investment moves. But if Adam found out, Charles firmly believed he'd do what he threatened and pull the rug out from beneath him. His world would tumble like a pack of cards.

'Do we have a deal on these terms?' asked Adam.

Charles' yes was produced with the sort of noise one might make while swallowing a fishbone.

'OK,' said Adam. 'Here's what we do! Tomorrow we liquefy the account. Sell everything. Get rid of all the rubbish you've accumulated. Stick the proceeds in an instant-withdrawal NOW account and borrow against it as much as the bank will lend on margin. The next day we'll move heavily into the options market and trade actively, buying 'puts' or 'calls' as the computer dictates. We'll do that for a day or two and then review the situation. Maybe we should make a few mistakes on purpose and take some losses so that people don't get too suspicious. I'll leave the mechanics up to you. But I want you to report to me on all the moves we make – let me have all dealing slips and a daily statement of account. Is that clear?'

It was clear. Unpalatable, but clear. Charles was as tightly trussed as if he was on one of his bondage trips. But already his fertile mind was at work and the germ of an outrageous idea was beginning to grow – an idea which, although dangerous, might just satisfy all his desires for the ultimate wealth, and for revenge, too.

Chapter Six

All day long Anne had agonized over how she would handle the session. She'd toyed with the idea of cancelling it. Breathing space. She'd also thought of handing Adam over to Peter Isaacs, of discontinuing therapy altogether, but somehow the appropriate speeches had sounded hollow and unconvincing. 'Adam, I've been giving this a lot of thought and have reached the conclusion that you may be better off with a male psychiatrist. My colleague Peter Isaacs has agreed . . .' or, 'I have the feeling, Adam, that therapy is not really what you need at this stage, and I think on the whole it would be better to discontinue it now . . .'

She knew that she should break it off, but her desire cancelled out reason. So, powerless to do anything, she did nothing as the clock on the wall ticked away the minutes to the hour of Adam's appointment.

Desperately she tried to regain that aloof professional calm which had always come so easily to her and had been the envy of her colleagues. In vain she tried to look at the problem in a dispassionate way. Mr X, the 23-year-old boy with the alcohol and cocaine problem. What should she be doing for him? It was hopeless. Even Anne's willingness to try any approach that might work, something she'd always considered one of her greatest strengths, now seemed only to complicate things.

The buzzer of the desk intercom made her jump. God, she was a nervous wreck. If she believed in the damn things, she might have been wiser taking a Librium.

'Send him up,' she managed at last.

Adam looked divine. Blond hair, shining and lustrous, was swept away from his full forehead. He wore a dark blue double-breasted navy blazer. Harvie and Hudson shirt, open at the neck, faded blue jeans and polished black Gucci loafers. Anne's heart danced wildly in her chest.

'Hello, Adam.'

He smiled his welcome. He didn't look like a psychiatric patient and didn't feel like one. The smile was the one he used when walking across the fashionable Le Ralais restaurant to greet a particularly favoured female acquaintance. It did strange things to Anne Carrrington's tummy.

'So, what's on the menu today?' he asked flippantly, perhaps unconsciously aware of the restaurant analogy.

'I thought we might try a little free association. It often helps to dredge things up that might be useful to examine. Of course this isn't psychoanalysis, classical or otherwise, but I often find it helps.'

Helps who, thought Anne. Helps sexy psychiatrists hide their ashamed faces from their patients. Helps cover up the emotions of incompetent and irresponsible doctors.

'Great. What do I do?' Adam made it sound as if Anne was about to explain the rules of a new card game. 'Patience' for patients.

'It's quite simple. You just lie down on the couch and let your mind go blank. Then you say the first word that comes into your head, and then another word that you associate with it. It's a pretty well-known technique. I expect you've heard of it before. The only rule is total honesty.'

'God, the full Freud trip,' said Adam irreverently. 'I didn't know that was your bag.'

'Oh, I'm not proud. I'll use anything – thumb screws, if necessary.' Christ, that was a Freudian slip.

Adam took up a languid position on the couch.

'Should I take my shoes off?'

'You can leave everything on.' Somehow that didn't sound very appropriate either.

Nor, indeed, was Adam's first word. With absolutely no hesitation he said, 'Casting couch.'

Anne fought back a mad desire to laugh. That just had to have been said on purpose. Or had it? After all, the surface veneer of their professional relationship was wearing pretty thin. Unconscious thoughts were now hovering around in the pre-conscious anteroom, waiting impatiently to be ushered into the chambers of consciousness.

'Lying down.'

Laid down, thought Anne. Laid.

'Story telling. Tall buildings. Hovering. Helicopters. Whirling blades. Flying.'

Intercourse, orgasms, thought Anne. And then she was off, her own thoughts flying, winging away, crashing back to reality – the reality of Adam's body lying on the couch in her consulting room, of being alone with the object of her frustrated desire. She felt her heart rate go into overdrive, intuited the shifts within her nervous system as the saliva dried her mouth, the insects fluttered in her stomach, the sweat poured from beneath her arms.

'Fucking,' said Adam unapologetically. And Anne knew she was lost.

Her knees began to tremble and she forced them together. Deep between her legs a tap was turned on, dripping at first and then running free as the awesome feeling began to spread in the depths of her pelvis. Like a nuclear explosion it radiated forth from the epicentre of her being, sending shock-waves up into her lower abdomen, down into the tops of her legs, back to caress her tensed buttocks.

Anne gripped the sides of the chair and tried to control her rapid breathing, running a dry tongue nervously over dried lips. Her eyes darted towards Adam. Thank God he couldn't see her, that she didn't have to say anything.

Adam was saying it all. 'Tongue. Licking.'

There it was. Anne could see the outline of his long penis, could make out its shape as it pushed up at the faded blue denim. He was hard as a rock. He was daring her. Laying down the gauntlet. Confronting her cruelly with the choice. It was brutal . . . and magnificent.

Anne was suspended, her mind wandering on some astral plane as the awful power of her physical desire racked her body. She was hovering on the brink of orgasm and yet no hand had touched her, no external stimulus had been received. Her body was obeying its own rules, and she had no strength, still less inclination, to attempt to influence or control it.

'Licking cunt.'

On unsteady feet, Anne crossed the two paces to the side of the couch. She knew what she must do, and she watched herself in fascination as she did it. She must taste Adam, put him inside her mouth. No other course of action was remotely possible. She'd never believed in determinism until this moment.

Adam sensed her movement and let it happen, lying still so as not to disturb her, frighten her away from the action that he willed with every fibre of his being. Like the stalker lining up the deer in his sights, he froze, knowing that the slightest movement might be disastrous.

Anne knelt down by his side and put out her hand and laid it flat on his hard penis. For a second she paused, savouring the surging sensations, loving him, loving it, vibrating in tune with the fiery music that played within her bowels. Slowly, with the deftness of a surgeon, she pulled down the zip, dimly aware of Adam's low-pitched moan. Still the boxer shorts concealed their mystery, and then he was in her hands. For what seemed like eternity she gazed at his erect penis. Reverently she moved her head towards it, nuzzling its side with warm, parched lips, smelling its musky scent, rubbing her hair gently against the shining glans.

Gently she took Adam in her mouth, running the tip of her tongue over his prick, her brain working feverishly to process the myriad of exquisite sensations being fed into it. She was aware of the enormity of her act. Yet the danger, the terrible threat of exposure, served only to intensify the delicious excitement of the moment. The time for caution had long passed. For now she wanted to do two things, and two things alone: she wanted to give pleasure and to receive it. If she could raise Adam to the heights of ecstasy she would own him, he would be hers. That would be enough.

Gradually, hesitantly, she began to suck, her eyes closed to maximize her senses of touch, taste and smell. Both of her hands caressed the base of Adam's tense penis, as in dreamy slow-motion her head began to move rhythmically up and down.

Adam could hardly believe what was happening and fought to imprint on to his memory the glorious panorama laid out before his eyes. The transcendent eroticism of the moment couldn't be separated from the extraordinary circumstances. Certainly he'd wanted this to happen – had done his best to bring it about. His fantasies about his beautiful psychiatrist, his dreams about her had been powerful sources of pleasure over the past few days. But for them to actually take place was another thing altogether. He was well aware of the risk Anne was taking – was aware, too, of the pent-up passion that had allowed her to gamble with her future in this reckless way. It wasn't as if such behaviour had come easily to her. Her whole demeanour denied that from the start, and the touching amateurishness of her performance was further evidence.

He arched his back and pushed himself towards her, giving himself up completely to Anne's welcoming mouth. He reached down, resting his hands gently on either side of her head, teaching her the movements that pleased him most. He wanted desperately to take her in his arms, to make love to her, to whisper words of tender reassurance in her ears. But that would come later. Right now he sensed that Anne wanted him to fill her up with the fluid of his desire, to climax into her, to show him the true extent of her feelings, the depth of her commitment. This knowledge served to intensify Adam's arousal and a sublime circle was set up as his excitement communicated itself to Anne's lips and tongue.

She took him in deeper, trying to accept the whole length of him into the very deepest recesses of her throat. Sometimes her teeth caught against the side of him, sending little messages of exotic pain to his clouded consciousness. Moving faster, she felt the already rock-hard penis grow further in her mouth. It wouldn't be long, and then Adam would be lost in the mysteries of his orgasm – her gift to him, and his to her.

Adam's hands tightened against her head, giving a delicious sense of coercion to this most-wanted act. He felt the familiar beginnings of his orgasm. It seemed as if the juices of his desire were summoned from every corner of his body to the universal meeting-place in the heart of his genitals. From his brain, from his buttocks, from the furthermost extremities of arms and legs the fluid came, leaving, it seemed, those areas dry, ennervated, as it journeyed south. Now all of his vitality was concentrated, ready to leave his body for Anne's and it felt as if his whole being was nothing more than an insignificant appendage tacked on to his throbbing penis, which alone was the centre of his universe. The moan started at the back of his throat, a distant roll of thunder heralding the onset of the storm.

Anne both felt and heard the warning signs of the culmination of the act, and she tensed herself to receive the offering. And then the fountain started to play in her mouth, gushing, pulsing, rushing, the liquid poured into her, soaking her parched and dry throat, cascading over her tongue, spurting over her teeth and lips. Liberation filled her soul as she gave herself up to the enjoyment of Adam's orgasm, swallowing and sucking voraciously as she savoured the taste, the texture, the smell of the delicious liquid. Then it was over. Adam lay limp in her mouth, his fingers playing gently with her ears, murmuring his love for her. Very quietly, she began to cry.

A few minutes before she'd been Adam's psychiatrist. Now she was his lover. It seemed incredible that such a dramatic change in roles could be brought about so comprehensively by one single act. Adam, too, as he got up from the couch, had been transformed. He was a patient no more.

Bending down towards the still-kneeling Anne, he lifted her up towards him. She turned her tear-stained face to look at him, her eyes searching for clues to his feelings, no longer as an expert but as a woman. They said nothing as they clung together, their souls suspended outside their bodies, communing in some wordless dialogue, merging in formless space. And then it began again.

Adam felt the stirrings, and Anne, pressed tightly against him, felt them too. He tasted his own desire as he kissed her, at first brushing her lips with his, then crushing them as the passion grew. He tasted her tongue, probing her teeth as he pushed against her. It seemed ludicrous that they were both fully clothed, but in some strange way that added to the excitement, and a secret and unspoken contract agreed that it would continue to be so.

Adam reached down and lifted up Anne's tight skirt, pulling away from her as he did so. His heart crashed against his chest as he saw what he had unveiled. Long white thighs were framed at the top by tiny silk Dior briefs, at the bottom by black silk stockings. A delicate white suspender belt formed a bridge between the two. Anne's body was no mystery to Adam. He'd seen it often outlined and accentuated by her tight clothes, had seen it in vivid colour in his erotic dreams. But he was hardly prepared for the reality. Anne's thighs and bottom were those parts of her anatomy which she'd always been most proud, and to come top of that particular list represented the heights of excellence.

Adam, erect once again, knelt down in reverence at the

beauty of the sight. With delicate fingers he slipped the white pants down to reveal the tight, proud buttocks pushing out at him. He ran his hands over them in wonder, feeling the soft, hot skin smooth and sensual beneath his touch. With the tips of his fingers he reached between Anne's legs, marvelling at the slippery wetness that testified to the extravagance of her need. Urgently they moved towards their shared objective.

Anne leaned back against the desk, symbol of her now vanished authority, skirt hitched up crudely around her waist. She was going to be fucked standing up by a patient fifteen years her junior in her own consulting room, her partner across the hall, her secretary downstairs, her American Psychiatric Association Board accreditation diploma staring down at her from the wall. Yet she didn't care – could only give a fuck. There would be time for worrying later.

She looked down at Adam's penis, running her tongue over her lips with anguished longing as her fingers manipulated the growing strength into hardness. She wondered how he could recover so quickly, how there could be anything left after the pent-up river had exploded against the back of her throat such a short time before.

Bracing her buttocks against the edge of the desk, she positioned herself to receive him, guiding his prick into the dripping core of her being.

'Fuck me,' she murmured. 'Fuck me as hard as you can.'

Adam tore into her, stimulated by her lewdness, her total capitulation. He sensed that for now she wanted cruelty not gentleness, a punishment, perhaps, for her precipitous fall from grace. Later there would be a time for tenderness but right now Anne wanted roughness, and he would give it to her.

He put both hands behind her back and grabbed hold of her straining bottom, pulling her towards him, forcing himself deep inside her, in the furthermost recesses of her pelvis as she moaned her satisfaction. The sharp corner of the desk wedged between her buttocks acted as a painful anvil to the hammer of Adam's penis. In between, pinned like a butterfly to the pages of a book, Anne's vagina lay bruised and throbbing under the delectable onslaught.

'How does it feel,' said Adam cruelly, 'to be fucked by a patient?'

The humiliation put Anne right over the top. Her knees began to give way as the crashing crescendo of the orgasm took her. Her vaginal muscles relaxed, contracted and relaxed again, milking Adam's thrusting prick of its second orgasm. She was vaguely aware of the noises she was making – whimpering, pleading, groaning as the climax rolled on and on. Would someone hear? It didn't matter – was of supreme unimportance. Then, suddenly, the madness was over and she sank down to her knees, her face level with Adam's glistening penis, his semen and her own moisture dripping from her on to her damp stocking tops.

'Oh God,' was all she could say.

In the dealing room at the investment bank, the employees exchanged knowing looks as Charles Phipps minced into the room. It wasn't, however, Charles' effeminate walk which was the object of their mirth and scorn. Everybody in the bank was used to that. What the looks signified was the growing realization among the hardened dealers that Charles was rapidly becoming a stock-market turkey, a man who could be relied upon to get it wrong. Never particularly lucky with the market, over the last few days he'd done nothing right at all. All his moves seemed to have been designed to lose the maximum amount of money. By betting against him one would've made a fortune. In fact, that morning one of the hard-bitten professionals had suggested that in future he was going to do just that, and use Charles as a barometer of what not to do in the market.

None of the men knew how close they were to the truth. Charles had been so wrong simply because he'd bet against Adam, whose system insured that he was always spectacularly right. Now, however, Adam and he were working in tandem and, although Charles couldn't profit directly from the market killing which was about to be made, he would certainly enjoy humiliating these dealers, who hadn't always succeeded in keeping their feelings about Charles out of their eyes.

'OK, fuck rats,' said Charles nastily. 'Open up the lines – we're going to play the options. Let's shift ass.' Charles liked to affect the hatchet man, macho image – to the almost universal disgust and distaste of all who witnessed it.

'Are we "putting" or "calling"?' The head dealer's voice was heavy with sarcasm. Whatever you do it'll be wrong, you prick, was the unmistakable inference.

'Don't you boys know anything? Can't you read the tapes? You losers wouldn't know dog shit from diamonds. The market's oversold, the corrections over – we'll buy every bleeding call in sight. Don't talk to me about stocks – I want everything that can handle big volume, and boy do I mean *big*.'

This was impressive bullshit from a market cripple. It sounded as if Charles had gone over the top, unhinged, perhaps, by his recent losses, determined to win everything back on a last throw of the dice, the gambler's last stand. There was something rather awe-inspiring about it, and across the busy dealing room an interested silence was established.

Like a drunken cowboy shooting up the town on payday, Charles stood his ground and babbled on, the words pouring out in an ecstatic stream, imagery drawn from the gutter peppering the stock-market jargon.

Custer's last fucking stand, thought one dealer. If he calls this one wrong he's finished, and he knows it, thought another, who found it strangely impressive nonetheless.

'We book this to the Phipps account, right from square one. Don't bother with the frigging details, buy everything that fucking moves. Just get quantity and no chickenshit on the cost. Chase them up, pay anything you have to as long as you accumulate the positions. Everything else goes on the back burner until we've cornered all the available Chicago, Philadelphia and American Exchange calls. Christ, I'm going to bust every option trader from California to the New York islands. They'll be out of their windows like confetti at a virgin's wedding.'

The heady excitement coursed through Charles. This was better than being beaten up by a truck driver. Adrenalin pumped and sweat poured. Before his mind's eye the magic figures danced. The exchange and the options market had not opened, but he, Charles, was one of only two people in the whole wide world who knew that the Big Board was going to have the second busiest day in its history and that, in the middle of a totally unforeseen buying panic, it was going to rise by 42 points in an unheard of 200-million-share volume.

The cowed dealers stared back at him. A helicopter ride over the sinking *Titanic* couldn't have provided a more poignant moment. It seemed clear that Charles was on the verge of market suicide, his own physical demise not long to be delayed. Certainly he had the authority to order this buying spree, ill-advised though it clearly was. His discretionary power over his nephew's account was absolute. There remained one question to be asked.

'What sort of money are we talking?' asked the head dealer. It sounded big – two or three million perhaps – hardly enough to unsettle the bigger boys in Chicago, but a significant punt anyway.

Charles puffed himself up. For a second he allowed himself a little strut along the dealing room floor. All ears were his. They would not be disappointed.

'Spend $150 million,' he said simply.

As pandemonium broke out, he knew he'd made his mark at last.

Peter Isaacs was in a cold, towering fury. Across the desk Anne Carrington looked more like a naughty schoolgirl than a famous and renowned psychiatrist.

'What can you possibly mean, Anne, you're "infatuated" with him? Christ, he's a *patient*. I don't have to tell you what that means. Tell me you're joking.'

'I'm not joking, Peter. God, I wish I was. It's out of my power. I'm out of my depth here. I guess it's neurotic, perhaps hysterical – I don't know. I don't think its psychotic. You tell me.'

'Don't confuse the issue with psychiatry.' Peter raised his voice. 'This isn't psychopathology, it's hot pants and wilful unprofessionalism. OK – here's what we do. You call in sick. I take over this Phipps character for a week or two and then I throw him out on his ear. It doesn't sound as if there's anything wrong with him anyway. Of course you don't see him again . . . ever, if you want to keep your licence.'

'No!' Anne almost screamed the negative. She wasn't going to give Adam up, whatever the consequences.

'What the hell do you mean "no"? There's no alternative.'

A sudden and ghastly thought occurred to Peter Isaacs. 'You haven't screwed him, have you?'

'It's none of your business.'

Christ, that meant yes. Peter's stomach churned. Hurt and anger raced through him.

'You'd better believe it's my business. We have a medical corporation here. You're my partner. What you do reflects on me. If you fuck patients, people are going to think that I fuck patients.'

Anne burst into tears, and Peter immediately regretted his cruelty.

'Oh God, Peter, I feel so guilty – don't shout at me.'

She was right. She needed understanding, not anger, thought Peter.

'OK, OK. I'm sorry. I didn't mean all that.' He reached out across the desk and touched her hand. 'I guess it's more than just the professional thing with me.'

Anne managed a watery smile through her tears at Peter's veiled admission of jealousy.

'It's more than just a physical thing, Peter. Much more. You can't just brush it away – and neither can I.'

As she said it, Anne felt better. She hadn't really thought about it before, but now she realized with absolute clarity that Adam was exactly what she wanted. How long the desire would last she had no way of telling, but she had waited too long for this experience to give it up for professional ethics or Peter's comfort. And if she gave Adam up as a patient – well, neither of them were married and it was a free world. Somehow this realization of her fundamental desire gave her feelings and behaviour a more acceptable perspective.

'Obviously you can't go on seeing him as a patient. You simply must realize that. It would be malpractice, criminal negligence.'

'Yes, I see that, of course.'

'And if you want to go on seeing him off-duty, I suppose that's no business of mine – although my advice to you is that you're putting everything on the line. If you feel you must do that, I strongly advise that we have regular meetings to discuss things. We have to think about your other patients, too. Clearly the whole thing has turned you upside down and I think it's important that we monitor your mental state as things develop.'

That was sensible, thought Anne. Demeaning, but sensible. Peter Isaacs was very wise, and, although perhaps a little vengeful, was basically kind and sympathetic. It began to look as if she would need all the support she could get. Falling in love with a 23-year-old playboy who snorted coke and drank too much was not the cleverest thing for a 38-year-old psychiatrist to do.

Then there was the problem of John Mitcham and the dreaded Aaron Ishmael, who seemed to have made it his calling in life to nail her ass. That was a slippery pole requiring careful negotiation and sure feet. To talk to Peter regularly would be a help. Nevertheless, there was no disguising the fact that in a way she herself was becoming a patient. Certainly the world seemed to have been turned upside down.

Back in her office Anne couldn't avoid the couch and the desk, both of which seemed to look at her accusingly. But the guilt only reigned for the shortest of moments, expunged from her consciousness by a much stronger emotion. The desire in her was stirring once again.

In the partners' dining room of Charles's bank the port and congratulations were circulating freely, the atmosphere thick with bonhomie and the smoke from Havana cigars. Although Charles' option deals had been done for the Phipps account, the bank had benefited from the substantial dealing commissions. In 24 hours the paper profits were pushing $200 million. All round the Street word was out that Charles Phipps and his bank had called the largest market upturn in history. Already the more volatile of the big private punters were thinking about pulling their accounts from First Boston and Hutton and heading for Seabury-Phipps, the big winners. All day long the telephone lines had been besieged as the brokers and the financial press had called up for the latest market predictions.

All of the partners had been prepared to overlook the extraordinary imprudence of committing such large sums of customer's money to the dangerous and volatile options market. In the world of Big Apple high finance, nobody was inclined to argue with the bottom line.

The senior partner, pompous, staid, portly and far from an admirer of Charles', was speaking:

'My dear Charles. Sometimes in the past we've had our little disagreements about market policy and investment strategy, but never, I repeat, never, in what I like to think of as a long and not undistinguished career in investment, have I witnessed such a display of pure intuitive investing brilliance.'

Buddha-like, Charles Phipps lapped up the unaccustomed compliments. Overnight Charles had become a winner, an instant market guru, the man who'd gazed into his crystal ball and seen a great vision, who'd had the guts to back his prediction with the hardest of hard cash. So now those who'd scoffed were converted to enthusiastic camp followers, disciples squatting at the feet of the master. Everyone wanted to know what the next play would be.

'We have to ask what your next move will be,' said the senior partner. Now, I suspect, is the time to unload those calls. In and out. Hit and run. Don't want to get too greedy.'

All eyes turned expectantly to Charles. For long seconds he gazed back at them, inscrutable, the man with all the answers keeping his cards close to his chest. He savoured the moment.

'Sorry, Jack. Must disagree with you once again,' he said at last. 'This market's going to hold yesterday's gains. I'm going to leave the positions open.' It sounded as if he'd invented the art of patronization.

Into Charles' mind flashed the memory of Adam's early morning prediction. Dow-Jones Industrials: up 1·43. And then a dreamy look came into his eyes as he lost himself in reverie. This was a triumph – like in ancient Rome when the slave by your side in the chariot had to repeat endlessly, 'Remember thou art but a man.' Well, Charles was a man all right, but he felt like a god, had god-like powers. Never before had he felt like this – omnipotent, the man who'd gambled and got it right, the man with balls, the voyager for whom no journey would be impossible. Nobody would ever take this glorious feeling away from him. This transcendent joy, this Nirvana.

And then it struck him like a blow from a sledgehammer. He hadn't got a thing. He himself possessed nothing. He was a fake, a poseur. Without Adam's forecasts he was a nothing, a nobody, a market loser. Slowly but surely and with an awful finality, Charles Phipps began to realize that he wasn't prepared to give this up. If Adam should ever pull the rug from under him, walk out on their partnership, he'd go to the ends of the earth to prise the secret of the market out of him. His present reliance on Adam was intolerable, a sword of Damocles suspended over him. No, he must have it all for himself – the power, the glory, the riches, the prestige, the entire kingdom. There and then Charles Phipps decided that whatever it might take he would get it. He would make his own personal pact with the devil and risk everything to gain the world.

Anne's heart sank as she struggled through the trendy crowd towards the bar of the Le Relais restaurant. Why on earth had Adam selected a hell-hole like this for lunch? The noise-level was almost to the pain threshold and the population density made the Black Hole of Calcutta seem spacious.

With mounting desperation she took in the closely packed tables, crammed together for maximum profit and social intercourse. Private conversation? Forget it. The lunch would be about as intimate as group sex in a Masters and Johnson laboratory. Still, this was probably what Adam's life was all about. She could hardly have expected a Chinese restaurant or health food bar. In the waters into which she'd allowed herself to fall, the people here were the typical fish. She had nobody to blame but herself.

Wedged tightly against the small bar by a seething mass

169

of humanity, Anne ordered a Campari and soda. She drank the fizzy, bitter liquid deeply and peered round her. Clearly Adam was going to be 'socially' late. Anne wondered what 'one-ish' had meant. To her it meant one o'clock. Damn. She should've asked. Perhaps to him it meant two. By that time they'd have to carry her out if she hadn't already died of suffocation.

All around her the glittering youth of haute café society shouted and screamed at each other, impervious to the fact that their remarks reached a far wider audience than the intended recipients. Perhaps it was intentional, all remarks being made for public rather than private consumption. Certainly Anne didn't feel like an eavesdropper.

A good-looking forty-year-old with a sunburned, stretched face and a voice like a foghorn was holding forth to a small, weasely looking man with hornrimmed glasses and what looked to Anne like high blood pressure.

'Word on the Street is that Charles Phipps called it right. Went over the top in the calls and murdered the option dealers. Apparently there's blood on the walls in Chicago and Philadelphia.'

'Christ. He'll be even more insufferable than usual. Remind me to avoid the Union Club bar for the next few weeks.'

Charles Phipps. Charles Phipps. Wasn't he the guy who 'kept' her hysterical patient Skip Demery – and was Adam's uncle, too? It would appear he'd made a killing on the stock-market. Clearly he was a man of many parts. Anne filed the information away in her mind. One never knew when such snippets might come in useful.

'Boy was I *zoned* after that week in Sun Valley,' offered another noisy reveller, 'everybody was *shit-faced* from dawn till dusk.'

Doesn't look as if you've managed to sober up yet, thought Anne. Where the hell was Adam? Why couldn't he have suggested somewhere more private?

There were so many things she wanted to say to him.

Anne's mind was a tidy place. She liked things settled, everyone to know exactly where they stood, without room for misunderstanding. They'd discuss things as two intelligent adults. Well, as two adults anyway. Intelligence was scarcely characteristic of anyone's actions at the moment. But if Anne wanted order, she also wanted, craved even, reassurance. What did Adam feel about her? Had it been just a meaningless fuck to him, interesting only because of its unusual circumstances? Would he use this lunch to humiliate her, to expose her as a hypocrite who'd thumbed her nose at her Hippocratic Oath? Anne shuddered at the awful thought.

And there were other questions to be answered, too. Whose was the casual, self-confident female voice which had answered the telephone when Anne had called earlier? Was she the famous Mariel, who scored drugs, liked to make it with girls while Adam watched? If so, Anne supposed she must be considered a rival. As the green twinge shot through her, Anne decided that jealousy was an emotion she didn't like one tiny bit.

As Anne caught sight of Adam in the doorway of the restaurant, all such confusing thoughts diappeared instantly. Once again her emotional engines were turned on. Like a burglar alarm triggered as a thief broke the circuit, the mighty klaxon of her desire began to wail, drowning all background noise of speculation and doubt. To see him was to want him. To want him was to love him. How to own him? When could she have him again? This afternoon? Now? In the lavatory? Against the crowded bar? The other customers were far too preoccupied to notice.

Anne had a minute or two to watch him as, sliding on a slippery sea of charm, he melted through the dense crowd towards her. Everyone seemed to know him, to want to say hello, to knead and pummel him, to crack a quick joke, to float the slick remark. But Anne was way past making judgements. She was in the dock, not on the bench

– a prisoner, a slave to her emotions – and when Adam bent down to kiss her lightly, sensually on the corner of her mouth, breathing out gently as he did so, she knew exactly why she had chosen to swap positions. At the touch of his lips Anne lit up as if an electric current had been passed through her body, making her shine like a beacon as she smiled her gratification. All round the fashionable restaurant the people-watchers took note. Adam Phipps had discovered a fox. Good old Adam. Mariel wouldn't like it. How soon could one decently telephone her to mention Adam's rendezvous? Boy, she'd be really *cross* – but she'd have to pretend she didn't care. Fantastic.

And so in one of those curious shifts of fate, Anne Carrington became most conspicuous at the very moment that she ceased to feel so. Previously she'd felt she stood out like a sore thumb in the strange restaurant, when in fact she'd been totally anonymous, invisible. Now, with Adam at her side, she was impervious to the hungry eyes which so suddenly had begun to devour her.

'Ready whenever you are, Mr Phipps.'

The eager head-waiter had put Adam at the top of the queue and nobody seemed to object to this flagrant favouritism. Droit de seigneur, the privileges of wealth by popular acclaim for this prince of the plutocracy.

'Great, Francisco. We're ready right now.'

With Francisco hovering attentively like a darting moth round a candle flame, the trio made their way across the restaurant to what was clearly one of the best tables. Envious glances followed their movements as they were seated at what the cognoscenti recognized as the place of honour.

'Let me order for you. It's about as easy to get hold of a waiter in this restaurant as it is to get the clap in a nunnery.' Adam laughed easily as Francisco made good-humoured objections to the slur on the efficiency of the hired help.

'Celery Remoulade, Carpaccio and a bottle of Beaujolais

Villages. Oh, and some Perrier. Now, you make sure the Carpaccio is cut thin, Francisco. The other day it was as thick as fillet steak.'

Anne smiled inwardly. He was trying to impress her. That was nice. She had to admit, too, that he *was* strangely impressive. It seemed after all that there wasn't a person there who wouldn't have been quite happy to have been used as a doormat by him. Whatever that said about their priorities and ambitions, the fact couldn't be avoided that there were few, if any, places on God's earth where she'd have inspired the same awe. And this was just one restaurant. What about Page Six, Café Luxembourg and all the other trendy places she read about in *New York* magazine? Clearly, in his own world Adam Phipps was a force to be reckoned with. Good. He might be top dog of a rather indifferent canine species, but at least he was out in front of the pack. With a little judicious encouragement he could be persuaded to upgrade himself. With Anne at the helm of his life . . . She caught herself. Not so fast, Dr Carrington. Maybe over the Celery Remoulade he's going to say that his family doctor has insisted he report her to the American Medical Association Ethics Committee, instruct his attorney to institute proceedings for malpractice. If he had a lawyer worth his salt that should be worth $100,000 minimum.

Adam was looking at her very hard. He leaned towards her conspiratorially, his voice low, suddenly serious, the bantering tone of the exchange with Francisco conspicuously absent.

'I loved what happened,' he said. 'It was wonderful, amazing. I want it to happen again and again.'

Relief and fear, in equal proportions, flooded over Anne. Again and again. That was exactly what she wanted – didn't want. Would she have exclusive rights, or would she have to share? What about Mariel? What about the ruins of their 'professional' relationship?

There was no delicate way to phrase any of the questions

to which she needed to know the answers. But she had to give some sort of response. A little speech about a momentary aberration, regretted and never to be repeated? No! Her heart screamed its defiance at this appalling prospect. Confessions of undying love and affection? Hardly. She was falling in love – that couldn't be denied – but she hadn't quite reached the destination. At the moment, her emotional state could probably best be described as sexual obsession – love of a kind, perhaps, but of a rather specialized variety. What she really wanted to explain to him was that above everything else, more than life itself, she wanted to play with his body, have it as her own private toy, to enjoy it, to use it, to have it use her. What would the people at the next table, who were already more or less sitting in her lap, make of that?

So Anne said nothing at all. Instead she stared fixedly at the shining white tablecloth, the demure maiden, little-girl-lost in need of rescue.

Adam sized her up, noting the twin spots of colour on her cheekbones. She was by far the most fascinating and intriguing woman he'd ever met but he didn't begin to understand her. Why had she let him pull her? It was clearly completely out of character – of that he was certain. The incredible intensity of the steamy encounter, the ecstasy of their lovemaking, had spoken its own language, scarcely requiring explanation in terms of cause and effect. She'd opened up to him like an exotic tropical flower to the rays of the sun as she had sucked the essence from him. The pleasure of that intensity didn't go away. It left its sweet reminders, its snatches of remembered feelings, smells and noises. And these memories cried out, demanded to be repeated again and again. He knew that he wanted her, that he *must* possess her.

Never before had he met a woman in whom extreme strength and total vulnerability had been more intimately mixed. On the one hand it was inconceivable that this highly thought of Manhattan psychiatrist could become his lover – on the other it was impossible that this beautiful, sensual woman, who'd given herself over to passion in a way he'd never before encountered, could belong to anyone but him.

For a moment they both sat in silence, contemplating the strange paradox of their relationship, knowing as they did so that events had taken over, that what would happen was in some weird way predetermined, out of their hands. Forces were at work that would manipulate them like puppets on a string. This mutual capitulation to the powers of fate seemed to help.

Having received no response to his declaration of intent, Adam tried again. 'Of course we'll have to just forget the whole doctor/patient thing.' There was the smallest hint of a question in his statement.

Anne looked up at him and smiled a big, open smile. 'I'm afraid we never did really get that off the ground, did we?'

They both laughed. Partners in crime. Lovers. Anne felt deliciously wicked. Suddenly she realized that she was actually beginning to *enjoy* herself. The beaujolais, fruity and fresh, was seeping into her veins and forming a delicious alliance with the pre-lunch Campari. The Carpaccio was a dream, Adam stunningly beautiful, the restaurant pretty and stimulating. She began to feel that she'd lived in the grey world too long, the world of snatched sandwich lunches, packed timetables, serious people, sick people. Now, at last, perhaps not to late, she was going to live a bit, allow herself to have a good time, indulge herself in what she'd always before considered less worthy pleasures. Certainly she appeared to have a willing and able tutor for a crash-course in hedonism. Being led astray by Adam would be a wonderful way to go. Reflecting her new-found confidence, her determination not to let guilt interfere with her pleasure, she sneaked her hand across the table and touched Adam's wrist with a light, playful caress.

'You know what you said just now – about wanting it to happen again and again – well, I'd like that too.'

The messages of excitement danced up Adam's arm, negotiated the complex pathways in his brain and roared downwards. Christ! This woman could make him hard without even trying. He caught hold of the delicate fingers, wrapping his hand round them gently.

'Where do we go from here?' he said.

'You mean literally?' asked Anne with a mischievous grin.

Again the laughter. Conspirators, sharing the same all but uncontrollable desire. Loosening up. Letting the latent sexuality bubble up to the surface. It was the beginning of intimacy. Both knew they were entering that strange world of tingling feelings, joys and disappointments, ecstasy and despair which characterizes the start of an affair. From now on nothing would be easy, but everything would be new, alive, super-real. Now both would look at life through the prism of emotion, through the distorting spectacles of passion. As a consequence they would draw wrong conclusions, compromise themselves and each other, make rash and unwise judgements. In recompense they would be allowed to drink deep of the drug of life, be filled with the vitality and excitement of living to the full. Caution and common sense, reality and prudence were to be exchanged for danger and dreams, illusion and recklessness. It was a trade that both Anne and Adam were more than prepared to make.

Adam's voice was suddenly husky and low-pitched as the humour evaporated, to be replaced by the unmistakable urgency of desire.

'I want you, Anne.'

With mild suprise both realized that it was the first time he'd used her name.

Anne smiled back at him, lips parted, her breath coming faster.

'You can have me – anytime,' she whispered, unable to keep the shakiness from her voice.

'Now,' said Adam simply.

Anne wondered if the whole restaurant could hear the beating of her heart. The colour rushed up into her cheeks. She was past speech. Weakly she nodded her head in acquiescence.

There and then they had left, the Carpaccio half eaten, the beaujolais half consumed. There had been no nonsense about paying the check: at Le Relais Adam didn't have to bother about such mundane things. The short walk to Adam's duplex had seemed to take an eternity, but an eternity full of the most blissful anticipation. They had walked in silence towards the union of their bodies, which both so feverishly desired.

This time it had been different. Before they had made love hungrily, greedily, pulling and tearing at each other as they fought to reach the Xanadu of passion. They had been violent and aggressive as they had ground their bodies together, extracting the maximum of sensation from the brutal friction. It had been deliciously degrading as they had exorcized the ghosts of too-long-thwarted desire. But now there was time for a different sort of lovemaking.

On Adam's soft Irish linen sheets Anne and he had danced to a more harmonious melody, their swaying bodies moving in gentle rhythm, responding quietly, luxuriantly, to each other's needs. Low-pitched moans of ecstasy had been the background music as Adam had entered Anne, sliding gratefully into the warmth of her as the smooth muscles of her vagina had gently caressed the skin of his penis, milking it tenderly, her long, powerful legs twisting round his. As they made slow love, he had kissed her, his tongue inquisitive, searching her mouth, tasting her taste, nuzzling her warm, dry lips as his fingers explored the smooth dampness beneath her outstretched arms. With infinite patience the two lovers had waited willingly for the pleasure peak, making it last, savouring every delicious minute of ecstasy. Each single second, each wonderful sensation was patiently analysed by two minds anxious to keep them forever alive in the vault of their memories.

Even the divine moment had seemed drawn out, endlessly prolonged, frozen in slow-motion as their hearts and minds had stopped in wonder to observe the extraordinary purity of physical love. Anne had felt delectable pulsations deep within her as Adam's love had bathed her inflamed passion, a soothing balm for her fevered fantasy. As he had filled her up with his offering, her own spirit had soared to meet his, flying above and around him. And then it, too, had taken physical form, cascading down, pouring out of her, soaking his hard stomach with the glorious wetness of her sublime orgasm. Afterwards, still, silent, they had communed in their state of grace, secure and certain that after this they could never be apart.

Charles Phipps was exhibiting all the symptoms of terminal panic. Over the last day or two he'd come to regard Adam's early morning, or late night, telephone call in much the same way as a junkie related to his fix. Just before the call was due he'd become increasingly nervous, strung out, tense, irritable, preoccupied. He'd hover round the telephone, willing it to ring like some lovesick teenager. Then, when Adam's voice finally came on the line, the adrenalin would rush through him and he'd experience an ecstatic high as the information was fed him – information which made him an instant hero in the eyes of his colleagues, which transfused life-giving fluid into his previously moribund self-respect. His foreknowledge of the Dow's behaviour allowed him to strut and pose in the corridors of Seabury-Phipps, to play oracle in the dealing rooms and hold sway in the partners' dining room. From being the Invisible Man he'd become the Statue of Liberty. When he farted, everybody sniffed.

Today the vital telephone call was conspicuous by its

absence. It was five minutes to ten. The market was about to open and the bank was on the other line screaming for Charles' instructions. What should be done with the gigantic open 'call' positions? Should they be allowed to run on? Or should they be closed immediately? The risk was colossal.

Of course the short answer was that Charles didn't know what to do. Without Adam's prediction he was a blind man. However, he couldn't, wouldn't admit it and was feverishly playing for time, pretending to the bank that he wanted a little more time to digest incoming information from overseas markets, especially the shortly to close London Stock Exchange.

On the other line, with trembling fingers, he dialled Adam's number for the hundredth time. The infuriating stone wall of Adam's answering service met him head-on once again. He'd already reduced three separate operators to helpless tears with interpretive remarks about their mothers' sexual predilections and their fathers' social diseases, but his objective nad remained unachieved. Now he scored the supervisor, who had added insult to injury by not only telling him that he wouldn't be connected to Mr Phipps number, but that he was being reported to the appropriate authorities for sexual harassment, threatening language and obscenity. In a towering rage, as impotent as it was furious, Charles had suggested that the supervisor perform a deed of sexual acrobatics as complicated as it was unappetizing. He'd proceeded to throw the telephone against the wall with all the force that his corpulent frame could muster.

He already knew what he must do: he'd have to close the position, take the profits. In the absence of certain knowledge, he couldn't afford to do anything else. Christ! The irresponsible little rat. Adam had pushed him to the edge of a heart-attack. At last count his blood pressure had been running 160/100. This sort of stress he didn't need.

If the market corrected after its remarkable gains of the

179

last few days, all the brilliant profits he'd so spectacularly achieved could be wiped out overnight. Hundreds of millions might slip through his fingers. OK, so it wasn't his money, but it would've been lost on his decision. Two days before he'd learned what it was like to be master of the market, the ultimate gun-slinger, the coolest gambler of them all. In that sweet moment of triumph he'd seen the whole world open up to him and the sublime feeling had changed his whole life. He would never be the same again. With a high like this permanently available to him, he might even be able to conquer his homosexuality, to dissolve his masochistic sexual desires. All would be possible if this ultimate pleasure could be had for the asking. But now his stinking, incompetent, irresponsible little nephew had shown him in the clearest way possible how insecure was his position, how totally dependent he was on somebody who had demonstrated in no uncertain terms his total untrustworthiness.

With a sinking feeling in the depths of his bowels, Charles barked his instructions into what remained of the telephone.

'Sell all the calls at the opening bell. Liquidate all positions. I think the market's going to turn round.' He slammed down the receiver.

Now, retribution. Charles Phipps waited only briefly for the elevator before taking off down the stairs. Ignoring the undoubtedly adverse effect of such peak exertions on his cardiovascular system, he charged out into Park Avenue like a fighting bull released into the ring. He half ran, half walked the few blocks to Adam's apartment building, his podgy legs consuming the distance at an uncharacteristic pace. Tornado-like he burst into the lobby and within seconds was hammering on the duplex's front door. In response to Wan-Tu's polite insistence that Mr Phipps was 'still sleeping', he put his hand firmly on the Oriental's breastbone and pushed as hard as he could, barging past him towards Adam's bedroom. Without knocking, he went straight in, a stream of invective flowing from his over-worked lips, a gunfighter shooting from the hip.

'Wake up, you little prick,' screamed Charles at the top of his voice.

The conversation that followed wouldn't have gone down well at a PTA meeting.

Adam took the view that Charles Phipps should get the hell out of his bedroom in the shortest possible time. Charles, in contrast, demanded a post mortem of Adam's failure to supply the daily computer prediction. Both pursued their own arguments in language which could've been described as lively and colourful or gory and obscene, depending on the point of view of the listener.

For a minute or two the tennis ball of abuse was hammered relentlessly over the net which separated the two antagonists. Adam, territorial rights severely violated, exploded wtih indignation. Charles, a man who'd experienced a guided tour of Nirvana, who'd seen the shining vision, who faced eviction from Paradise, pulsated with hatred.

Such was the furious pace of the verbal battle that it became clear that physical action of some sort was bound to intervene. Adam, strong and fit, had the disadvantage of nakedness and the fact that he was still in bed. Charles, a mugger's dream, was at least clothed and standing up. In the event it was no contest. Adam leaped from the bed with an infuriated shout and fell on his uncle like an angry wolf attacking a rabbit. Pinioning his arm behind him and grabbing him by the seat of his pants, he frog-marched Charles towards the door, rushed him along the corridor and projected him amid screams of protest out into the apartment's marble foyer.

It was a marginally chastened Charles Phipps who retraced his steps along Park Avenue to the cold comfort of his apartment. Disconsolately he flicked on the stock-exchange tape. Maybe the market was on a down tick, perhaps, after all, he'd been right to close the positions. If so, his new-found reputation would survive for at least another day. Eagerly his eyes followed the tape. Disaster. The market was running away like there was no tomorrow. A bull run. A bear massacre. The tape was half an hour behind. First-hour volume was a record. The Dow was up 22 points and rising. By closing his 'call' positions an hour and a half before, he'd blown the chance of making millions.

It was little recompense that it was Adam who'd blown his opportunity. The fact was that at the bank he'd now be called chicken. The man who'd gone part of the way but who couldn't hack it when the stakes were raised. Poor old Charles Phipps, reverting to type, running for cover after a fluke call.

Condescension would be the staple diet at the board meeting the following morning – the senior partner prominent in ladling out liberal doses. Patronization, scarcely concealed contempt, latent aggression – all would be in evidence as the board members over-compensated for their short-lived and now apparently misplaced faith in silly old Charles.

Cold and clammy, appalled at the ghastliness of his predicament, Charles knew that the time for action had come. No more pussy-footing. Adam couldn't be trusted with his secret. If he wouldn't part with it voluntarily, then it must be prised from him. Thoughtfully, and with ice-cold malevolence coursing through his body, Charles picked up the telephone and dialled.

Anne had left strict instructions that if Mr Phipps called she was to be interrupted whether or not she was with a patient. This counteraction of one of her strictest rules meant that when the telephone light flashed she knew exactly who was on the line.

'Good morning,' she breathed down the line, with all

the enthusiasm that the presence of a patient in the room permitted.

Adam sounded rather shaken. 'You'll never guess what's just happened to me. I've had to throw that extraordinary uncle of mine out of my bedroom. Can you believe it?'

'Not the famous Uncle Charles? Hey, I hope he wasn't staying the night,' Anne joked in mock jealousy. Through Skip Demery Charles' habits were well known to her.

Adam laughed. 'No *way!* He came barging in here, ranting and raving. It was an amazing scene.'

'What on earth did he want?'

Suddenly, Adam appeared wary. 'Oh, nothing really. We've been working together on a system for playing the stock-market. I handle the computer side of it. He was a bit pissed-off that I hadn't done my homework. Still, that doesn't give the idiot bedroom visiting rights. They're reserved for you!'

Anne felt a flush of pleasure rise on her cheeks. At the same time she remembered the overheard conversation at the packed Le Relais bar about Charles Phipps' 'market killing'. Perhaps Adam's 'system for playing the stock-market' was a lot more successful than Adam was letting on. Certainly it seemed to have been the cause of violent emotions in Adam's uncle.

'Listen, Anne, the real reason I'm calling is to ask if you'd spend the weekend with me. Monday and Tuesday are both holidays, and if you could get them off we could make it a long one. It'd be really good if you could.'

That sounded wonderful, an answer to a prayer. Anne knew there were houses in Southampton and Palm Beach. Which would it be?

'I'd simply love to, Adam. Can't think of anything nicer.'

'Great. Superb. Have you ever been to the Oktoberfest in Munich?'

'No,' said Anne cautiously. 'Why do you ask?'

'Well, none of us have, and I've always wanted to see it.

Anyway, we've got a plane organized so there won't be any hassle. There's a fantastic hotel, apparently, called the Bayerischerhof with a pool on the roof. So if we eat too much we can always burn it off.'

Anne knew what it felt like to be the country cousin. She could hardly believe her ears. She was to be flown to Europe in a private jet to the Munich Oktoberfest simply because 'none of us have'. For the moment she ignored the rather sinister implications of the phrase, its intimations of plurality, that it was apparently to be a team outing. Instead she concentrated on the extravagance of the gesture, the conspicuous consumption. Was this how the really rich lived? Was this how the name 'jet-set' became coined? Apparently. There wasn't a shred of evidence that Adam had laid this on especially to impress her. Presumably this was how they all filled up their lives. The Rio carnival, Le Prix de l'Arc de Triomphe at Longchamps, partridge shooting in Estremadura, salmon fishing on the Dee – the list was presumably endless to the inventive hedonist, whose highest creative activity was to construct an itinerary of sufficient taste and originality to impress and amuse his friends. Hiking in the Himalayas, crocodile shooting in Lesotho – well, now that it was the end of September, what was more natural than to be in Munich for the Oktoberfest? Anne wracked her brain to remember what the festival was all about. Something to do with drinking very large quantities of beer, she seemed to remember. What the hell! It sounded like terrific fun, and she'd be with Adam. It was a drag they couldn't be alone. Anyway, at some stage she'd have to learn to get on with his awful friends.

'I'd love to come, Adam. It sounds incredibly exciting – and very glamorous. Tell me what I have to do.'

'Just pack – nothing else. The limo will pick you up on Friday about six, and with the time difference we'll be eating black bread and liver sausage in the Bayerischerhof for breakfast on Saturday morning. Back in the Big Apple Wednesday morning, if that's all right with you.'

Anne flicked through the big appointment book on the desk in front of her. She knew she'd kept Wednesday more or less free, reckoning she'd earned an extra day off. Damn. John Mitcham, nine o'clock Wednesday morning. The only appointment of the day. She made the decision instantly. She'd call him and change the appointment to Thursday. Twenty-four hours wouldn't hurt, and it would give her a chance to recover from the return trip.

'Sounds fine. I'll be waiting.'

Mickey and Fritz looked about as comfortable on Charles Phipps' sofa as two cockroaches caught in a spotlight. They shifted uncomfortably from side to side and their eyes darted about the characterless, but to them enormously opulent, apartment. To say they were out of place was a gross understatement. It was two in the morning, a time deliberately chosen for its anonymity. The two homosexuals had obeyed Charles' instructions and left their leathers at home. This, he'd said on the telephone, was to be a strictly nonsexual encounter, although a far from unprofitable one.

So now the two men were on their very best behaviour – a fact that did little, if anything, to disguise the throbbing waves of evil emanating from them, as if they hadn't washed for a year and had tried to hide their smell with liberal splashings of eau de cologne. They wore nondescript suits of the sort that any bank clerk might have been reasonably proud, and these effectively camouflaged the hard, endlessly exercised bodies, the muscles honed and built to perfection in ceaseless workouts. The cold, wicked eyes – dead, humourless, purged of any emotion – couldn't be so easily concealed and left Charles in no doubt of the dangerous nature of the men with whom he was dealing.

Like Dr Faustus, his was a pact with the devil. He chose his words carefully.

'I've asked you here tonight to see whether or not you might be interested in helping me out with a little problem I have.'

Mickey suppressed a snigger. Both men had first-hand experience of this man's 'little problems'. What did he want – to be screwed in his own bed? To give head in front of his mother's portrait? The possibilities were endless.

Seeing the sneering eyes, Charles toughened his pitch.

'In the past our dealings have been – how shall I put it – on a physical basis. Small sums of money have changed hands. Very small sums. Tonight my needs are rather more comprehensive. I have a lot of money to spend. A great deal, in fact.'

Both men shifted imperceptibly to the edge of the sofa as if attracted towards Charles by some invisible magnet.

'How much money?' said Fritz nastily. He'd heard that line before. One man's idea of heavy cash wasn't necessarily another's. Five hundred? A round grand? Never for one second did it occur to either to ask what was required of them in return. They'd do anything if the money was right. Literally anything. That had never been the problem.

Charles puffed himself up. Tonight *he* was into domination. Mickey and Fritz were about to become employees. They'd have to learn how to act the unaccustomed part.

'I'm talking $100,000,' he said, peering at the two men closely.

Four fish-like eyes sparkled with greed at the unexpected enormity of the sum, and Charles Phipps knew at once that he had them hooked. They'd cheerfully torture their baby sisters to death for a fraction of that amount. No question.

Like naughty children caught in the act of tearing the wings off flies, Mickey and Fritz sought desperately to camouflage their excitement. No geniuses, both men were street-sharp and knew that displays of enthusiasm could be costly.

Mickey picked thoughtfully at a dirty nail, his eyes avoiding Charles' as he tried to appear casual. 'That's a lot of money. Seems like you must have a big problem.'

Until this moment Charles had committed no crime. This was the point of no return. He took a deep breath. Life would never be the same again.

'I'm talking about kidnapping. Possibly a little more.'

'Possibly a little more.' That could only mean one thing, thought Mickey. The little prick's taking out a contract and he's paying ten times the going rate. Still, he wasn't about to educate him about current tariffs in this field. When you stepped outside your area of expertise, you always got taken for a ride.

'Suppose you tell us about it. We may be able to help,' he said after what he hoped was a pregnant pause.

'There is a certain person, a young man in fact, who possesses some information that I'm anxious to obtain. It would be your job to get hold of that information by whatever means you think necessary and hand it over to me. It would please me greatly if this particular person became permanently unavailable afterwards, if you get my drift. It would be a pity if he was able to point his finger at any one of us after the event, as it were.'

Charles slipped naturally into his banker's role. Never say outright what could be wrapped up in a fog of veiled innuendoes. That way one could wriggle out of commitments, blame others later for 'misinterpreting' one's instructions, for getting the wrong end of the stick.

Mickey and Fritz exchanged questioning glances. Both were surprised by Charles' forceful manner, a far cry from the whining, snivelling, grovelling nonentity who'd take their lengths on the floor of the Snake-Pit and then cried out for more. He looked like he meant what he said. Mickey proceeded carefully. This was big business – the biggest.

'This information. What sort of information?'

Charles was on his guard. Nobody must know the exact nature of the discovery, of its supreme importance. Anybody who did would realize that $100,000 was chicken-feed, a joke figure compared to the value of the information it was buying.

'It's rather complicated, a little technical. This man has used information provided by myself to construct a computer program that has a limited use in predicting stock-market movements.'

It never hurt to put oneself in the position of the wronged party. Even reptiles like Mickey and Fritz preferred to have a modicum of 'right' on their side.

'In effect, he's cheated me and stolen what should've been mine. I want it back, and I want him punished.'

He gave added emphasis to the last word. Adam's last moments on earth wouldn't be good ones, might be very bad ones indeed, thought Charles, a sadistic frisson of excitement racing through him. What would they do to him? How would they misuse him? He suppressed a flicker of sexuality. His mind must be ice-cold, clear and uninfluenced by such considerations. He was playing a deadly game.

'I propose,' he continued 'to pay you $25,000 on our agreeing a deal. You get a further $25,000 when I get the information I need. The balance of $50,000 you get on the final solution of the problem, the details of which I would leave to you.'

'Final solution'. That had been used before, thought Charles. He'd always rather liked the euphemism.

'Used banknotes.' Mickey spoke out loud but the half-question, half-statement was more a thought.

Charles nodded. They were going to go for it.

'So this thief guy – is he hot?'

Charles imagined that Mickey meant is he famous, is he protected.

'He's about twenty-three and he keeps late nights. I'll

provide you with all the details of where he can be found and when. Picking him up should present no particular problem.'

It was true, thought Charles. With good timing one ought to be able to mop Adam Phipps off the sidewalk of Park Avenue, pour him into a bottle of brandy and spirit him away into the night. By that stage his 'friends' would probably be too drunk to notice.

'Have you somewhere where you could take him?' asked Charles.

Mickey nodded thoughtfully. The downtown loft would do. The warehouse was deserted. It would only take an hour or two to beat the information out of him before they stuck him in the river. One hundred thousand dollars. Christ. And of course it would only be the beginning. This mother could turn into a meal-ticket for life. The 'hit' would tie them into him closer than copulating dogs. And then there was the whole sexual thing. The idiot was a natural for blackmail.

Mickey's eyes flicked hungrily over the art work, the signed photographs of Presidents, the expensive furniture. Now that they knew where he lived, who he was, they had him by his scrawny little balls. One hundred thousand would just be starters, for sure. He felt himself harden in the tight red G-string beneath the shiny trousers of his suit. Money had that effect on him.

As if reading his mind Charles added, 'The way I have planned it is that the information and the money should all be exchanged at drop-off points, left-luggage lockers or something. That way we needn't ever meet again after tonight. That must be safer for all of us.'

'Of course,' chorused Mickey and Fritz, a second or two too quickly.

Charles saw it all in their minds, knew exactly what they intended to do. Never for one second did he imagine that they wouldn't go for the shake-down. In their position he would've probably done exactly the same. Possessing no morals himself, he was well placed for recognizing the characteristic in others, and that these two snakes had no value systems at all was totally plain to him. They'd do anything for money, and after they'd done it they'd come back for more . . . and more. And the beauty of the situation was that he didn't care in the least. With Adam's computer program in his grasp he could rise above little problems like blackmail. He'd have money, power and riches undreamed of. At worst he'd always be able to afford to pay them off, as their imaginations would be incapable of conjuring up a sum he'd be unable to afford. At best he could have them wiped out, blotted from the face of the earth like the vermin they were. If $100,000 bought him Adam's death, it would be far from difficult to arrange the early demise of these two far from valued members of society.

So, as Charles read their mental processes, watched them size up the quantity of gravy on the meat in terms of the potential for continued extortion, he preened himself on the beauty of the situation. Nobody on earth could tie him to these two men because nobody knew of his forays to the leather-bars except, possibly, the suspicious Skip Demery, and he didn't know for certain. Charles had always gone out of his way to keep his identity a secret and to avoid being followed as he journeyed back uptown. Nor could anybody connect Mickey and Fritz with Adam. They'd neither met nor seen him before. On learning of Adam's disappearance, the police would think he'd disappeared on one of his periodic jaunts round the world. Perhaps it would be months before he was missed. And if for some reason it was suspected that he'd been kidnapped, then the natural assumption would be that it had been for ransom. The cops would sit on their asses waiting for a ransom demand which would never arrive. By the time they got to searching New York, and the rest of America for that matter, Adam would be in an automobile compactor at the bottom of the East River, or wherever was to be his ultimate destination.

For an hour they discussed details. Charles showed them both a photograph of Adam, explained the layout of the Park Avenue apartment, gave them telephone numbers from which they could monitor his movements. He explained, too, what he needed from Adam. Something called a floppy disc, which looked like a 45 rpm record and a list of the all important 'weightings' of the market data which Adam had told Charles he kept 'in his head'. Adam would be held for just long enough so that Charles could check the accuracy of the information he'd provide against movements of the Dow-Jones Index. And then it would be the Big Sleep, the Long Good-bye.

The three men began to quiver with excitement as they contemplated their suddenly rosy futures. From their own secret viewpoints all of them began to see how they could become the masters of their own private worlds, and the aphrodisiac effect began to build in each simultaneously.

It was Fritz who gave voice to the universal but latent feeling.

'Seems to me we ought to celebrate the deal – kinda one for the road.' He leered at a suddenly flushed Charles Phipps.

'Yeah,' agreed Mickey. 'You should have something to remember us by.'

Like a conjurer his hand darted downwards. But it was no rabbit, no coloured ribbon that he produced from his fly. With that well-known mixture of horror and fascination, Charles stared down at the growing, rearing phallus.

'You were just made to eat cock, man. Come here and do your duty.'

As the butterflies took off in his stomach and his heart began its wild dance, Charles Phipps did as he was told.

The *ancien régime* splendour of the Bayerischerhof Hotel

in Munich provided a dramatic contrast to the New World so recently departed. As a bridge between the two, the private jet had combined elements of both – the airplane itself typical of the former, the fine wines, delicious food and respectful and unobtrusive service indubitably characteristic of the latter.

The start of the weekend had been inauspicious. Adam, planning being not one of his strongest suits, had been late and as a result the private jet had missed its take-off slot, entailing a two-hour wait in the special lounge at Kennedy. With a sinking heart Anne had discovered that the infamous Mariel and somebody called Peter Danforth were to be fellow travellers.

However, the moment they were airborne things had got dramatically better. Adam had ordered the most brilliant dinner, pieced together apparently from Anne's chance remarks over the last few days. The flinty, ice-cold Sancerre had beautifully offset the smoked salmon from the Dee in Scotland; the 1961 Cheval Blanc had perfectly complemented the delicate lamb cutlets, tender and pink in the middle the way Anne loved them. Afterwards there had been a puffy, tangy soufflé Grand Marnier with which they'd drunk a sweet, heady wine from the Barsac region south of Bordeaux; a fine Chateau Coutet, less obvious, but no less magnificent than Yquem. To eat and drink like that was always a sublime experience for Anne. Doing it at 20,000 feet, sitting at a proper dining table with sparkling cutlery and heavy, spotless Irish linen, and waited on by two quietly efficient and immaculately uniformed stewards, made it infinitely more pleasurable.

After dinner they'd sat in the vast salon and watched a movie which Anne knew had only just been released in New York a week or two before. Adam and she had sat side by side on one of the comfortable sofas, and while they had held hands like teenagers Mariel had kept her distance and, more important, her silence. That, and Adam's proximity, had been the very best of omens and

Anne, relaxed by the wonderful dinner, was beginning to let herself go. Even Adam's lateness at the airport, irritating and threatening at the time, had begun to seem charming and reassuring. He needed her to look after him, to organize his life, to make things work for him. She had squeezed his hand tightly at the comforting thought.

The big, black Mercedes had been waiting on the tarmac as they had gone through customs without leaving the jet, a deferential official boarding the plane and asking the routine questions.

They had mounted the magnificent wide staircase of the Palais Montgelas – the former Bavarian State Chancellory until bought by Falk Volkhard, owner of the Bayerischer-hof Hotel – and marvelled at the beauty of the vast, sparkling eighteenth-century chandelier. An assistant manager, effusively subservient, had ushered them into their suite. Huge bunches of flowers were everywhere and, as the hotelier proudly demonstrated the fully stocked antique drinks cabinet, Anne had taken in the unselfconscious, understated luxury of the heavy, dark mahogany furniture, the thick silk curtains, the huge, inviting bed.

Anne had never questioned the sleeping arrangements. Of course she'd be with Adam. But at the back of her mind there had been a niggling insecurity. It had been an outside possibility that she would've been asked to share with Mariel, while Peter shared with Adam. She needn't have worried.

Mariel, apparently cheerfully, seemed prepared to admit defeat.

'Well, I guess you two love-birds get the best room. Poor Petey and I will have to sleep on the floor.'

In fact, the suite's two single rooms were almost as opulent as the master bedroom, and everybody laughed – Anne with not a little relief.

'What we all need is a swim, a massage and some breakfast before hitting the party.' Better move things on while the conciliatory mood lasts, thought Adam.

It was a good idea. Anne's high spirits, dented to a certain extent by jet-lag, were thoroughly revived by the exercise and cold water. God, over the years she'd missed so much. Before, she'd always tested the water, paddled on the periphery of life and experience, always holding back because of career and ambition. Now she'd at last plunged head-first into the deep end without first looking for the sharks, piranhas and barracudas. And the feeling was good. She was making up for a lifetime of caution. At last she was looking after number one.

One thing seemed totally clear and was a significant contributor to her happiness and security. For whatever reason, Mariel had quite definitely decided to extend the olive branch of friendship. From the moment they'd met for the first time at Kennedy she'd been charm personified. Anne had expected to loathe her but was already half way to liking her. She was funny, amusing, light – and above all had seemed to concede all proprietorial rights to Adam. It was a highly promising start. However, Anne remained on her guard. It would be unlike Mariel's type to throw in the sponge without a struggle. The new friendliness should be taken with a pinch of salt.

What Anne couldn't know was that, despite her reservations, she'd seriously underestimated her opposition. In the clear blue, meticulously chlorinated waters of the Bayerischerhof roof-top pool swam a creature far more dangerous than any carnivorous inhabitant of the ocean deep. Nor were its teeth its most valuable weapon. Mariel intended to conquer and consume Anne with her tongue. And it would be done without any words at all.

The waiting game didn't come easily to Mariel O'Sullivan, but then ease was something she'd never taken for granted. To get what you wanted in this life, to protect what you had took hard graft. The glittering prizes fell to the toughest and most persistent of the competitors, were kept only by the ceaselessly vigilant. Those lessons, infinitely more valuable than Ivy League degrees and other academic honours, had been learned in the vicious, unrelentingly competitive world of the Bronx streets. There she'd gained insights into realities of life which seemed permanently unavailable to those exposed to a more sheltered education, over whom she always reckoned she had a head start.

So Mariel had learned how to recognize an enemy, and now the enemy was Anne. She knew, too, that frontal assault was likely to be counter-productive. Every atom of her considerable native cunning would have to be used in the battle if she was to avoid losing her one-way ticket to a better style of life, but it would have to be a manipulative, Machiavellian campaign. Adam was on the verge of falling in love with Anne, there was no doubt about it. He'd more or less admitted it to her, and his every action and gesture pointed to it. It was plain that he admired her and was attracted to her. What was worse, he was coming to rely on her, to depend on Anne the way he'd previously depended on Mariel. Once that happened, it would be boot hill for Ms O'Sullivan, the slag heap, the used car lot. The millions, which for months had danced tantalizingly in front of her eyes, would disappear like a hologram at the flick of a switch.

And Mariel was not about to let that happen. To lose one fortune to another woman might just be considered bad luck. To blow a second would be bad judgement. What's more, there might never be another chance. She'd be the laughing-stock of high society New York – no longer second-hand goods, but third. At best she'd have to try LA, get out of the Big Apple altogether. At worst she'd have to lose herself in Europe and build from scratch: all the contacts, the telephone numbers, the endless false starts, as one learned to separate the con-men from the real thing, the mini- from the mega-bucks.

In Europe it would take her forever to infiltrate the ranks

of the seriously rich. It had been difficult enough in New York. But in Paris and London the game had so many different rules and the way ahead was littered with cunning sociological traps for the unwary. All those aristocratic noses, permanently sniffing the air for the scent of insecurity, for the whiff of dodgy credentials or a dubious background. The cards would be stacked against her. She might even have to go back on the game – the flaccid bodies, the drunken impotence of the nocturnal punters, the bounced cheques, the sporadic violence, the humiliations and pathetic perversions. 'Meet me on the train wearing nothing but a fur coat.' 'Spit in my face when I come.' 'Make an obscene call to my wife.' 'Have you ever made it with an animal?' Mariel shivered at the thought.

Trading her body for hard cash had shown her a different world – a world of fashionable discos, expensive clothes, travel – and she'd been young enough and enthusiastic enough to think it was great. Now, however, she was all of 23. Not, some might think, a particularly advanced age. Hardly geriatric time. But Mariel felt old and therefore was, in a way, old. Into her two dozen years had been crammed experiences which had given her the perspective of an old-age pensioner. In comparison Adam and Petey were suckling babes in swaddling clothes. She'd seen it all and done it all. If there was anything left unseen or undone, then Mariel no longer wanted to know about it. All she wanted at this moment in time – wanted passionately – was to be rich. Revoltingly, disgustingly, obscenely rich. As rich as Adam. Richer, even. She no longer wanted to be secure, comfortable, free to do her own thing. She wanted the power that stupendous wealth alone could bring. 'Will you fund my campaign for governor, Mrs Phipps?' 'Will you build my hospital, Mrs Phipps?' 'I got done for speeding. Can you fix the judge, mummy?' She'd find out if it was true that Hobe Sound was smarter than Palm Beach, Connecticut than the Hamptons, the University of Virginia than Harvard, and make her dispositions accordingly. Houses would be sold, others bought, businesses expanded and taken over, brilliant investments made until she, Mariel Phipps, bestrode America like a colossus – had the whole fucking country between her legs, sniffing, licking, thrilled to be there. Mrs Phipps. Mrs Phipps. Mrs Phipps. That was the key. To get it she needed one small scrap of paper: a marriage certificate. Nothing more. It didn't seem too much to ask.

But somebody else was after her meal-ticket, was trying to screw up her future, steal the millions which were, she felt, rightfully hers, and Mariel was quite prepared to kill as a last resort. It was merely a question of the most efficient method of obtaining her objective. Murder might easily compromise matters – and it was delicate tapestries, not mail bags, which she'd planned for the sewing activities of her declining years. No, Mariel would fall back on that one attribute which had never let her down, which had been responsible for all the considerable successes of her life up till now, which had enabled her to come so close to her desired goal. As she'd always done before, she'd win by sexual manipulation, by destroying the opposition in the sweaty, lathered intensity of the sex act. She'd use her incredible body to conquer.

So far her plan appeared to be working. She'd lulled Anne into a false sense of security by her impeccable behaviour. Going out of her way to be friendly, she'd signalled Anne's victory by apparently dropping all claims on Adam, and she'd done it with good grace. Anne had responded with the gratitude which Mariel had expected. On that acceptable base of 'friendship' Mariel was now building fast. She paid special attention to Anne, laughed enthusiastically at her jokes, listened seriously to her serious remarks, was suitably deferential when she spoke. But all the time, cobra-like, she was waiting for the moment to strike, to gauge that split second in time when the gap appeared in Anne's defences. When that instant came she would destroy without any compunction, as she might crush a cockroach beneath the heel of her boot.

After a huge breakfast in the cellar restaurant of the hotel – eggs, cheese and black bread – they had made their way through the almost deserted streets of the town towards the vast fairground, the Theresenwiese, which was the traditional site of the Oktoberfest celebrations. It seemed that the whole of Munich emptied itself to join the party, perhaps 150,000 people, which now vibrated and throbbed beyond the banner bearing the legend *Willkommen zum Oktoberfest*, under which they now stood.

'OK,' shouted Petey. 'Boy, they'd better not run out of beer. I've got one thirst on me.'

They all laughed at his bravado. Petey was always the first to pass out or throw up. Despite this he cherished the illusion that head- and stomach-wise he was an iron man.

'Let's *do* it,' screamed Adam in support of his friend. And so it had begun. With the unspoken but combined awareness that all hell was about to break loose, that strange things were about to happen, they plunged into the heart of the Bavarian bacchanalia.

On the balmy, warm breeze of the late Indian Summer the heady smell of hops melded gracefully with that of schnapps, the sweet smell of burnt caramel from the sugar-roasted almonds on sale at countless booths and the familiar smell of barbecued chicken.

'Where do we start?' Petey gave voice to everyone's question, the excitement mounting within him.

'There's Löwenbrau,' said Adam, latching on to a familiar landmark with a certain amount of relief.

'No. Too obvious,' said Mariel. 'Let's try this one, Paulaner. By the end of the day we'll get to see them all.'

By the end of the day, Adam my love, you'll be well and truly shit-faced was what she meant. What she intended. She knew his weaknesses well – had, after all, helped to create them. Alcohol could be relied upon to work its demon way with Adam. At a certain stage of drunkenness he'd be like putty in her hands. Then he could be handled with ease. Not by direct commands or ridicule, but by egging him on, by encouragement, by sharing his whims and appearing to enjoy his fantasies. At such times Adam's somewhat bizarre sexual predilections could be relied upon to surface. That would be her opportunity. But the moment would have to be judged with the very greatest care.

'Come on, Anne, let's hit the party,' said Mariel, smiling pleasantly and giving Anne's hand a little squeeze. 'There's some space over there.'

Like an enthusiastic younger sister trying to embroil her elder in some exciting but juvenile activity, Mariel led Anne through the maze of closely packed revellers to a partially empty table.

Getting a drink posed no problem at all. A thick-set waitress, tight black bodice plastered over a frilly shirt, materialized in seconds. Her red, shiny face and heavily beer-stained green apron testified to the fact that she was working flat out. A few minutes later she was back, five litre-full mugs of beer held effortlessly in her spade-like hands, the glasses beaded with condensed moisture from the cold liquid.

Thank God she'd always rather liked beer, thought Anne. There appeared to be nothing else to drink, and if she wasn't to put the skids under the party spirit she'd better not hold back. Not that she really wanted to. There was something about the whole atmosphere of the place that demanded that one let oneself go, let it all hang out. The Germans were setting about the project of 'having a good time' with their characteristic efficiency. Anyway, any remaining inhibitions she may have felt were already beginning to dissolve, to melt away as the delicious beer infiltrated her bloodstream. At the three-quarter litre stage, Anne was beginning to feel very good indeed, her feet tapping to the music as she returned the smiles of her cheerful Teutonic neighbours and began to enter into the spirit of the festival.

She was vaguely aware of Mariel's eyes upon her, watching her closely. What could be seen in their green depths? Jealousy? Hardly. The cold glint, the hard hatred was totally absent. No, it looked more like tenderness, respect perhaps. There was something there but it was impossible to say exactly what. Contrary to popular belief, psychiatrists were no better at reading minds than anyone else. To hell with it. Who cared? For whatever reason, Mariel had quite obviously withdrawn from the competition and didn't seem to be bearing any grudge. Quite the opposite, in fact. She was going out of her way to be charming. Despite herself Anne was actually beginning to like her. She had one hell of a personality and was incredible-looking.

Anne realized that her glass was empty. So, apparently, was everyone else's.

'I can't think why, but I seem to have room for another one of those,' she heard herself say.

Across the table Mariel watched, listened and waited. Everything was going according to plan.

The brutal truth was that Mariel intended to get Anne drunk and then to pull her like she'd never been pulled before, to sweep her from the pedestal she occupied in Adam's mind and cast her to the ground in the gritty reality of homosexual lovemaking. After seeing it happen, Adam would lose all respect for Anne. What's more, Mariel predicted, Anne would lose all respect for herself. In the cold grey of dawn's light there would be an excellent chance that Anne might split for good, leaving the field free. Victory snatched from defeat's gaping jaws.

To achieve her objective two things were necessary. First, Anne would have to be more than a little drunk. That side of things seemed to be going well – the beer was strong and she didn't seem to be holding back. The second prerequisite was a psychological one, and already Mariel was working on it, already beginning to achieve it.

For the truth of the matter was that the emotion lurking at the back of Mariel O'Sullivan's pretty green eyes was a very simple and very primitive one. It went by the name of lust. Over many years and in countless situations Mariel had come to the realization that if you were to control, conquer, manipulate and rule by sexual means, then it was absolutely vital that you should enjoy it and be seen to do so. Not for her were the simulated orgasms of the tired old street-walkers. That was the loser's way. In the end the counterfeit was always exposed and discarded as a sham. Instead, Mariel had learned the art of extracting the maximum enjoyment from all of her sexual escapades, finding that in the taking of pleasure she was far better positioned to dispense it.

In the past she'd discovered how to be excited by wrinkled old men as well as by their sallow grandsons; by dog-faced dykes and bull-necked policemen; by greasy Italian drug pushers and impotent aristocrats. Now, as she gazed across the table at Anne, she found it no problem to turn herself on, no problem at all. In her imagination she began to take Anne's clothes off piece by piece, visualizing the slopes and curves of the delectable, firm body beneath, conjuring up the indefinable magic of the feminine smells which would spring from it, tasting in her mind the nectar which would flow. And as she did so Mariel could hear the grunts and groans of Anne's passion, feel the warm breath, see the splayed legs, the dripping opening of love, the proud buttocks thrusting at her, the strangled voice begging her for satisfaction. Would she scream obscenities as she came, as Mariel's fingers played deep within her? Would she cry afterwards with the intensity of the experience? Would she want it again and again?

As the familiar music began to play inside her, Mariel felt the force-field of sexuality which always surrounded her begin to glow, to pulsate, to beam across the table towards Anne. She allowed her hand to snake out across the table, her fingers lightly touching Anne's in an affectionate caress.

'You know, you're really *all right*,' she said, her voice low, husky, innocent yet extraordinarily suggestive.

Anne felt it immediately. It was like testing a battery with your tongue, only now the buzzing vibration was felt in the tips of her fingers, where the younger girl's hand rested. Already it was travelling up her arm, spreading across her chest to the nape of her neck. It was a far from unpleasant sensation, but unsettling, unexpected, inexplicable. Suddenly Anne wasn't quite sure what to do with her eyes. Somehow she didn't want to look directly at Mariel, and so she looked upwards instead. Green and white striped streamers, stags' and boars' heads stared back at her. What on earth had that little interaction been about? Mariel had told her she was 'all right'. So what? Why the electricity? Why did she feel so uncomfortable? And why was it so pleasant to feel uncomfortable in this way?

Petey's shout of 'Fräulein, beer, bitte' blasted the intriguing thoughts from her mind. Her stomach was going to be asked to hold a second litre of beer. Great.

Adam's hand replaced Mariel's. Why was she so eminently touchable this morning? Why wasn't Adam's hand wired to the mains like Mariel's had been? What a funny thought. Hey, was she getting a little bit high?

'Enjoying yourself?' asked Adam encouragingly.

'Fer sure.'

She smiled back at him, imitating Mariel's Valley-Girl chat.

'What does the psychiatrist say about Germans letting off steam?' asked Adam.

'It's so controlled, so regimented. You know that more or less everyone in this room is a little bit drunk or completely stoned, and yet nobody's fighting, nobody's falling over. If this was New York the whole place would be swarming with cops, guns everywhere, knife-fights, fist-fights – you name it. The air would be stiff with pot smoke, the pushers would be pushing. You'd almost certainly end up with a police riot. It's incredible when you think that there must be about 80,000 people drinking too much beer in a space that can't be much bigger than 100 acres.'

'Hey, that's *really* interesting, Anne. I hadn't thought of that. Of course you're right. I saw one security guy and he didn't even have a gun,' agreed Mariel with enthusiasm.

It was always nice to be appreciated. Anne felt herself warming towards Mariel all the time. What an inordinately attractive mouth she had. No wonder Adam had been so heavily into her. He had good taste. But then he tasted good. Hah! Anne laughed out loud at her own joke. This beer was really getting to her.

Anne stretched upwards with both arms, cupping the back of her neck in a languid cat-like gesture of contented relaxation. As she did so, Mariel caught a glimpse of the tantalizing patch of wetness beneath Anne's outstretched arm, visualized the moist recess, imagined its musky perfume, allowed herself the luxury of imagining what it would be like to taste it. She ran her tongue over the voluptuous lips that Anne had noticed a few moments before.

Anne caught the gesture. It was odd but she seemed to have become curiously sensitized to Mariel's movements and actions. She smiled openly at her new friend, blissfully unaware that she was hovering on the brink of a disaster.

Now that Mariel seemed to have dropped all claims on Adam, Anne could see her in an entirely new light. Liberated from jealousy she found it quite possible, even a little exciting, to imagine them making it together, Adam pushing himself between those full lips, emptying himself into Mariel as he had into her. With a tiny shock of alarm Anne felt the motor of her sexuality turn within her. Somebody, something – perhaps the beer, perhaps she herself – had pushed the starter, had fired the engine.

Although now it was relatively cold, Anne had a premonition that before the day was out it would warm up and, firing on all cylinders, achieve maximum revolutions. It was far from an unpleasant prospect.

Adam, Anne and Mariel were alone at last. A stomach-churning trip on the Big Dipper, known as the Doppel Looping, had proved too much for Petey. White and shaking after the ordeal, he'd jumped at Mariel's suggestion that he return to the hotel for a little R and R. Now, to prove their superiority to their recently departed friend, the trio decided to take a ride on the heart-stopping Muncherbahn – the hard core of the party heading, if Mariel was to get her way, towards hard-core activities.

'I feel *great*!' shouted Mariel. 'How ya doin', Anne?' In a playfully exuberant way she bear-hugged Anne from behind, clasping both hands across her new friend's chest. At first the gesture was spontaneous, totally natural, pure schoolgirl bonhomie. But then, quite suddenly and unexpectedly, it metamorphosed into something quite different. Mariel's hands parted but she didn't remove them from Anne's body, allowing them instead to rest lightly on Anne's thrusting breasts. At the same time she moved in close to Anne's back, pushing herself hard against the small, tight bottom.

For the second time that day Anne felt it all happen inside her, felt her nipples come instantly alive beneath the warm palms of Mariel's cupped hands, heard the playful laugh die in her throat. For a long second the spell held, woman and girl locked together, unable to move, prisoners of the moment. Unbidden by any higher mental process Anne, a surprised observer of her own bodily actions, felt her bottom push back against Mariel as the tips of her breasts hardened further. And then at once it was over. This wasn't the time nor the place. Just part of the softening-up process. With a careless laugh Mariel released her prey, noting with satisfaction the colour that had sprung up on Anne's high cheekbones, the momentarily downcast eyes, the stiff nipples pressing visibly against the silk shirt. Things were right on schedule. No question.

Anne Carrington listened to the thumping of her heart. The Big Dipper hadn't got her pulse rate up this high. Through the swirling mists of alcohol, dissipated but not abolished by the fresh air, she fought to make sense of what was happening.

It began to look as if the young girl had taken a fancy to her. What's more, her own reaction hinted that, at the very least, she was flattered by Mariel's feelings. Meanwhile the tingling sensations which continued to dart across her chest suggested a less neutral emotion.

Mariel liked her. You could see it in her eyes, in all her gestures and attitudes. People often lied with their tongues, it was a rare thing for them to lie with their actions. All psychiatrists knew that. No, it was all cool. It was a party. The Oktoberfest. A different country with different customs. She'd never allowed herself to be young and irresponsible, to go where the spirit took her. For once in her life she was going to let go and have a good time. If Mariel wanted to cuddle her then why the hell not? She'd enjoyed it. Letting go. That was what it was all about. Others had spent their lives doing it and Anne felt she deserved it – just this once. Symbolically the experience was expressed by the Big Dipper: for a split second, suspended above the inevitable abyss, one hung on for dear life. Then the trick was to surrender entirely to the wild thrill of the descent into the depths – to give up control for freedom.

Anne sat in the middle on the scuffed black imitation-leather seat flanked by Adam and Mariel. The fit was, for a variety of reasons, mercifully tight and the three voyagers were crushed together, their bodies one as the thrill of the roller-coaster encouraged them to fight for even closer proximity. Fear and other less innocent motives. She couldn't remember when she'd been happier. Her childhood was rediscovered, liberated by passion from the heavy shackles of reason, from the cautious voice of conscience. A child of the universe at last, she had a right to the simple pleasures and enjoyments, the ones she'd considered previously to be only for lesser mortals. Adam's hand on her shoulder and Mariel's warm, hard body both reassured and enabled her to share the joy of the moment under the late afternoon sun.

At such times of ecstasy there is often an overwhelming desire to reward those who have made it possible, to honour and please the teachers who have shown the way, and Anne was not immune to such feelings. And so, at the moment of her greatest danger she was wide open, a giant flower whose petals were spread back to the warming rays of the sun. Porcupine-like she'd always been curled in a tight ball of inhibition and repression. Now, inches from the vulture's grasp, she was allowing herself to unwind.

Beside her, Mariel watched. It was time to raise the ante. Feigning fear, she burrowed in close beneath Anne's protective arm, her head nestling in against her neck, her mouth almost touching a delicate ear. With both hands she held on to Anne's thigh, squeezing with all her might during each precipitous decline from peak to trough of the roller-coaster ride. Big sister/little sister. Mother/daughter. It was as innocent as nuclear war.

'I really like you, Anne. You know, *really*.'

Mariel's voice was husky. It was a question, almost a plea. Hardly a statement at all. Despite the howl of the wind and of the other riders, the words were distinct, urgent, the closeness of Mariel's mouth sending them bullet-like directly into Anne's consciousness.

There was no appropriate answer.

As dusk gathered and the fairground lights came on, the giant party became visibly more animated. People had been drinking heavily all day, and as the blanket of darkness descended on the Theresenwiese inhibitions were shed beneath its protective anonymity. In the crowded beer halls strangers overcame their natural shyness and friendships were struck, while outside the multicoloured neon painted patterns of magic on the glistening faces of the revellers. All the time the loud, insistent music forced the already soaring spirits of the participants ever upwards.

Anne, Adam and Mariel were a part of the madness, deeply at one with the collective unconscious of the Oktoberfest. There were no individuals, no singular ambitions, desires or objectives. All shared the same destination: to merge together in the melting-pot of communal alcohol, to live completely and utterly for the pleasure of the moment. It was an atmosphere tailor-made for Mariel's purpose, as she'd intended it to be.

Towards 10 o'clock they'd discovered one of the few wine halls, and now made the hazardous transition from hop to grape. Both Anne and Adam were flying high, leaning heavily on each other, lost in the heady atmosphere, tired but happy.

This was the difficult part.

'You know, I think we ought to split back to the hotel,' said Mariel cheerfully. 'The whole thing apparently winds down in another hour, and it's never cool to go out with the dregs.'

She anticipated objections. References to the 'cool' thing to do usually carried a certain amount of weight with Adam.

'Must we go yet?' Anne was having such a good time, she didn't want it to stop, but somehow Mariel's exuberance made the hotel sound a fun place to be, too.

Adam looked undecided.

Mariel would play her trump.

'The guy at reception said that apparently the party goes on in the Bayerischerhof bar until breakfast-time next morning.'

With difficulty they found a taxi.

Back at the hotel Mariel stage-managed proceedings immaculately. Suddenly she was a little tired. She wanted to relax, take in a little champagne in the suite. Both Anne and Adam would hit the bar, from which noises of boisterous high spirits could already be heard.

'Hey, Anne, why don't we give Adam a minute or two on his own. Come up and keep me company. I think it's a pretty masculine scene in there. In half an hour he'll come running back to us.'

It was a subtle appeal. The insinuation was that if Anne went with Adam she'd be a clinging vine, over-protective, out to spoil his fun. If, on the other hand, she sided with Mariel, then she'd cement an alliance which it was in her interests to keep sweet. There was, too, the veiled inference that if Adam was a real man he'd avail himself of an hour or two with the boys.

It worked.

'You're right, Mariel. Go on Adam – see you later. Some champagne upstairs sounds divine.' Anne had fallen for it.

Anne peered deep into the champagne bubbles. Wasn't it a beautiful colour? Just the best. Really the only thing to drink. Maybe she'd write something about the colour of champagne. For *Harper's* perhaps, or *Esquire*. Perhaps she'd knock it off tomorrow. It was such an original idea.

'You know, Mariel, somebody ought to write about the colour of champagne.' She laughed. It was sort of funny. 'It's soooo wonderful.' Through the delicious mists she tried to focus on Mariel.

Mariel watched her closely. The timing had to be perfect. She had about half an hour. At some time during those short thirty minutes Adam would come back to the room. He wouldn't want to stay away for longer than that. Also, there was the question of Anne's blood alcohol level. Right now it was spot on target. One or two more glasses of wine and she'd be right over the top. Passing-out time.

Mariel threw her head back and laughed. 'Anne, that's a great idea. You know, you're so brilliant. God, I'd like to be clever like you.'

'Listen, who needs brains looking like you?'

Anne thought it was a compliment, her critical faculties having been dissolved by the alcohol. She felt deeply sensual, totally relaxed. She leaned back in the armchair, both legs thrust out in front of her, the champagne glass dangling from her right hand, the occasional drop falling to the carpet.

Slowly, Mariel walked towards her. She knelt down between Anne's outstretched legs.

'Listen, forget about me. You're the most beautiful woman I've ever seen. Models, anyone – you name it.'

Both of her hands rested on Anne's knees. As she spoke, as if to emphasize her point, she moved Anne's legs in towards her, crushing them against her sides.

Physically, mentally, spiritually Anne was primed for it. A sacrificial lamb, she'd been fattened for the slaughter. All day long, without her conscious knowledge, she'd been schooled and tutored in her responses, had learned the appropriate reaction for the moment of truth. Now, her defences demolished by the alcohol, she was ripe for it. She felt as horny as hell, and this incredible-looking girl, who'd been making passes at her all day, was now kneeling between her legs.

Like divers who cast themselves from high cliffs, relying on the perfect timing of the incoming waves, Mariel had got it right.

Mariel gave a quivering sigh of naked desire, and her hand plunged towards its long-contemplated destination. With unerring accuracy the back of her hand slid along the inside of Anne's warm, soft thigh, her fingers finding the elastic edge of her panties.

Almost in relief Anne allowed her legs to splay open as her body gave permission for the bold, invading hand to please her, the uninvited but far from unwelcome guest.

Anne was open at last, wide open to fate, to love, to the forces of destruction. Her legs were open. Her heart was open. Her vagina was open. With indecent speed her body had signalled its capitulation and Mariel, her hand pressed down hard on the warm pants, felt the slippery moisture of Anne's instant arousal begin to flow. Deftly she reached up, her fingers snaking around the edge of the already soaked panties, and plunged them into the heart of the warm, slippery, welcoming recess. With unerring accuracy she sought the centre of passion, touching it at first gently and then increasing the pressure – pushing, caressing, loving, stroking the instrument of Anne's desire.

Head back, mouth open, eyes closed, Anne welcomed the probing, knowing fingers, powerless and unwilling to resist the sublimity of the moment, wanting it to go on and on. So intense, so unexpected was the experience, so overwhelming its strength and power that Anne soon realized that, like some violent explosion, it could neither be controlled nor prolonged. She was only seconds away from climax.

Mariel felt Anne's orgasm coming as if it was some physical thing – a tangible object which her fingers could hold, shape, mould to their purpose. She knew it, loved it, had created it. It would be her own work of art and then it would be gone, leaving its shuddering legacy, its uneasy aftermath of doubt and desire. Beneath her fingers she sensed the balloon of Anne's orgasm grow, divined the precise moment it would burst, showering its accumulated wetness down the perfect white thighs. Almost before Anne herself was able to anticipate her own bodily response, Mariel's voice was screaming at her.

'You're coming, Anne. You're going to come.'

Mariel O'Sullivan braced herself to receive the offerings of passion. Fingers still at last, she waited patiently for the inevitable thunder after the tell-tale flash of lightning. And then Anne's legs began to vibrate, to throb with the inevitable orgasm as she thrust herself out hungrily at the pleasure-giving hand, wishing she could be more exposed, that she could be turned inside out, the better to be stimulated and explored. As the full force of the gale hit her, she went rigid, her vagina closing clam-like over the intruder, her musculature imprisoning Mariel's hand deep within her, forbidding it to leave. On and on it went, breaking her heart, raping her soul with its intensity as her legs began to thrash and leap about, out of control like the dancing feet of a hanged man. Trembling and quivering, she felt the orgasm pour out of her like champagne out of a shaken bottle, soaking her stocking tops, drenching her upper legs, the heavy scent of her abandonment lingering briefly in the breeze. And then, at last, it was over. It had seemed like an eternity of bliss. It had lasted twenty seconds.

It was at that moment that she saw him. Adam stood in the doorway, horror and disgust all over his face. He had seen it all. Anne, legs wide open, Mariel's hand buried deep within her, was still throbbing with the aftermath of her orgasm as she saw the end of her world in Adam's accusing eyes She opened her mouth to speak as the awful humiliation rushed into the vacuum created by the evaporation of passion. But no words came out. There was nothing to say, nothing at all. White with anger, Adam turned on his heel and left them alone – the bang of the slamming door sounding the death-knell to Anne's future happiness.

Eyes still tightly closed, Anne clutched at straws. There was just one chance left, and it was a slim one. Maybe it had all been a nightmare, a complicated bad dream, an hallucination. In fear and trepidation, knowing that she'd discover the worst, Anne opened her eyes. A pink nipple, innocent, proud, perfectly conical, filled her field of vision. She'd been sleeping in Mariel's arms – was now lying awake in them. They were alone in the big four-poster bed. Christ! What had she *done*? What had she allowed to be done *to* her? What had *happened*?

With an aching head and a heavy heart, Anne lay stock-still as she forced herself to remember. Bit by horrendous bit she recreated the painful mosaic, slotting each piece into place, appalled and shocked by the picture that her disjointed memory remorselessly revealed. They'd all got drunk. Of course they had. And she'd felt so good, so safe, so loving, so free. She'd allowed Mariel to play with her, to make her come. How on *earth* could she have done that? Wine after all that beer. Champagne and Mariel's eyes peering into hers, face close, the warm, sweet breath on her cheek – the same breath she could now feel. Then it had seemed alluring, exciting, infinitely promising. Now, in dawn's early light, it seemed to Anne like the fetid odour of some evil dragon, a foul, fiendish thing which had violated and destroyed her.

Anne felt the nausea rise within her, revulsion working with the crippling hangover which engulfed her. She'd allowed Mariel to make love to her and Mariel had made her pay for those exquisite sensations, made her pay cruelly, charging exorbitant interest on the delight she'd so imprudently borrowed. Adam had seen and heard it all – every second of her degradation, every moment of her debasement.

There and then, lying in the arms of a devil who looked like an angel, Anne Carrington realized that she had hit rock bottom. Bed-rock. She'd blown it, given it all away – Adam, her profession, her pride, her self-respect. For the rest of her life she'd have to live with the terrible memory of this sordid room. She'd destroyed herself, and for what? For lust? For passion? For impermanent ecstasy? For a moment's pleasure she had given up her all.

Once more Anne closed her eyes, praying that the beating of her heart would not betray her wakefulness or disturb Mariel's sleep. Explanations, apologies, jokes – worst of all, attempted intimacies – all would be impossible at this moment of the intrusion of rude reality. Cold nausea gripped her at the thought of the awful possibility. Adam's red, hungover eyes fixed balefully upon her, full of contempt, pity – patronizing sorrow, perhaps, for the psychiatrist who had fallen by the wayside. She saw Mariel laughing, savouring her triumph, full of reminders of the previous evening's debauch.

And then, quite suddenly, deep within, Anne found a little piece of her former self, a small part of her that had survived the tempest of lust, the madness of the last few weeks. It was composed in equal parts of energy and practicality, and it screamed one unequivocal message to her psyche. The metaphysical angst could and would be indulged in later. For now there was one pressing necessity if she was to extricate herself from the quagmire into which she'd fallen: she had to get out of bed, out of the room, out of Munich, out of Germany, out of Mariel's and Adam's lives for good.

Very slowly, and with infinite patience, Anne began to wriggle free of Mariel's embrace, peeling back the thin, strong arms, slipping out from beneath the shapely leg that straddled her. Mariel stirred and moaned and, like some sleepy baby putting thumb to mouth, her hand fumbled for the triangle between her legs, its arrival there seeming to quiet and comfort her. Mariel O'Sullivan: the ultimate sexual object, who had last night become for Anne the ultimate sexual subject, a girl who used her body without shame to get what she wanted – to destroy and manipulate.

Free at last, Anne looked down at her as she stood naked by the side of the bed among the discarded clothes. Then, with quiet determination and an increasingly steely resolve, she made for the shower.

No longer did it seem important whether or not Adam or Mariel were asleep or awake. She was her own person once more. Cold water was what she needed to purge her soul, to cleanse her body, to wash away the heavy scents of her own secretions which the younger girl had drawn from her like a honey-bee the pollen from some exotic flower. For five long minutes Anne stood beneath the icy stream, punishing herself, atoning for her sins. As every second passed she became stronger as the process of re-discovering herself continued. Like a butterfly escaping from its chrysalis, Anne was undergoing her own rebirth.

Dripping wet, she walked back into the room, impervious now to its connotations. From the closet she selected faded blue-jeans, white sneakers, a simple white T-shirt, a big Claude Montana leather jacket. She stepped into the soft Levis, the dampness of her body making it difficult to pull them over her tight bottom. Slowly and deliberately she did up the heavy silver conch belt. She didn't pack. They could have her clothes. Throw them away. Anything. She was starting afresh. A new day was dawning and she wanted nothing which could remind her of this disgusting little escapade.

Already Anne was building a wall which would contain the potential damage of the experience. It was a question of having the right attitude. Things couldn't harm you unless you let them. She would learn from her mistake and understand more about life, other people and herself as a result of it. That way she could avoid its repetition and emerge from disaster stronger than before. Defeat could be turned into victory. It was the winner's way.

She slipped her Cartier wallet into the pocket of the jacket, checking first for the Gold American Express card. Thank God for plastic money. Had there ever been a better invention?

At the door she paused. Lot's wife looking back? Pillar of salt time? Forget it. All Anne saw was the tail-end of a sad little scene. One in which, lightyears ago, briefly, she'd played a part. It was foreign to her now and it would never be repeated as long as she lived. The going had got tough and this fully paid-up member of a tough fraternity was getting going. During the taxi ride to the airport there were no regrets, during the two hour wait for the plane there were few recriminations. In more senses than one, Anne Carrington was going home at last.

To John Mitcham it seemed that he was dead already. The final act was in a way superfluous, dotting the 'i's, crossing the 't's, almost a pedantic afterthought. His suicide would be the ultimate admission to the fact he'd known for so long – that in any meaningful way he'd ceased to live many years before. John Mitcham's 'deadness' was, however, far from painless. From the tip of his head to the toes of his feet he hurt, the dull aching pain filling him up, unbearable, unremitting, constant. It prevented him from sleeping, made food taste like excrement, sapped his self-confidence, turned the slightest activity into the most Herculean of tasks. His energy and zest for life were but distant memories mocking his present misery. Yet he knew that in some way he'd deserved this dreadful retribution. It seemed appropriate that he, most miserable and pathetic of men, should have been singled out for this fate, and the guilt, global and ghastly, was the cruellest pain of all.

Not to be, that was the answer. Fortune's missiles he could, and would, withstand no more. Sleep. But he'd murdered sleep. A murderer, too. Murderer of himself, contaminator of good men and women, a burden to his wife and two children. Macbeth and Hamlet. The thoughts shot round his agitated mind. Great, silent tears of sadness flowed gently down his craggy cheeks as he thought of those he loved – had loved, anyway, before he'd become too evil, too wicked to love, unworthy of receiving love in return.

One of the big, wet tears fell upon a piece of paper at which he stared intently with unseeing eyes. With effort he focused on the blurred typewritten note, trying to take in the meaning of the words written there.

'So I must ask you to give your immediate attention

215

to this long overdue account, failing which I shall be forced to take legal action to recover these professional fees. I need hardly remind you of how much time and effort I put into your case, and of the considerable benefit you gained from treatment. The fact that you have seen fit, against my advice and in your own worst interests, to discontinue treatment, gives you no right to ignore my account.'

Aaron Ishmael's hard, tight signature brought the letter to an end.

Three thousand nine hundred dollars. John Mitcham couldn't have afforded $390. A million years ago he would've laughed at the bill – filed it in the wastepaper basket, told the pompous doctor in a cleverly worded letter to get knotted. But the laughter had long since died, helped to its demise by the painful insights into his own inadequacies which Ishmael's psychoanalysis had so relentlessly spotlighted. Today, his last day, John hadn't even the power to feel anger. The deadness had seen to that, strangling and suffocating his emotions with its icy touch. The only feelings that were left were self-destructive. He had no money to pay his doctor's bill. He was fifty-five and he had no money – in a land where to be poor represented the ultimate failure.

Emotionally blunted, his mind worked on. Irrational, half-crazed by his all-consuming grief, he fought to make sense of events, to see the way forward, to interpret what was happening to him. Although he could feel no hatred, he knew that Ishmael was the villain of the piece – to the extent that anyone but himself could be allowed to share the blame. The psychoanalysis had ruined him, both mentally and financially. His increasingly black mood had made him incapable of dealing with the harsh insights as Ishmael had stripped away the vulnerable defences of his psyche with an unfeeling and surgical precision. He'd wanted sympathy and understanding – the warmth that

Anne Carrington had imparted so generously – but he'd received only cold intellectual steel, hard and sharp. Sometimes he'd lie there weeping quietly, a man thirsty for comfort in a desert of sterile rationalizations, but Ishmael's tone had never softened.

As the depression had taken control, his decision-making capacity had vanished and with it his will to resist the powerful analyst. Slavishly he'd accepted that the expert knew best. After all, what did *he* know?

The bills had kept pace with the unpalatable and disturbing interpretations. Manfully he'd struggled to pay them. Sixty dollars an hour – the same rate as a prostitute. Could that be a coincidence? Twelve hundred dollars a month for four long, hard years. He'd borrowed from the bank, imagining that if he could just get himself together then his former money-making capacity would be restored and the loan could be repaid. Always Ishmael had divined improvement when he could feel none, and he'd allowed himself to be persuaded, sinking deeper into the quagmire of debt, feeling worse because of it. Finally his bank had called a stop, but it had been too late.

Anne Carrington had made all the difference. For a time he'd felt that she'd be able to save him. Now he knew she'd arrived too late. He remembered how she'd told him from the very beginning that there would be no charge for her treatment, and the enormous relief he'd experienced. But it had been more than just the money, more than the tablets. In Anne he'd sensed genuine concern, the humanity of a person who hadn't, like him, lost the ability to feel. Now he would be letting her down, and, as far as he was able, he felt sorry about that. What, he wondered, did doctors feel about patients who killed themselves? The truth was that John Mitcham was way past caring what anybody else thought. His own feelings of hopelessness claimed all of his limited powers of concentration.

Once again he read through the letter and between the lines saw it for what it was – the death warrant of John

Mitcham, wretched failure, miserable blot on the face of humanity, a man for whom even the most appalling fate would be too good. Then, somewhere deep within, a little flame of anger flared and was briefly directed outwards at the world that had done this to him. Aaron Ishmael was its recipient. Hardly knowing what he was doing, he snatched up a biro and scrawled across the letter, 'You killed me, and you try to charge me for my death.'

Then, slowly and steadily, as if attempting to conserve vital energy, John Mitcham stood up. The piece of paper stayed in his hand as if stuck to him and he looked down at it as if it was an alien object – at once important but also, paradoxically, irrelevant. With an impatient gesture he thrust it between some books on a shelf. He'd taken to doing that sort of thing recently. It seemed to represent some half-way house between filing and destroying, having the advantage of side-stepping the decision as to which course of action to follow.

Action – that was the answer. He had to take action, to fight against the raging torrents of despair, to dam them up, divert them from his tortured psyche. But action was so difficult – it was so hard to move, to do anything, even to think, perchance to dream. God, what was this ridiculous Shakespeare thing? The thoughts were coming in like bullets now. It was a change. For months his thoughts had been slowed, sometimes stopped altogether, as the dead-ness and lethargy had gripped him. John wondered what was happening. It was as if the letter had removed some blockage to the pent-up stream of ideas which now cascaded into his confused mind. The lead weights which had seemed attached to all his limbs now appeared lighter as he walked dreamily around the empty house, planning his resignation from an intolerable world.

Suicide, that was the word and that would be the verdict, the world's comment on his miserable little failure. John smiled bitterly. Was there an element of revenge in his action and in the violent method he'd already chosen? If so, against whom was it directed? Ishmael? No. Of course it would be against Mary. Once again tears filled his eyes at the thought of his young wife. God, he'd loved her in the days when love was possible, now lightyears away. Even through what Anne Carrington described as his 'illness' and Ishmael had insisted on calling his 'neurosis', she'd been the prime mover, the force that kept him struggling on against the black despair. At the same time it was she who had represented the pressure. All his worries had centred on her, and through her, on the children. For himself the financial problems were bearable. He didn't mind discomfort, selling the house, cutting back mercilessly on living standards, eating eggs and bread, staying at home for vacations. But Mary minded. God, how she minded. Appearances – neighbours, friends – those were the things that Mary cared about. He didn't blame her for that. Somehow it didn't seem to be her fault. Caring about the thoughts of others was built into her genes, as much a part of her as the colour of her deep blue eyes. In the beginning it had even been part of her charm. Her ambition, her bubbling enthusiasm for life and materialism had made the back-breaking hard work worthwhile, as together they'd planned their American Dream. But the cup of life had never been full enough for Mary. Try as he might, John had never been able to fill it up, and over the years the drink had acquired a bitter taste. He'd had to run just to stand still as the economy had nose-dived, and he'd borrowed to finance the expensive life-style to which they'd grown accustomed and which Mary was not prepared to, couldn't even, give up.

As the dreams began to fade with the realities of early dawn, the bickering and recriminations had started. She blamed him for his failure, for his mediocrity, for his ordinariness. That had been the problem, for John knew that all he'd ever been was an ordinary man with extraordinary ideas, ambitions beyond his status. Then of course she'd begun to castrate him, to break his balls and, obediently, he'd become impotent. Unable to afford Acapulco, unable to get it up. Gradually he'd come to see himself through Mary's disappointed eyes, and that was when the depression had begun to bite. He'd always been unworthy of her. She should have married a high-flyer. There had been one once, as Mary had never ceased to remind him. Well, now she'd have her chance. At the thought John Mitcham began to sob.

Self-pity began to surge through him. Why him? How had it come to this? Would he be brave enough for this act? Or would he botch it up as he'd botched up his life? Never had he believed it would come to this. It was wrong to kill yourself. Weak. But to do it was brave, too. Brave or weak, good or bad, to live or die. The questions would only be answered in the action. After, there would be no questions anymore, no answers. Nothing.

It was what he wanted – nothingness, an end to pain. It would be his gift to the living. He'd grant Mary and the kids freedom from the sentence of their lives with him, a chance to play in Aspen and Palm Beach, to be with and to become the rich and famous. Mary was so pretty. God, she was pretty. The men would . . . A strangled cry burst from John's lips. No medieval torturer, no inhuman interrogator could have beheld the agony he was suffering in the lonely house.

He'd show them his suffering. They should know about it. Mary, always so sensitive to the thoughts and opinions of others, should be aware of the feelings of her own husband. Perhaps, in the dreadful confrontation which was about to take place, she'd come to know him at last, understand the horror that was going on inside his head.

He walked to the cupboard where he kept the rope and his heart began to beat faster as his mind began to scream. Up the stairs. The knot tied roughly with sweaty, slippery fingers around the brown, polished banister rail. He peered down into the stairwell. Usually when he did this it was to see Mary peering up at him. 'John, telephone.' But Mary was with her mother. Wouldn't return until tomorrow. For John tomorrow was already an eternity away.

He put the other end of the rope round his neck. No hangman's noose, just a simple reef-knot.

Sitting on the banister rail, legs dangling into the well of the stairway, John Mitcham took one last inventory of his thoughts and was surprised to find that he didn't have any. And in this way, with a blank mind and the mild sensation of surprise, he propelled himself into oblivion.

Anne dialled Peter Isaacs' personal number the moment she was through the front door. Her mind still woolly from the long flight and dog-tired, she wanted him to know immediately that her ordeal was over, that from now on it was going to be all right, that he need worry no more.

Peter barked his hello. Damn, it didn't sound as if she'd caught him in a very good mood.

'Peter, it's Anne. You don't sound too kosher.'

'God, Anne, when did you get back? Never mind. Did you cancel John Mitcham for Wednesday? For God's sake, did you?'

The room began to revolve gently as the terrible feeling of impending doom spread upwards from Anne's stomach. The saliva in her mouth disappeared like a dew-drop in a sauna. She somehow knew what was coming, wanted to delay the awful truth.

'What's happened?' she managed at last.

'He's just hanged himself, at least he's just been found. We've got terrible trouble, Anne.'

Anne knew it all. Disaster stared her in the face. But even as her career and her solvency hovered on the brink of the abyss, she felt burning sorrow for the sad man whose life had been so dreadful that he'd freely chosen a violent death.

Peter was talking fast.

'The wife walked in and found him hanging in the

stairwell, incontinent of urine and faeces. Not a pretty sight. She called Ishmael and he went right round and cut him down. The wife's hysterical but apparently on the make already. Ishmael's stuffed dollar signs in her eyes, and already the place is crawling with lawyers. Ishmael's been on to me, wanting you. He says you're done for and he's glad. Says the wife's been advised to go for malpractice, and to go hard. He's already agreed to back their claim. Says he'll relish the job. The poor sod's still in the back room – hasn't even made it to the morgue yet – and they're talking millions in the lounge. Christ, you're in trouble, Anne. Why on earth did you cancel that fucking appointment?'

Anne forced her tired mind to think as adrenalin pumped through her.

'I've got to get round there immediately. You'd better come too as a witness to anything that's said. I'll pick you up at your place and update you on the circumstances on the way to the Mitcham house.'

'Yes, it's got to be done. You realize it'll be unpleasant. You're going to be called every name in the book, and a lot that aren't – that's if the wife doesn't try to assault you.'

Anne knew. Knew, too, that she'd have to see the body. Already there was guilt. Had she missed the warning signs of an impending suicide? Was there a connection with the cancelled appointment? Had Mitcham felt abandoned, revenged himself on her by his act? It was a situation far from unknown among psychiatrists. Had she been right to insist he discontinue the analysis, to put her faith in the antidepressants? With the benefit of hindsight many would conclude 'no'.

Anne needed to know the answers to all these questions, but there would be others who wanted answers as well. Malpractice – every doctor's nightmare. She had insurance but there was a limit. Anne couldn't remember what it was. If they went in really big and won she could be wiped out financially. Any verdict against her would be an irretrievable blight on her career. And there was the medical ethics question, too. Ishmael had promised to pursue that one mercilessly. If malpractice was proved, her crime would be compounded. There might even be the question of suspending her licence.

But at the back of Anne's mind was an even more unwelcome thought. When had John Mitcham died? Sometime over the weekend. But when, precisely? And what had she, Anne, been doing at the time? Had his misery, increased by loneliness, climaxed on Saturday night, or in the very early hours of Sunday morning at the very time when Anne had been lying on the big double bed at the Bayerischerhof with Mariel? She shuddered with disgust at the dreadful possibility.

Peter Isaacs, harassed, worried, was pacing the sidewalk outside his apartment building, anxious eyes scanning the street for signs of Anne's approach. When the taxi drew up he didn't waste any time on preliminaries and as he got in the words came spewing out of him.

'When exactly did you see him last?'

'Last Wednesday.'

'You were seeing him on a weekly basis?'

'Yes.'

'Was that wise?'

'Christ, Peter. I don't know. With the benefit of hindsight, apparently not. I didn't know he was going to top himself. You know how it is. It's always a risk. You can't have them sleeping in the office.'

Anne's tone was irritable. She was tired, angry, upset, sad and she felt guilty. Peter's attitude wasn't helping at all.

'Look, Anne, you know you've got to get used to people asking these questions. Prosecuting counsel is going to ask them. We can't lose this one. It'd be the end of everything. You know that.'

Peter was being brutal but it was all true, and Anne recognized it. Wearily she forced herself to remember the details as the grumbling taxi-driver headed for the suburbs and the Mitcham home.

'Did you question him about suicidal intentions during the last session?'

'Of course. As far as I can remember he said something like, "Oh no, I'd never do that".'

'Did you write that answer in your notes?'

'I'm sure I did, but I can't be one thousand per cent certain.'

Anne inwardly blessed that pedantic, almost obsessional side of her personality which dictated that she write everything down. At times like this it could be a life-saver. They'd go through her notes with a fine-tooth comb. If there was no mention of her asking about suicide, any court would assume that she'd omitted to ask the question. With a severely depressed patient that would amount to negligence. The case would be lost before it had even begun.

'Well, that's something.'

Peter was relieved. He knew Anne wouldn't have omitted the vital question in normal circumstances, would certainly have noted the answer to it, but these were far from normal times. The Adam thing had really unsettled her.

'How was his mental state?'

'As you can imagine, he was depressed, Peter. That was what I was treating him for, remember?' Immediately she regretted her sarcastic tone. Peter was right to ask. She knew what he meant.

'The most worrying aspect of his mental state was the guilt,' she continued. 'He felt he was a bad person all right, but it fell way short of the delusional.'

'What about alcohol?'

'Yes, he was hitting the martinis a bit.'

That was a bad sign. Fifteen per cent of suicides were

alcoholics. A far higher proportion had taken alcohol before the act.

'Was he particularly agitated? Any evidence of anger?'

'I can't remember a depressed patient who wasn't a bit anxious, but his was far from an agitated depression, if that's what you mean. Anger didn't seem to be a major factor in our sessions.'

'What made you decide against admitting?'

'He hadn't got insurance, wouldn't have dreamed of using a public facility. No way could he have paid the bills. That was one factor and an important one. And he was definitely improving. There was a good response to the medication. If he could've held on he would've been out of the woods in a couple of weeks. I suppose at the end of the day it's a gut instinct. He was obviously a risk, but I didn't think he was going to do it. He just didn't *feel* like a suicide, especially not at the last session. God knows what happened to tip him over.'

Peter was on to it in a flash.

'Could it have been your cancelling the session?'

'Unlikely, but yes, in the light of what we now know, I suppose it's an outside possibility.'

It was a weak point in her defence and they both knew it. There would be questions as to why the session had been cancelled. If the opposition went the whole hog and employed private investigators, all sorts of unpalatable creepy-crawlies might emerge from beneath the stone.

For a few minutes Peter and Anne sat in silence, digesting that one.

The taxi came to a shuddering halt. They had arrived.

John Mitcham's suburban house said a lot about him – and more about his wife. It wasn't exactly pretentious, wasn't luxurious enough for that, but it was formidably neat, unashamedly middle-class. There were clipped, symmetrical hedges, an ironed lawn and regimented rows of small, inoffensive flowers. Not grand itself, it stood close to much grander houses. Little fish in a big pond. The Mitchams were going to get as close as possible to the heavy cash. A closer look showed signs of financial strain. The paint was beginning to peel. Money needed spending on the roof. The car in the driveway was ten years old.

As she walked towards the front door, Anne took it all in. She knew what the monthly mortgage payments had done to John Mitcham, and it seemed to her that the prim garden, faded shutters and uneven roof were covered with a thin film of his blood. Inside there would be a stereo, a full wardrobe of expensive dresses, a video recorder – all paid for in the currency of John Mitcham's mental anguish. He was in pain no more, but the angst hadn't died with him. Like a relay-runner his race over, his energy spent, he'd passed on the baton of his agony. Anne had grasped it, was now the unwilling recipient of his unwanted legacy. It had ended his life – and threatened to do the same to Anne's career.

A dainty, refined chime sounded somewhere in the house as Anne pressed the bell. Almost immediately the door was opened. Mary Mitcham possessed the remains of what had been cheerful, if rather brittle, good looks. She was in her late thirties, possibly early forties and was locked in deadly combat with her advancing years.

Beneath the tight jeans and blue cashmere sweater was the body of a much younger woman, and Mary Mitcham worked hard keeping it that way. She wasn't going to surrender to Father Time without putting up a fight, or to anybody else for that matter. Beneath the neat fringe the blue eyes were cold and the down-turned mouth hinted at a formidable temper, if not semipermanent irritability. From the state of her makeup it looked as if she'd been crying, but a general air of steely purpose proclaimed that she was totally in control of herself and far from hysterical.

'I'm Dr Carrington. This is my partner, Dr Isaacs. We came as soon as we heard. I'm most terribly sorry . . .'

226

'You killed him,' said Mary Mitcham simply. It was a statement of fact. Two plus two equals four. No element of doubt clung to her words, hardly an insinuation of reproach. The situation was, for her, clear-cut and plain for all to see. Her husband was dead and the person who bore sole responsibility for his death was standing on her doorstep.

'I know how you must feel . . .'

Anne could guess exactly how Mary felt. Guilty. Unbearably guilty. So guilty that she wasn't prepared to accept the guilt. It had to be re-located, displaced. Anne was the obvious candidate.

'You'd better come in.' Anne was cut off in midsentence.

There were three men in the small living room. One, small, hook-nosed, closely resembling some unspecified but malevolent bird-of-prey was, Anne knew intuitively, her chief adversary Aaron Ishmael. The other two – neat suits, unremarkable faces, black attaché cases parked by the sides of their chairs – were obviously lawyers. It was not encouraging.

Anne took a deep breath and spoke first.

'I felt that I should come to see if there was anything I could do to help.'

Anne had known that she would be about as welcome as a fly in a jar of face cream, but it was vital that she did everything that could possibly be expected of her. Already she could imagine the prosecuting counsel's sarcastic tones.

'Am I to understand, Dr Carrington, that on hearing of your patient's death, a death, I shall argue, due in no small measure to your negligence and lack of professional competence, you took no steps to console the widow, offered no help at all?'

At Anne's entry into the room Aaron Ishmael had bounced excitedly out of his chair, gesticulating frantically with a well-used briar pipe.

'I can't believe your presence here will do anyone any

good,' he said rudely. 'We are at this moment in time discussing the appropriate action to be taken against you for the way in which you have mishandled this case.'

'It would certainly appear that there is a strong *prima facie* case for malpractice here,' agreed one of the lawyers as he, too, stood up. 'We have been retained to act for Mrs Mitcham and will be contacting you or your lawyers formally in due course.'

'Have the police been informed of my patient's death?' said Anne sharply. Nobody was going to browbeat her anymore. She'd had enough of that lately. If there was going to be a fight, she would fight tough.

'They came immediately. The body goes to the morgue in a couple of hours,' said Mary.

'Where is the body now?'

Mary gestured towards a door leading off the living room. All three men looked prepared to object but the determination in Anne's eyes quieted them. She was going to say goodbye to John Mitcham, and nobody was going to stop her.

In the gloomy twilight of the den, John Mitcham was lying beneath a white sheet on a studded leather Chesterfield. A layer or two of old newspapers separated the corpse from the worn leather. The stench of faeces and urine explained the necessity for that. Despite her medical training, the long hours in anatomy dissecting rooms picking over the entrails of greasy cadavers, fighting back waves of nausea and enduring the appalling smell of the formaldehyde, Anne had never really got used to the physical side of medicine. Few psychiatrists ever had. People were people to her, not merely bodies or lists of symptoms. She turned back the sheet.

Death by strangulation. Never a pretty sight. It was almost impossible to conceive how anybody could have chosen this method of dying, its violent eloquent testimony to the mental horrors which had precipitated the desire for death. Few who hadn't experienced it could begin to understand the quality of that suffering. But Anne knew, had recognized the anguish during her psychiatry post at medical school at Johns Hopkins when the other medical students had appeared impervious to it. From that moment on she had been driven by a burning ambition to destroy that most subtle and unbearable of pains before it consumed and destroyed the sufferer. There had been many successes. Now she was confronted by a spectacular failure. She wanted to see it, to learn from it – she knew that she mustn't shrink from it.

There it was. The end product of depression, most terrible of illnesses in which the very soul of man was scarred and bruised. The eyes, fish-like, protruding and blood-shot were rolled up as if in those last terrible moments John Mitcham had been trying to read some ghostly graffiti on the ceiling, its inscrutable message never to be revealed. His face was still predominantly blue, gorged and full, distended with the unoxygenated blood as the noose had cut off venous return from his head. But already the red cells were beginning to break down, releasing their coloured pigments, and the blue was already infiltrated with yellows, greens and browns so that his face looked bruised and battered. His mouth was distorted, lips pulled back over uneven teeth as they had in vain tried to form the soundless scream. The rope was still in position, buried deep in rolls of fat around his neck, defying removal without cutting into the surrounding skin. Both forearms lay across his chest, rock-solid with rigor mortis, hands clasping pointlessly at the buried rope as, in reflex action, John Mitcham had attempted to put a stop to his dance of death.

Anne could visualize the churning legs, the fight for breath, could imagine the mounting panic, the final moment when it had all gone 'pop' deep inside John Mitcham's brain. A great wave of sympathy welled up within her as she remembered the kindly, craggy-faced stockbroker with the cares of the world on his shoulders.

His death had placed her in peril, but she bore him no malice and her heart went out to the restless spirit which had inhabited this broken and empty shell, this grotesque caricature of a human being. Fighting back her tears, she bade him a silent farewell, apologized to his wandering soul for her failure to help him.

She didn't stop to trade insults or threats with the grim little crowd in the living room. Instead, Peter gathered into her wake, she made for the front door. There might be many theories about who was to blame for John Mitcham's suicide. As far as Anne was concerned both Mary Mitcham and Aaron Ishmael were the prime contenders.

Paula was getting tired of telling Adam Phipps that Dr Carrington was unavailable. First there had been the flowers. For two weeks, she imagined, he'd turned the rooms of every hospital patient in the Big Apple into instant florist shops. The drag had been that it had been her job to re-locate the floral tributes to Dr Carrington to the rooms of the city's needy. Now there was the telephone assault. Five or six times a day she had the job of fending off the telephonic kamikaze attack, and she was fed up to the teeth with it.

'May I speak to Dr Carrington?' said Adam, his voice achieving the monotony of a recording with the constant repetition of his request.

Damn, it was the pissed-off secretary again.

'As I've told you before, Mr Phipps, Dr Carrington is busy and cannot speak with you.' The intimation was as clear as it had been all morning. Anne had left instructions that she didn't want Adam's calls put through.

Adam sat down heavily on the sofa. The last two weeks hadn't been good. When he'd woken from his drunken stupor in the Munich hotel room to find a triumphant Mariel crowing at Dr Carrington's humiliation, he'd reacted violently. Although his eyes had been thick and bleary, he'd seen through her as clearly as through the uncertain manipulations of a three year old. Mariel had intended that he despise Anne for her sexual abandonment. Well, she'd got it wrong. He despised only one person – Mariel O'Sullivan.

He'd watched her wake, beautiful and deadly, and seen the mischievous smile play round the full lips as she looked round the room and took in the fact that Anne had gone, that her scheme had worked. And he'd heard the hungover, sexily husky voice drawl,

'Hey, baby, where's the psychiatrist? Christ, did she come like a ton of fucking bricks. Years since I saw a chick have an orgasm like that. Wonder if they teach them how to do it in med school.'

Adam had hit her with the flat of his hand, hard, across the face, and wiped the smile from her lips. There and then he'd told her to get out of his life, to blow, get lost, to return to the gutter from which she'd crawled.

In those few short hours he'd lost both the women in his life. One of them he wanted back. But it was beginning to look like that increasingly strong desire was going to be insufficient to bring about its objective.

In the earliest days of their relationship Anne had been a plaything, a brand new toy, an exotic status-symbol, an ego-boosting experience – but he'd grown to love her. Now, the memory of her passion, of their lovemaking, the superb contours of her sculpted body and secret scents filled his consciousness. He remembered, too, her kindness, her concern, her empathy and sympathy – the delicious way she laughed, the way she discharged her professional duties, her vulnerability, her child-like enthusiasm at the Oktoberfest. And then there was her amazing mind – inventive, analytic, filled with remarkable information, interesting and interested, absorbing and absorbed.

Adam had come to see that his initial reaction to his discovery of Anne and Mariel together had been horribly

231

inappropriate. He'd been shocked, terribly shocked, but now he had a more accurate perspective. He'd lost count of the times over the last two years that Mariel had organized similar 'scenes', and he'd always been an enthusiastic voyeur. What possible right had he to be angry? Anne hadn't been to blame. She'd been hopelessly manipulated, outmanoeuvred by a mistress of the art. She'd been a stranger to the wanton and dangerous hedonism of his world. He'd wanted her to join it, and she'd tried enthusiastically to do just that. It was his fault, not hers.

He had to talk to her. To explain himself. To apologize. But how could he penetrate the wall she'd erected around herself? He loved her. That was it, that would be enough. He'd never loved anyone before. She'd have to accept his love. It would make everything all right.

He picked up the telephone once more. Paula's truculent voice answered.

'If you'll put this call through to Dr Carrington's private office I'll give you $25,000 in cash,' he said firmly. 'This is Adam Phipps calling.'

He heard the sharp intake of breath over the telephone as Paula weighed the options. The internal debate didn't last long.

'Putting you through,' she warbled.

'Dr Carrington speaking.' The voice was cool, a little crisp. Usually Paula introduced the caller. For some reason this time she'd omitted to do so. Another black mark for the tricky secretary.

'Anne, it's Adam. I'm sorry to break through to you like this. I had to talk to you, to say how sorry I am.'

Anne fought back the desire to slam the telephone down. She'd tried to escape this part but somehow she realized it had always been unavoidable. She said nothing.

Internally she audited her feelings. What was there? Was her anarchic spirit still in chains after the counter-revolution? Did reason rather than emotion still rule her world? Over the past two weeks she'd thought a lot about Adam,

232

but she'd thought of other things more. He'd been replaced, to some extent devalued, in her affections. There were other far more pressing considerations, like the Mitcham case. But the storm of passion had left its legacy of destruction, and lingering memories of its raw power remained. How would she react to him, either on the telephone or in person? Apparently, calmly.

'Hello, Adam,' she said.

'Anne. I must see you. Please let me. I know I've really blown it, but I want to make it up to you. I really need to see you. I've been so miserable. I love you, Anne. I love you.'

The wave of his declared affection broke precipitously against the sea-wall of Anne's iron resolve.

'There was a time for all that, Adam. I'm afraid it's over. It's finished, completely finished.'

'No, Anne. It's not. It's not over. Don't say that. Please don't say that.' There was a catch in his voice.

Anne softened up a little.

'What happened in Germany wasn't important. It was just a symptom. I can't be involved in your sort of life. My own is too important to me. It wasn't your fault. You aren't responsible for my inadequacies. But I intend to make sure that I never let things get out of control again. So for us it's over, Adam. You've got to come to terms with that.'

'No, no. I don't want that. I need you, Anne. Please don't block me out. Please don't. I need your help. I can't live without you.'

'Adam, Adam, don't.' Anne experienced an uncomfortable feeling in her chest at his naked appeal. She steeled herself inwardly.

'Listen, Adam. It's just that I can't deal with my own life and yours at the same time. I tried to and it's been a dismal failure. You've got to understand that. Surely you can see that.'

'But if we start again we can change all that. Give me another chance. Please. Just let me see you. I know we can work it out. I've got rid of Mariel. She's not around anymore. And it would be just us. Nobody else. You've got to see me.'

She had to let him down gently, but firmly.

'Adam, if you care at all about me you've got to leave me alone for a bit. Give me some breathing space. Who knows, maybe another time, sometime in the future we could be friends and laugh about all this. For now it's impossible. Too much has happened for me to let you back into my life. You must promise not to see me again, or try to contact me. Will you promise me that?'

'Oh, *God*,' sobbed Adam. 'Please change your mind. Please, for my sake.'

'Goodbye, Adam. Help me to be strong,' said Anne.

She hung up.

She had handled it well, let him down gently. But why the hell were her hands shaking?

Chapter Seven

At the best of times door-opening in New York City was a not unhazardous occupation – the more so when the door guarded the entrance to an apartment containing the extraordinary art treasures which Adam Phipps had accumulated. To minimize the risk of uninvited guests, a set procedure had been worked out: potential visitors had to present themselves to Frank the doorman in the lobby. Through the video hook-up the hall porter would announce their names to Wan-Tu while they waited in the downstairs anteroom. On this occasion there was no exception to that rule. Over the closed-circuit TV Frank said quite clearly, 'Mr Templeman and Mr Waterfield to see Mr Adam Phipps, on introduction from Mr Charles Phipps.' It was true that Frank had sounded a little strange, but then Wan-Tu put that down to his well-known drinking habits. Clearly old Frank's thickness of voice was the result of over-indulgence at lunchtime.

Little did Wan-Tu know that Frank's introduction was made under duress, and the snub-nosed ·38 that Fritz had pointed at his right temple from just outside camera-range was indeed duress.

Routine procedure in such circumstances required that Adam now be approached with the news of his visitors' arrival to discover whether or not he was 'in'. However, Adam Phipps was locked in his computer room, having given instructions that he wasn't to be disturbed 'on any account'. Past experience dictated that this command wasn't to be disobeyed lightly.

So the oriental was faced with something of a dilemma. Mr Templeman and Mr Waterfield could be asked to go away in view of the fact that Mr Phipps was 'out'. But their business might be important. After all, they came with an introduction from Mr Charles, always a difficult person to ignore and ever-ready to take offence. Clearly some sort of compromise was called for. The two gentlemen might, for instance, be invited up, given a drink and placed effectively 'on ice' until Mr Phipps emerged from his den. That decided, Wan-Tu hardly gave it a second thought. Like many of his race he believed in fate. He was correct to do so: it was to be a fateful decision.

'Send them up,' he said into the intercom as the TV screen went blank. In terms of their immediate effect, his words might well have been 'kill him instantly'.

Without a second's hesitation, Mickey took a step forward and, with a little grunt of triumph, plunged the six-inch stiletto blade into the doorman's solar plexus. For a second Frank stood his ground. Why had he been hit in the stomach? He'd done what they wanted. Why were they beating him up? And then, suddenly, he felt very faint, very far away, light-headed, a rushing in his ears. He was floating on air, first speeding down a dark tunnel and then inexplicably soaring, flying up into the air, above the building, above the city. Quite clearly he heard someone say, 'Is he dead?' And somebody else reply, 'You'd better believe he's dead.' Frank believed them. They were telling the truth. He *was* dead.

At the door of the apartment Wan-Tu had a brief moment of doubt. Checking the two men on the monitor, he didn't quite like what he saw. It wasn't that they looked odd, more that they appeared nondescript, anonymous, lacking that indefinable aura of money and class which characterized the majority of visitors to the Phipps apartment. Still, he was only a poor bloody foreigner who still hadn't even come close to understanding the natives. Maybe he'd got it wrong.

The instant the door was open he realized he'd got it right.

'Where's Phipps?' said Mickey shortly.

The 'Mr' was conspicuous by its absence.

'I am afraid Mr Phipps is tied up for the moment,' Wan-Tu offered hopefully. 'If you would like to wait . . .'

He had to bluff this out. Who *were* these people? Policemen? Denizens of the shadowy drug world in which Mr Adam liked occasionally to immerse himself?

When the knife appeared in Mickey's hand, Frank's blood was still all over it and instinctively Wan-Tu knew its source. It hadn't been Jack Daniel's which had made Frank's voice shake. Suddenly, he found himself thinking of Formosa, of his wife and four small children, whose sole ambition it was to join him in America the moment he was awarded the precious prize of citizenship.

Mickey stepped in close and nuzzled the sharp point of the blade up against Wan-Tu's chest. His voice hissed through clenched teeth.

'Show me where he is this second, you frigging little chink, or you're chop-suey – so help me.'

Wan-Tu knew that he was in mortal danger and that the odds were heavily against him. But he didn't panic.

'I'll take you to him,' he said, trying to disguise the naked terror which leaped and jumped within him.

At the door of the computer room he paused, the blade of the knife scraping greedily at the side of his neck like some hungry animal which had decided perversely to toy with its prey.

'Mr Phipps. Mr Phipps!' he called insistently.

For a long moment, an eternity, there was no sound from within.

'Mr Phipps. Mr Phipps.' Wan-Tu shouted more loudly as the steel scratched and pricked at his neck, its shaft vibrating in tune with his quivering vocal chords.

Adam flung the door open.

'Wan-Tu, I've told you before . . .' The explosion of anger died in his throat at the sight in front of him.

Wan-Tu, his formerly yellow, parchment skin now a

peculiarly unhealthy shade of grey, stood quaking in the doorway, the gory knife plastered tight against his throat.

Mickey spoke fast, urgently. 'Adam Phipps?'

Adam nodded and fought to stay calm.

'You have a computer program, stored on tape. One which predicts stock-market movements. I want it. *Now*.'

The adrenalin surged through Adam, speeding his thought processes. The disc. The market disc. Charles Phipps. They were going to steal his program. He'd deny he had it. Say it was in the bank. Say he'd destroyed it. He'd prepared for this moment. The program by itself was useless. The vital weighting information was stored in his memory, where nobody could get at it. He'd tell them that.

Mickey watched Adam's thoughts as they tumbled incoherently through his consciousness. He had a contingency plan for such anticipated resistance. Mickey's left hand snaked out and upwards to grab Wan-Tu by the hair. Roughly he jerked the unfortunate butler's head backwards, exposing his straining neck, the full jugular vein. Everybody knew what was about to happen and the dreadful horror of anticipation gave to the moment a strange surreality, the movements of each proceeding with clockwork precision, as if each member of the group in some perverse way willed the terrible conclusion.

Adam saw Wan-Tu's eyes pop wide open, his pupils dilate with anguish, his lips purse for the scream which would never come – saw, too, over his shoulder the cold, expressionless eyes of the psychopathic killer, took in the excited flush on the cheeks of his accomplice. Adam knew he had to find words to avert the catastrophe, but even as he searched for them he realized that they didn't exist. They could have his disc, but it wouldn't save Wan-Tu – probably wouldn't save him, either. And so, like a mesmerized rabbit, he watched the blade embark on its slow-motion journey across his butler's exposed throat, saw the thin red pencil line of blood widen and then gape as it sliced effortlessly through the tissues and stared in fascinated impotence at the thick crimson stream which began to spurt and bubble from the awful wound, listening spellbound to the gurgling, suffocating sound as his servant drowned in his own blood on the carpet in front of him.

Rooted to the spot, Adam fought against the nausea and faintness which threatened to engulf him.

From some distant alien place he heard his own voice say,

'I can give you the disc, but it's useless without the weightings.'

It was his reflex bid for survival. If they thought the disc was enough by itself they'd kill him there and then. Wan-Tu would reach heaven just long enough before him to open the door. The perfect butler, even in death.

'I know,' said Mickey with a sadistic leer. 'Your uncle told us. You'll probably want to tell us all about it.'

As he spoke Mickey launched himself forwards and aimed a vicious kick at the head of the lifeless corpse at his feet. Adam heard the sickening crunch of broken bones, a dead man's bones, as he felt his legs begin to crumple and the bile rise in his gullet. Then, mercifully, the carpet came to his rescue. Miraculously it launched itself up off the floor and rushed up to meet his face. He buried his head in it gratefully, sinking into it, escaping to a safe haven from the horror which had invaded his world.

What was it Hitler had said about lawyers? Anne tried to remember. Something about not resting until there wasn't one left in Germany. That didn't seem a bad idea. This desk jockey was really getting to her. OK, so it wasn't wise to pretend there were no weaknesses in her case, but there were limits. This man's tongue dripped neat, undiluted pessimism. The way he was laying it down, it looked as if Anne had actually strangled John Mitcham, or at least had bought him the rope.

'Of course, the plaintiffs are going to emphasize your

self-appointed role as the scourge of the psychodynamists. I gather from sources within your profession that you've been quite vocal on that one. And quite recently, too.'

Anne groaned inwardly. Some prick of an office boy had dug out the scurrilous *Daily News* story. For sure no one had bothered to check-out the original *Journal* article to discover what she'd really said. Anne was beginning to lose her temper. For the moment she was just about managing to hang on.

Some warning gleam in Anne's eye led the attorney to offer a brief defence of his tactic.

'The thing to do is always to peer at the case through the eyes of the opposition. That way we're ready for anything It's a useful exercise, especially in a situation like this in which they appear to be holding so many trump cards.'

There he goes again, thought Anne. What was he trying to do? Probably trying to get her to agree to an out-of-court settlement. Admit negligence. Pay up and shut up. The overweight lawyer would do a bit of wheeling and dealing, have a liquid lunch with his opposite number and then put in an eye-watering account without having to go through any of the hassle of preparing a court case. Everybody would be pleased. Ishmael, Mary Mitcham. The psychodynamic fraternity. But *she* would be guilty. No way was she going to fall in with *that* plan. She'd fight every inch of the way – in court and out – to preserve her reputation and career. She was right and she'd prove she'd been right all along.

Anne waved her hand wearily, signalling for the lawyer to continue his dreary monologue. To a certain extent he had a point: it might be painful but it was important to anticipate the effect of the plaintiff's case on the jury. That was always hard to predict, but the photographs of John Mitcham's corpse would be powerfully emotive. Human reaction would be to look for a scapegoat. Who better than an overpaid doctor?

'I suppose that one of the aces they hold – if I might

extend the playing card analogy – is that you saw fit to cancel the appointment on the day before the suicide. I think I'm right in saying that you did this because you were travelling abroad with a young man-about-town of considerable means and of a certain notoriety.'

He picked up on the surprise and outrage in Anne's eyes. Apparently a bit of back-peddling was in order.

'I hope you don't mind my mentioning this aspect of the case. Certainly it must appear to be an intrusion into your private life. However, the existence of this . . . affair . . . is, I am told, well known to certain of the society columnists. The plaintiff's attorney would be incompetent if he didn't know, too. May I ask how you met Mr Phipps?'

Peter Isaacs, protective instincts strongly stimulated, leaped in. Without hesitating he lied outright.

'I introduced them,' he said simply, in a voice which brooked no argument.

Luckily the lawyer failed to pursue the matter. It was obvious he had no idea at all of the circumstances of Anne and Adam's meeting. Peter decided to follow up.

'And I can't see how this friendship is relevant to the case. Nobody suggested, nor can they legitimately suggest, a connection between the cancellation of the appointment and the suicide itself. Psychiatrists often have to cancel sessions, and of course the patient's themselves are always cancelling. Mitcham himself cancelled a total of four times. It's no big deal.'

The lawyer puffed himself up like a toad.

'With respect,' he intoned, his manner clearly indicating that respect was in fact neither due nor felt, 'that may well be the case. However, I suspect it won't be the way a jury sees it. They expect their doctors to earn the very high fees they charge – not to short-change their patients.'

Peter exploded with rage.

'But this doctor wasn't charging her patient one red cent. She was giving away valuable time for free. One wonders how many times you yourself work for charity.'

The lawyer reddened. It was certainly true that Anne's generosity would work for her. On the other hand, the opposition would argue that Mitcham had in fact paid the highest price of all for his reliance on Anne Carrington's expertise.

Anne smiled across the polished mahogany table at Peter. How had she deserved him? He was one hundred per cent behind her, as he'd always been.

The insurance company representative, quiet for some time, decided to put his oar in.

'To my mind, the great strength of the plaintiff's case is the aggressive stance being taken by Aaron Ishmael. It would appear that he's an outstandingly charismatic figure, and a very powerful one. He can produce documentary evidence in terms of the letter he wrote you of his prediction that the precipitous ending of therapy would be disastrous for his patient.'

It was a good point. Ishmael's finger of suspicion had indeed been pointed before the 'crime' had been committed. Capital would be made out of that. But it could be answered.

'I don't think there's much problem about exposing Ishmael's motivation in all this. He's a self-centred, self-important man, whose methods and approach to treatment had been called into question. Mitcham's depression was going biological. My notes prove that. I know we can put up powerful expert witnesses who will say it is negligent, cruel, little short of malpractice to deny such people medication and to keep them in analysis. I'm sure we can get the Johns Hopkins professor to attest to that – probably the Harvard one, too.'

As Anne spoke she realized she wasn't carrying half her audience with her.

The lawyer, unwilling to surrender his pessimistic approach, answered her point.

'To a certain extent what you say is true. If this business comes to court the wider issue is going to revolve round the talk therapy versus physical treatment controversy. The problem is that this argument has never been convincingly decided before, and it isn't going to be decided now. The jury will go for the bottom line. The treatment may have been well intentioned, but the dead body says it didn't work. And Ishmael said it wouldn't work beforehand. You can't get away from that.'

'But the fact that the pills didn't "work" isn't the same thing as saying that to prescribe them was malpractice. Our experts will say it wasn't,' interjected Peter.

'And theirs will say it was. Stalemate.'

The lawyer judged that the time was ripe to make his play.

'My opinion, and that of one or two of my colleagues, is that we might do well to settle this thing out of court. Keep it as quiet as possible. If we make them an offer in this early stage, before things get out of hand, positions too entrenched, we might well get away more lightly than if we go to trial. Frankly, I think there's a better than even chance the jury will find against us, perhaps spectacularly so.'

He leaned back watching Anne closely. He didn't really expect her to go for it. She didn't.

'There was no malpractice,' she said quietly, 'and I'm damned if I'll say there was when there wasn't.'

The lawyer and the insurance man exchanged furtive glances. At last the lawyer spoke.

'I'm not quite sure that you understand the situation, Doctor. You see, I'm employed by your insurance company to represent you and to give you my advice.' He inclined his head towards an increasingly uncomfortable-looking insurance executive. 'If the company takes the view, on my advice, that our position is a poor, if not hopeless one, then it's their duty to their shareholders to obtain the most advantageous settlement possible in the circumstances. I'm sure you see the logic in that.'

Anne saw the logic all too clearly. Her reputation was to

be sacrificed for the company's bottom line. So much for all those years of premiums. She had as much chance of winning the case with this attorney as of making it to the moon on gossamer wings.

She made the decision at once, without thinking of the consequences, and stood up abruptly.

'Gentlemen,' she said curtly, 'our dealings are at an end. I don't want to be represented by you, or by anybody else you may want to appoint. I'll hire my own counsel and pay for my own defence. I don't think there is anything else to say except that, if you'll excuse me, I have patients to look after. I'm sure you have other more pressing business to attend to.'

Her pronunciation of the word 'business' carried with it the unmistakable inference of sordid, grimy activities.

Peter got to his feet as a warm glow of admiration spread through him. It was her finest hour. Horatio at the bridge. She'd just sacked her lawyer, but more importantly, she'd also fired her paymaster. How the hell would she finance the case? It could cost her millions, even if she won. She'd be in hock for the rest of her life. But that was of subsidiary importance compared with the matter of principle on which she wasn't prepared to compromise. She wasn't guilty and wasn't about to say she was, whatever the financial advantages of so doing. No wonder he loved her. Perhaps even more, now that she'd demonstrated her frailty, shown that she was human after all, stepped briefly from her ivory tower to commune with lesser mortals. As he thought, hope surged once again through Peter. He would have her yet. By providing the shoulder to lean on during her greatest crisis, he could build up a credit which she might be prepared to repay with her love.

As they both turned haughtily and left the conference room, Peter felt better than he had in years. Together they would pull through this. Anne had done no wrong. If she was found guilty of malpractice it would be a total travesty of justice. To avoid that miscarriage any behaviour would be justified. Somehow, somewhere it could be proved that Anne was not responsible for Mitcham's suicide. But how? Where was the evidence?

The judicial machine, normally grinding like the mills of God at a snail's pace, had acquired for once super mobility. The trial of Mary Mitcham *v.* Dr Anne Carrington had been wedged into a recently vacated spot two short weeks ahead, and neither plaintiff nor defendant had objected to the unaccustomed speed of the judiciary. The plaintiffs, confident that they could prove malpractice beyond a reasonable doubt, saw no reason to delay the huge financial settlement they anticipated. They were eager for blood, Ishmael the enthusiastic conductor of the orchestra of retribution. Anne, too, wished matters to be brought to an immediate head. She was still without an attorney, and was playing with the idea of conducting her own defence. She'd have to rely on the testimony of the expert witnesses she would call.

Naïve in the ways of the legal world, she'd failed to grasp the nature of the adversary system of American justice. She knew she wasn't guilty, and therefore was not unduly worried that a jury would find her so. Right would triumph in the end. It was the American way. The opposition, however, had demonstrated a less worldly view of things. Through their distorting spectacles they, too, thought themselves to be in the right, but they'd taken the precaution of speculating in order to accumulate. Out of their anticipated winnings, a substantial sum had been set aside for the hiring of James Masterson III, the silver-tongued attorney who'd been known to reduce the most respected and erudite of witnesses to bundles of blabbering humanity, mouthing desperate and incoherent rubbish in response to his cunning questions.

Both Peter Isaacs and Anne Carrington, giants in their own profession, had misunderstood the fact that a courtroom was little more than a theatre in which the jury were an audience, who would applaud the best and most flamboyant actor. In this area Anne had no expertise, John Masterson III buckets. And so, while Peter and Anne sat after work in their office discussing the strengths of their case, they had little real conception of the incredible weakness of their position.

'Smith of Johns Hopkins will have them for breakfast,' said Peter confidently. 'Can you imagine what would happen if an intern suggested treating biological depression with psychoanalysis on one of his ward rounds? There'd be blood on the walls.'

Anne could imagine. It would not be a pretty sight. She warmed to the theme.

'And the psychoanalytic jargon will be totally incomprehensible to any of the jurors.'

The knock on the door was insistent.

'Come in,' said Peter absentmindedly.

Paula had a strange look on her face, her cheeks flushed with excitement. In her hand she clutched a copy of *The Daily News*, which she thrust at Anne without a word.

The headlines screamed up off the page: PHIPPS HEIR ABDUCTED: TWO SLAIN. Her eyes raced over the article as Peter peered at her quizzically. Her heart rate took off into the stratosphere.

The newspaper concentrated on the gory nature of the murders and contained little in the way of hard information. It was obvious to the police and to the FBI, who had been immediately called in, that Phipps had been kidnapped. Everyone was expecting a ransom note, and in the meantime were playing a waiting game.

'Adam Phipps has been kidnapped. The butler and the doorman were murdered,' she managed at last in answer to Peter's look.

Peter stood up immediately and went to her. That was all she needed after the horror of the Mitcham suicide.

Christ! Couldn't the little turd have got himself kidnapped some other time? He put a steady hand on Anne's shoulder.

'My God, how awful. Poor Adam,' Anne said. But inside she was already deep in prayer.

Adam felt the scream begin in the deepest depths of his bowels. Chased mercilessly by the white, searing pain which had been its cause, it travelled upwards to make its escape. Within inches of freedom, however, its exit was block by an old and far from clean rag. And so the scream and the pain collided in a maelstrom of violence, a sizzling cauldron of horror which exceeded his mind's capacity to process. Hovering on the borders of consciousness, Adam lay motionless, scarcely able to struggle against the ropes which bound him.

'Sock it to him, Mickey,' said Fritz, cheerleader to violence. But Mickey needed no encouragement. No encouragement at all.

Like some deranged musician, he played Adam's body like a drum, regretting only that the sound-accompaniment was lacking. For that he had to rely on his imagination, a delicate, poor, truncated thing. Luckily, he could both see and feel when the pain was biting hardest, knew when he could relax his efforts because at such times Adam would escape briefly into unconsciousness.

He hadn't even bothered to ask for the information he was being paid to extract. On the principle that actions spoke louder than words, a little pain was worth a dictionary, and Mickey had never been much of a talker anyway. After this, Adam would probably offer the computer weightings without being asked. He wouldn't be strong enough to go through it a second time.

The evening papers and the TV news services had no progress to report on the Phipps kidnapping. A ransom note, widely expected, hadn't been forthcoming and already some of the more inventive journalists, ever searching for some new and saleable angle which might increase the circulation of the rags for which they worked, were beginning to allow their imaginations to run riot. Had Phipps really been kidnapped? Perhaps he was the murderer himself, or was involved with the killers. Could it be some sort of a drug killing? Angel Dust, perhaps? Everybody knew rich-kid freaks were into everything these days. Free-basing, snowballs, magic mushrooms.

Anne's day had been a nightmare, and by early evening she was feeling no better. A kidnap had seemed the obvious explanation. In Europe, of course, it was as common as nose-picking. Every half-penny Greek shipowner, had his own personal bodyguard, and one for each of his children. Sooner or later it had been bound to cross the Atlantic, and what more obvious target than someone like Adam? Any minute now a ransom note could be expected, plus, probably, a bit of Adam. Nothing essential. A fingertip, an earlobe. Just enough to concentrate the minds of those who held the purse strings. The thought had made Anne's blood run cold, but it hadn't stopped her mind from working.

All day long she'd felt that her subconscious had been trying to tell her something. It was an irritating, nagging feeling, the knowledge that you had forgotten something important but couldn't remember what it was. The more she tried to isolate it and to shine the search-light of consciousness upon it, it scurried away, out of reach of the beam. She knew something about Adam's abduction. Something vitally important. Something that could save him, but what the *hell* was it?

Throughout the long afternoon the feeling had persisted. She'd tried to make her mind go blank, to think of other things, to free-associate, but it had all been to no avail. She was no nearer to the solution of the frustrating problem.

She'd already contacted the police department, offering

to help, and had been referred to the FBI, who were now handling the case. Peabody, the officer heading the investigation, had been polite but patronizing.

'Don't worry, lady. This is being looked after at the highest level, you know. The Phipps family are heavy-hitters in this town. It has to be kidnap. For sure he wouldn't have known the abductors. We should have a ransom note soon. We can't do much until we do.'

It had made sense. You couldn't search every corner of New York State. Every policeman had a picture of Adam. That had certainly been handled at high speed. And you couldn't turn on the TV without seeing his face. Somebody was buying up prime-time like it was packets of peanuts. Uncle Charles probably. Uncle Charles. Uncle Charles. Uncle Charles Phipps. Charles Phipps, who'd made a stock-market killing, according to the man at the Le Relais bar. Charles Phipps, who'd had a furious row with his nephew about some computer program which was useful in predicting the movements in the Dow-Jones Industrials. Charles Phipps, who liked to fuck her hysterical patient Skip Demery, who kept him in a Village love nest, who, on his nights off, according to Demery, wasn't averse to a little S and M in the downtown leather-bars. The pieces of the puzzle slipped neatly into place. Anne had broken the mystery which had plagued her all day. Christ. That could just be it. Charles Phipps had his nephew kidnapped for the market information he could provide. Normally he'd be above suspicion, but Anne knew about his little peccadilloes, about his squalid, secret life. He was the man with the motive, and his sexual forays into the homosexual underworld suggested he had unsavoury friends. Friends, perhaps, who for a fee might be prepared to help Phipps get what he wanted. It was still a long-shot, but it was definitely a lead.

With shaking fingers Anne punched the intercom on her desk. Paula answered.

'Paula, read me out Skip Demery's number.' Anne could

scarcely hide the excitement in her voice. She checked herself. This had to be handled incredibly carefully. If she let Skip think that he had valuable information, and that she wanted it, he'd run all round the houses to avoid giving it to her.

The thin, mincing voice answered immediately.

'Skip, this is Dr Carrington.'

'Well, *hello*. To what do I owe the honour of this call? Don't say you're going to cancel me, Doctor. My ego just couldn't stand to be cancelled at the moment.'

Anne laughed and tried to sound casual.

'No way. No, I was just ringing up to see how you were, to check things out.'

She sensed the immediate suspicion in his voice when he replied.

'How very kind. But what's up, doc? You don't usually do that.'

'Well, I just thought that with this Phipps thing going on that Charles Phipps might be under a lot of pressure, and that you might be getting some of the fallout.'

'Don't even *talk* to me about that piece of *shit*,' Skip screamed theatrically into the mouthpiece. That meant, 'Talk to me as much as you like about him. I've got all day.' Great. Anne had got there.

'What's he done now, Skip?'

'The frigging, warped little toad. I tell you, the next time he comes round here I'm going to put his balls in the liquidizer and drink 'em in a piña colada. Can you believe he hasn't called me, not even fucking *called* me for two-and-a-half weeks? Can you believe the *gall* of the asshole? The runt, the rotten stinking *faggot*.'

'He must have a lot on his mind right now with this kidnapping.' Anne tried to sound reasonable rather than devious.

'He doesn't even *have* a mind. All he has is a butt and a miserable apology for a prick. I can't even get hold of him. His answering service is full of *shit* and his rat-bag of a secretary pretends he's busy all the time. I tell you, the only time that *pervert* is busy is when he's taking a length from some off-duty policeman.'

That was getting warm. Anne moved ahead cautiously.

'Is he still into all that stuff?' she asked, keeping her tone off-hand.

'Is he still *into* it,' Skip's voice was almost a shriek. 'You *bet* he's into it – like there's no tomorrow. The smart money says that's why he's neglecting me. I wouldn't fucking mind if American Express weren't on the line every ten minutes about my frigging account.'

Anne knew that was only partly true. Feelings had obviously been hurt, feathers ruffled.

'But I thought he just hired passing trade in that other scene. You know, ships that pass in the night, that sort of thing.' Anne was rather proud of her mastery of the jargon.

Skip's voice was low now, conspiratorial.

'Word is . . .' he paused theatrically, 'word is he's met up with a couple of thugs on a more regular basis.' He waited, anticipating tremendous interest. Self-respect might be low, self-centredness was always high.

Purposefully, Anne failed to respond, a fish hovering around the bait, finally deciding not to go for it. Skip would have to add a juicier morsel to get her to bite.

'In fact – and you won't believe this – my little dickie-bird tells me there was actually a *fight* over him one evening. A fight over that stinking piece of blubber. Can you imagine? They must have been *blind* men, or *starving* or something.' Again he paused.

Two men. The sort who got into fights. A regular basis. She was almost there.

'You don't think he's got himself shacked up with those guys, do you? I mean that would be bad for you.'

'Too right it would be bad for me. Who the hell would pay my bloody *bills*.' Again the shrill voice rose, only to fall again.

Here was a new Skip Demery. Cold, implacable foe.

Hero of western mythology. The man who'd track down the guy who'd wronged him even if it took a lifetime. In what he hoped was a steely, unforgiving voice he said,

'It just so happens that I've made it my business to find out where these two pieces of rubbish hang out. A seedy little loft on Second Avenue and Vine. Let me promise you this, Dr Carrington, because you might be called as a witness of some sort at my trial. If I find that Charles fucking Phipps has put one podgy leg across the door of that poxy apartment, I'm going to splatter him all over the Village – so help me.'

The address sprang off the blotter where Anne had hurriedly written it. Second Avenue and Vine. That could be it. She had to get this prick off the line. No problem. She'd just put the telephone down. He'd think he'd been cut off.

She buzzed down. 'Give me a line, Paula, and if Demery rings back tell him I've had to rush out to an emergency, OK?'

In seconds she was through to the FBI.

Anne pushed through the rapidly gathering crowd towards the barricade which was being hastily erected at the Second and Vine intersection. The whole place was swarming with cops and with other, more sinister figures dressed in drab, paramilitary uniforms, tinted glasses covering darting, alert eyes. SWAT teams. Christ! It was the real thing all right. Secrecy was clearly being given the very lowest priority in this operation. Anne prayed the FBI knew what they were doing.

She cornered a sweating police sergeant.

'I'm looking for Peabody. He told me to contact him here. I'm Dr Carrington.'

'Right over there, lady. The guy in the suit by that squad car.'

Peabody looked as if he was enjoying himself, fighting to

disguise the excitement in his voice, to appear the laid-back, competent professional, coolest pip in the heart of the cucumber.

'Well, Dr Carrington, you sure as hell hit the bull dead-centre. We've got them located in that apartment building over there. They're holed up in a loft. They probably know we're here, but we've made no contact yet. As you can see, first priority is to seal off the entire area. If we get into a shooting war we don't want pedestrians in the firing line.'

Great, thought Anne. What about Adam? Was he expendable while the cowboys, Canadian Mounted Police-like, got their man? She held on to herself. In psychiatry, as in the classic TV series 'Dragnet', it was important to get the facts before one started sounding off.

'How do you know where they are?'

'The street's full of information. The two turkeys are well known round here. Mickey and Fritz. Body-building homos, fond of throwing their weight around. Apparently there's enough leather up there to start a shoe factory. The guy two floors below says it sometimes sounds like a torture chamber when the boys are entertaining friends. Every-body's terrified of them so no one complains.'

'But how do we know Adam is there?'

'He's there all right. A couple of winos saw someone who matched his description being dragged in there last night. Anyway, they're all corked up tight for now. We've got SWATS on the stairs and the roof, and sharp shooters in the neighbouring buildings.'

Wap-wap-wap. The noise of a chopper drowned Pea-body's report. He shouted above the roar of the rotor blades. 'The whole thing's covered from the air, too. Those boys have nowhere to go.'

From his manner it was clear that he was getting something out of this. Promotion? The satisfaction of more primitive lusts? It wasn't clear. Whatever, Adam Phipps' survival appeared to be of something less than paramount importance.

'What's the next step?'

Anne's question seemed to throw Peabody and for a moment he appeared perplexed. Immediately Anne picked up on his number. This was a guy for whom the game was the thing. He was an organization man. In one short hour he'd put together an immensely complicated operation. He'd discharged his duty with consummate skill and was now prepared to bask in the reflected glory, which, in his opinion, such expertise undoubtedly justified. That the prime objective was to rescue Adam Phipps and capture his abductors had been lost sight of along the way. In short, he appeared not to know what was next at all.

'Oh, I guess we'll talk to them on the megaphone. Tell 'em they're surrounded. If they don't come on out I guess we go right in and waste 'em.'

Anne could see Peabody on the megaphone playing small-town sheriff to the robbers holed up in the bank. His role as part of the 'we' who would go in to 'waste' the opposition was far less convincing.

'Listen,' said Anne firmly, 'I'm a psychiatrist and I've studied the behaviour of criminals in a siege situation. There are things to say and things to avoid saying. Will you let me talk to them?'

'Hell, no, lady. This is my baby. I'm in charge here. It's my responsibility.'

Anne felt the beginnings of panic. Christ! This mother was going to blow it. He didn't know how to drive, but no way was he going to give up the reins. He'd rather take the whole coach over the cliffs than give up his precious authority. Anne knew she was fighting for Adam's life. One wrong step and she'd be signing his execution order. What did she know about the Peabodys of this world? First off, it was a no-no to antagonize them. To be able to get away with that you had to be a superior. Then there was no limit to the amount of shit they'd take. But Anne wasn't Peabody's boss, and, what was worse, she was a woman. Peabody would be a chauvinist for sure. Somehow she had to appeal to his own self-interest. And she had one trump card: she was a doctor and a psychiatrist. That meant that as far as Peabody was concerned she was an 'expert', a species for which a man like him would have uncritical respect.

'It was just that I thought it would be really efficient if we could use my expertise and knowledge of human behaviour in a situation like this.' She saw a thoughtful look come immediately into his eyes. It acquired a dreamy quality.

In his mind's eye, Peabody was already reading the report: 'Mr Peabody, demonstrating considerable initiative, arranged for an expert in the psychology of the siege mentality to be present at the scene, and this, despite the shortness of the time available . . .'

'OK, doctor,' he said at last. 'You talk to them. We'll go up to the floor below and reach them with a megaphone. You'll be surrounded by SWATS in case they make a break for it, so you'll be OK.'

Anne tried to slow her racing mind. What the hell had that article on the London spaghetti shop siege recommended? She'd lied to Peabody in pretending to know all the answers, but then he'd had to be stopped. If there was a break-in followed by a fire-fight, Adam's chances of survival would be less than 25 per cent.

Bit by bit her memory served up the details. She must keep up a dialogue. Procrastinate. That was it – you had to keep them talking, get them to relate to you, even manage the odd joke. You had to become a person rather than a disembodied voice. Trading was important, too. I'll send in food if you do this or that. Shift the focus away from the basic issues to more peripheral ones and let fatigue go to work on them. Build trust. Do what you say you're going to do. Most important, avoid precipitous action until there was real evidence of an imminent threat to the hostage.

Surrounded by a phalanx of bodyguards and a rather less confident Peabody, she mounted the rickety stairs of

255

the converted warehouse. On the landing below the top floor a sandbag barricade had already been erected. Two men, Uzi submachine guns at the ready, crouched behind it.

Peabody handed Anne the megaphone. 'Good luck,' he whispered.

Adam Phipps knew as surely as he'd known anything in his life that he wouldn't live through another day. It wasn't pessimism which led him to this conclusion: it was ice-cold logic. The only questions were how he'd be killed and when. As his final act of defiance in this increasingly intolerable world, he vowed that he'd take his secret with him. Come what may, Charles Phipps wouldn't get the information he craved.

For the moment, both of his captors slept. Trussed up like a chicken on the filthy sofa, Adam envied them their escape from the awful reality of existence.

Anne Carrington's voice – metallic, crackling, but unmistakably hers – roared into the room. OK, he'd flipped. He had to be hallucinating. What the hell was she doing here?

'Mickey, Fritz. I want you to stay calm for your own sakes. It's in your own best interests to do nothing at all till you've heard what I have to say. This whole building has been cordoned off by the police and the FBI. There are armed men at all the entrances and they have orders to shoot at the slightest provocation. If you wish to remain safe, do absolutely nothing.'

Appeal to their self-interest. Emphasize the helplessness of their position. Talk only to them. Leave Adam out. Bolster their authority.

'We know you're holding Adam Phipps. Is he still alive? If he is, you have nothing to fear from us. Nothing at all. We are here to help you. But you are totally surrounded.' Carrot and stick.

Mickey came off the bed like a jack-in-the-box, Fritz following closely behind. Sweeping up the ·38 he bounded towards the window, peering out cautiously into the street.

'Fucking *hell*,' he screamed, 'they've rumbled us. There's Feds everywhere. The street's crawling with them.'

'What'll we do, Mickey?' Fritz was as white as a snow drop.

'Shut up. Let me think, will ya?'

Anne Carrington's voice, calm and even, continued its disembodied monologue.

'Can you let me know if Phipps is OK?'

Mickey darted towards Adam. Roughly he thrust the barrel of the revolver into Adam's mouth, chipping front teeth with the gunsight.

'You'd better believe we've got the mother. And he's chewing on a ·38 right now. Make a move and I scramble his brains – so help me.'

'Is that Mickey?' Establishment rapport. 'My name's Anne. As long as you don't harm him you'll be quite safe. I promise you, Mickey. We have no intention of forcing our way in – none at all.'

'You let us out of here. Do ya understand me? Get us a car. And we take this prick with us, OK? OK?' he screamed the question.

'What sort of a car do you want, Mickey?' Confuse the issue. There was a pause.

'Any fucking car, man. Just get us a car!'

'Perhaps you might be wiser to let us give you a helicopter. But only on the condition that you release Phipps unharmed. We might be able to consider that.' Silence. 'What do you say, Mickey?'

'Shut up. I'm thinking.'

Mickey's mind was in overdrive. They'd blown it. They were surrounded. Trapped. Already there were two corpses. The Chink and the doorman. Murder one. At best they'd do thirty years. With Adam as hostage there was the slimmest chance they could make a break for it. It was worth a try. A helicopter sounded possible. But that meant a pilot – a police pilot. A car would be safer. But to get clean away in New York's crowded streets? There had to be a better way. Play for time.

'Who the hell are you? Are you a cop?'

'My name is Dr Anne Carrington. I'm a doctor, a psychiatrist.' Be honest. Build up confidence. What would Adam be thinking?

Mickey's fevered brain sought to process the information. A fucking shrink? What the hell was she doing there? Why on earth had they called in a head doctor?

'Mickey, why have they got a psychiatrist? Do they think we're crazy?' Fritz was on the verge of panic.

And then, quite suddenly Mickey saw the opening. A shrink. Insanity. Why not? They just might be able to beat the rap if they went the insanity way. Like Hinckley. He was a smart guy. A year or two in some cushy clinic and then back on the street. Yeah, yeah. Insanity was the newest game in town. Anyone could play. What a rip-off. Zap the President and get to finger nurses in the hospital. Sucker the suckers. It was worth a try, and the alternatives looked terrible. Out on the street they'd have to run the gauntlet of a bunch of uniformed trigger-happy fascists just longing to bust out like bandits. One false move, perhaps even no false moves, and they'd be in a fire-fight. It'd be Bonny and Clyde time. Butch and the fucking Sundance Kid. How the hell did you act crazy?

'You're really a shrink?' he shouted.

'Yes I am. I work at the university.' Anne sounded straight.

'Fact is, I ain't been feeling too good lately.'

Anne's heart leaped as, immediately, she saw the opening. Christ, the transparent naïveté of it. This Mickey was thinking of an insanity plea. Her brain worked fast.

'That's what we thought. That's why I'm here. It seems to me that from the way you carved those guys yesterday that something is going badly wrong. It's very probable that you're emotionally ill – sick – not really responsible for your actions at all. I want to help you both. In my professional opinion, you need treatment, not punishment.'

If she could con him into thinking he might cop a guilty but insane plea she might have him hooked. Then the awful thought struck her. Was it really such a con? Might he not actually swing a verdict like that? It was happening all the time. To hell with it. Her mission was to get Adam out of there in one piece. She was living for the here and now.

'Hey I ain't sick, Mickey. We ain't sick. What's she trying to pull?' Fritz was way behind Mickey on this one.

Mickey whispered back, his voice hissing out through clenched teeth. The Phipps creep shouldn't hear this.

'Listen, idiot. It's a scam. We pretend we're crazy and they let us off the hook. We do time in some laid-back funny-farm and make like we're loons and then they let us out when we decide to be better. Otherwise they got us for thirty years. No sweat.'

From the look of pure horror on Fritz's face, Mickey saw in an instant that he was failing to carry his audience with him.

Fritz began to gabble.

'Hey, man, they ain't sending me to no fucking madhouse. I had this uncle. They cut his brain, man. They wired him up, like in the electric chair. I seen that movie. We gotta get outa here.'

Fritz stood up, his face white, fists clenched, naked fear beaming from him in waves. Prison to him was the devil he knew, a familiar, almost reassuring place. The State mental institution represented unknown horrors, confronted only in his most appalling nightmares.

Mickey was not about to argue. With an economical movement, the sort you might use to flick an unwanted fly off your leg poolside, he turned the short barrel of the ·38

259

to point at the centre of Fritz's stomach. He said, 'You're a pain, Fritz,' and pulled the trigger.

The roar of the hand-gun set off different thoughts in different minds.

Fritz had lift-off. No longer attached to the ground, he was flying through the air, his whole body merely a complicated package for the ·38 calibre bullet which propelled him. When he'd seen the black barrel aiming at his abdomen he'd taken a short step backwards, so he was already travelling in the direction of the missile which was wreaking such havoc in his bowels. He wanted to say something. Wanted to correct Mickey. Mickey had got it wrong. He was not a pain. He was *in* pain. There was a difference. People should get things right.

Mickey enjoyed hurting people. Even a friend like Fritz, a guy whose body he'd enjoyed. Perhaps that was why he'd blown his stomach away rather than his brains. Already his thoughts were on the main chance. If Fritz wasn't going to make like he was crazy, then Fritz was a problem – and problems had to be obliterated. And if he was going for insanity, it would be good to go the whole way. He'd just wasted his friend. What sane man would do a thing like that?

Anne Carrington felt a cold wave of nausea break over her as she heard the shot. So near yet so far. They'd murdered Adam. It was all over. Next to her she was vaguely aware of the SWAT team bracing themselves for action, heard the click of safety catches.

Micky's voice screamed out. 'I shot Fritz. I shot Fritz. Phipps is OK.'

Fritz, as if on cue, provided the corroborative evidence. He began to scream. And then quite suddenly his screams stopped. Mickey's bullet, before exiting just to the right of his spinal column, had nicked the wall of his abdominal aorta. For a second or two the tissues of the mighty artery had held. Now they gave up the unequal struggle

'Hey, lady. I'm coming out. First I send out Phipps.

Then me. OK? OK? Don't shoot. I'll throw the gun first. I ain't got no weapon.'

Anne held her breath. In her heart she formed a mighty prayer: 'Oh, Lord, give me this. I'll never ask for anything again.'

Slowly, the door opened, the handgun clattered on the stair. And there was Adam standing shakily and totally naked on the top flight of the stairs, bruised, battered, bloody, hands still tied behind his back, and, in Anne's eyes, completely magnificent. In that split second she knew that far from being over, it was a new beginning.

At Peabody's insistent gesture he stumbled unsteadily towards the sandbag barricade and fell into Anne's arms. For a minute or two she held him tightly.

Tiptoeing sheepishly, like a naughty schoolboy, Mickey edged through the door, peering uncertainly for the reception committee, naked except for a filthy pair of Y-fronts.

Over Adam's bare shoulder Anne watched her out-smarted adversary. Why did psychopaths have such cold eyes? Why did psychopaths have *three* eyes? And why were all those guns going off and Mickey's third eye spouting blood like that. He should see a doctor. It was strangely beautiful, that couldn't be denied. Superb choreography and dazzling colours. Grey matter. It was so long since Anne had seen it. And she'd forgotten how incredibly white bone was. Red, white, grey – God should've put a little blue into the body somewhere. It began to look as if Mickey wouldn't be having his day in court after all, or anywhere else for that matter. Technically of course it was murder, but you didn't bring charges against a SWAT team. Certainly not on behalf of an ex-citizen of Mickey's quality.

So Anne just switched off her mind and concentrated hard on the here and now – the unmistakable reality of Adam in her arms once again.

Charles Phipps sat awkwardly in the small, comfortable consulting room of Dr Evans' medical offices. Everything had come completely unstuck for him, but he had, through incredible luck, avoided the ultimate disaster. For some extraordinary reason best known to themselves, the Feds had blown away the only man on earth who could tie him into Adam's kidnapping. If Mickey had been alive to implicate him, nothing was surer than that he would've done so. Those two would've talked like they had some canarial disease. Chirpese time. But both Fritz and Mickey were comprehensively dead. He'd seen the gory photographs in *The Daily News*.

When the FBI had arrived to interrogate him he'd put up a defence which would've made Stonewall Jackson look flaky. Sure, Adam had fingered him and said the two men had mentioned that he'd hired them to secure some computer program. But Adam was a young man who had taken too many drugs, who had an alcohol problem, who had, on Charles Phipps' own recommendation, been visiting a psychiatrist. He'd always been jealous of his uncle and shown somewhat paranoid reactions towards him. Clearly the awful experience of the kidnapping had pushed him over the brink. His fantasies had become reality.

And as for the two ruffians who had abducted him and murdered that unfortunate butler and the nice doorman – well, a man who occasionally escorted the First Lady when her husband was held up with the affairs of state, a man whose social and business credentials were beyond reproach would hardly have numbered them among his friends, would he? Charles had seen to it immediately that Skip Demery had become a close ally once more, his vicious tongue garaged safely behind buttoned lips. The promise of the three-month rented house in Mustique, the new wardrobe, the immaculate new car had seen to that.

In the leather-bars the patrons had been unhelpful when the FBI had shown Charles' picture. Honour among perverts. At the end of the day it had become clear to all that any jury would clear Charles if charged with kidnapping, and the inescapable implication of that would be that Adam was indeed of unsound mind. So he'd been given a clean bill of health. Almost.

To have a cough in New York City was not exactly a big deal, but this one had been unusually persistent. In the last two or three days it had got worse, and Charles had been running a temperature and feeling rotten. He'd even been slightly short of breath. Not one to visit his doctor indiscriminately, he'd decided to consult Dr Evans. He was glad now that he'd made the appointment because this morning in the bath he'd noticed some strange new bruises which seemed to have appeared on the back of his legs. He couldn't remember bumping into anything and he wondered if they were connected in any way with the mild fever. Anyway, Evans would know. He was a good doctor.

It was a pity they'd have to discuss the Adam thing. Maybe Evans would know Adam had accused him of complicity, maybe not. He'd stick to his story. If it had been good enough for the men with suspicious eyes from the FBI, it would certainly do the trick for old Evans. After all, he was still a Phipps, still on the board of the bank. Damn! He'd been trying not to think about the bank. His job there was about as safe as a rope bridge in a hurricane. Adam had pulled the account and had made no bones about why he'd done it. In the corridors of Phipps-Seabury he might just as well have been a dead man who had started to smell, from the reaction he got from his colleagues. Still, he was out of jail and his reputation and, for the moment, his job, were intact. He might be able to swing a position with a smaller firm. After all, he was well connected. It was definitely true to say that events had turned out badly, but it was also easy to see how they could've been worse, far worse.

The white-coated receptionist was calling his name.

' 'Morning, Charles. My God, what a business with Adam. Terrible thing. Terrible. It all happened so fast. No sooner had I heard he'd been kidnapped than I heard he was safe. Got to hand it to the Feds. Frankly, I'm glad those two pieces of shit got wiped out. Save the money on the trial. Good thing in my book. Very good thing. Wish they'd do it more often.'

For a minute or two the two men discussed the kidnapping. Evans clearly hadn't been contacted by anyone. Presumably Dr Carrington was now taking care of Adam's medical needs – and other needs as well, if Charles knew anything at all.

'Now, Charles, what can I do for you this morning?'

Briefly Charles outlined his symptoms. Evans listened, relaxed and at ease, until Charles mentioned the bruises on his leg. Suddenly he stiffened. Cutting Charles' monologue short, he interrupted,

'I'd better take a look at those right away, Charles, if you don't mind. Just drop your trousers down.'

Charles did as he was told. Taking his trousers down was always rather a pleasant experience, whatever the circumstances.

Dr Evans bent down behind him. For a few seconds there was silence.

'Can't think how I bruised myself,' said Charles uncertainly.

'And you say you've been running a fever with this cough. Any shortness of breath?' asked Evans from his kneeling position, his voice strangely serious.

'Yes, funny you should say that. In the last two days I've been out of breath on quite minor exertion. You know, walking upstairs and things.'

Dr Evans resumed his place behind his desk. His face was rather white.

'Charles, I have to ask you an embarrassing question. It's very important you answer me honestly even though it may be difficult for you. Have you ever had any homosexual experiences?'

Charles gulped, the blood rushing to his cheeks. The

doctor was trying to peer into his closet. It just wasn't done.

'What an *extraordinary* question,' he exploded. 'Why on earth do you ask?'

Evans took the bull by the horns. 'Because, Charles, I'm extremely sorry to have to tell you this – you have Auto-Immune Deficiency Syndrome, AIDS. You've probably heard of it.'

Charles had heard of it. Everyone in the gay community, in or out of the closet, had heard of it. It was the homosexual death sentence. God's pestilence on those who shared the brown habit. AIDS. Only 14 per cent of those who got the illness were alive at the end of three years. The statistic was as well known in the bathhouses of big-city America as the percentage of human beings in the world who were male.

'No,' said Charles softly, as the nausea gripped him. 'No,' he repeated more loudly, like some incantation to ward off evil spirits.

'I'm afraid the lesions on your legs are KS – Kaposi sarcoma – lesions. There's no question about it. The lung infection may be PCP – *pneumocystis carinii*. I won't know until I've cultured some sputum. I'm very sorry, Charles. Very sorry.'

PCP, KS lesions. To the general public the initials meant nothing. To homosexuals they meant the end of the world. KS. Charles would die of cancer if the lung disease didn't get him first. There was no cure for AIDS, the total breakdown of the body's immune system which rendered the sufferer defenceless to normally benign infections which the ordinary person would throw off without a second thought.

'Are you sure?' asked Charles hopelessly.

Evans nodded slowly. 'You may know that the groups of people who get this thing are intravenous drug users, haemophiliacs, Haitians and, occasionally, very young children. I know you don't fit into those categories, which is why I asked you about homosexuality. I need to know, Charles.'

Charles spread his little hands in despair and resignation. 'I may have . . . once or twice . . .' His voice tailed off. 'What causes it?' he managed. He already knew the answer. Cause unknown. Anything to avoid the discussion of prognosis. Charles knew the answer to that, too: death.

'It's probably passed on in the sperm.'

Passed on in the sperm. Mickey? Fritz? Skip? The hundreds of others who'd emptied themselves into him? Why him? Why him? He felt the panic rise within him, replacing the numbness of the initial shock.

'I read somewhere that Interferon could delay . . .'

'We'll try everything, Charles. Of course we will. They're working flat out to find a cause and a cure, you know. They're bound to come up with something sooner or later.' Dr Evans stopped short. The 'later' bit had been a mistake. If Charles had PC pneumonia he'd be dead in six months, and the symptoms certainly pointed to it.

'I'm going to die, and there's nothing I can do about it. That's the truth, isn't it, Dr Evans?'

'I'm afraid that's the truth, Charles.'

A large tear rolled down Charles' podgy cheek. His homosexuality had killed him.

Mariel O'Sullivan sat alone in the small roof-top room of a run-down Paris pension staring disconsolately at the telephone. It had to ring soon. She just had to get some bread. Three weeks behind with the rent and now no money for food, and, more important, no money for the clothes she'd need to make the money to fill her stomach.

When Adam had pulled the plug on her in Germany it had been a comprehensive operation indeed. Back in the States nobody had wanted to know. The word was out that she was the baddest of bad news. The big bucks had got wise to her, and she was too proud to return to the lower rungs of the ladder. The modelling, too, had dried up, as if word had got out that she'd become a pariah, an untouchable. With all the doors closing in her face, she'd decided to go to Europe to make a new beginning. But Europe was in the grip of depression and in Paris the model agencies were on their knees, getting rid of their own models rather than taking on new ones. So she'd decided to try a little high-class prostitution. There again she'd had no luck. The punters weren't punting, and she didn't speak French. Now she was beginning to get desperate.

The jangling of the telephone cut into her thoughts.

'Miss O'Sullivan?'

'Speaking.'

'I decide to give you the job.'

Relief flooded through her.

'You do blue film before?'

'No.'

'Listen, you have to do exactly what I say. Understand? You want it, you obey me. If not, then I got many peoples who want to do it. Yes?'

'No. I mean yes. I want it. I agree to what you say. Have I got the job?' Mariel was fighting for her existence.

The cackling laugh over the telephone was one of the nastiest things she'd ever heard.

'OK. You start tomorrow. Come to the address I gave you. Eh, and Miss O'Sullivan, just to show you mean what you say, your first job, you like midgets? Ha? Is a very pretty midget.' The line went dead.

There was no sound in the room except that of Mariel O'Sullivan weeping.

The impanelling of the jury in the case of Mitcham *v.* Carrington had been uneventful. Both sides had been keen to exclude anyone who'd been treated by psychiatrists or psychologists for even the most minor conditions.

To Anne and Adam, the jury selection had been a nerve-bending preamble to the trial itself. But their togetherness made it infinitely bearable. Anne had been determined not to let Adam back into her life on any condition, but circumstances, and her own emotions, had overruled her. In the terrible ordeal of his kidnap she'd discovered the true strength of her feelings for him – her heart going out to him in a way which proved to her that she was deeply in love. To deny it was pointless. She'd prayed to her God to give him back to her, and her prayer had been granted. A greater force had been pulling the strings. In the crucible of torture, death hovering at his shoulder, Adam had been forged anew. He'd been transformed, and the new forcefulness and sense of purpose showed in all of his thoughts and actions. As soon as he'd heard about the Mitcham case he'd taken control. His brilliant mind and the power of his love bringing mighty reinforcements to her cause.

Behind Anne now stood not only Adam and the staunch Peter Isaacs, but the phenomenal resources of the Phipps fortune. To offset the formidable Masterson, the patrician James Drury had been hired to mastermind the defence, and the full resources of the Phipps family law firm had been put at his disposal. Now the defence table fairly bristled with the biggest of the big guns, reeking with the smell of power, money and influence – the immaculately suited WASP attorneys chuckling confidently among themselves, exchanging invitations to lunch at their various clubs.

On the Mitcham side of the court Masterson sat quietly at his table, Mary Mitcham, tear-blown, tense, the wronged wife from the tip of her head to the soles of her Gucci shoes, beside him. She'd been carefully instructed and she was going for an Academy Award.

'You're on display for every second you're in this courtroom. I don't want you to relax for one single second. Not one. Whatever happens, don't smile – not ever. I want tears, lots of them, but don't get noisy. Suffer in silence. Stiff upper-lip. And your clothes. Black, black, black· And no makeup. Hair tied up tightly in a bun. Everything must be neat and tidy,' Masterson had said. She'd obeyed him to the letter. Already she was working over the jurors one by one with her filmy eyes, her proud, defiant grief, as she sought recompense for the terrible wrong which had been done – the $2,000,000 which would be such a poor substitute for her beloved husband, whose only mistake had been to put his faith in the bogus expertise of Dr Anne Carrington.

Two million dollars. It was a huge suit, but Masterson was confident they'd get it, and was totally determined that they would.

Briefly he looked across the room to where the law establishment were appearing for the defence. Turkeys. They might belong to the best clubs but he'd walk all over them in the courtroom, where it counted. Then his roving eyes sought out Anne Carrington. She was very pretty. That would go against her – he'd see to that. He'd paint her as the gorgeous dilettante doctor flitting round the world while the city's morgues filled up with her patients; fiddling while the hangman's noose tightened. Next to her was the Phipps boy. Rich as Croesus. He'd been on holiday with her. The doctor and the young playboy. Old enough to be his mother. Boy, it was a juicy case. It was sitting ducks.

Not for one second did Masterson consider the possibility that Anne might not be guilty of malpractice. That was beside the point. In the adversary system of justice, you fought your own corner and fought to win. If you won, you were right. It was as simple as that. Another famous victory for Masterson. A fatter fee next time. And then, and then . . . the house . . . the Senate . . . higher . . .?

He cut short the pleasing reverie. The trial was about to start. Judge Ruckelhauser signalled to Drury to open for the defence.

The clipped Boston Brahmin tones wafted reassuringly across the courtroom. It was all going to be fine. Drury's words oozed out, a soothing balm, healing all wounds, bringing together the commonsense consensus, pointing the way towards sweet reason. A terrible tragedy had undoubtedly occurred. A fine man had been taken cruelly from us in his prime, despite the very highest professional competence of the brilliant young doctor who had been treating him. And treating him without charge because of his unfortunately straitened financial circumstances. A marginally pained expression passed over Drury's aristocratic features at the very mention of fees and money. It was, in fact, totally comprehensible that Mrs Mitcham, racked by grief and sorrow, should cast round her for a culprit, when no culprit existed, apart from the vicious illness of depression. It was natural that she should do so, he maintained with a curled lip. Natural that she should, perhaps, want to share the guilt for her husband's unhappiness.

Masterson smiled to himself. Drury was good. Very good. The implication was clear that Mrs Mitcham had failed to make Mr Mitcham happy, wanted to redistribute blame which in a large measure was hers. It had had to be said obliquely, the idea planted surreptitiously in the jurors' minds. If he'd made the point openly and in a hostile manner the jury wouldn't have forgiven him for terrorizing a weeping widow. From the drift of the speech he could tell what was coming next. He'd have handled it the same way himself.

'It isn't unnatural, too, that in her despair, and still suffering the financial misfortune which contributed to such a large extent to poor John Mitcham's unhappy state of mind, she might seek to solve that problem as well, as her unfortunate husband had tried unsuccessfully to overcome it.' He paused. 'Two million dollars. Two million dollars,' he repeated, allowing a hint of his former distaste to surface once more. 'I'm sure none of us can really conceive of an amount of money like that, can we?' Drury suppressed a little frisson of guilt. That was about the value of his children's trust fund.

From the jury's faces it was clear that none of them were in Drury's position. All eyes turned accusingly on Mary Mitcham. The golddigger. The wife who'd pushed her husband to the brink. Through her own extravagances, perhaps. The hard-hearted harridan, who sought to achieve in his death what she'd failed to achieve in his life.

Mary stared back at them. She'd been tutored to accept this. It would be like a game of tennis, Masterson had said. At the moment, the other side had the advantage of service. Later it would be their turn.

Drury was still on the subject of money. For one who apparently disliked it, he appeared to be obsessed by it.

'Yes, it's certainly a great deal of money. There would be a lot left over after payment of the debts. Really a very substantial amount.' He fingered his Brooks Brothers tie. Fine red stripes against a navy-blue background. You could trust this man. He wouldn't mislead. As comforting as the Constitution. Visions of Mary Mitcham stepping into her Lear jet, leasing the Palm Beach house for the season, socking it to them at Cartier were inexorably conjured up.

'And while we are on the subject of the debts, we should realize that one of the most substantial debtors is a man who will be, I suspect, the most important "expert" witness for the plaintiffs in this sad affair.' The word 'expert' was a masterpiece. The implication was that this man, whoever he was, possessed no expertise whatsoever.

Masterson was on his feet at once. 'Objection, your honour. Counsel is attacking the credibility of an as yet uncalled witness and suggesting that this person has a vested interest in misleading this court for financial gain.' Damn. It had been a reflex action. He bit his tongue with frustration.

Drury beamed at him. One up for the Old Guard.

Masterson had put into the bluntest words the veiled insinuation he'd just floated over the courtroom. Now he'd withdraw, but the point had been forcefully expressed. Ishmael was on the make. Couldn't be trusted.

Judge Ruckelhauser upheld the objection and told the jury to disregard Drury's words, but he, too, saw the ploy. Good old James. One in the eye for the flamboyant Masterson. They'd have a laugh about that one on the links one day.

To counter his private thoughts he said out loud, 'This court does not take kindly to blatant misuse of the defence counsel's opening speech. Please see that it doesn't happen again.'

Drury bowed in gracious acknowledgement and continued:

'Whatever the motive behind the bringing of this case – and I for one am not suggesting that the motive is actually a dishonest one – the outcome will hinge on the treatment methods employed by Dr Carrington. In a sense, therefore, it isn't she who is on trial today but psychiatry itself. You will be asked to decide whether that profession should move into the twentieth century, or whether instead it should look backwards to the obsolete treatment methods of sixty years ago. Whether it should be a science or an uncertain art. Whether its most proficient exponents are to be found in our own most august institutions, such as Harvard and Johns Hopkins, or in Mid-European centres or those modelled upon them.'

'As I look at you now,' he continued, 'I have complete faith that you will make the right choice and choose science over mumbo-jumbo. That will not be a difficult decision. However, your task is by no means an easy one. John Mitcham is dead. Through no conscious fault of her own,' the word 'conscious' was emphasized, 'Mary Mitcham is alone in the world, burdened by debt. Your natural kindness will want to help her in her hour of need. The insurance company can pay, might be your attitude. And who knows, I can't believe there's anyone in this courtroom who doesn't occasionally like to see an insurance company refund some of the premium income which they so gleefully extract from us.'

Drury chuckled gracefully. Mr Nice-Guy. One of the boys. Joe Citizen down-trodden by big business. Mary Mitcham was about the only person in the room who didn't smile.

With a crack of his ringmaster's whip, he brought back seriousness. His voice now earnest, he continued:

'But in voting to recompense Mary Mitcham, you would be voting to condemn a fine young woman doctor, one of the finest in the land. You would put a blight on a brilliant career and condemn as wrongly incompetent one who gave her precious skills as charity. That would indeed be a terrible and uncalled for thing. My client did the right thing by her patient. Professors of psychiatry at both Johns Hopkins and Harvard will say so. Never for one single second did she depart from the highest standards of her profession. And yet, you will ask, why is John Mitcham dead? Again and again, I suspect, the counsel for the plaintiff will ask it. There is an answer to that question, and it is that depressive illness is a disease that kills in the same way that cancer kills. Physicians can cure it sometimes, but they are not infallible. When death occurs in depressive illness, it is not of necessity malpractice. If that were to be the case we would have to say that every practising psychiatrist in the country is guilty.' Again the smile. 'And despite our natural inclinations, I think we would all fall short of saying that.'

Play on the popular prejudice against psychiatry in order to defuse it. Laughter rippled through the jury. They were eating out of his hands. Soon, thought Drury, they will be eating out of Masterson's.

'God, he's good,' whispered Adam excitedly to Peter. 'I think we're home and dry. He's turned the jury against the

Mitcham woman.' At the defence table, Anne was thinking the same. It had been a virtuoso performance.

Drury sensed it was time to quit while he was ahead. Don't bore them. That was the kiss of death.

'And so, ladies and gentlemen, I leave you with the future of a kind and generous young woman in your hands. I am quite confident that you will see that justice is done.'

For a while after Drury had sat down Masterson didn't get up. All eyes turned expectantly towards him. He had his audience. Slowly, deliberately he stood. At first his voice was hesitant, his manner subdued, almost unsure. The court strained to pick up his words. Apart from the thin voice, there was total silence in the room.

'What does it take . . .? I wonder what it takes to make a man walk up the stairs. Walk up the stairs and take a rope. One that he'd bought a few days before. And to take that rope and tie it round his neck. Think of it, tying a rope round your own necks, and then tying it round the banister, and then . . .' He paused. The jury shifted uncomfortably. Round twelve necks were twelve nooses. Masterson's voice was suddenly strong, vibrant, searching out into the very corners of the room. 'And then leaping headlong into eternity. What does it take? *What does it take?*'

As one man the jury made their leap with John Mitcham, experienced his despair. Drury's speech, clever and polished, already seemed strangely irrelevant. This was about life and sudden and violent death, not about money, jokes and insurance policies, about professional reputations and professors of psychiatry. Somehow everybody felt the stakes had been raised significantly.

Drury's heart sank. It was Masterson's turn now and he was taking the unashamedly emotional route. Mitcham's death was actually beside the point. The question was, had he been properly treated? But the jury were already following Masterson down the road of feeling. Somebody had died in misery. Somebody must have caused that misery, or at least have allowed it to happen. That somebody would have to be punished, made to pay for their cruelty. A sacrifice was called for. What did it take? Masterson was going to tell them.

For three brilliant minutes he dwelt on John Mitcham's misery while the tears cascaded endlessly and silently down Mary Mitcham's cheeks. A black woman in the back row of the jury was the first to jump on the bandwagon. Masterson saw her go for her handkerchief and he zeroed in on her. In two short minutes the courtroom was filled with the woman's sobs. Abruptly, Masterson changed tack.

'Let us not despair at this man's senseless, purposeless death. Now he is in pain no more. Today he walks in paradise, free of his earthly torment, at one with the universe in which he was treated so cruelly. But we have a debt to John Mitcham. A sacred obligation. If we discharge it faithfully he may not have died in vain. We have the duty, the absolute moral *duty*, to expose the dreadful incompetence, the blatant professional neglect which led to his death. The world must know what they can expect from the treatment of *Dr Anne Carrington*.' He shouted Anne's name. He hadn't mentioned it nor referred to it in any way before.

Anne's head flipped back as if she'd been struck full in the face. Intellectually she'd known it would be bad, but she hadn't been prepared for this. She'd been cast as the devil incarnate. Nothing less. And it hurt like hell.

At the defence desk James Drury surveyed the damage, his eyes appraising the jury one by one to see the effect of Masterson's words. It was not a pretty sight. The lawyer next to him didn't like it either. He leaned over and whispered in Drury's ear, 'I think we're in big trouble, James.'

'Only the biggest,' was the lead counsel's pessimistic reply.

Lunch in the Italian restaurant across from the court-house was hardly a festive occasion. Anne, Adam and Peter took turns to give voice to their irritation and frustration. James Drury, the old pro, was trying desperately to keep up morale. Adam's language was the most colourful.

'But, James, that creep of a lawyer is turning the whole fucking thing into a *circus*. All that crap about God and divine retribution. Hell, this is a malpractice suit, not the day of the Last frigging Judgement. Is he allowed to get away with all that?'

'As long as he stays within the rules of the game he can say what he likes. I agree with you totally. His methods stink. It's rotten law. Not at all the sort of way you and I have been brought up to behave. And old Ruckelhauser hates it, but he doesn't count. It's the jury who decides the issue, and they're lapping it up. Too many soap operas, I guess.'

'Maybe we should be taking his tack – making their hearts bleed for the beautiful young doctor,' said Peter, mildly irritated by Drury's attitude. It was all very well to pour patrician scorn on a cheap lawyer's tricks, but it didn't appear to be winning the case.

'No, I think not. Anne's beauty will go against her, I'm afraid. The great American public like their female doctors ugly. The only good-looking ones are on "General Hospital". Look, we mustn't get down about all this. We've got our experts this afternoon. I've had a long session with Smith, the Harvard professor, and he's going to say all the right things as far as we're concerned. And he's going to say them forcibly.'

Anne smiled. Smith said good morning forcibly. He'd be a good man to have in their corner. The best. The thought of him cheered her up. No jury, however imbecilic, could fail to be impressed by Smith, and Robinson of Johns Hopkins. Suddenly she knew it was going to be all right.

'I wonder what the hell Masterson will find to do with

276

them in the cross-examination. I wouldn't dare question either of them myself. I think he'll meet his match there.' Peter's spirits, too, were lifted by the thought of their powerful allies.

'I sure hope so,' said Drury, with rather less confidence. Masterson had a formidable reputation for being able to turn men into mice. 'We'll follow up with you, Anne, and then rest our case after that, apart from the summary.'

'Do you know,' said Anne, 'you'll find this really strange, but I think I'm actually going to enjoy this afternoon. I'll be watching that asshole Ishmael right through the whole thing. It'll be a real pleasure seeing him publicly castigated by the biggest names in the business.'

Smith was indeed saying all the right things. Roundly he had condemned the treatment of severe depressive illness with psychotherapy, leaving nobody in any doubt that he considered it irresponsible and cruel. Ishmael shouldn't have been treating Mitcham. What he'd needed was physical treatment methods, such as the Mianserin, which Dr Carrington had prescribed. It was the standard approach. At Harvard, Mitcham would've been given an antidepressant like Mianserin. Her approach had been faultless – without the least suggestion of malpractice. She'd kept more than adequate notes and had inquired closely about suicidal intentions. The doctor could not be blamed for Mitcham's decision to kill himself. Psychiatrists were not mind-readers and had never pretended to be. Probably Mitcham himself hadn't known he'd kill himself until the split second he'd launched himself from the banister.

Drury watched the jury closely. They were impressed, but they didn't like Smith personally. His manner was too pompous, elitist. He lacked the common touch. However, they were taking note of what he said. After all, everyone had heard of Harvard. This was clearly a top man.

Anne and Peter were watching Smith and not the jury, and they liked what they saw and heard. Neither could see how this man's testimony could possibly be ignored. He was a giant in their world. But they weren't experienced enough to know that in the courtroom world, lack of charm was a serious deficiency.

Masterson rose, serpent-like, for the cross-examination.

'Professor Smith, I would like to ask you a very simple question and I would like you to answer it with either yes or no. Do you understand?'

'I think I can follow that complicated instruction,' replied Smith arrogantly. It was the patronizing tone of voice he used to such devastating effect on his young interns at ward rounds.

'Would you say that Dr Carrington's treatment of John Mitcham was successful?'

Smith paused. Successful? Well, hardly successful in view of the fact of the corpse. It was the right treatment but it had failed to save the patient. That was par for the course in medicine. He wanted to qualify his reply, pointing out the deficiency in the question. But he'd just promised the upstart lawyer that he'd answer either yes or no. Damn. He'd been manipulated into giving a hostile answer.

'No,' he said after a pause.

A murmur rippled through the courtroom. Nobody appeared to be actually saying anything, but somehow the noise was there.

Masterson emphasized the point. 'You're telling me that Dr Carrington employed an unsuccessful treatment method on her patient. Yes or no, please.'

'Yes,' said Smith testily.

Drury groaned. Two questions and the pompous ass was already on the ropes and Anne's case with it. The jury wouldn't understand the subtle difference between correct treatment and unsuccessful treatment. Unsuccessful implied a botched job. The net effect was that the Harvard professor appeared to be saying that Anne had screwed up, and this despite his earlier testimony when he'd said she was blameless. It looked like the expert witness was contradicting himself. It was a disastrous beginning. Perhaps a fatal one.

Cat-like, Masterson came closer to the witness. 'I think, professor, that you have said Mitcham suffered a severe depressive illness in which biological features, such as profound sleep disturbance and weight loss were significant. Is that the case?'

'Yes.'

'Would you tell the court what, in your opinion, is the safest and most effective treatment for this condition?'

'Electro-convulsive therapy.'

'If we could keep to the yes and no answers. Did Dr Carrington use shock therapy on her patient Mitcham?'

'No.' Smith was beginning to sweat. Drury could see it standing out on his forehead.

'So Dr Carrington failed to employ the safest and most effective treatment for this condition?'

'Yes.'

In the back of the courtroom both Adam and Peter were beside themselves with frustration. It was all they could do to keep from shouting out to put the record straight. Mitcham hadn't wanted shock treatment. He hadn't been prepared to go into hospital because he couldn't afford a private one, and couldn't bear the stigma attached to a public ward. Both he and his wife had lived their lives according to what the neighbours thought. Somebody should make that point. It was a travesty of justice that the jury shouldn't hear about that.

'In your opinion, Professor Smith, would the chances of John Mitcham killing himself have been diminished had he been admitted to hospital?'

'Yes.'

Smith was on a tramline. Every time he wanted to answer favourably to the defence he came up against the

279

iron rail of professional truthfulness. Mitcham hadn't been ill enough to be forced into hospital against his will. Presumably Dr Carrington had offered hospitalization, but for some reason it had been turned down. He would've liked to have said that, but he was restricted to negatives and affirmatives, and he knew enough about the law to know that counsel had the right to insist on that in the case of genuine questions in which no statement of fact was included or implied. Thus 'Have you stopped beating your wife?' was a question that implied the statement, 'In the past you have beaten your wife'. None of Masterson's questions had been of this type.

Like a hunted hare, he began to look round for help. From Drury. From the judge. From the jury. None was forthcoming. He was on his own.

'So, despite the fact that the chances of John Mitcham killing himself would've been diminished by his admission to hospital, Dr Carrington did not in fact engineer a hospital admission.'

'Yes.' The formerly assertive voice was now strangely quiet.

'In your opinion, Professor, would it be possible, and I emphasize the word "possible", that the cancellation of Mitcham's appointment by Dr Carrington was a contributory factor in the worsening of his state of mind which led to his suicide?'

Strictly speaking, anything was possible. 'Yes,' said Smith unhappily.

'Has it been your professional experience that Mianserin is a less effective antidepressant medication than tricyclics like Amitriptyline and Imipramine?'

'Yes, but it's less . . .'

Masterson's voice cut in sharply. ' "Yes" will do, professor. I want to keep this simple.'

Drury could hardly believe his ears. Masterson was a virtuoso. He'd crucified Smith in his cross-examination. The professor had been trying to say that Mianserin, despite being marginally less effective, was a much safer drug to prescribe for out-patients because it lacked the dangerous side-effects of the tricyclics. He'd been headed off in the nick of time by the astute lawyer. Masterson might be a parvenu, but he was shit-hot. Drury was going to avoid him like the plague in future. Defeats weren't good for one's reputation, and there were bills to be paid. This case looked as if it was headed down the tubes for sure.

'From speaking to members of your profession, I've heard it said, Professor Smith, that you have often been a vocal critic of psychoanalytic treatment methods. Would you say there was some truth in that?'

'Yes.'

'One last question and then I will let you go, Professor. Who would you say was the most famous and influential psychiatrist of this century? Famous and influential. Just one name, please.'

'Freud.'

'Thank you for your very interesting testimony, Professor Smith. That will be all.'

James Drury was on his feet. 'Your Honour, my next witness has been delayed unavoidably. May I ask for a recess until tomorrow?'

He had to stop the carnage. Delay was the best he could hope for. Masterson had eaten Smith for breakfast and the case was in ruins. If he could do that to Smith he could do the same to the Johns Hopkins professor. He was turning the defence experts into witnesses for the plaintiffs, and *their* doctors were still to come – among them the redoubtable and vindictive Dr Aaron Ishmael. He prayed Ruckelhauser would do this for him.

He would. 'Court is recessed until tomorrow morning,' he said.

The large screwdriver had made mincemeat of the flimsy

catch on the downstairs window, and now Adam, hidden by the trees of the yard from the eyes of honest citizens, from whose ranks he had so recently defected, eased himself over the sill and into the kitchen of the deserted house. According to Drury, Mary Mitcham was staying with friends. He should be OK. But he'd forced an entry. Technically he was a burglar. If he got caught he was in deep trouble, and it would do Anne's case no good. No good at all. Not that things could get much worse.

As the defeated and deflated Smith stepped down, Adam knew that they'd lost. He'd turned towards Anne and seen the hurt and the beginnings of tears in the proud eyes. She was teetering on the brink of disgrace and financial ruin, and only because she'd risked everything for her patient, put herself on the line to cure John Mitcham's misery. It was cruelly unfair, totally and completely unjust and he couldn't stand idly by and watch it happen.

So far, everybody on their side had played by the rules, while the opposition had used every low trick in the book, and several that weren't. Even their decision to file suit against Anne had been an exercise in cynicism. Mary Mitcham was on the make. Always had been, even when her husband was alive, from what he'd learned about her. And Ishmael – the pompous, conceited egotist, who just couldn't bear the fact that his judgement had been called into question. At the moment of Smith's humiliation Adam had declared war on the whole despicable lot of them. He would take the law into his own hands. Do whatever needed to be done to get Anne off the hook. The end justified the means.

One of the unsolved mysteries in this case had been Mitcham's mental state at the time of his suicide. Somehow, for some reason, it had worsened dramatically. On his last visit to Anne he'd denied suicidal intentions. What had changed his mind? Maybe, just maybe, he'd written something down. Apparently there had been no suicide note. But if there had been one it was quite possible that

Mary Mitcham had destroyed it, or, more likely, hidden it. There might be letters, too. Last despairing missives penned by the desperate man. Written, but never sent. It was a slim chance, but it looked like the only one.

With the aid of a pencil flashlight, Adam was able to find his way easily around the small house. He'd started with the big desk in what must have been Mitcham's den. The drawers were stuffed with papers, most of which turned out to be bills. It seemed the unfortunate man owed money to just about every tradesman in the State of New York. That wasn't news. There were market letters – Zweig, Dow, Theory; catalogues – Smarter Image, Synchronics, Bachrach; piles of old magazines – *Forbes*, *Fortune*, *Business Week*. Nothing remotely relevant to the contents of Mitcham's poor, tortured mind.

Adam felt black despair well up inside him. Anne was going down and he was powerless to help. He could pay her damages, marry her, insulate her from the world which was about to misuse her so comprehensively, but he could never make amends for the dreadful blow to her pride if the malpractice was proved. He might win her, but she'd never be happy. Anger coursed through him. Fuck that self-centred wimp of a man who'd opted out and caused him so much trouble. He forced himself to continue his methodical search, but as each room failed to provide the answer he sought his spirits descended towards the depths. The bedroom and the den contained nothing of interest – bathrooms, spare rooms, kitchen were all far less likely to contain what he sought. He checked them anyway. Nothing.

Sunk in gloom, Adam threw himself into a chair. It had been a long-shot and it had failed. In a few short hours it would be dawn, and the trial. The end of everything for Anne. Morosely, he stared up at the bookcase. What sort of books had that worm Mitcham and his dreadful wife read? *Crash of '79*, *How to Survive the Coming Depression*, *How to Buy Real Estate with Nothing Down*. Gloom and

Doom. Something for nothing. Typical. Mitcham sure hadn't survived his coming depression. How well would Anne survive hers?

And then he saw it. A tiny white piece of paper sticking out between two books. He plucked it out, and in the flashlight's dim glow devoured its contents with mounting excitement. It was a letter from Aaron Ishmael, rude and abrupt, demanding immediate payment of a vast account. Across it was Mitcham's scrawl, 'You killed me and you try to charge me for my death'. That was it. From the grave Mitcham made his accusation. No jury on earth would ignore his words. From the date on the letter it was clear that they'd been written on the day of his suicide.

Adam moved over to the telephone and dialled Drury's number.

James Drury stood before the court. 'I propose to call no more witnesses for the defence in this case,' he said shortly.

Again the hum of controlled excitement buzzed round the room. No more witnesses. Had Drury given up? Had he chickened our after the beating Masterson had given Smith? And why on earth wasn't he going to call Dr Carrington to testify in her own defence? Was he worried about what creepy-crawlies might emerge from beneath the stone in the cross-examination?

Masterson, a quizzical expression locked onto his face, wondered all those things. It was unlike Drury to give up. Had he got something up his sleeve? If so – what? Certainly the case looked to be open-and-shut, the two million in the bag. The jury might even take it on themselves to award more. It was unusual, but it had happened before. Pity. He'd have liked to get the Carrington woman on the stand. He'd have made her look like a high-class hooker with as much right to a medical licence as a homicidal maniac to an axe. He stood up. Time to get the show on the road.

'Call Dr Aaron Ishmael,' he said.

Masterson hardly had to do anything at all. The vitriol dripped from Ishmael's tongue freely and unbidden – a poisonous fountain of venom corroding and poisoning the atmosphere of the courtroom.

Dr Anne Carrington had plumbed new depths of behaviour. John Mitcham had been getting better, confronting the root cause of his problems, the only way a lasting solution could be found. And then this meddling doctor, this self-appointed scourge of Freud and Freudianism, had lured him away from the one treatment which could have saved him. The siren voice, seductive and scheming, had drawn him remorselessly towards the rocks. He, Aaron Ishmael, had predicted tragedy, and events had proved him right. Now he wouldn't rest until the world knew of the disaster that had occurred, and how it had occurred. If his words sounded harsh it was because of the pressing necessity of righting a great wrong. Others must be discouraged from behaving as Dr Carrington had. She'd brought discredit on a great profession. But, far more important than that, she'd contributed directly through her own negligence and conceit to the death of a patient. In his book there could be no greater crime. The abuse of trust, the disrespect to a, dare he say it, eminent colleague, the rampant doctrinaire approach – all were the sins of Dr Carrington.

It was a tour de force of aggression as Aaron Ishmael pulsated his hatred. Normally this would have counted against him, but so gigantic was his passion and so vehement his accusations that the faces of the jury seemed to show that they felt there must be some sort of fire behind all this smoke. If Anne was blameless, why was this doctor so worked up? If she had any points to lose she'd lost them. Not one of the twelve jurors doubted they would find her guilty. Not one person in the room doubted they would do just that.

James Drury watched, waited and hoped. He had a big

problem. Somehow Ishmael's letter, which Adam had so mysteriously 'found' the night before, must be entered into the court record. Drury hadn't been certain of its origins, although he could've hazarded a guess. For the moment that wasn't the problem. The question was how to get the letter with its damning accusation accepted as evidence. As things stood, the plaintiffs would be within their rights to object to its production at this late stage of events. It was, after all, standard courtroom procedure that all evidence had to be disclosed and examined by the other side in advance. But there were exceptions. In murder and other serious cases, when lives were at stake, the judge could overrule counsel's objections in the interests of justice. In a malpractice suit it was extremely unlikely he would do such a thing. And so Drury hung on Masterson's every word to see if he would open a back door through which the defence could push through to victory.

Masterson was coasting along. He couldn't remember when it had been easier. Ishmael was a performing seal who could be made to do tricks at will. For once he wasn't even bothering to watch the jury. He knew they were with him all the way. Dr Carrington would be lucky if she prescribed an aspirin for the rest of her life. What was his contingency fee? Thirty per cent: $600,000. He thought about a Hatteras Sport Fisherman 50-metre. It would look well docked outside the Boca-Raton house. Very well, indeed. He forced himself to concentrate. Better anticipate Drury's cross-examination. He'd harp on the question of Ishmael's fees, contrasting them with Anne's failure to charge any.

'At this point, ladies and gentlemen of the jury, I would like to confront an issue of which the defence has already made much, and of which I suspect they will attempt to make more. I am referring to the question of fees.'

Drury let out a great sigh of relief. They were home and dry. In the direct questioning, Masterson, for the plaintiffs, had himself brought up the question of fees. That entitled him to bring evidence on the question of fees in his own cross-examination. He'd drive a coach and horses through the gap Masterson had unwittingly opened up for him.

Blissfully unaware that the Hatteras yacht was to remain a mere vision, Masterson cruised on.

'You charged John Mitcham fees, Dr Ishmael?'

'Why certainly I did.'

'Would you say those fees were exorbitant, in any way excessive?'

'Certainly not.'

'And yet you knew that Mitcham was in a poor position financially?'

Masterson was proud of himself. He was undercutting the defence's cross-examination. By asking the questions Drury would ask, he was effectively defusing them. The sense of déjà vu as he went over ground already covered would turn into boredom and irritation. And his first rule was never to bore or irritate a jury.

'Mitcham's financial position wasn't examined in the psychoanalysis. We were dealing with matters far more weighty. The economics were peripheral. Once we had righted the imbalances in Mitcham's psyche, the economics would have looked after themselves. As we now know to our cost, and, as I predicted before the event, paying no fees to Dr Carrington was the most extravagant and ill-advised gesture of Mitcham's career. He paid with his life.'

'Precisely, Dr Ishmael. Could you, perhaps, tell the court what Freud's attitude was towards the payment of fees?'

'Yes. He used to insist on payment in advance at the time of the session. He felt that the payment of money was an excellent way of concentrating the patient's mind. That way the patient would work harder in the often difficult and demanding analysis.'

'Thank you, Doctor. Your witness.' With a dismissive flourish which said 'follow that', Masterson sat down. He couldn't remember in the whole of his career when he'd felt more confident of the outcome of a case.

James Drury rose for the cross-examination.

'Dr Ishmael, you told this court just now that your fees were not exorbitant?'

'That is correct.'

'Your Honour,' said Drury, turning towards the judge, 'Counsel for the plaintiffs and this witness have maintained that the doctor's fees were fair and reasonable. I would like to introduce evidence into the court as to the nature of those "fair and reasonable" fees. May I add that the defence in this case relies heavily on the assertion that John Mitcham's debts, and specifically his debts to Dr Ishmael, were to a large extent the cause of his unhappy mental state. A brilliant young doctor's career is dependent on this court forming an opinion on that matter.'

His heart stood still. Ruckelhauser could rule against him. If he did, he'd never play golf with him again.

'Well,' said the judge, 'this "evidence" has not been properly disclosed, but, on the other hand, counsel for the plaintiffs did bring up the question of fees in the cross-examination. May we ask the nature of this "evidence"?'

'An account for services rendered, submitted to John Mitcham by Dr Ishmael.'

Masterson's antennae, finely tuned instruments at the best of times, were now twitching like mad. He was picking up the baddest of bad vibrations. His natural inclination was to object, but to what? To a bill? That would look like he had something to hide. Still, his gut told him to object, and he always obeyed his gut.

'Objection, your Honour. Plaintiffs haven't had a chance to examine this evidence. We are asking that it be withheld.'

The WASP in Judge Ruckelhauser began to buzz. He didn't like Masterson and he liked the shrink even less. What's more, his emotions were in tune with his legal duties. A case could be made for upholding the objection, but there was a stronger one for overruling it.

'Come now, Mr Masterson, I don't see why this court shouldn't be in a position to know how much Dr Ishmael charges for his services. I'm quite fascinated to know myself, and I'm sure the jury is, too. After all, he has said his charges are "not exorbitant". That's a value judgement with no facts to back it up. Surely you're not against a few facts, Mr Masterson? After all, we're talking about a young doctor's reputation here. Objection overruled.'

Masterson sat down, staring with some unreasoning foreboding at the piece of paper which fluttered in Drury's hand.

'May I ask that you read this letter out to the court, Dr Ishmael? You will note that the letter was sent on the day before John Mitcham's suicide. He must have received it on the very day he decided to kill himself.'

Ishmael was chalky white. With shaking hands he took the letter, peering down at it as if it contained his death sentence.

'It is your letter, signed by yourself, isn't it?'

Ishmael managed a nod.

'And you do agree that poor John Mitcham read this letter on the day he decided that death was preferable to life?'

Again, with downcast eyes, Ishmael bobbed his head up and down.

'May I have an answer to that question, please, Doctor?' There was a cutting edge to Drury's voice.

'Yes, I suppose so.'

'Please read the letter to the court, Dr Ishmael.'

Ishmael's thin, reedy voice insinuated its uncertain tones into the pregnant silence.

'Dear Mr Mitcham, Despite repeated attempts to obtain payment, you have not as yet complied and so I must ask you to give your immediate attention to this long overdue account, failing which I shall be forced to take legal action to recover these professional fees. I need hardly remind you of how much time and effort I have put into your case, and of the considerable benefit you have received from treatment. The fact that you have seen fit, against my advice, and in your own worst interests, to discontinue treatment gives you no right to ignore my account. Yours etc.'

Ishmael stood stock still. He'd stopped speaking, but he didn't look up.

'Please read out the amount of the account, Dr Ishmael.'

'Three thousand, nine hundred dollars.'

Drury turned to look at the jury. They had all at one time or another received letters like that, and they all knew what they felt about the senders. At the mention of the money, two or three of them drew in their breath sharply.

Ishmael was going down the drain. The defence bandwagon was rolling once more. It was time for the coup de grâce.

'Down in the right-hand corner, Doctor, you will recognize some handwriting. Would you please tell the court whose handwriting it is?'

Ishmael was all but inaudible. 'It appears to be that of John Mitcham.'

'Certainly it is Mitcham's handwriting. Two independent handwriting experts verified that at eight o'clock this morning. These must have been the last words he ever wrote. His last will and testament, you might say. Dr Ishmael, will you please *share them with this court*.' Drury almost shouted the last words.

Ishmael's head jerked back and everyone could see the tears of despair in his eyes.

' "You killed me and you try to charge me for my death." '

Pandemonium broke out in the courtroom as the implications of John Mitcham's accusation sunk in. A voice from beyond the grave, the writing on the wall, the last despairing defiance of a desperate man as he scribbled the agonized words on what was effectively his death-warrant. At that split second in time each and every one of the members of the jury knew that the wrong doctor had been accused. Anne Carrington was safe at last.

'No further questions.' Drury's statement was triumphant as Ishmael, scourged and flayed, beaten and bowed, slunk from the witness box.

Judge Ruckelhauser did not hesitate. 'Will both counsels please approach me. Gentlemen, I am going to instruct this jury to reject this suit in view of the evidence this court has just heard.'

Both Anne and Adam could feel the stillness as if it were a tangible thing. For so long their hearts and minds had raged and roared with catastrophic emotions – with passion and ecstasy, with pain and sorrow, with fear, with terror. Now the peace of God had descended on them, and in the calm tranquillity of the church their souls walked and talked together, not requiring the medium of language. Anne had taken Adam to St Patrick's the moment they'd escaped from the excited courtroom. It was a part of her life he'd never seen, and it was the most important part. In that communion of sweet mysticism they sat side by side, hand in hand, enjoying the sublimity of closeness, needing and wanting nothing more.

Everything had come right. God had intervened, and He had been merciful: Adam's torturer consumed in the fire of His wrath, Charles Phipps dying of his terrible disease, Anne's tormentor Ishmael cast down as a result of his overwhelming pride. Before both lovers stretched a lifetime of opportunity and happiness – and both were acutely aware of the gift they'd been given as they offered up their prayers in thanks.

On the street outside it was quiet no more.

'What now?' said Anne, her face glowing with the joy of the moment.

'Will you marry me?' said Adam simply.

'It felt like we were just married in there.' They both laughed. Her answer had been yes.

'On one condition, Adam.'

Adam knew what she meant. He smiled wryly.

'Don't worry, it's gone. The secret died with those two creeps. It'll die with poor Charles. I've wiped it out of my mind. I'll never use the program again.'

Then and there, on the wind-swept sidewalk of the Big Apple, he picked her up in his arms and kissed her tenderly, as their souls met in that union which would never be put asunder.

SPARKLERS

Pat Booth

A story that races from the Olympic ski slopes of Colorado to the inner councils of the Mafia, from the exclusive haunts of the rich and beautiful to the machinations of the international diamond business.

Caroline Montgomery is fresh, young, stunningly attractive and heiress to an American business empire. She has one overwhelming ambition: to become the fastest woman on skis in the world.

Until she meets . . .

Miles Parmere: ex-Harrow, the Guards and the SAS. Bored, idle, a little dissolute, he's a man looking for something to happen.

When they come together as lovers, theirs is a story that explodes across the page. But it also becomes the story of a viciously corrupt Mafia banker who will seek to destroy Miles and Caroline in a maelstrom of intrigue and violence.

FUTURA PUBLICATIONS
FICTION
0 7088 2156 1

RULING PASSIONS

Susan Crosland

When Daisy Brewster landed in London she was just another pretty young American out to enjoy a year abroad before returning home to marry. But before the year was out, Daisy would take on the scheming world of London journalism, and be taken on in turn by London's most eligible bachelor MP.

Though she couldn't know it, she would also take on a dangerous enemy when she casually flicked off the sexual gropings of her lecherous boss, pushing a button that would detonate fifteen years later in vicious innuendo and blackmail – all aimed at destroying her husband's career and her own happiness.

Meanwhile Daisy will become a not-so-innocent abroad as she manoeuvres through the shoals of political intrigue and sexual misadventure – taking us behind the scenes at Buckingham Palace receptions, dinners at No. 10 and top-secret meetings in Whitehall.

'Has all the ingredients . . . sex, ambition, political intrigue'
Guardian

'A big slick book . . . plotting and intrigue well conveyed'
Sunday Times

'The conflict between politicians and journalists is beautifully portrayed'
Evening Standard

'Elegant, sophisticated . . . knowing, gossipy'
The Times

'A racy dip into the shenanigans of Fleet Street and Parliament'
Today

FUTURA PUBLICATIONS
FICTION
0 7088 4471 5

All Futura Books are available at your bookshop or newsagent, or can be ordered from the following address: Futura Books, Cash Sales Department, P.O. Box 11, Falmouth, Cornwall TR10 9EN.

Alternatively you may fax your order to the above address. Fax No. 0326 76423.

Payments can be made as follows: Cheque, postal order (payable to Macdonald & Co (Publishers) Ltd) or by credit cards, Visa/Access. Do not send cash or currency. UK customers: please send a cheque or postal order (no currency) and allow 80p for postage and packing for the first book plus 20p for each additional book up to a maximum charge of £2.00.

B.F.P.O. customers please allow 80p for the first book plus 20p for each additional book.

Overseas customers including Ireland, please allow £1.50 for postage and packing for the first book, £1.00 for the second book, and 30p for each additional book.

NAME (Block Letters) ....

ADDRESS ....

....

☐ I enclose my remittance for _____

☐ I wish to pay by Access/Visa Card

Number   ☐☐☐☐☐☐☐☐☐☐☐☐☐☐☐☐

Card Expiry Date   ☐☐☐☐